Mia Emme

Unvisited Tombs

Book 3 The Watchers Trilogy

Excerpt from *Middlemarch – out of copyright, and used with grateful acknowledgement to George Eliot.*

ISBN: 978-1-9161399-2-3

Book design: The Art of Communication book-design.co.uk

Images: Shutterstock

DEDICATION

For my Gran
with respect, love and admiration.

"For the growing good of the world
is partly dependent on unhistoric acts;
and that things are not so ill with you
and me as they might have been,
is half owing to the number who lived
faithfully a hidden life,
and rest in unvisited tombs."

George Eliot, *Middlemarch*, 1871

CHAPTER ONE

Oxford, August 2007

Iris Shaw drove along Foxcombe Road, anxiety spiking at the blue lights illuminating the night and houses. In the passenger seat her husband, Michael, ended a phone call.

'No answer from Zoe?' Iris asked.

'No, it's probably on silent this time of night.'

'Shit.'

The gates of Ash House were open, and Iris drove straight in. She got out of the car only to reel back as paramedics wheeled out an elderly woman on a gurney. The patient's eyes were closed, mouth covered by an oxygen mask and her skin ghastly in the weird lights.

'Oh my God,' Iris said. 'What's happened, will she be all right?'

'And you are?'

Iris walked beside the gurney.

'Iris Shaw. She's my great aunt, Josephine. Please, is she going to be all right?'

'It seems your aunt took a bad fall and hit her head. She was unconscious when found by a Miss Ruth Dunn, the housekeeper.'

'Ruth's my aunt's companion. She rang me after she called you.'

Iris glanced at Ruth Dunn's slight form at the front door, pulling her coat on and talking to Michael. The gurney reached the ambulance, the wheels were collapsed, and the paramedics loaded her aunt into the vehicle.

'Please, what's happening?' Iris asked.

'We need to get your aunt to the hospital. She briefly regained consciousness and seemed confused when we reached her. We're worried about the head wound and there's a suspected broken ankle, maybe a couple of ribs.'

One paramedic held the door open while the other climbed inside.

'I'm coming with you,' Iris said.

The paramedic nodded and helped her into the ambulance. A hand caught hers and Michael was at the door.

'I'll bring Ruth and follow in the Land Rover,' he said. 'You're going to the JR, yes?'

Iris looked at him, her mind a blank. The paramedic holding the door nodded.

'Yes, Accident and Emergency,' he said. 'She'll be admitted straight away.'

The doors shut and Iris sat next to the still form of her aunt. The ambulance moved, turning out of the gate, and gathered speed almost silently with its sirens now off. Its strobing lights coloured the night while inside the white lit interior seemed an alien place to Iris. She clung to a rail in the queer light, found Josephine's hand and held on. The paramedic attached monitors and a bag of clear liquid, pushing a cannula into her aunt's wrist.

'Can I just check her details with you?'

'Yes, of course.'

'Josephine Guard, ninety-three years old. Has diabetes for which she takes Metformin and angina for which she takes paracetamol. Is that right?' Iris nodded. 'Is there anything else we should know about, such as allergies?'

'She's allergic to shellfish. Not that that's relevant. I'm sorry, I'm rambling. Will she be all right?'

'I'm most concerned about the head wound. I'll get her stable and to the hospital. Just keep talking to her.'

Iris swallowed, suddenly mute, and squeezed her aunt's hand.

'What do I say?'

A slight pressure on her palm made her look to her aunt, whose other hand batted feebly at the oxygen mask.

'She's awake!'

The paramedic lifted the mask clear.

'Josephine, can you hear me?' The old lady managed a nod and the man continued, 'You've taken a tumble and hurt your head. We're taking you to hospital.'

The pressure on Iris's hand increased and the watery gaze found hers.

'Iris,' the old lady managed.

'I'm here, Aunt Josephine.'

'There's Sam,' the old lady murmured. 'And you must find Amy Dudley.'

Iris felt alarmed and glanced at the medic, who made a 'keep talking' gesture.

'Of course,' she said. 'I'm here and I love you. Just hold on.'

Her aunt's eyes closed, and the frail hand slackened.

'Aunt Josephine?' Iris's gaze flew to the paramedic, who checked her aunt's wrist.

'It's all right,' he said, 'just unconscious.' He replaced the oxygen mask. 'She mentioned those people when we found her. Are they family members?'

Iris's gaze was pinned to her aunt; she held her breath while watching the rise and fall of the old lady's chest, reassuring herself that Josephine was still alive. She glanced at the paramedic, trying to order her thoughts.

'I don't know anybody called Sam or Amy Dudley; could it be her head wound? How much longer until we get there?'

The paramedic adjusted the blankets around Josephine.

'A few minutes at most. And yes, even the most minor head wounds can cause confusion, especially in the elderly. It's probably nothing to worry about at this stage.'

Iris nodded, barely hearing him, and prayed to any gods listening not to let her aunt die.

Iris didn't remember reaching the hospital or transferring her aunt to the intensive care unit. The queer smell of mass food production and antiseptic, wholly exclusive to hospitals, gradually seeped into her consciousness. Suddenly a nurse touched her arm and Iris sat straighter, staring at the woman's lips trying to make sense of what she was saying. The nurse smiled and seemed to understand.

'You can go in now,' she said again.

Iris nodded and gathered herself, willing body and soul up. She managed to stand and stared at the door, trying to get her legs to obey and move through it. The fluorescent lights gave everything a metallic, surreal quality that prompted unwanted memories. Abruptly an image of hair matted with blood and a collapsed face and neck, skin and bone eaten away ripped free from its bonds. She gulped and shook her head, shoving the fear down. Tears smarted and she dashed them away.

'It's not the same,' she whispered, forcing herself to believe it.

A hand on her elbow made her start and Michael was there with Ruth Dunn's anxious face hovering behind him. Iris swallowed and with false courage led the way into Josephine's room. Her aunt looked tiny and washed out against the white bedding, bandaged head and myriad of wires and tubes. Once again Iris felt as if reality had been banished. Familiar, nightmarish thoughts and more past images threatened her. She struggled against them and with an effort denied the panic and terror they invoked to sit next to the bed. She gazed at Josephine, wholly different and yet still the same. She heard crying and feared it was her own distress and weakness made real. But her eyes were dry, and she glanced at Michael sitting the other side of her aunt. He shook his head. She looked at Ruth, whose tears were bright in the ghoulish light.

'Ruth, what happened?' she asked.

The older woman sniffed and struggled to control herself.

'I'm not sure,' she whispered. Her breath hitched and her fingers were white on the bed frame. 'I got up to go to the bathroom and saw a light on in Josephine's room. I went in and, and found her.'

She put her face in her hands and sobbed hard enough to threaten Iris's fragile control. Michael rose and put an arm around the older woman's shoulders.

'It's all right,' he said.

He gestured to the door and Iris fought the fear of being left alone. She managed a nod in return and her husband led Ruth from the room speaking of hot tea. Iris's gaze locked on her aunt and she blocked out all else except willing Josephine to live.

Michael returned carrying steaming Styrofoam cups. Iris found a smile and took one, sipping the pasty-looking tea. Her husband did the same and grimaced at it.

'Ruth's calmed down,' he said. 'I've asked her to make a list of things we need to collect for Josephine. How are you holding up?'

Michael's hand warmed her shoulder, and she fought the urge to cry, unwilling to show any upset. She managed a smile and patted his hand.

'I'm okay, just worried.'

She sipped more tea finding it sweet and tasteless, but it seemed to revive her a bit. Michael sat once more on the other side of Josephine's bed.

'I finally got through to Zoe,' he said. 'She's on her way.'

Iris glanced at her watch; it showed 1.30am and exhaustion suddenly weighed against her fears and worries. She estimated their daughter's journey from London would take an hour and a half and went to speak, but a doctor came in. The next fifteen minutes were taken up with explanations of the head wound and the inability to x-ray for the suspected broken ankle and ribs until Josephine was stable. Iris tried to take it in, but the man's words ran into each other making formless sounds she couldn't understand. Iris barely noticed when the doctor left nor when Michael went to find Ruth. Her whole being was focused on Josephine's fragile breaths misting the oxygen mask. Time seemed suspended in the airless room and Iris's hand felt warm compared to her aunt's. She gazed at the lined face and begged Josephine not to give up.

When Zoe arrived at the hospital an hour later, Iris and Michael met her at reception. Iris held out her hand, shaking her head, and her daughter gave a gasping cry, too shocked and bewildered for tears.

Chapter Two

They buried Josephine a week later. Iris stood next to Michael and their daughter at the graveside while light rain fell from scudding grey clouds providing extra solemnity. Iris placed the carefully selected gladioli and poppies for remembrance onto the coffin. Zoe added a bunch of freesias, Josephine's favourites. The priest intoned a prayer and those gathered bowed their heads as the coffin was lowered into the ground. A few minutes later the service was over and the mourners broke up, exchanging sombre words as they walked to their cars. Michael moved amongst them letting those that didn't know the way to their home where the wake was being held.

By unspoken agreement Iris and Zoe remained at the graveside saying a private, silent goodbye to Josephine.

'At least she's with Uncle Walt now,' Zoe said.

'It's hard to believe he's been gone nearly seven years.'

Zoe wiped her eyes.

'I can't believe they're both gone. I'm going to miss Aunt Josephine so much.'

'I know, me too.'

Suddenly the cemetery was obscured by more tears. Iris turned away so Zoe wouldn't see her crying and forced the surge of grief down while surreptitiously drying her eyes. Turning back, she hugged her daughter, feeling Zoe's arms, softer, less muscled than her own, tighten around her waist. She held on and let Zoe cry for a few minutes before leading her to where Michael was waiting. Once in the car Iris rubbed her hands together trying to engineer warmth, wondering why she always felt cold lately.

'How many are coming to ours?' she asked.

'About twenty from what I can gather,' Michael replied.

Michael started the car. Iris looked at her reflection in the visor mirror, making sure there were no tell-tale marks from her tears. Her hazel eyes were a little reddened and puffy, but nothing she reasoned anyone would notice. She rubbed a sleeve over her short, auburn hair, drying the worst of the rain off. In the reflection she watched her daughter wipe her face and rub at her damp chestnut locks, an exact mix of Iris's auburn and Michael's dark brown.

'We did Aunt Josephine proud today,' Michael said.

'I hope so,' Zoe replied.

'Everything was exactly as she wanted,' Iris said. 'And there's plenty of her favourite for the wake.'

'Champagne?' Zoe asked.

Iris twisted around in the passenger seat so she could see her daughter.

'Naturally. Would you expect anything else?

Zoe shook her head and smiled through fresh tears. Iris resolutely held her own tears at bay, refusing to give in to them, and was glad when Michael started the car to drive home to Whitebarn Farm.

Close to Oxford, Whitebarn Farm nestled in its own thirty-six acres of pastures and copses. The rambling farmhouse was over a hundred years old, built of thick, solid stone walls and floors, and painted white like its namesake. The roof of grey slate and pitted chimney gave it a serious air and, despite modern touches over the years, such as double glazing and central heating, it retained its weathered character. It was the only home Iris had ever known and, approaching it now, she opened the window and drew a cold breath that held earthy scents of grass and animals. The familiar love for her home softened the grief a little.

Nothing ever stays the same except Whitebarn.

Now, more than ever, she knew that to be true.

Half an hour later Iris made sure everyone had a full glass and raised her own. The murmuring of the twenty or so people stilled, and all faces turned to her expectantly. It was a strange sight; the silent, dark-clothed people standing and sitting in the primrose yellow living room. Iris managed a smile despite her grief that seemed to come in waves that flattened all else.

'I'd like to thank you all for coming and honouring my great aunt, Josephine. Josephine meant more to me, to my family, than I can possibly put into words. It suffices to say that her generosity of spirit and her vibrant character touched countless lives. I know she'll be missed by so many. Please raise your glasses, to Josephine!'

Everyone echoed her aunt's name, and they all drank. The murmuring began again against a background of jazz that swelled and lifted the atmosphere. Iris, listening, realised Michael or Zoe had put on Charlie Parker, Josephine's favourite. She moved amongst the mourners, paying special attention to Ruth Dunn. Everyone spoke kindly and lovingly of her aunt, telling stories and anecdotes. She finally reached a platinum blonde woman whose navy dress starkly contrasted against the spring green sofa. With a start she noted the woman had taken a photograph album from the shelf and was perusing it, glass of champagne in one hand. Pasting on a smile Iris settled next to her.

'Rosalind, thank you so much for coming,' Iris said,

hoping she sounded sincere.

The woman, Iris knew, was in her early fifties, a similar age to herself, but the resemblance ended there. She doubted Rosalind ever left the bedroom without make-up. The woman's neat figure, as she frequently extolled, was due to strict diet and gym routines, whereas Iris's toned muscles and sun-browned face were due to a lifetime working outdoors at Whitebarn. Rosalind smiled, showing perfect white teeth, and inclined her head. She had the buffed and polished look of the very rich and smelt of something cloying.

'It was a lovely service,' Rosalind conceded. 'You did Josephine proud.'

'Thank you. We did everything as she wanted. You know Josephine never left anything to chance.'

'Oh indeed. Grandma always said Josephine was a force to be reckoned with ever since they were prefects at boarding school.'

Rosalind turned back pages of the album and pointed to a black and white photograph showing two women standing proudly next to an ambulance outside a smart townhouse.

'I didn't know you had this one of them together. Do you know they even drove that ambulance through the Blitz?'

Iris wished she would put the album away.

'I did know, yes.'

Rosalind sipped her drink still looking at the photograph. She moved a fingertip onto the townhouse.

'Isn't this the Russell Square house; the one that got bombed?'

Iris glanced away and her gaze found the framed sepia photo of her aunt and uncle on the wall. It showed them on their wedding day on the front steps of the same London townhouse.

'I believe so,' she said.

Rosalind peered closer at the album.

'Such a shame,' she murmured. 'It was a gorgeous house. You know, despite it being so badly damaged I'm not surprised they managed to sell it after the war. Fantastic location.'

'If you say so. It was way before my time.'

Iris wondered how she could get away from the woman and take the album with her. A small crease marred Rosalind's forehead.

'And mine, of course,' she said. 'But Bloomsbury was, and is, so expensive. Grandma's flat went for nearly half a million after she died. She's buried at Highgate cemetery, you know. Of course you do, you were at the funeral with Josephine.'

Iris recalled the lavish funeral four years ago and tried not to compare it to the simple, elegant service Josephine had just had. Rosalind sipped wine and turned the pages, commenting now and then, forcing Iris to remain. Then her hand stilled at a photograph of an elegant woman looking disinterested and holding a baby Iris.

'Now that's a nice one of your mother.' She glanced about. 'Trudi couldn't make it today?'

Iris didn't look at the picture, striving to keep the rancour from her voice.

'No. She couldn't. My mother is in her seventies now and it's a long way to come from Leith.'

'Of course,' Rosalind murmured, looking unconvinced. 'But she's still managing to work, I see. Her latest collection for Yarn and Tweed is selling well. I bought one of her designs only a few days ago.'

Iris tried to smile but her face felt too rigid.

'That's nice.'

The following silence deepened and lengthened while Rosalind continued to turn the pages. Iris desperately wanted to excuse herself but was loath to leave the woman pawing the album unsupervised. Now the pictures showed Iris as a toddler at Whitebarn. Amongst them Iris was with various animals, Josephine and her husband, Walt. There were few of Trudi. A sick, tight feeling gripped Iris and she longed to stop the turning, dreading the next page. But it was too late. The picture of a rugged, long-nosed man appeared. He was laughing while running alongside her as she rode a pony. Suddenly Rosalind snapped the book closed and looked vaguely around, twirling her empty wine glass.

'So, Zoe tells me Whitebarn is doing well,' the woman said in a bright tone. 'Something about horses?'

Iris thankfully chatted about the farm and animals while removing the album from Rosalind's unresisting fingers. Abruptly a man in his early thirties, aquiline featured and with feline grace, settled on the other side of Rosalind and refilled her glass.

'Sorry, I got held up talking to some old fellow.'

The other woman smiled at him and this time it reached her eyes.

'Iris, you must remember my stepson, Theo?'

Iris did indeed and the man's insincere smile reminded her of how much she disliked him. Still, she graciously accepted Theo's condolences and used his presence to escape the sofa, taking the album with her.

'I hope you'll both stay for the buffet,' Iris said. 'It should be ready very soon.'

She moved purposefully away, stopping briefly to thank people for coming, and gained the kitchen. Inside Zoe and Michael were putting sandwiches and cold meat onto plates. Iris side-stepped the door, resting her back against the wall, and took a moment to watch them. Gus, her Picardy sheepdog, rose from lying half on his bed by the Aga. He greeted her with wet nose and wavy tail. Iris stroked his black tufted ears while Gus rested his tawny body against her legs, and she drew comfort from the large dog. She took a deep breath and, as always, the long, low room with its wooden beams, flagstone floor and whitewashed walls engineered a sense of calm.

A shadow moved from the back door to become a broad-shouldered man carrying bottles of wine from the cellar followed by his brown and white springer spaniel, Peg. The man put the bottles on the table, the dog obedient at his knee. Iris put the album atop a stack of cookbooks on the kitchen side and moved forward. Gus kept pace and greeted Peg with a happy tail. Despite Gus being one and a half times the size and weight of the spaniel it was the older Peg who led the relationship. Having known Gus since he was a puppy, Peg imparted her wisdom daily, especially trying to teach the now three-year-old Picardy about work and its importance. Gus tried hard to please Peg and Iris but was not always successful in curbing his playful nature in preference to learning. Now he play-bowed, tail picking up speed, and while Peg's tail responded, clearly wanting to romp, her dark eyes flicked to Thomas and told the Picardy, no, not in here. Iris, noting the exchange, debated letting the two friends out into the back garden but could imagine only too well the mayhem they would cause if some well-meaning guest let them back in to the living room. For while the seven-year-old Peg was the picture of obedience when Thomas was around and they were working, she was still a bundle of energy capable of nearly as much mischief as Gus when she thought Thomas wasn't looking. Iris patted Gus with a whispered 'later' and looked to find Thomas's blue gaze on her. He winked and dropped a hand to Peg, who turned her nose to his touch.

'I'll take them both when I do the feeds,' he said.

'Thomas, thank you,' Iris said.

The farm manager was generally a taciturn man and as much a part of Whitebarn as the stones it was made from. He nodded, scratching his salt-and-pepper beard, his expression sympathetic.

'Wanted to say, sorry about Josephine,' he said. 'She was a kind and lovely lady. I liked her.'

It was a long speech for him, and Iris knew he meant every word. Zoe handed Thomas a laden plate and an empty glass.

'Here you go, Thomas,' she said. 'We've got to go and distribute the food and wine out there, but please could you just stay in here and do the very important job of looking after the dogs?'

Zoe grinned and ruffled Peg's ears. Thomas grinned back and nodded his thanks.

'Pheasant and rabbit down in cellar,' he said.

Iris smiled, knowing better than to ask where the bounty had come from. Michael opened red wine and poured a measure into Thomas's glass before setting the bottle on the table.

'Good man,' Michael said. 'And don't feed them too much chicken.'

Thomas's eyes twinkled and he pretended he hadn't already picked meat off a bone for the dogs. Peg waited patiently while Gus stayed beside Iris, who picked up two salvers. Her husband did the same and Zoe carried bottles of wine. Telling Gus to stay with Thomas, Iris negotiated the door and returned to the wake.

Two hours later and most of the mourners had left. Iris stood at the French doors that led out onto the back lawn, enjoying a moment of stillness. The afternoon was lengthening toward early evening causing shadows from the orchard to spill across the grass. Behind her, strains of jazz muted the few remaining conversations and she sipped wine, wishing everyone had gone. Michael was suddenly topping up her glass and darting glances at her.

'I'm all right,' she said.

He raised his eyebrows.

'Honestly,' she lowered her voice. 'I just wish everyone would leave. I've still got to check on the Boreray and bring in Blue, Shiloh and Honky.' She gestured to her black formal wear. 'I can't wrangle sheep and bed down horses and a donkey like this.'

'Can't Thomas do it?'

'He's out there now with Gus and Peg doing the last feed for the chickens as well as sorting out the Oxford Sandy and Blacks. He spends more time bedding down those pigs than I do. I'd really like to get this all over with today.'

'He's not driving, is he?'

'No, Natasha's coming to get him.' Iris smiled, recalling Thomas's wife's comments when she had rung earlier. 'She said he would never leave the animals until they were all done and dusted, red wine or no, and that she'd be here to collect him at five.'

Michael glanced at the grandfather clock.

'Half an hour. He won't have long enough to help you with the sheep or the others. How about I wind everything up here and you go upstairs and get changed? If it's not all finished by the time you're ready, you can slip out the back door to the flock. Zoe can get the mares and Honky in.'

'But I'm the hostess.'

He kissed her on the forehead, his sparse six-foot frame making it easy.

'And I'm the husband and perfectly capable of being the hostess with the mostest.'

'Host with the most.'

'I'm a progressive type and if I feel like being a hostess then I'll carry it off with grace and panache.' He took her glass. 'Go on, go and get changed.'

She squeezed his arm and managed to escape the living room without being stopped. She hurried up the stairs and along the hall to their bedroom, only to stop in the doorway, staring. Silhouetted against the darkening sky Theo turned from the bedroom window.

'What are you doing in here?' Iris asked.

He moved and was suddenly only inches away, causing Iris to step back and let him pass.

'I'm sorry. I got lost looking for the bathroom.'

'There's a downstairs toilet for guests to use.'

'Right, I must've missed that. Where is it again?'

She told him and he left, apologising for intruding. Iris waited, making sure he went downstairs, and then shut the bedroom door. His citrus cologne still clung in the air and uncaring of the chill she opened a window. Getting undressed and into her work gear of blue jeans and a long-sleeved t-shirt she kept glancing at the closed door, feeling strangely vulnerable. Back on the landing she could hear Michael and Zoe saying goodbyes and paused, unwilling to be seen. The front door closed, bringing blessed silence, and she went to see to her animals.

CHAPTER THREE

Three days later Iris stood in Josephine's cream and apricot living room in Ash House feeling stunned. From the hallway she could hear the rise and fall of voices as Michael spoke to Josephine's solicitor but couldn't bring herself to move. They were alone in the house. Ruth, despite being a beneficiary, had declined to attend the meeting fearing it would upset her too much. Something Iris completely understood. She stared unseeing out at the lawn and the trees beyond it. Half a mile away, she knew, lay Foxcombe Valley, a horseshoe-shaped vale some six miles wide and ten miles long of untouched woodland and sloping hills. It was a place she knew well from her walks and picnics there with Aunt Josephine and Uncle Walt. *A place I now own.* At a weight against her legs, she looked down and let her fingers trail on Gus's tawny fur. He stared back, his deep brown eyes understanding, and she took comfort from his steadfast presence. It never ceased to amaze her how Gus always seemed to know her mood or what she was going to do next, almost as if he could read her mind. The dog sighed and lay down on her feet, his robust, shaggy body warm and heavy. She raised her fingers to the window, framing the ash trees that swayed green and gold beneath the blue sky.

'Why didn't you tell me?' she murmured.

'Who, me?'

Iris turned, disturbing Gus, to see Michael carrying in a tray that held a cafetière and espresso cups. The smell of coffee was enticing.

'Not you. Aunt Josephine. Has the solicitor gone?'

Gus ambled over while Michael nodded, put the tray down and settled on the sofa. He greeted the dog with a head stroke and a chuck under his bearded chin. Iris's gaze returned to the garden and sky without really seeing them. She suddenly turned, gesturing to a framed aerial photograph of Foxcombe Valley which hung over the fireplace.

'Why didn't she tell me about the valley, about the money and Uncle Walt?'

'Maybe she thought you knew, at least about Walt. It was no secret he'd been in the jewellery business.'

'But they sold all that over thirty years ago. How was I supposed to know how successful it was? You didn't.'

'True. But he did have a few shops and staff, didn't he?'

'Internationally, apparently. Which was something else I didn't know. I was only twenty-two when they sold it all.'

'And we had only been married a year then. So, my knowledge is tiny compared to yours. *You* lived with them.'

She made an exasperated sound.

'For six months when I was eighteen. My stepfather had just died.' She said it quickly and ignored the stab of pain beneath her ribs. 'I wasn't exactly paying attention to what Uncle Walt was doing business-wise.'

'Didn't he inherit the jewellery business from *his* father?'

'That's right, his father died in the First World War and it was just Walt.'

She huffed a breath and paced, her footsteps muffled by the thick carpet. Gus sat and watched while Michael poured coffee.

'It's not really about not knowing though, is it?' her husband said.

Iris stopped and sank into an overstuffed armchair at which Gus promptly tried to climb on her lap. She evaded him, telling him 'down' and he sighed, lying at her feet instead.

'What else could it be?' she asked.

'If you had known, you might've been better prepared to deal with all this. Despite her age, Josephine dying was a shock.' He shot a concerned glance at her which she pretended not to notice. 'And now, today's shock of finding our lives have changed beyond belief.' He held out a cup for her. 'Perhaps everything coming so fast and so suddenly is why you're feeling off balance. Shell shock.'

Iris took the cup, putting her fingers around it to warm them, and wondered if he were right. That so much so suddenly had fractured her usual diamond-hard control.

'I feel so helpless,' she said and hated the admission.

'For Josephine? There was nothing you could've done,' he said.

She suppressed a shiver and nodded, pretending that was what she had meant. And it was, in part, but only a small part. The abyss that caused her to feel inadequate and worthless was something she held back every day and it had a far older permanence than her aunt's death. Images of ruined and blackened skin amidst blood made her swallow against a tight throat. Feeling breathless she rubbed the back of her neck and with practiced ease hid her distress in a truthful diversion.

'And you're right, I am shocked. It's so much money,' she murmured.

'Seventeen million is a lot of money.'

Iris groaned and rested her head back, staring at the ceiling. Relief washed her when she heard Michael move to the window knowing the diversion had worked. Then she really did think of the money and tried to sort out her fractured thoughts.

'With power of attorney I only ever dealt with one of Josephine's accounts,' she said. 'There was never more than two or three thousand in there. I had no idea she had so much.'

'I know, it's unbelievable.'

Iris closed her eyes and thankfully the darkness only pinwheeled with orange and pink.

'You could give up work if you want,' she said. 'Finish writing your book about Lord Marlborough.'

'Be a kept man? No more students, no more lectures. It might be a relief.'

Gus shifted, turning on his side but keeping his paws on her foot. She opened her eyes and the white ceiling seemed too bright.

'But you love teaching.'

'Can't fool you, can I?' She heard the smile in his voice, then he sighed. 'As much as I love teaching history, I admit the academic side has become challenging lately. There's talk of redundancies.' He sighed again. 'Not that it's a worry for us now.'

She moved forward, sipped coffee and glanced at her husband. He seemed to sense her gaze and turned, coming to sit on the sofa and refilling her espresso cup. She smiled her thanks and a sudden thought struck her.

'Did you ever hear Aunt Josephine mention the name Sam, or Amy Dudley?'

'No. But I know the name, Amy Dudley. She's famous or, rather, infamous. Why?'

'Aunt Josephine mentioned them in the ambulance. Who is Amy Dudley?'

'Was. She died hundreds of years ago shrouded in

mystery and a royal scandal. Not far from here, actually, in the village of Cumnor.'

'Why would Aunt Josephine want me to find a woman hundreds of years dead?'

'What did she say, exactly?'

'It was just after we got in the ambulance. She said "There's Sam" and then she made me promise to find Amy Dudley. The paramedic said it was probably confusion caused by the head wound, but it's very strange that she was a real person. How did this Amy Dudley die?'

Michael shrugged.

'Now that is the million-dollar question. No one has ever been able to properly say whether it was murder, accident, or,' he hesitated for a heartbeat, 'suicide. But whatever the cause, Amy Dudley's death changed the face of British politics and royalty.'

Iris nodded, posing ease she didn't feel.

'How so?'

'Amy Dudley was married to the man many believe to be the lover of Queen Elizabeth I. And even though it was never proven, many believed Lord Robert Dudley murdered his wife so he could marry the queen. Ironically, this meant Elizabeth could never marry him. The nobles and commoners alike would have rebelled if she had, threatening the Crown and stability of England.'

'Goodness. But what has all this got to do with Aunt Josephine?'

'Perhaps she read something about Amy Dudley, and it stuck. Talking of which, have you read the letter yet?' he asked.

She could feel the envelope in her cardigan pocket and still see her name on it in Josephine's spiky writing.

'No, I…'

Someone knocked on the front door, making Gus huff a

woof. Husband and wife stared at each other. Then Iris rose and went to the hall with Gus following. She opened the front door to a man she didn't recognise wearing a smile she didn't like. He stepped forward as if trying to gain entry. She pulled the door closed, filling the gap with her body and feeling her dog right behind her, nosing her legs.

'Can I help you?'

'I'm looking for Mrs Guard. We have an appointment.'

He had a slight accent she couldn't place and was a bit shorter than her five foot eight, wearing a dark grey suit and tie that complemented his black hair and hard shoes. His brown gaze was curiously flat and somewhere his smile never reached.

'She's not available, I'm afraid,' Iris said. 'What's the appointment for?'

'Oh, forgive me, my name is Stephen Sloane.' He produced a card which Iris took, reading 'S. Sloane. Fine Antiques and Unique Furniture of Reading'. 'I'm to speak to Mrs Guard about some furniture she's thinking of selling. I rang and made the appointment a fortnight ago.'

'I'm sorry, but my aunt, Mrs Guard—' she paused, catching a breath that hurt, 'recently passed away.'

Mr Sloane's expression became sympathetic although his gaze never wavered from Iris's.

'Oh dear, I'm very sorry to hear that, Miss?'

'Mrs Shaw.'

'You have my deepest condolences, Mrs Shaw. I apologise for bothering you. But without seeming indelicate, are you the beneficiary?'

'Excuse me!'

Unseen, Gus gave a low growl at her distressed tone. The man looked startled, taking a step back while his gaze raked her legs.

'I just wondered. I mean…' He straightened his tie and

stepped forward, closer this time. 'It's just that if you are the beneficiary and do decide to sell any items please keep me in mind.'

Iris stared, the door handle became sweaty in her grip and nausea rolled her guts. She felt Gus nosing to move past her. Mr Sloane seemed not to notice her discomfort and he continued, 'I was particularly interested in two inlaid end tables and a vintage steamer trunk. If you could just...'

Stephen Sloane disappeared as Michael shut the door. Her husband took her hand and led Iris, with Gus following, into the living room, putting the refilled coffee cup in her hand.

'I don't care who that was,' he said. 'Just sit down and drink that while I go and make lunch. Ruth will be here soon, so we'll need to make some decisions then. But for now, drink your coffee and breathe.'

Iris did as she was told, her thoughts bashing like a fly against glass. She sat forward on the sofa, one hand in Gus's scruffy coat, and watched Michael leave. She heard the faint, familiar sound of a radio in the kitchen and gratitude flooded her. Her husband, she recognised, was managing to be calm and rational for her. Giving her space to sort her thoughts and feelings out while he did the same. Gus laid his whiskery chin on her thigh and she sipped coffee, stroking his ears while trying to ignore the familiar feeling of inadequacy. But it was no use and the usual, secret sense of failure rose up, now aided and abetted by grief at Josephine's death. She fought away the panic the emptiness engineered by focusing on the practicalities of probate and Ash House, desperate not to show any vulnerability should Michael return. She let the practicalities consume her, relegating the emptiness to a dull ache, and so maintained the usual pretence of strength and confidence.

An hour later Ruth cried when they told her Josephine had left her an oil painting, the china figurines she loved and a monetary bequest. They seemed to talk for a long time and yet decide very little. In the end Ruth agreed to continue living in Ash House until probate was done so Iris and Michael could decide what to do with it.

Back at the farm Iris left Michael to phone Zoe and walked to the paddock and its three occupants. She opened the gate, pleased to see Honky hadn't let himself out again and went inside with Gus at her heels. Iris whistled, making Blue and Shiloh, the Andalusian mares, raise their heads from grazing, intelligent gazes sweeping the paddock. Gus trotted to the left and lay in the grass watching, tongue lolling. Blue, the dappled grey, gave a whinny and ambled over. Shiloh, her chestnut belly heavy with the foal she was carrying, came more slowly, snatching at grass. Honky had no such patience. The dark brown donkey trotted to Iris, braying a welcome. Gus rose and quartered behind the mares, wanting everyone to stay together. Honky started nudging Iris's pockets and hands, seeking carrots, or his favourite, Polo mints. Disappointed, the donkey raised his head and started investigating Iris's hair with soft lips in case any hidden treats were in there. Laughing, Iris pushed him away, then put her arms around Honky's neck and gave him a hug. Blue then reached them and demanded attention. Soon Iris was stroking the three broad faces, enjoying their comforting equine scents and feeling their warm breaths on her skin with Gus at her feet.

'You'll never guess what,' she murmured. 'We're rich.'

Not that we've ever been poor exactly.

Along with Michael's salary, the turnover from Whitebarn's rare breeds meant they were comfortably off. She acknowledged that the farm had been a struggle, especially in her early years. But it had been her stepfather's dream and so making it success was something she would never give up on. Never. Her determination over Whitebarn filled the internal emptiness somewhat and any successes filled it momentarily, pushing the fear of failure away for seconds at a time. The generally solitary, physical work provided mental and emotional respite from having to pretend to be someone she wasn't, someone whole and balanced.

But now what, as we're going to be multi-millionaires?

Abruptly she felt overwhelmed, suddenly terrified she would somehow lose it all or be found wanting over any expectations Josephine might have had. She took calming breaths, focusing on the movement of stroking her donkey and horses.

What on earth am I to do with it all and Foxcombe Valley as well?

Someone hailed her and turning she saw Thomas and Peg. She waved and gave her horses and donkey a final pat before going to see what he wanted.

'Problem with Lottie's farrowing,' he said, speaking of one of the prize sows.

'Oh goodness she's early and her first as well. Do we need to call Pete?'

She knew their vet, Pete Maddox, would come at a moment's notice. He had been tending Whitebarn animals for years and was a close family friend.

'Not as yet,' Thomas said. 'Best come and see.'

Iris and the two dogs followed Thomas round the back of the farmhouse and down through the orchard to where the piggery and pigsties were sited. After checking on the sow, Iris left Gus with Thomas and quickly went to the house. She changed into her work clothes, anticipating a long night ahead.

In the kitchen she opened a cupboard and retrieved her

orphan pouch. A nylon webbed harness that fitted like a jacket and fastened at the front beneath a removable woollen pocket securely fixed there. The unique design enabled lambs and piglets to be carried safely and warmly from and around the sheep pastures or pigsties leaving Iris's hands free. It was equally invaluable while waiting for the vet or when attempting to feed wriggly orphaned animals bottled formula. From her stepfather's original invention Iris had developed the pouch throughout the years and its sturdy design had saved many a rare breed baby at Whitebarn. Now, slipping the orphan pouch on and fastening it, she hurried back to Lottie.

It wasn't until late that night that they managed the full, challenging delivery of eight healthy piglets. After settling Lottie with her babies, Iris returned wearily to the house, Gus a following shadow. In their bedroom her dog stretched out half on his doggy duvet, half on the floor. He gave a sigh, clearly pleased to be abed, but Iris knew Gus wouldn't sleep until she was finally settled. Having showered, she slipped beneath the covers a little after eleven and was asleep in moments. She was woken by Michael shaking her and switching on the bedside lamp with Gus at his side. The alarm clock showed 5am and she was instantly alert.

'What is it? Are the animals all right?'

'The police are here, downstairs.'

Iris stared at him.

'What? Why?'

'Someone's broken into Ash House.'

'Oh my God, is Ruth all right?'

'They're not sure. They don't seem to know where she is.'

Iris swung her legs out of bed, bones suddenly heavy and mind full of cotton wool.

'I don't understand, how's that possible?'

'I don't know.'

They stared at each other and in the dim light Iris could see her worry reflected in Michael's gaze.

CHAPTER FOUR

Iris knew she should move, get up and go downstairs but she couldn't seem to feel her hands to put on her slippers or her robe. Michael helped her, his gaze distant and skin grey. Somehow, they made it to the kitchen where a tall, fair-haired man in a suit was making tea. Seeing the stranger Gus backed and hid behind Iris's legs. She stared at the unknown man with her kettle in his hand, and the sight was so odd she nearly laughed. A woman in her late forties wearing a white blouse and fawn trousers was sitting at their table flicking through a notebook; she glanced up and stood.'Good morning, Mrs Shaw, I'm sorry to wake you. I'm Detective Inspector Louise Fields and this is Detective Sergeant Dens.'

The man smiled and it lit his broad, pleasant face while they shook hands. Iris and Michael took chairs at the other end of the table while Gus slipped underneath and rested his head on Iris's knee. DI Fields resumed her seat.

'I've already apprised your husband of the situation and he was kind enough to suggest we had a cup of tea while we waited for you. I hope you don't mind?'

'Not at all. I think I'll need some myself. Please tell me, what's happened?'

'Of course. The silent alarm at Ash House was triggered at 3.55am. Attending officers discovered the front door open and entered the property. They found the downstairs in disarray and on further investigation ascertained the house was empty of any occupants or intruders.'

Iris gripped Michael's hand, a coldness in her chest.

'I don't understand,' Iris said. 'Where's Ruth?'

DI Fields looked at her notebook.

'You're referring to Ruth Dunn, your late aunt's companion? Your husband told us Miss Dunn agreed to live at Ash House for the next few months. Is that correct?'

'Yes, until probate is done.'

'Are you sure Miss Dunn was in residence? It's hard to ascertain how the alarm was triggered because the front door was open and there's no sign of forced entry.'

'This makes no sense. We just saw her there yesterday afternoon. Ruth has no family and Ash House is her home. Why would she go anywhere else?'

'That's what we're trying to ascertain.'

Abruptly, Iris stood, causing the chair to squeal across the flagstone.

'We should go there. I need to go there.'

Michael nodded and rose to stand next to her. DI Fields' raised hand stopped their momentum.

'You can't, I'm afraid. The forensic team is still going over the house. Please, you'll be more help here for the time being. Once the team are finished this morning, we'll certainly need you to go over and tell us if anything is missing.'

'Ruth is missing.'

'We don't know that she hasn't just left of her own accord. If the alarm hadn't been triggered no one would be the wiser as to her absence or the state of the house.'

Seeing Michael's frown, Iris sat again as the inspector's meaning became clear.

'Wait,' she said. 'You think Ruth messed up the house

and then just walked out? She wouldn't do that.'

DS Dens put mugs of tea, a pint of milk and the sugar on the table with spoons. Iris watched Michael, his expression thoughtful, make one for her, putting in extra sugar. She was grateful of the warm mug and sipped, feeling the sweetness wake her. DI Fields sipped her own drink, tucking a strand of dark hair behind her ear, and tapped the notebook.

'Can you go over what happened yesterday afternoon. You were both at Ash House?'

'Yes, we met the solicitor about my aunt's will there at 3.30. We then saw Ruth about an hour later. We all stayed talking until six or just after and then Michael and I came home. After that Michael was in the house and I was with my farm manager attending one of the pigs until about eleven last night.'

'And your farm manager is?'

'Thomas Wade. He and his two sons, Danny and Luke, work here. Luke's taking a year off from university so they're both living at home at the moment. I can give you their address.'

'Thank you, that would be appreciated. And what were *you* doing once you got home, Mr Shaw?'

Michael's gaze narrowed but he answered readily.

'I phoned our daughter to let her know what the solicitor had said and then I spent the evening on my laptop preparing lectures for next week. I work at the university teaching history. At about seven o'clock I went to the piggery and fetched the dog to feed him. I took him back with sandwiches and coffee for Iris and Thomas. I popped down with coffee refills throughout the evening. I finally visited them at about ten o'clock to say goodnight. I was asleep when Iris came to bed.'

'I see, thank you. Now, did anyone else know that Ash House would, essentially, be empty?'

Iris frowned, noting Michael's knuckles were white on his mug.

'My aunt's funeral was a few days ago,' she said. 'So, plenty of people were aware she had passed.'

'I'd like a list of who attended, please.'

'You can't honestly think anyone who came to the funeral would be involved,' Michael said. 'They're friends and family. It's absurd.'

Gus's whiskery face emerged from under the table, eyes wary and nose questing. DS Dens dropped his hand to the dog, who retreated back to Iris.

'Lovely looking dog. Rescue, is he?' Constable Dens asked.

'He's purebred Picardy sheepdog,' Iris replied tersely. 'One of only a few in the country. Now look, whatever has happened Ruth wouldn't have done anything to the house and certainly wouldn't have walked out. You need to be out looking for her.'

DI Fields read something in her notebook, flicking the page back and forth.

'Has Miss Dunn been prone to seizures or mental illness that you know of?'

'So now she's having a psychotic break of some kind? This is ridiculous.' Heat flushed through Iris and her shoulders tightened. 'Someone has broken into the house and hurt Ruth or taken her. Please, you have to find her!'

Michael put a hand on her arm. She stared at him and he spread his fingers in a 'wait' gesture. He looked from the inspector to DS Dens.

'Why are you here?' he asked.

DI Fields and the sergeant exchanged a look. Michael nodded as if confirming something.

'It seems odd that a Detective Inspector would be attending in the early hours to what seems to be a simple burglary,' he said. 'That's if anything has actually *been* stolen, and perhaps or not, a missing person? And forensics already on the scene? What aren't you telling us?'

DI Fields took a sip of tea, her expression pensive, and then she seemed to reach a decision.

'Very perceptive, Mr Shaw. I was trying to find out what you knew about Miss Dunn. How you felt about her before telling you all the facts in case you were biased.'

Iris stared at the woman and her stomach clenched on the tea.

'In case we're suspects you mean?' she said. 'That's why you wanted to know our movements yesterday afternoon! What, you think we burgled our own house, or helped Ruth do it?' DI Fields met her gaze steadily. Iris's stomach knotted. 'And there's more, isn't there?'

'I'm afraid we found some evidence of a struggle in what we believe to be Miss Dunn's bedroom.'

'Oh my God. I told you something's happened to her. You have to find her!'

From under the table Gus gave a huff that was almost a growl and Iris tried to calm down.

'We do indeed need to find Miss Dunn,' the inspector said. 'She could be a victim, certainly. But she could just as easily be involved in whatever happened. An older woman, fearing for her security and realising she's going to be out of a home in…'

'Let me stop you right there, Inspector,' Iris said. 'We told Ruth earlier that my aunt had left her five hundred thousand pounds. So, she had no need to steal anything and certainly no worries about her future.'

DS Dens let out a breath and DI Fields raised her eyebrows.

'That certainly changes things. Sergeant, get on the radio and let the officers at Ash House and the station know that Miss Dunn is now considered a victim and to adjust their search accordingly. And find out what the situation is with the forensic team, please.'

The man nodded and left. Iris heard a crackling radio as the door shut and stared at the inspector while her hands clenched to fists.

'You come in here, practically accuse of us being criminals and try to blame Ruth. Wasting time when you should've been looking for her!'

Beneath the table Gus's body was heavy against her knees. Her fingers, buried in the fur of his back, could feel the Picardy tense at her angry tone.

'Please, Mrs Shaw, try to stay calm.'

Iris stood, her legs and arms shaking, and fists still clenched.

'My husband and I are going upstairs to get dressed. Then we're going over to Ash House. You and your sergeant can wait outside in your car or meet us there. I don't care either way, but you're not staying in here.'

She got up and held open the kitchen door. Michael rose and walked out, down the hall. Iris heard him open the front door. DI Fields picked up her black woollen coat, bag and notebook and walked toward Iris looking as if she might speak.

'Just leave, please,' Iris said.

The inspector shrugged and moved past, gathering the sergeant as she went. Iris followed them with Gus at her heels and watched Michael close the front door behind them. She went to her husband, welcoming his quick, tight hug, trying not to give in to anxiety. She broke away, looking at him, and the worry etched in Michael's face fuelled her own fears.

'We need to get over there as quickly as possible,' she said, starting up the stairs.

'Agreed, but I have to make a phone call first.'

Iris turned and stared at him.

'To whom, for heaven's sake? It's not even seven o'clock.'

'Our lawyer. I don't like the way that inspector talked to us. And if anything has happened to Ruth, we were probably the last people to see her before she went missing. I want him to know what's going on.'

Iris felt as if the stairs had vanished and she was falling. She suddenly sat down and tried to look as if she were thinking and not panicking. She closed her eyes and rubbed her temple but couldn't banish the image of a crumpled figure lying in a field. Michael pulled her up.

'Come on. We just need to keep practical and keep moving.'

Iris nodded and got to her feet, feeling as if the stairs were shifting beneath her, but she managed to get to the bedroom and get dressed. All the while her thoughts were filled with pulpy, blackened skin and fear of what might have happened to Ruth.

CHAPTER FIVE

Three hours later and Iris sat, hollowed out, in the living room of Ash House. She and Michael were finally alone, the police having left. The place was a mess. Furniture was upturned and moved while paperwork was strewn everywhere. She was glad Gus was safely at Whitebarn with Thomas. The walls, doors and furniture were covered in black fingerprint powder and light dustings from it covered the carpets. The forensic team had taken everything they thought relevant including cutting a section from Ruth's bedroom carpet; something Iris had been too afraid to ask about. She heard Michael finish on his phone, and he came in looking tired.

'Josephine's solicitor has agreed with the police. We can move all the furniture out and store it until probate is over.'

'Good. That place I spoke to can get a storage container on the farm in the next couple of days. The stable surveillance system can monitor it and I'll get some more cameras set up before the container arrives. I'd just feel better having Aunt Josephine's things at Whitebarn rather than using a storage company.'

'I agree. We'll get a removal company to move everything over in the next couple of days.'

'In the meantime, I'll ring Thomas and ask if he can

bring our livestock truck over this morning. Luckily, it's just been cleaned after the last show. We can line it with plastic or something and that way we can take anything we're worried about today. We'll just have to keep everything in the house or barn until the container arrives.'

Michael sat next to her and she rested her head on his shoulder.

'We should clean up,' he said. 'And decide what to take.'

Iris sighed and rose, looking around.

'I'll phone Thomas now, if you find some cleaning stuff?'

Michael got up and gave her a hug.

'Sounds like a plan. I'll put the kettle on too.'

He went to leave, and she caught his hand.

'Michael, why isn't anything missing?'

'I don't know. I don't understand any of this.'

'I'm worried about Ruth.'

'Me too, honey, me too.'

He lifted and kissed her hand, then left. Iris stared about the wrecked living room trying to decide where to start.

Just after two o'clock that afternoon, Whitebarn's laden truck left Ash House for the second time that day. Standing on the drive, Iris watched it turn out of the gate and then went back inside. The house looked strange with several large items of furniture, paintings and ornaments missing. But at least it was tidier and cleaned of any fingerprint powder.

The only untouched place was Ruth's bedroom by order of the police. The room was situated at the top of the stairs and the blue and white tape caused Iris's worry and fears to spike every time she passed it. Keeping busy had helped prevent the imaginings and anxieties from overwhelming her. Now, going upstairs once again, she tried not to look at the door, but breathing hurt and fears for Ruth tumbled in her thoughts. She closed her eyes and deliberately slowed her breathing, trying to engineer some calm. After a few moments she felt better and passed Josephine's room, already emptied of everything she couldn't bear to leave, and gained the smaller of the two guest bedrooms. She gazed at the furniture, pictures and ornaments, moving about, touching things and wondering if there was anything that couldn't wait for the removal men. She went to where a white and blue embroidered throw had been draped over a boxy item and lifted the cover to see what lay beneath.

'Good Lord,' she murmured.

Pulling the throw clear she stared at the old trunk. It was a large wooden chest bound in brass strips with a brass keyhole but no key. She heard a step and Michael came in carrying a small landscape painting.

'I think we should take this. Wasn't it one of Josephine's favourites?'

'Yes, I think so.' Iris gestured to the trunk. 'This definitely needs to come with us today.'

Michael rested the painting against the wall and eyed the chest. He bent, running his hands over the wood.

'I don't think I've ever seen this before, have you?'

'I have, but not for years and years. I always wondered what Aunt Josephine had done with it. Wait until you see what's inside.' Iris tried lifting the lid, but it was locked. 'I think the key's in Josephine's jewellery box, which has already gone to Whitebarn.'

Michael straightened from the chest and looked about the room.

'I don't think there's much left to take today. I reckon we can fit this trunk and everything else in the Land Rover and not worry about bringing the lorry back.'

Iris agreed and replaced the throw over the chest.

'Then let's get loaded up and go home.'

Michael caught her shoulders, his expression concerned. 'How are you holding up?'

'I'm okay,' she lied. 'Just worried about Ruth and about leaving this place with no one watching it.'

'I don't think whoever broke in will be coming back anytime soon.'

'Then why are we moving everything out? And why did they take Ruth?'

Michael pulled her into a hug, and she knew in his silence that he had no easy answers or reassurances.

It took them the rest of the afternoon and early evening to deal with Josephine's furniture, rugs, paintings and ornaments at Whitebarn. Thomas's sons helped with the loading and unloading, lifting and shifting into the barn. While she worked Iris took comfort in the fact that the container was arriving in two days and the removal was booked for the same day. Finally, just after six o'clock, everything was safely stored, and the animals had been taken care of. In the kitchen Iris gratefully accepted a glass of red wine from Michael and set out a takeaway for dinner.

'Did you manage to sort the extra cameras for the surveillance?' he asked.

'Yes. Thomas and I moved two to the barn. I've got a chap coming out to supply and install five more tomorrow morning.'

'I spoke to Zoe and told her what's happening. She wanted to come up, but she's got work tomorrow so I told her not to and we'll see her next weekend.'

Iris nodded. They ate in silence for a while; Gus slept on Iris's feet under the kitchen table. Iris felt as if tiredness and worry were engrained in her bones with each movement needing extensive concentration and focus. Conversation with Michael was sporadic but comfortable. Neither of them mentioned Ruth although Iris kept checking her phone to see if the police had called. When they finished eating Michael cleared everything away, loading the dishwasher and feeding the dog. At his insistence, Iris took her wine and went into the living room where the fire had been lit. She shrugged into her cardigan feeling the need for comfort more than warmth and stopped in the living room doorway, arrested by the sight of the old trunk. Putting down her glass, she went upstairs and fetched Josephine's jewellery box. Back in the living room Iris rummaged through it until, right at the back under some brooches, she found the brass key. Michael came in with his own glass of wine, followed by Gus, who trotted over, sniffing the chest and wandering around it.

'Ah the mysterious trunk,' Michael said. 'When did you first see it?'

Her husband settled on the sofa.

'When I lived with Aunt Josephine and Uncle Walt. Mother had already left for Scotland and Thomas was looking after Whitebarn.'

Michael took a sip of wine and nodded, his expression sympathetic. Try as she might Iris could never properly recall the first three months she had lived at Ash House after her stepfather's funeral. They were a blur of grey days and sleepless nights that were only alleviated by her aunt's constant presence, holding her through the numb silences, sudden tears and angry outbursts. She shook her head, dispelling the memories and continued.

'One day, about four months after I'd gone to stay, Aunt Josephine made me get out of bed, shower and dress. Then she took me up to the attic. As you know, it's vast and Uncle Walt was such a pack rat. She somehow convinced me to help catalogue and tidy everything. Keeping busy helped.' She swallowed some wine, recognising that that had been when she had first learnt to hide the newly raw emptiness and pretend to be confident about things. She gestured to the trunk. 'This was one of the things up there.'

Michael topped up her wine glass.

'Don't keep me in suspense,' he said. 'What's inside?'

'Old letters from Josephine to Walt during the war, clothes and books as well as hopefully, a large wooden box inside which is a pocket watch. It's very old, ivory and rosewood, engraved brass and silver.'

'That sounds intriguing. So come on, open it up. Let's get a look.'

Iris unlocked the trunk and opened the lid. Gus immediately looked inside, snuffling at the contents. She pushed his large Picardy nose away and, there, underneath some letters and books lay the box. It was scratched and scarred with one corner splintered off just as she remembered. She took it out and slid the wood cover off, lifting out the pocket watch. Gus, tufted ears pricked, was intent on her movements while Michael let out a low whistle of appreciation. The watch's ivory rim was yellowed with age, the silver and brass tarnished, and the rosewood dulled. Yet, it seemed to glow in the firelight. She turned it this way and that enchanted anew by its beauty. Michael put his wine glass down.

'It's beautiful,' he said. 'Can I see it?'

Iris handed it to him and smiled at his expression.

'How on earth did Josephine get this? It must be hundreds of years old,' he said. 'Was it something Walt found as part of his jewellery business?'

'No, actually it's an odd story. According to Aunt Josephine, after their Russell Square house was bombed, she went through the rubble and found the box. It had some warped iron casing attached to it.'

Gus moved to Michael and sniffed at the watch before settling next to Iris.

'Lucky the box wasn't blown to pieces.'

'Truly. But the oddest part was that Josephine swore blind she had never seen it before.'

'That's strange. Didn't Walt own the house before they got married – maybe it was his?'

'That's right, being a few years older than Josephine I guess he'd already made quite a bit of money and bought the house just before the war. But apparently he'd never seen the box or the watch before the bombing either.'

'That is odd. Perhaps it belonged to a neighbour?'

Iris shook her head. From somewhere outside a fox barked. Gus looked toward the sound and gave a huffing woof, subsiding when Iris rubbed his head.

'Josephine asked around and at the time only one other house was bombed on the square. They didn't claim the box so it couldn't have been from there.'

Michael turned the watch to study its edges.

'Do you know, I think this opens,' her husband said. 'There's a funnel at the side and a seam that runs around the whole thing and a hinge.' He put his nail to the seam and pushed. 'It's going to need oiling or greasing to help it.'

'Oh, I think I have something,' Iris said.

She rose and went to the kitchen, returning with a pot of Vaseline that they used for Gus's pads when they cracked. Michael rubbed some of the jelly into the watch seam and hinges and reapplied his nail. The watch gave reluctantly, and Iris imagined it creaked. Slowly it yielded to Michael's pressure and he peered inside.

'I was right, it's hollow but there's something in here. Hold out your hands.'

Iris did as bid. Michael's fingertips were white as he

tightened his grip and applied more pressure. Suddenly the watch opened and something fell, landing heavily into Iris's hands. She gasped, staring at the thick gold locket studded with diamonds and emeralds. She held it up for Michael to see and noticed a boar's head engraved on the back. She stared at her husband, whose expression was incredulous, and then back to the locket.

'What on earth is this doing in there?' she asked.

'I have no idea. Didn't Josephine ever show it to you?'

'No. And I don't remember the watch opening before. Do you think she knew about the locket?'

'Again, I have no idea,' he said. 'We'll probably never know if she did.'

Michael put the watch down and Iris gave him the locket to inspect. She looked into the trunk thinking about her great aunt and moved some papers about, uncovering an order of service booklet. With trembling fingers, she lifted it out, staring at the picture on the cover. Newspaper clippings fluttered from inside scattering to the floor.

'What's all that?' her husband asked.

Iris scrabbled the clippings together, putting them back into the booklet.

'Nothing,' she said. 'Just something Aunt Josephine kept.'

Iris rose, still gripping the booklet and with tears stinging her eyes only just managed to gain the downstairs toilet before a sob broke free. Sitting on the toilet seat she muffled her crying in a towel and rocked on the weeping. After long moments she forced some control, gasping deep breaths and wiping her eyes. Then, flushing the toilet to cover the sound of blowing her nose, Iris washed her face and shoved the booklet into her cardigan pocket before returning to the living room. Michael rose and hugged her.

'All these years we've been together, why didn't you tell me?'

Keeping her head down she moved from him and stroked Gus's ears.

'Tell you what?' she said with forced brightness.

He held out a newspaper clipping she must have missed in her haste. She looked away but couldn't avoid the printed headline; 'Local Farmer Dies After Drinking Industrial Drain Cleaner'.

'That you were the one who found your stepfather after he committed suicide.'

She shook her head, unable to speak. Michael's arms were around her in a moment and Gus nudged her hand, leaning against her legs. Iris refused to give in to tears in front of her husband, despising herself for the vulnerability and feeling like a failure for it. She pushed him away and settled on the sofa, hating that she finally had to explain things.

Nearly an hour later Iris felt emotionally drained and unknotted as if muscles she never knew were tense had eased. Michael covered his shock well, but she knew hearing what had happened that day upset him almost as much telling it had. Dry eyed, she watched her husband read through the newspaper articles, his expression full of concern and sympathy. Her heart ached with love for him, but it also twisted with familiar fear at the thought of admitting to the emptiness spawned from that day. To reveal it, she had long recognised, meant he would know she pretended confidence and strength, making her ultimately vulnerable. That things she barely acknowledged, like inadequacy, self-condemnation and worthlessness, made her constantly unbalanced and insecure; abnormal. He would discover the ugly truth of her. That to be seen as confident and strong she projected a technicolour version of herself while hiding the real black and white Iris from everyone, including him. She knew he would see her differently, love her less and in all likelihood leave. A thought that, while illogical, was more terrifying than any other. Yet Michael's current understanding and support, even though she had hidden the truth of that day from him, made her wonder. So, against instinct and will she managed to say, 'I should've been here. I could've stopped him.'

His fingers found hers and he shook his head.

'You can't think like that. There's nothing you could've done even if you had been here.'

'You don't know that,' she muttered. 'No one does.'

He held up a clipping.

'I need to ask; why do none of the reports mention Trudi? Had she left for Scotland already?'

Anger at her mother, a bitter old friend, rolled through the emptiness, filling it for a welcome moment.

'No. They were still together when he died. She was actually meant to be here with him that weekend.'

'Where was she?'

Iris touched the order of service booklet.

'I don't know. She's never told me or anyone else, except the police. But that's Mother all over, she never talks about anything she doesn't want to.'

Michael frowned and seemed about to say more but she couldn't bear it and stopped him by gathering the cuttings. Slotting the articles into the order of service booklet, she deposited it back into the trunk.

'I'm sorry,' she said.

'What for?'

'Not telling you about it all. We only met eighteen months after and I just couldn't bear to.' By that time the emptiness had already become too much. The pretence too important. 'Then as time went on it just became too hard to even think about.' That much at least was true.

He pulled her close, murmuring comfort and understanding. She let herself relax against him and tried to believe what he said while wondering if anything would ever fill the emptiness and stop her having to pretend to be somebody she wasn't.

Later when Michael carried the trunk upstairs Iris curled on the sofa feeling rinsed of emotion. Gus joined her and pushed his head against her arm, so she ran her fingers through his fur, and he gave a contented sigh, his head in her lap. She pulled her cardigan out from under his chin and felt something in the pocket. Taking it out, she stared at the unread letter from Josephine and the business card of Mr Stephen Sloane. Binning the card, she took a breath and opened the envelope, taking out three tightly written pages. She held them still folded and studied the elegant whorls of Josephine's handwriting, feeling comforted by its familiarity. Then, with the pages trembling in her fingers, she unfolded the letter dated the previous year and read,

May 2006 at Ash House

My Darling Iris,

If you're reading this then I've finally exchanged worlds. Don't be too sad. I'm with Walt now and forever beyond any pain, care and worries. I know with my passing you'll discover I've been keeping secrets and I'm sorry I didn't tell you everything while we were still together. I suspect now my solicitor has told you about Foxcombe Valley and my fortune you might feel I have no more secrets to share and how I wish that were true! Again, I'm sorry – not for keeping secrets this time – but for having to tell you these after I'm gone. It's selfish of me I know, but I must tell someone, and you and Michael are the only ones I trust. My darling, what you do with these secrets is your choice. Please remember that. But if what I reveal is too much, too hard or too dangerous for you then leave it as it is, but don't forget it all and just keep everything safe for someone else to discover and champion.

So, I'm sure you remember many years ago I showed you an old pocket watch and told you the story of how I found it in a box among the rubble of our old house in Russell Square. Thanks to a man called Gordon McCraken I discovered the iron casing that had preserved the box had been a safe, buried in the basement of our old house.

Back in 1840 Gordon hid the pocket watch in this safe, along with a satchel containing extraordinary things including his notebook and a large, leather tome. These things were also in the box preserved from the bomb by the iron safe. I couldn't believe what I'd found or how long it had been there. The more I discovered the more intrigued I became. I was amazed to find that the leather book held the most remarkable secrets. A notebook, documents and accounts about the death of one Lady Amy Dudley.

When I discovered the artefacts and read everything it broke my heart. I was appalled at what happened to Amy Dudley. It gave me a fierce determination to put things right and I set out to find her. I wanted to reveal what really happened and let Lady Dudley rest in peace. Not just for her, but for poor Gordon and Amy Dudley's most ardent and stalwart investigator at the time of her death, Samuel Banks. Reading the accounts, I felt I must try to do the same, for all of them.

But it was not to be. For there were, and perhaps still are, people called Watchers who wanted to keep anyone from investigating Amy Dudley's death or revealing the truth of it. Somehow, they found out what I was doing and threatened me. They said they would kill Walt, who knew nothing of what I had found bar the pocket watch, if I kept investigating. They even tried to force me to give up anything I had relating to the death. I convinced them all I had was a couple of pages from Gordon's notebook with diagrams of Amy Dudley's skull. I gave them two pages from the notebook, and it seemed to work. But I was terrified and stopped my search, hiding everything.

Thankfully the Watchers seem to have left me alone throughout the many years since. Although I've never been certain of it and I was too afraid and suddenly grew too old to continue the quest. Now, as my life is drawing closed, I feel I must pass on all that I have held secret about the poor woman's death to you. The book and other artefacts are in a safety deposit box at a private bank in London called Goodwins. Not even my solicitor knows about it. The form passing ownership to you on my death is filed at the bank. All you need do is go with two forms of identification and my death certificate. The security code to unlock the box is four digits. You'll find them with you, imprinted on my wedding day where this all began. You'll forgive a foolish old woman the puzzle, but I've been scared of the Watchers all these years so even writing the code here seems incautious to me. You'll work it out and discover the code, I'm certain.

One other thing. As I've been coming toward the end of my life, I've wanted something of Amy Dudley's close by. The watch is the least fragile of the artefacts and has nothing to do with her death. It's not mentioned by Sam and only in passing by Gordon, but it did belong to Amy Dudley. So, when we went to London for Penelope's funeral at Highgate cemetery a few years ago, I took the opportunity and went to Goodwins.

I only meant to keep the watch with me for a little while, but it never seemed the right time to take it back. I kept it hidden in my bedroom, not wanting questions about where it came from or having to speak about Amy Dudley, but I took it out nearly every day and held it. Now, my fingers are too weak to open the watch to see the treasure inside, so Ruth has helped me when I feel the need. Open the pocket watch and find the beauty inside, my darling. I've no idea how or why it came to be in there and you'll see that neither Gordon nor Sam mention it. So, perhaps it's just a token. Something Amy Dudley treasured and hid. Who knows? But I've left it in there, just as she did. I kept the safe box from Russell Square and put the watch in it only recently, leaving it where you saw it all those years ago.

As to the other things, please, Iris, go to Goodwins, read and see everything and keep it all safe. If you feel the Watchers are no threat or perhaps no longer exist, you might try to achieve what the rest of us failed to do – solve the mystery. Find Amy Dudley and let her rest in peace with her soul untainted by suicide. Such an ugly subject that I know you've struggled with over the years and still do, although you pretend otherwise. But I only ask that you try. Now, my darling, I truly must leave you and I'm sorry for it. Remember me with only good memories, not sad ones. Know that I love you beyond words and worlds, and that you are and always will be, a true child of my heart.

Your ever loving,
Josephine

Chapter Six

The following day Zoe swiped her security card and left Arrant forensic laboratories, heading for the park. She took the route by the Thames enjoying the bustle of the thoroughfare and the fresher air after the sterility of her workstation. She found Will seated at their usual bench eating a sandwich. He handed her a smoothie from their favourite cart and exchanged hellos while Zoe unwrapped her lunch.

'You got out a bit early today?'

Will's black curls bounced as he nodded, giving him an enthusiastic air.

'I finished the Cornwall excavation data early. Turns out the bones are over a thousand years old.'

'Blimey, that's impressive.'

'That's not what Western Housing said. I've already flagged the site as national importance and issued a protection order while we see who else is down there. What about you? How's the blood splatter on that Wandsworth case?'

Zoe bit into her sandwich, chewing reflectively and ordering her thoughts.

'Intriguing. I can't seem to get the weapon right. I thought at first it was something with a metal rim, but now I'm wondering if it's wooden like a cricket bat edge. How's that Southampton skull coming?'

'Good. I should be able to finish the reconstruction this afternoon now the Cornwall bones are done.'

They smiled at each other and Zoe studied Will while they ate. He seemed to have barely changed since they had met at university eight years previously. His grey eyes still had a mischievous glint despite the seriousness of his job. Zoe felt a familiar surge of gratitude that they had ended up working at the same company. For her, it meant being able to talk to a friend about complex cases, often criminal, that she dealt with, without having to worry about confidentiality. Will's expertise in bones often coupled him with her blood analysis work, making it especially easy to talk shop. A breeze picked up off the river and the crying gulls seemed loud. She took a deep breath, revelling in the autumn sun.

'It's so nice to be out here every day for lunch,' she said.

Will eyed her with amusement.

'Except when it's raining or snowing or too cold, Princess.'

'You can talk, Mister, it's far too hot to sit outside.'

He chuckled and raised his smoothie in a salute. Zoe sipped her own drink, her thoughts slipping back to work.

'If you're free sometime tomorrow,' she said, 'there's some cut marks on a tibia I'd like your opinion on. The blood stains on the clothes seem all wrong for what I've been told happened. I think…'

'Zoe?'

She looked up. A man dressed impeccably in a tailored suit had stopped nearby. He was framed by the sun making his blonde hair glow and his face difficult to make out. He moved forward and she suddenly recognised him.

'Theo? Oh, my goodness what a surprise.'

She rose and he leant forward to kiss her cheek.

'Fancy meeting you here,' he said.

'We're here quite often for lunch. It's only a short walk from our office.'

Theo glanced at Will placidly eating his sandwich and Zoe made the introductions.

'Why are you here?' she asked.

'Funnily enough my work has just relocated nearby.' Theo looked around. 'I was taking a stroll, seeing what's about. It's very pleasant isn't it?' His gaze found hers. 'I heard about Ash House. Is there any news about Miss Dunn?'

Zoe looked away, filling her gaze with people and the Thames, managing to keep her voice steady.

'I spoke to Mum this morning and the police still don't know anything.'

She hated this, talking about someone she knew who might be hurt or worse. It was an unspoken agreement between her and Will that they hadn't speculated on Ruth's disappearance. They both knew too much about death and wounds to make it an objective conversation. She looked and found Theo's gaze intent on her. His expression suddenly clouded as if he understood her reticence.

'Well, it's nice seeing you,' he said. 'Perhaps we could get coffee sometime?'

'Sure, why not.'

She resumed her seat, expecting goodbyes and leaving. Theo moved closer.

'Oh great,' he said. 'I'm dying to find decent coffee. I tried that place *Bean Expecting You*. It was not good. How about tomorrow lunchtime?'

Zoe stared at him trying to think how to politely refuse but nothing came.

'Okay,' she said slowly. 'We could meet here just after

midday, if that suits?'

'Excellent. See you then.'

Theo grinned, his eyes crinkling with it, and took his leave. Zoe watched him lope away, her thoughts unruly. She sat back and found Will's gaze on her.

'What?'

'He likes you.'

Heat flooded her face and she silently cursed her pale skin.

'Does not. And doesn't matter even if he does. I'm not interested.'

'Good.'

'Good?'

Will's gaze lifted and she glanced to where he was watching Theo's retreating form.

'There's something, I don't know, fake about him.'

'You sound like my mum. She doesn't like him either.'

Will nodded, still watching where Theo had gone. Zoe ate her lunch trying to concentrate on work and banish thoughts of Ruth and Theo.

The next day Zoe took Theo to *Home of the Joe*. The coffee shop was a little too far from Arrant to visit regularly, which was why she chose it for this lunchtime meeting. They settled at a table near the window and ordered.

'I'm afraid I've only got half an hour,' Zoe lied. 'We're so busy.'

Theo gave her a crinkly-eyed smile.

'No problem. I'm just glad to see you and thank you for showing me this place. If it tastes as good as it looks, I'll be happy.'

Thankfully their coffee arrived, and Zoe didn't need to reply. She surreptitiously studied Theo while she added sweetener to her black coffee. He looked striking in dark grey suit and white shirt and seemed utterly relaxed, stirring his latte while gazing out the window.

'You said your company had relocated nearby. What is it they do?' she asked.

He turned his gaze to her with a serious expression.

'It's a large international company specialising in commodity brokerage. That's what I do, I'm a commodities broker.'

She felt her eyebrows draw in and tried to school her expression to something resembling interest. Theo laughed.

'Don't worry, it's as dull as it sounds,' he said.

The tightness in her shoulders eased and she managed a smile.

'I'm perfectly prepared to hear all about it, honestly.'

'Well, I'm not prepared to waste our lunchtime being boring about it. So, tell me, how did you get into blood analysis?'

She frowned.

'How do you know that's what I do?'

He dropped his gaze and seemed very interested in his coffee.

'I sort of asked your mum about you at the wake.'

Sudden warmth sprang across her chest.

'You did?'

He nodded, still not meeting her gaze. Zoe stirred her drink and found herself watching his hands as they lifted the cup, then his lips as he drank. She looked away.

'I wanted to say thank you for coming last week,' she said. 'I know it would've meant a lot to Aunt Josephine to have Rosalind there, and you, of course.'

She heard the clink of cup on saucer and looked back to find his gaze on hers, frank and open.

'Thank you for inviting us. Rosalind was terribly upset about your aunt passing. Josephine was so close with her grandma. I just wish our visit had been under better circumstances. But even so, I have to say Whitebarn seems fantastic, what little I saw of it.'

'It is amazing. Mum's worked so hard and now it's one of the top rare breed farms in Europe.'

'That's impressive. I imagine it was a wonderful place to grow up.'

'It was. I love it there and because of it I initially wanted to be a vet. But, to answer your earlier question, while I was at uni I became fascinated with criminology and switched degrees. From there I specialised in forensic blood analysis. Did you always want to be a commodities broker?'

He laughed again, easily and from the belly, making other customers look over.

'No. I wanted to be a spy like James Bond or an astronaut. But while I was at boarding school, I started a black market sweet business from my dorm. I soon realised I have a knack for reading people and selling things. So, here I am. Do you miss having animals around?'

'All the time. But London and my long hours aren't ideal for keeping pets.'

'Not even a cat?'

'I've thought about it.'

'It would have to be a rescue,' he said.

'Of course.'

They smiled at each other. Zoe's heart tripped faster and she sipped her coffee, focusing on the smoky taste. A mobile phone rang. Theo fished it out of his pocket and glanced at it.

'Sorry, I just have to…'

She nodded, shocked by a throb of disappointment. Theo answered the phone.

'Hello? Look, can I call you back? I'm in a meeting. Great.'

He ended the call and pressing a button switched off the phone entirely, leaving its blank eye on the table.

'I believe we were talking about whether we should rescue cats,' Theo said. 'And I'm starving so I'm going to order some food. Would you care to join me?'

Zoe laughed and found herself agreeing to a toasted sandwich and a second cup of coffee.

In the end she didn't return to Arrant until nearly 1.30. Apologising to her supervisor for the unusually long lunch she hurried to her workstation. Her phone buzzed and taking it out, she opened the text message and read, 'Thanks for a great lunch, I really enjoyed it. I'd love to take you to dinner. Are you free Friday night? Theo.'

She stared at it, thinking about her mum and what Will had said. She remembered Theo's hands and laugh, the way he really listened, and his easy manner. She tapped a reply. 'Thanks, I enjoyed it too. Dinner would be lovely. Pick me up at 7pm Friday. I'll text you my address. Zoe.'

Later that night Zoe rang her mum. Like Iris, she was upset and disappointed the police had no further information about Ruth's whereabouts or the Ash House break-in. They talked about the arrival of the storage container and moving the rest of Aunt Josephine's belongings. Yet nothing shifted the dull ache Zoe felt about Ruth's disappearance. It seemed to hang between her and Iris during the conversation like a third party listening in and whispering. She arranged to stay at Whitebarn over the weekend and with goodbyes and much love, they hung up. For a few minutes afterward Zoe stared at her phone wondering why she hadn't told her mum about seeing Theo.

CHAPTER SEVEN

Later that night Iris and Michael were woken by someone knocking at the front door. Gus trotted onto the landing giving short barks. Switching on lights Iris went to the hallway, calling her dog to quiet. She looked out the landing window and hurried to the bedroom.

'That unmarked police car is outside,' she said.

They looked at each other and Michael nodded, squeezing her arm. Iris led the way downstairs, Gus at her heels. She held her dog and opened the front door, so the porch light came on. It illuminated DI Fields, her expression blank, and DS Dens, looking sympathetic. Iris's heart buckled at the sight of them.

'Ruth,' she whispered.

'We believe so,' DI Fields said. 'I'm sorry to tell you this, but a woman's body, matching the description of Miss Dunn, was found an hour ago.'

She felt Michael at her side and swallowed, clinging to the door, forcing herself to stay upright with her gaze locked on the inspector.

'Where?'

'The woman we believe to be Miss Dunn was found near Sandford Lock.'

'Please, not in the water?' Iris looked at Michael. 'It's so cold at the moment. I can't bear to think of it.'

'I'm afraid I can't tell you anything more at this stage. But we need someone to make a formal identification.'

Iris looked at Michael, fear like a living thing in her breast.

'I'll do it,' her husband said.

'Thank you,' DI Fields replied. 'We can make an appointment for the morning.'

The shower didn't seem hot enough, no matter how high Iris turned the lever. The spray pounded her skin and bowed head, digging into her muscles, and suddenly she was weeping great hiccoughing sobs drowned by the water. She put hands on the wall and leant her forehead there to keep from curling to the floor. She couldn't seem to stop images of Ruth – gentle, kind Ruth – merging with those of her stepfather's ruined face from her thoughts. Abruptly the water sluiced off and she looked through blurred eyes and steam to see Michael holding a towel. Gus's whiskery face, concerned eyes and droopy tail just behind him. Her husband helped her out of the cubicle and dried her, rubbing vigorously while she stood, feeling light and cobwebby, Gus a weight leaning behind her. She managed to put on pyjamas and crawl into bed, lying down with one hand in her husband's, the other on her dog, and fell asleep between one breath and the next.

Iris woke with a slow feeling, blinking from the darkness behind her eyes to the semi-darkness of their bedroom. She glanced at the clock, which showed 3.16am, and took a moment to consider her state.

Awake and crowded with thoughts.

She sighed; as a chronic insomniac she knew sleep was over for the night and slipped out of bed. She put on slippers and gown while feeling oddly surreal and forcing away thoughts of Ruth and her stepfather. She picked up her book and, along with Gus, went to the kitchen. A few minutes later she took a hot chocolate and the dog into the living room where she lit the fire, already laid for the morning. On impulse she picked up Josephine's letter from the mantle, taking it to the sofa and curling up under a blanket.

Gus scrambled to join her. The big dog turned a circle on the sofa and nestled next to her, head on her thigh. Her throat tightened at his warmth and never-failing presence. Lifting her aunt's letter Iris re-read it, feeling weightless in mind but clay heavy in heart.

'Imprinted on her wedding day,' she murmured.

Moving her dog's head, Iris rose and got a pad and pen. When she settled back on the sofa Gus resumed his lap/sofa position and Iris wrote,

07/05/1934

She stared at Josephine's wedding date trying to figure out which four numbers might be the code, realising with a start that she had already made the decision to go to Goodwins.

'All right let's think about this,' she said to the dog. 'It wouldn't be as straightforward as just the wedding date. Besides that's not what Josephine wrote. I have it to hand, apparently. Imprinted on her wedding day where it all began. Where what began? Amy Dudley's death?'

Gus yawned and his tail waved, brown eyes earnest and interested. Iris stroked his ears.

'Okay so neither of us are historians.'

She considered waking Michael but decided against it. Instead, she rose and went to the study for her laptop, pausing to look at the two new monitors recently installed. One cycled through the five cameras that showed the stables and pigsties. The other rotated through the four cameras pointed at the shipping container. The images were monochrome, but good quality. Blue, Shiloh and Honky were white, grey and black respectively lying amidst their straw beds. The pigs were pale and black shapes in their homes. The grey shipping container was bright against the night. A fox, small by comparison, crossed in front of it and disappeared off camera. Iris took the laptop to the living room and curled back on the sofa, tucking a blanket around her legs. She switched on the machine and was soon connected to the internet. She typed 'Lady Amy Dudley' into the search engine and gave a surprised huff when it returned over two million results, including ones of Amy Robsart. Frowning, she clicked on a Robsart site.

'It was her maiden name,' Iris told Gus. 'And one I know. Amy Robsart is the woman who fell down the stairs and broke her neck.'

Scrolling down Iris clicked on a random site and read an account of Amy Dudley's strange death at a manor house called Cumnor Place. She opened another tab and brought up a map of Oxfordshire, putting in Whitebarn and then Cumnor, finding that, as she thought, they were only thirty minutes apart by car, with Foxcombe Valley in between.

'I must have driven through the village so many times,' she said. Gus shuffled, putting his bearded chin on her arm, dark eyes fixed on her. 'We've walked there,' Iris told him. 'There's some lovely footpaths around Cumnor. I don't remember a manor house though.'

She found a site about the house and discovered it had been demolished in 1810. Then she flicked back to the map finding roughly where Ash House was situated, on the same valley side as Whitebarn, but on the edge.

'Fancy Josephine buying a house right there,' she said with a smile. 'Almost as if it were planned.'

She returned to the Amy Dudley sites and spent the next

half an hour reading various accounts of the mysterious events at Cumnor Place. When finished she found what was thought to be the only real image of Amy Dudley. Iris stared at the pale face with its stern expression, bow lips and pristine tawny hair. Yet she thought Amy Dudley looked fiercely alive, ready to laugh or debate, passionate and poised. Long dead but still restless, it seemed.

'What have I got myself into?'

She studied the image, imagining shutting the laptop and leaving it all as it was. She closed her eyes, thinking of the poor woman falsely under the suspicion of suicide. Raw images of her stepfather rose unbidden and her breath became short. Something twisted, a pinching of guts and nerves, and the emptiness roared. Half closing the laptop, ready to leave, she glanced at her aunt's letter and straightened, forcing the feelings of inadequacy and guilt away.

'It's not fair,' she whispered. 'The poor woman. It's not right.'

She pushed the laptop open and scrolled back, searching the sites for numbers that Josephine might have turned into a code. Yet after forty minutes there seemed to be nothing significant. No numbers that fitted everything Josephine had written. Iris rubbed her temple where the puzzle irritated like a mosquito in the dark. She drew a breath and stroked Gus while trying to tidy her fragmented thoughts. She re-read her aunt's instructions and looked at Amy Dudley's image again. Gus stretched his legs, paws spreading, expression content, and she idly smoothed his ears.

'Where did it all begin, Gus? Perhaps not with Amy Dudley, but where it started for Josephine? With the bombing and finding the box. Okay, maybe that date is the code, but I don't know what that is. And how would I have it to hand?'

Gus yawned and closed his eyes. She sipped the remnants of hot chocolate, uncaring that it was cold, and stared into the fire. Still nothing came. She shook her head and felt her legs numbing under Gus's weight. She shifted slightly, easing the Picardy more onto the sofa. Gus opened an eye and gave an aggrieved sigh. Iris let her gaze wander, silently repeating her aunt's puzzle until she reached a familiar photograph. Her heart unexpectedly quickened, and her breath caught. She rose, causing more canine disconcertion, and went to the picture, taking it down from the wall. She studied it. Uncle Walt in his uniform and Josephine in a long-sleeved wedding gown outside the Russell Square town house. No matter how much she peered there were no visible numbers. Gus jumped off the sofa and wandered to the fire, stretching out in front of the heat. Iris knelt next to him and turned the photo toward the firelight hoping to see better. He sniffed the frame and nosed it, licking the wood.

'Maybe,' she said to the dog, 'this isn't it. But it is to hand and their wedding day, plus it is the Russell Square house and that's where it all began for Josephine.'

She frowned, peering at the picture, and rubbed a thumb over the glass. Needing to see the house more clearly she rose and turned the frame over, releasing the catches and taking the back off to reveal the browned reverse of the photo. She stopped and stared at faded blue ink:

7/5 outside 19 Russell Square Park.

Iris placed the photo face down on the coffee table and wrote the sentence on the notepad. She stared at the pad, then underlined the four numbers.

'It looks like we're going to London,' she said.

CHAPTER EIGHT

When Iris next awoke the bedside clock showed 7.31 and she felt the mere two hours' sleep in every fibre. Michael was already up and the smell of toast coming from the kitchen made her hungry. She rose, a sudden need to talk to her husband jolting her tired mind. She put on a dressing gown and went to find Michael.

He was in the kitchen reading Josephine's letter with her note explaining things next to his plate that held peanut butter on toast. Gus was eating his breakfast and waved his tail at her entrance without moving from his bowl. She poured a cup of coffee from the cafetière, adding sugar, took a piece of Michael's toast and, eating it, settled to wait. Her husband finished a few moments later and sat staring at the letter and then looked at her.

'So, this is why Aunt Josephine mentioned Amy Dudley. Bloody hell,' he said.

'Big, huh?'

'Huge, if the documents are real and why wouldn't they be?'

Gus, food finished, rubbed his wet bearded face on his bed making chuffing sounds and then settled next to Iris who tickled his head.

'Josephine believed them to be real and so did these Watcher people.'

Michael put the letter down.

'Obviously we have to go to London,' he said. She nodded and her husband continued, 'but it can't be today, I've got to go with the police before work.'

He paused and pushed his plate away. Iris squeezed his hand and tried to think of something to say. But Michael shook his head and touched the letter.

'What about tomorrow,' he said.

'Right. Tomorrow I've got the buyers from Germany coming for the piglets.'

'What about Friday? I haven't got any classes, only marking and a student meeting first thing. I can work from home afterward. We could go mid-morning, be there by lunchtime. Or there's a possibility of Monday for me.'

Iris rose and consulted the day planner on the wall.

'I've got nothing that needs me here Friday. Thomas can have Gus, deal with the feed delivery and the land agent who's dropping paperwork and keys off for the valley, so it should be fine. It can't be Monday as Thomas has the morning off for a clay shoot.'

'Friday it is then. Have you checked this Goodwins out? We might need an appointment.'

'We do. I looked them up before I came to bed. They're very exclusive. In Mayfair no less. I've got the number, so I'll ring and make an appointment.'

Michael nodded and glanced at the wall clock. Iris sipped coffee, hoping the caffeine would help her dragging thoughts.

'We're doing the right thing, aren't we?' she asked.

'What, going to London?'

'No, not just that. The whole thing, looking into Amy Dudley. What if the Watchers Josephine was so scared of still exist and come looking for us?'

Michael's expression turned thoughtful.

'I can't imagine they're still around. I mean, who knows who they were anyway? They might have been some hyper-competitive antique dealers after the documents to sell.' He touched the letter again. 'Besides we only have to read the documents and look at everything. We can leave it all at the bank and never see it again, if we don't want to.'

Iris eyed her husband, absolutely doubting his ability to leave such things behind.

'We'll see,' she said. 'But we won't know until we get there, I suppose.'

'Exactly.' He glanced at the clock again and pushed his chair back. 'I have to go.'

She rose and hugged him.

'Are you going to be all right?' She swallowed. 'Do you want me to come with you?'

He kissed her on the lips and rested his forehead against hers for a moment.

'No. I don't think that would be a good idea. I'll be fine. Are you okay to phone Zoe and tell her about Ruth or should I do it tonight?'

'I'll do it after breakfast. I'd rather she heard it this morning than risk waiting and have her read about it in a newspaper or two.'

'Good point. I suspect there might be a few journalists looking to speak to us and her.'

'They can try.'

Michael kissed her again, his expression sombre, and left for the morgue. She binned the toast, having lost her appetite, poured coffee then went to call her daughter.

For Iris, the day passed with slowness steeped in tiredness and sorrow. Michael rang mid-morning to let her know that he had made a positive identification of Ruth. He sounded as tired as she felt, and she could tell he was upset but could find no words of comfort. Later that evening she and Michael discussed everything but came to no further conclusions about Ruth or Amy Dudley. Despite sleeping heavily Iris had nightmares of drowning and being chased by empty-eyed men. She woke feeling unrested and unsettled. Her time that day was taken up with the German buyers who wanted to establish their own rare breed piggery featuring Sandy and Blacks. A very good price and a date for shipment of the piglets was agreed. Iris should have felt happy and pleased, but there was only a blankness of emotion.

In the red and gold twilight she went to bed down the mares and Honky to find the donkey missing from the paddock. She stared at the horses then the latched gate and despite the heaviness felt a smile on her lips. It was Honky's newest game. The donkey had learnt how to unlatch the gate and push it open, slipping out before it closed again on its own weight. In this way Honky could escape the paddock without the mares, who showed no interest in gallivanting about the farm searching for mischief. Recently she had resorted to tying the gate shut with baler twine to foil him, but either Honky had worked that out too or someone had forgotten to tie it. At her side the Picardy watched her expectantly waiting for his part in the game.

'All right,' she said. 'Gus, where's Honky? Find Honky.'

The dog bounded up, raced around the paddock and set off toward the orchard. Sometimes she wondered if Honky and Gus worked the whole thing out between them as a bit of fun. Gus never failed to find Honky no matter how far the donkey had gone or where, even into the barn to hide behind the caravan they used for shows. The game of hide and seek could last anything from five minutes to half an hour. Once found, Honky would happily be herded by Gus to the stable or paddock. This time Gus returned with the donkey in under fifteen minutes. Honky was living up to his name. The donkey's coat was matted with mud and slurry, so clearly he had been enjoying himself rolling in the stinky stuff. He ambled to Iris searching for treats. She rattled a feed bucket with a few pony nuts at the bottom while trying to breathe through her mouth. Honkey greedily followed the sound of food and she led the rascal into the yard to hose him down. Honky stood with a look of bliss on his face as she washed and brushed him with Gus close by keeping an eye on the wanderer.

Iris was leading a now clean Honky into his stable when Gus started barking. She looked over the half-door and her jaw tightened on seeing a familiar car parking next to her Land Rover. A moment later DI Fields and DS Dens alighted. Iris made them wait while she bedded down Honky and her mares then led the officers to the kitchen.

She offered them tea or coffee, which they declined, and deciding to hell with it poured herself a glass of red wine, wishing Michael was there. She sat, while DS Dens stood next to DI Fields, who settled at the other end of the table. Gus lay at Iris's side where he could watch the police. DI Fields seemed particularly grave and Iris's numbness became leaden.

'What is it now?' she asked. 'It can't be anything good or you would've rung. You only turn up if it's bad news.'

'We wanted to let you know that we're holding a press conference next week about Miss Dunn's disappearance,' DI Fields said. 'And we've established a cause of death.'

The glass felt hard in her grip and she consciously loosened it, taking a sip of wine.

'And did Ruth drown?'

'No. I'm afraid Miss Dunn was strangled.'

The kitchen darkened, fading away, and the inspector's

face smudged white into the blackness. Iris blinked, re-focusing, and tried to think. But her mind was blank, suspended in a void. Something nudged her leg and Gus's head was on her thigh. Her fingers dropped to his ears and whiskery face. She drew a shuddering breath, mentally shaking off the inertia and shock.

'Strangled,' she whispered. 'Ruth was strangled. Murdered by someone? But who, why?'

'We don't know. Which is one of the reasons we're holding the press conference. We're hoping it might nudge someone's memory about Miss Dunn's disappearance. Where she was in the days before we found her.'

Iris took a slug of wine, trying not to think. DI Fields opened her notebook and flicked through the pages until she found what she wanted.

'When we spoke previously you mentioned Miss Dunn had no family.'

'That's right. Her husband passed away some years ago, and they had no children.'

'Can you think of anyone who would want to hurt Miss Dunn?'

'No, I can't, honestly. Ruth was with my aunt for three years and in that whole time she was only kind and gentle. Do you think whoever broke into Ash House killed her?'

'We don't know. Forensics have so far come back with very little, I'm afraid. Although it's early days.' The inspector put a business card on the table. 'This is the contact details for family liaison. You're not strictly Miss Dunn's family or even next of kin, which is why no one's been assigned to you. But if you call them, they've been advised to keep you informed.'

She slid the card along the table. Iris took it, placing it square with the table edge, not wanting to look at it. DI Fields's expression was understanding. Iris wished the woman would leave and take the sergeant with her.

'I understand you've removed all your aunt's belongings from Ash House,' the inspector said.

'Yes, it's stored in the container you passed on the way in.'

'And you're certain nothing's missing?'

'Positive. My aunt had an inventory done for her will. The solicitors have confirmed everything is accounted for.' She looked at the inspector noting the intensity of the other's gaze. 'Why?'

DS Dens shifted, glancing at Gus, who watched the officer from Iris's side. DI Fields looked uncomfortable.

'We have reason to believe that whoever murdered Miss Dunn was looking for something at Ash House.'

'Why do you think that when nothing is missing?'

The inspector's eyes narrowed, gauging Iris.

'What I'm about to tell you, Mrs Shaw, is not being released to the general public. However, given your connection to the victim and the fact that the property broken into is to all intents and purposes yours, I've been authorised to give you certain information regarding Miss Dunn's injuries. This is in the hopes that you might be able to help with our inquiries.'

Iris frowned, not liking the official speak.

'Should I call my lawyer?'

'If you would like to. But we only need some help at this stage, nothing more.'

Iris studied the inspector, feeling wary.

'Okay. Tell me and ask the questions. If I don't want to answer, then that's that.'

DI Fields inclined her head in what Iris took for assent.

'Did you know if Miss Dunn was in the habit of self-harming?'

'Not as far as I was aware.'

The inspector produced a photograph of a large key, the type that Iris imagined unlocked old church and castle doors.

'Do you recognise this?'

She took the photo, studying the long haft and solid-looking teeth.

'No. Why, what's it for?'

'It was found on Miss Dunn's body. I'm sorry to say it, along with what we believe to be spoons and a knife blade, was used to brand her.'

'Brand her. I don't understand.'

DI Fields just looked at her steadily. Iris glanced at the photo.

'Oh my God, she was *branded*.' Iris suddenly wanted to be sick. 'Someone burnt her with this key and other things? That's disgusting, barbaric.'

'Indeed. We believe someone did this to Miss Dunn to force her to tell them the whereabouts of something they couldn't find at Ash House or didn't have time to find. Cash or valuables are the most likely. But with nothing missing we've no idea what it could be.'

'My aunt never kept cash in the house.'

Abruptly Iris's chest turned icy, her heart seemed to falter while her thoughts flashed to Josephine's letter and the Watchers.

'This can't be right,' she said.

'The alternative is actually worse,' the inspector said, misinterpreting her.

Iris's thoughts flailing on Amy Dudley and the Watchers, she looked at the inspector with confusion.

'What do you mean?'

'Someone doing this to Ruth Dunn for no reason at all. Just because they can.'

Iris stared at her and then looked at the sergeant, who

glanced away. Nausea rippled through her cold core, tearing at her throat, and she swallowed. DI Fields reclaimed the key photo.

'No one's been near the storage container?' the inspector asked. 'No strangers have been to the farm?'

'Only some buyers from Germany today, but they've been expected for weeks and were only interested in the pigs. They left about two hours ago.'

'I'll need their details. But otherwise, there's been no one suspicious or odd here or at Ash House since the break-in?'

'No one.'

Her thoughts tilted back over the days, analysing and trying not to think about Ruth, Amy Dudley or the Watchers. She pictured Ash House on the afternoon before the break-in. Imagining the rooms refilled with furniture, paintings and objects. She recalled sitting and drinking coffee, trying to come to terms with Josephine's first secrets. Suddenly she rose and went to the living room, fishing a card from the bin. She returned to the kitchen, handing it to the inspector.

'I've just remembered this man,' she said. 'Stephen Sloane. He came to Ash House the day of the break-in. He said he had an appointment with my aunt about some furniture she wanted to sell. He was very persistent.'

DI Fields examined the card, pocketed it and turned her study to Iris.

'I noticed you now have security cameras.'

'Yes, linked to monitors in the study and a silent alarm linked to the police station. Why, do you think the person who murdered Ruth might come here, looking for God only knows what?'

'We don't know. For the time being a patrol car will do regular passes of the farm overnight. If you see anyone acting suspiciously call me. Do not engage them. In the meantime, I'd like to inspect the container and check your security measures.' She rose. 'I'm sorry not to bring better news. Will your husband be home soon?'

Iris nodded, her head feeling too heavy for her neck. She led the way into the hall and opened the front door just as Michael was putting his key to the lock.

CHAPTER NINE

The following morning the Shaws travelled to Grosvenor Street in London where Goodwins was sited. Arriving an hour early for their appointment, Iris and Michael settled at an outside bistro table on the corner of Davie Street with a view of the bank. They ordered coffee and Iris studied Goodwins.

'It doesn't look like a bank.'

Michael glanced at the white Edwardian building with its colourful window boxes and then returned his attention to his bag.

'Well, it's an exclusive facility,' he said. 'They probably try to keep themselves under the radar of normal folk like us.'

Iris looked at her husband, who was rummaging in his oversized bag checking its contents.

'All right,' she said. 'Give it up. What's in the bag?'

Michael looked startled and snapped the holdall shut.

'Nothing. I don't know what you mean.'

'Michael, you've been coddling that thing since we left Oxford. It had its own seat on the train for heaven's sake. So, tell me, why the love affair?'

'I just thought it might come in handy, that's all.'

'Handy for what? Smuggling a small child or a medium-sized dog into the bank? Are you planning some sort of heist I should be aware of?'

Her husband looked away, suddenly interested in people-watching.

'No. It's just my bag.'

'Just your bag? What, do you think this is my first day?' She smiled. 'Open it and show me what's inside or you don't get to come into the private, posh bank and see the secret stuff.'

Michael's mouth dropped open and his eyes widened in mock shock.

'You wouldn't!'

'Try me, you shifty historian. I'm not going to jail for you. Open it up.'

Her husband grimaced and tilted the holdall toward her, undoing the clasps so she could see inside.

'I knew it!' Iris reached for the contents, but Michael closed the bag and hoisted it out of her reach. She continued, 'Those are your special document wallets. The ones with the protective linings. Shifty and sneaky historian. You've no intention of leaving anything at the bank, have you?'

'I just want to be prepared.'

'Prepared to take everything and run.'

'No running will be involved.' He patted the holdall, placing it on an empty chair. 'But I do think we should get a taxi back to the station rather than the tube.'

'I see. Just being prepared, are we?'

'Yes, I'm a regular boy scout.'

'You were kicked out of the scouts.'

'Ah, but the lessons never left me.'

He grinned and she did too. Their coffee arrived and Iris savoured it, feeling better than she had in weeks.

Nearly an hour later, the tall wood doors of Goodwins closed behind them with the shush of an expensive mechanism. The interior shone with polished steel and glass and a white and gold marble floor glistened. Iris walked to the reception desk pretending she did so every day. A paper-thin man greeted them and asked for their credentials. Iris explained about Josephine's death and handed over her passport, driving licence and the death certificate along with Michael's identification. The man perused them, typed on the computer and made copies of everything.

'Look here, please,' he said, pointing to a tiny black nub at top his computer screen. Iris and Michael shared a confused look and the man smiled slightly. 'It's a retina camera. For the scanner.'

'Of course it is,' Iris murmured and lowered her head.

Fragile-seeming red lines flickered and were gone. Once Michael had been scanned, they were asked to take seats. A few moments later a woman appeared with high heels clicking across the marble and she smiled a greeting.

'Mr and Mrs Shaw? I'm Lana Mitchell, please come this way.'

Lana Mitchell turned, as delicately as if figure skating, and clicked toward a handleless, brushed steel door which exuded heaviness and privacy. She paused at an oval panel set into the frame, red lights strobing her eye, then she stepped aside and gestured for them to do the same. Once their eyes had been scanned the door swung open. They entered a windowless and seemingly endless room. The door closed behind them with noiseless efficiency. Thick, pale carpet replaced the marble floor. Hidden lights gave the illusion of day in a muted, sunshine fashion and potted Ficus trees were tastefully and uniformly arranged every ten feet or so. From the walls, gleaming eight-foot tall columns of brass drawers protruded. The drawers ranged from letterbox slender to kitchen cupboard sized and each had a centred number pad. Down the middle of the room a table was sliced into compartments by ten-foot steel screens and doors. Iris did some calculating and realised with shock that Goodwins must encompass the whole row of buildings on the street. Lana Mitchell handed them glossy booklets.

'These are your client handbooks. All relevant information regarding this facility is contained within but please feel free to ask any questions.'

She smiled and flowed forward into the room. Iris followed with Michael at her side, gazing about. Some twenty feet later, they halted beside one particular column of various-sized drawers.

'Number 1053,' Lana Mitchell said. 'Once you've removed the drawer you can take it into booth 95, just there.' She gestured to a compartment in the centre table. 'The door lock of cubicle 95 will, for your time here today, correspond to your box security code. If you require anything else, please use the courtesy phone in the booth. It connects to reception only. They will be happy to answer any questions, provide access and escorts to bathrooms and any refreshments. When you're finished please use the retina scanner to leave this room.'

Iris stepped forward.

'Could I just ask,' she said, causing the other woman to pause in her leaving, 'what if we want to take things home? Is there a procedure?'

'We only require notification if you wish to close the account.'

'Right. I'm also curious as to the security arrangements in here, such as cameras and the like.'

'Our cameras are only used overnight when the bank is closed to ensure client privacy during opening hours. There are, however, motion, heat and light sensors throughout the entire floor, ceiling and walls which are active at all times. A member of staff comes through the room every two hours and there's a panic button in each booth under the table which activates a camera, providing audio and visual for that booth in case of emergencies. All the information is in your handbook.'

'I see. Well, it sounds very secure. Thank you.'

Lana Mitchell inclined her head and glided away. Iris stared at Michael, who pulled his 'what the hell face', and they waited until the woman was out of earshot.

'This is unbelievable,' she murmured.

'Unbelievable.'

'I had no idea such places existed.'

Her husband touched a drawer face.

'Me neither,' he said, 'except in films and books.'

'Lana Mitchell would be a Bond girl.'

'Which would make us the villains or the unsuspecting canon-fodder?'

Iris gazed at the column of drawers.

'Neither I hope.'

'Why did you ask about the security?'

She glanced at him.

'I've got no idea what's in this drawer and I don't like the idea of some random bank person watching us find out. What was that number? I should've written it down.'

Michael joined her and held up his palm on which was written 1053.

'Boy scout,' he said.

She elbowed his ribs and scanned the drawers seeking the right number and found it three from bottom. Iris stared at the pad in the centre of the foot-tall drawer, her guts twisting.

'I didn't ask what happens if I use the wrong code,' she said.

'Do you think it's the wrong code?'

Iris took a long breath.

'No. But…'

'Only one way to find out.'

She gave him a sideways look.

'Really? Goodness I don't know what I'd do without you.'

'Nervous sarcasm, wow, you are worried.'

'Oh, shut up.'

'You shut up.'

They smiled at each other.

'It'll be fine,' her husband said. 'Josephine wouldn't have left that puzzle if she didn't think you could figure it out. Everything fit. It's the right code.'

She nodded, took another long breath and, bending forward, punched in the numbers memorised from the photograph. Nothing happened. She swallowed and stepped back glancing at Michael, who watched the drawer intently. Suddenly there was soft click and the whole drawer slid out, perfectly balanced to stop just in front of her thighs.

Inside booth 95 they removed and arranged the drawer contents on the table. They consisted of: a large leather book; a document wallet containing a bundle of silk-wrapped parchment; some letters and a notebook; a dark wood and silver candlestick holder and cracked glass panels wrapped in a sheepskin pouch. Michael produced two pairs of cotton gloves and after donning one each they settled in comfortable chairs and began to read. The next hour was broken only by the occasional gasp and murmuring. When Iris finished reading, she stared at the candleholder, overwhelmed with sadness that had a tight fist of anger at its core that filled the emptiness like nothing ever had. She glanced at Michael, noting his set expression and tense jaw.

'We have to find Amy Dudley,' she said. 'I can't leave her alone in the dark. I just can't.'

'I agree,' Michael said, studying the notebook. 'I can't

believe all the supposition about Amy Dudley's death is wrong. Utterly, devastatingly wrong. That poor woman.'

Iris rose and went to the table to touch the sheepskin pouch.

'Do many people think she committed suicide?' she asked, striving to keep her voice steady.

She turned to find Michael watching her and found a smile for him which he returned.

'It's a common theory, I'm afraid.'

'We need to put that right.' She fought away memories and touched the wrappings again, seeking distraction. 'According to Gordon McCraken these plates are photographs of the coroner's report. Could they help prove Amy Dudley's murder if they're still readable?'

Her husband rose to stand beside her and studied the wool-bundled glass.

'It's possible they're still legible,' he said, sounding doubtful. 'But they would be terribly open to interpretation.'

'What do you mean?'

He moved the wrapping slightly, exposing a glass edge.

'Well, the academic community have been fooled about important ancient documents too often not to decry cracked glass daguerreotype as proof positive. Especially over something as controversial as Amy Dudley's death.'

'I've been meaning to ask, why is it still controversial? I mean, at the time I understand. And even when Gordon McCraken was looking into it given his explanation of Katherine Grey's involvement, which I'm still not entirely convinced of.'

Michael resumed his seat, huffing out a breath and steepling his fingers.

'All right, we know from Gordon's notes that he believed Katherine Grey could easily have formed the Watchers and orchestrated Amy Dudley's murder as revenge against Lord

Dudley. Possibly to implement him in her death and get the man hanged.'

Iris supressed a shiver at the depth of such anger and loathing.

'Do you honestly think that Katherine Grey could have hated Robert Dudley that much?'

'If Gordon was right and she held him responsible for the death of her sister, Jane? Yes, I believe Katherine Grey could certainly loath the man enough to kill his wife. And don't forget it seemed as if Robert Dudley was going to be king, given his relationship with the queen.' He shook his head. 'Can you imagine how angry that would make Katherine Grey? Robert Dudley was the only one left of his family. A family responsible for Katherine's sister being bullied into becoming queen, then poor Jane Grey was branded treasonous and executed, and that man was now tipped to take the very throne her sister died for.'

'Okay, maybe it was Katherine Grey, but that was centuries ago. Why would it matter now?'

'For a start, if we prove Amy Dudley was definitely murdered and Robert Dudley's innocent of it, it could invoke a royal scandal.'

'Because it's possible that Elizabeth I extended family, like Katherine Grey, had a hand in it? But the whole thing is hundreds of years old. Who would care?'

'The royal family. Look, since the abdication and the Second World War the royal family have worked tirelessly to maintain and evolve their relevance in an increasingly modern world that views such institutions as redundant. But manage it they have and very successfully too. Imagine suddenly having a member of the royal family revealed as organising a cold-blooded murder. Not a battlefield death but the ruthless killing of an innocent, and now much maligned, woman.'

Iris could well imagine the newspaper headlines, social media frenzy and television reports. Michael continued, 'Think how history, modern media and the public vilify Richard III for his supposed killing of the two princes in the tower, and that's even older than Amy Dudley's murder. The royal family can shake off Richard III because their direct ancestor, Henry VII, supposedly meted out moral revenge and Richard was killed in battle for the throne, not murdered in cold blood.'

Iris abruptly sat, staring at her husband.

'Goodness, so Katherine Grey ordering the murder of Amy Dudley could make our royal family very unpopular.'

'Indeed. Add on to that the fact that Amy Dudley's murder has essentially been covered up for hundreds of years. All that time the poor woman has laboured under the dreadful suspicion of suicide. Religious leaders will have a field day and the press will tear the royals apart. It could mean a serious scandal and severely damage the royal family's standing.'

She picked up the notebook and turned to the pages showing the Tudor family trees, tracing Elizabeth I to Katherine Grey.

'But we've no idea if Gordon McCraken was right about Katherine Grey's involvement. So, after we find Amy Dudley, we can't just say she was murdered. We have to make sure we know who ordered her murder and why.'

'More, if we're going to succeed in letting Amy Dudley rest properly, we have to make sure every proof of murder we have is unshakeable or at least too convincing and provable to quash.'

Iris gazed at the letters, notebook and Sam's notes. She flicked her attention to the candleholder and the just-visible daguerreotype plates.

'Otherwise,' she whispered, suddenly appalled at a

notion, 'it could all be made up. That's what they'll say, the academics, the royalists, the royals themselves.'

'Unfortunately, yes, that's exactly what they'll say. And even when we prove the documents are original it won't make what they say true.'

'We have to find Amy Dudley.'

'And the original coroner's report.'

'Bugger, and that.'

Iris studied Michael's face, determination etched in every line, and she knew it mirrored her own.

'We're doing this,' she said.

'Absolutely.'

'Thank all my gods you bought that stupidly big bag.'

He grinned.

'See me? Bloody genius boy scout.'

They gathered all the artefacts, stowing them in Michael's bag and left the booth. Her husband then returned the empty drawer to its slot and locked it back in place. Their footsteps were silenced by the dense carpet as they made their way to the door. Abruptly Iris stopped, legs unsteady. Michael caught her arm, his expression concerned.

'What's the matter?'

'What if this is what they were after at Ash House? Why Ruth was…' Nausea swept her making her stomach cramp while her thoughts whirled. 'What if this whole thing is as dangerous as Josephine believed?'

Michael looked grim, his hand clenching and unclenching around the bag strap across his chest.

'It's possible,' he said. 'Especially after reading what we just did and Gordon's account.'

'I wonder what happened to Gordon. Why do his notes end with his trip to Oxford? Do you think the Watchers killed him?'

'I don't know. I don't know if the Watchers still exist or

if us digging into Amy Dudley's murder will be dangerous, or if Ruth's death had anything to do with it all. But I do know we can stop if you like. Put everything back right now and just walk away.'

Iris imagined putting the documents in the drawer, tucking the candleholder next to the leather tome and shutting it all away. The emptiness gripped her making her collapse inwardly at the thought of leaving Amy Dudley behind and returning to Whitebarn. She straightened, breathing deeply, and shook her head.

'I can't leave Amy Dudley tainted anymore; it's not fair. I won't abandon her soul to that appalling, false accusation of suicide.'

'And the Watchers?'

'If they exist and come after us then we'll go to the police and the press. Just expose everything, evidence be damned.'

'All right, at least that way Amy Dudley will still have a chance of resting peacefully even if the whole thing is wrangled over for years.'

'Exactly. But if we put it all away now, she'll never be saved.'

'So, we're definitely doing this?'

'Yes. We'll try it the proper way first by getting all the evidence, Amy Dudley and the report. But if we can't or the Watchers come at us, we'll just publish everything anyway. Deal?'

He kissed her forehead and grinned.

'Deal.'

She could sense excitement like a bright wave coming off him. Things like this, she realised, must be what historians dream about. Holding hands, they continued to the steel door.

At reception the thin man called a taxi and twenty minutes later they got into a black cab, heading for the train station. The taxi passed the bistro where they had stopped for coffee. Iris watched it go by thinking how everything had changed since they had sat there. She didn't notice the expensively dressed man wearing sunglasses, seated nearby and watching them leave Goodwins.

CHAPTER TEN

That evening at dinner Zoe found it increasingly difficult to pay attention to what Theo was saying. The waiter placed Dover sole on their table and the smell made her throat close, panic welling. She rose, murmuring an apology and headed for the ladies. On passing the coat alcove, tears blurred her vision. She stopped, fighting not to cry and jaw clenched against the sobs. Suddenly Theo was there. He pulled her into his chest, hiding her from the restaurant, and stepped them into the alcove.

'Hey now, what's wrong?'

She gulped.

'It's Ruth,' she managed. 'She was murdered.'

'Oh no. Oh sweetheart, I'm so sorry.'

'I only found out yesterday.'

'Why on earth did you agree to come out?'

'I wanted to see you and ... and I should be better than this. What I do should make me better at this.'

He wiped her tears with the ball of his thumb.

'No, it shouldn't and we're not staying here. You need to go home.'

'But what about our food?'

'Doesn't matter. Do you want to wait here while I sort it out and get us a taxi?'

'Yes, please.'

'Stay here and I'll be back in a minute.'

He bent and kissed her lips, soft, lingering and filled with strength, then he was gone. She stared at the dark mass of coats, trying to steady her breath.

Twenty minutes later and the front door lock kept moving under her teary sight making it difficult to get the key in. Finally, Theo took the keys from her, unlocked the door and steered her to the living room, switching on lights and settling her on the sofa. He stood, gazing at her with concern, his hands spread out as if stopping a fleeing deer.

'Do you want some water or something stronger?' he asked. 'Do you have anything stronger?'

She managed a smile.

'It's lovely of you to offer, Theo, but you don't know where anything is.' Her eyes were hot, and insides balled out, leaving her oddly vacant and unsure of everything. She rose. 'I'm so sorry for being such a mess. Thank you for looking after me.'

He took her hands.

'You're not a mess. It's completely understandable that you're upset. I wish you had told me earlier.'

'I'm sorry I wasted your time tonight.'

He stepped closer.

'That's not what I meant. I meant I could've helped. Talked it through or not, whatever you needed.'

She moved until they were only inches apart.

'I'm sorry,' she whispered, caught in his blue gaze.

'Stop apologising,' he murmured.

She kissed him, feeling heat flood her, driving any thought of murder away. He deepened the kiss, closing the space between them so their bodies touched everywhere. Her hands were in his hair and all thought had stopped when suddenly he pulled away, breathless, and put inches between them again.

'Zoe, I don't want this.'

It took her a moment to understand and then she felt slapped, her heart shrinking to dust. She half stumbled away.

'I see. Well, you should go. Thank you for everything.'

He caught her hand, and she resisted the urge to pull away.

'Zoe, I'm sorry. That came out wrong. What I mean is you're too important to me.'

She stared at him, her heart restarting and warmth filling her chest.

'I'm important to you?'

He stepped to her again, smiling but also shy faced.

'Yes. I know it's probably too soon to say things like this, but you're important to me and I don't want to do anything while you're upset or because you're upset. Then you might regret it, be embarrassed or something and never want to see me again.' His voice dropped. 'I couldn't bear that.'

His expression was tender and uncertain. She closed the gap, kissing him and pulling at his jacket. He returned the kiss and then drew back.

'Are you sure?'

For an answer she kissed him again and this time he didn't stop her.

Zoe woke early the next morning with her legs slotted comfortably through Theo's. She shifted, disentangling them, and he sighed in his sleep but didn't wake. She slipped out of bed, pulled a robe on and looked at him, lying on his front. Her gaze wandered, taking in his broad shoulders and easy breathing.

'Are you watching me sleep?' he asked without opening his eyes.

She grinned.

'Maybe.'

He opened his eyes, turning to look at her and returned the grin.

'Do you want to come back here and watch me not sleep?'

'Definitely.'

Later, they showered together and then Zoe made breakfast. Pouring coffee, she watched Theo spread jam on his toast.

'What are you up to today?' he asked.

'I've got a hair appointment in a couple of hours.'

He ran fingers through her sleek bob.

'Really? Your hair looks fine to me.'

'Thanks, but it really needs a cut otherwise it gets scruffy and long very quickly.'

'Do you ever think of growing it? I bet you'd look great with long hair.'

She shook her head and smiled, pleased by his interest.

'Gosh, I haven't had it long since I was child. I don't really think about it.'

He kissed her.

'Maybe you should.'

Desire curled her guts and sent a fluttering through her. She swallowed coffee as distraction.

'After my appointment I'm due at Whitebarn for lunch,' she managed. 'Staying over until tomorrow evening. Back to work Monday. You?'

'Nothing planned. I might have lunch with my father and Rosalind tomorrow, but otherwise I'm at a bit of a loose end.'

'Oh, that sounds lonely. I'm sorry I'm not here.'

He looked away, his expression wistful. She touched his hand.

'I'd invite you to come with me, but it's the first time since Ruth…'

He covered her hand with his and smiled.

'That's so sweet, but I'll be fine. I'll call a couple of friends to go out tonight, maybe go to the gym this afternoon. But would you like dinner Monday evening?'

'Yes please, and next time I go to Whitebarn you can definitely come.'

'I'd really like that.'

He raised her hand, kissed her fingers and turned her wrist to softly brush her palm with his lips. She shuddered, warmth rolling her belly and heat springing between her thighs.

'Theo,' she whispered.

'What time do you have to leave?'

'Not for an hour or so.'

He rose, pulled her to him and led the way upstairs.

CHAPTER ELEVEN

The same morning Iris parked the Land Rover in front of a five-bar gate. Beyond it Foxcombe Valley stretched away, amber, green and gold while long grass marked the edges of the track that wound through the trees. The woods spread out and back as far as she could see. She and Michael got out; Gus followed, sniffing the grass and looking through the gate bars.

'I haven't been here for ages,' she said.

'The last time was over ten years ago for Walt's birthday picnic.'

'What a great day that was. We had so much fun here.'

Michael leant on the gate, gazing at the valley. Iris picked up the padlock, feeling its hefty weight.

'What did we think?' she asked.

'About what?'

'About how we were able to just come and walk or picnic here. Did we ever ask?'

Michael frowned. Gus had wandered the dirt track away from the gate. Iris called for him and took the keys out.

'When we got here the gate was always open,' she said.

'I don't know what I thought,' her husband said. 'I mean, even with the gate open it's clearly private land. I don't think I ever asked Josephine about it. Did you?'

Iris tried the first key and when that didn't work used

the second to unlock the gate, taking off the padlock and handing it to her husband.

'If I did, I can't remember what she said. I guess because I've been coming here on and off my whole life it just seemed normal to do so.'

Michael swung the gate open, slotting the stand into the pre-drilled hole to hold it. Gus trotted through, disappearing into the long grass at the side of the track.

Iris drove the Land Rover in and in the mirrors saw Michael close the gate, clicking the padlock shut on the chain. Her husband opened the passenger door just as Gus ghosted through the grass, his tawny shape barely visible while he stalked.

'I expect he's found a mouse or something,' Iris said.

From a bag in the passenger footwell she took out an old towel. She called her dog and a few moments later Gus emerged carrying a dead rat. He bounded to the car and jumped in, tail wagging to happily present Iris with his kill. Michael smothered a laugh while Gus dropped the rodent onto the towel. Iris found a smile, knowing any disgust would deflate the dog.

'Good lad,' she said and ruffled his head.

Gus's tail wagged faster, and he turned to Michael for more praise. Iris grimaced and tossed the bloodied rat out of the window so the Picardy wouldn't notice it was gone. Michael, still grinning and telling Gus what a good boy he was, got in. Iris, used to her dog's prey drive, liberally used the hand sanitiser fixed to the dashboard before driving on. After a few minutes she steered the vehicle left onto a barely discernible, overgrown track, that if you didn't know was there you would easily miss it. Driving slowly, bouncing and swaying, they reached the gravelled car park space and turning circle. Iris stopped and switched the Land Rover off. They all alighted. Gus investigated the trees and trotted about, sniffing. Iris inhaled the autumn forest scents, looking up at the delicate blue sky, and felt some of her constant tension lessen. Michael shouldered the rucksack, fishing a compass and piece of paper from his pocket. Unfolding it, he studied his hand-drawn map.

'According to Gordon's notebook Foxcombe Manor should be in…' He turned to the left, pointing. 'That direction.'

'Are you sure?'

'Trust me,' he said and winked.

'Well, it's a nice day for a walk,' she replied. 'Although Zoe's due for lunch at one so we've only got about five hours to get lost and then we'll need to call it a day.'

'Ye of little faith. Come along.'

He set off, following what Iris could only think of as a little-used deer track. Gus bounded after her husband and then stopped, waiting for her. The Picardy's excitement and impatience evident in every line of his body and grinning face.

'All right, I'm coming,' she murmured. 'But remember where we parked.' Smiling, she followed her husband and dog into the trees.

Just over an hour later they emerged into a large glade and stopped. Michael looked about with satisfaction.

'Here,' he said.

'Really? Fifth time lucky, are you sure?'

He pulled a face and continued walking, peering through the grass.

'Aha! Bricks. This must be it.'

'Where, show me.'

She reached him and crouched, parting the grass with Gus's help. She found the unmistakable old bricks and then more, the foundation line of a wall. She straightened and gave Michael a hug, feeling suddenly light.

'I was so scared it wasn't real,' she said.

He held her close while Gus nudged her leg, wanting to join in.

'Me too,' her husband breathed, sounding relieved.

Nearly an hour later they had identified all the foundation lines of Foxcombe Manor. They marked out the library with tent pegs and twine from Michael's rucksack. Iris paced the library with Gus at her heels and orientating herself from a photograph of Michael's map on her phone.

'The trapdoor should be here somewhere,' she said, planting a tent peg, 'but it's just earth.'

The Picardy sniffed through the grass, tail wagging as he picked up and followed a scent.

'I guess the trapdoor must have caved in at some point or grown over,' Michael said. 'It has been nearly two hundred years since Gordon was here.'

Iris dropped her head, rubbing the back of her neck and imagining bulldozers rumbling in. The notion of ripping Foxcombe Valley open and destroying where Sam had lived sickened her. She stared at the woods, picturing the destruction and trees cut down to get the machines in.

'There has to be a way to find the tunnel without disturbing anything too much. No machines or men or anything. I couldn't bear it.'

'I'm with you there,' Michael said. 'Okay, so Sam built it as an escape route so it must have another entrance, exit, whichever. We just need to find it and hope it's still accessible unless we start with just shovels here?'

Iris glanced at her watch.

'We've got time to look for the other entrance before we need to head back. If we can't find it, we can bring spades on Sunday after Zoe leaves. How does that sound?'

'Good to me.' He turned a circle staring at the woods. 'Except we don't know which direction the tunnel goes in.'

'How about you take your best guess, and we'll go the other way.' She grinned at him. 'Save us all that time wandering around?'

He made a mock shocked face.

'Well, just for that, I won't share my coffee and doughnuts with you.'

'How rude, especially as I made the coffee!'

'Yes, but I'm carrying the Thermos and the doughnuts. So, I get to decide who has what.'

'All right, I take it back. You're an excellent woodsman. Super direction-finder and all-round fantastic husband. Now, dole out the coffee and doughnuts or I'll set the dog on you.'

Michael glanced at Gus rolling in the grass, legs flailing, and making chuffing sounds.

'Oh, I'm terrified.' He picked up the rucksack and unzipped it. 'And I love you, so I'll share.'

During the impromptu picnic they discussed the tunnel and reasoned it couldn't have gone beneath the manor house. Using the library wall, they drew a semicircle on Michael's map from where the entrance should have been, out into the woods. They decided to start walking at the semicircle apex for half an hour and watch for anything unusual such as more bricks, sunken ground from cave-ins or ruin debris. If they found nothing they would come back and work their way around the semicircle, walking for half an hour away from the imaginary trapdoor each time. They finished eating and packed the Thermos, dog's food and water bowls away. Michael paced out from where they believed the trapdoor should have been and orientated himself with the compass before leading the way into the woods.

Nearly an hour and a half later, despite the lack of tunnel evidence, Iris was enjoying herself. According to the paperwork, the land agents had for years followed specific instructions from her aunt to do only what was necessary to keep the valley wild and balanced. As a consequence, the woods were well coppiced, now turning red and gold. Blackbirds scurried in the undergrowth and crows called and fussed in the treetops. Squirrels darted and leapt amongst branches teasing Gus, who happily chased, stalked and barked at them at every opportunity. She had already spotted one potential badger sett and earlier, through the trees, two deer had leapt across their path. Now Michael halted a few feet ahead of her.

'That's half an hour,' he said.

Iris gestured to a fallen tree and they settled there with Gus laying at their feet. Michael took the Thermos from the rucksack.

'Fancy finishing the last bit with me?'

Iris nodded, leaning back to stare up at the burnished oak leaves while listening to the soughing wind rustling and rattling branches.

'Spades tomorrow I guess,' she said, accepting the cup from Michael.

'Seems that way as we need to start heading back to the farm.'

Gus suddenly half rose and became still, intent on a squirrel crawling round a tree trunk. It scampered up the tree and Gus rushed it, paws on the trunk, barking and watching it scurry away. The Picardy dropped his head, following a scent nose to ground, moving purposefully but without haste. He turned circles, snuffling on one spot, then tail wagging, abruptly dug at the ground giving small whines.

'What's all that about?' Michael asked.

‘Probably fox scat or something.’

She called Gus, but he only flicked his tufted ears and continued digging.

‘Some working dog,’ she murmured, smiling.

Handing Michael the cup, she rose and went to Gus. Shooing the Picardy from his quarry, she moved leaves with her foot, trying to see what the fuss was about. Something dark lay there and she crouched, sweeping forest debris away.

‘Michael, there’s a hole here.’

‘An animal-type hole?’

‘No. A brick-type hole.’

He was at her side in a moment. Together they cleared leaves and soil until they had uncovered a large cavity with brick teeth. Iris wiped loam from her hands and stared, unable to move, delight like Christmas morning filling her.

‘It’s only the bloody tunnel,’ she said.

Michael let out a whoop, startling Gus who rushed him, giving kisses and leaping about. Iris took a torch from the rucksack and shone it in the hole, but it revealed only dark edges.

‘Rubbish,’ she muttered.

She lay on her belly at which point Gus bounded over and licked her face. Much to the Picardy’s disgust Michael caught and held him while Iris wiped her cheek on her sleeve and wriggled forward over the hole. The light picked out a mound of mossy bricks stretching down and down. She moved further forward, ignoring Michael’s worried grunt and Gus’s unhappy noises. She squinted, managing to see the opposite tunnel wall and moved the light, seeking the floor and trying to gauge how deep it was. Her breath suddenly hitched while icy tendrils seemed to catch her throat.

‘Oh shit…’

'What, what is it?'

Iris's fingers shook as she put the torch down and took out her phone, taking a photograph. She scrambled up and gave her husband the phone.

'Is that what I think it is?' she asked.

Michael let go of Gus, who danced about Iris while her husband stared at the photo.

'It looks like bones,' he said. 'Like rib and leg-type bones.'

'That's what I thought.'

Michael turned the torch on and lay down to shine the light once more into the hole. After what seemed an age he got up, brushing soil and leaves from his trousers.

'Oh yes, there's bones down there,' he said. 'Could be a deer fallen in. No wonder Gus was so interested.'

'Well, we need to get in there anyway, bones or no. We'll bring spades and, I don't know, rope I guess or something.'

Michael looked at the hole with a gauging expression.

'I'll work something out. But it'll have to wait until late tomorrow, unless…'

'Unless we tell Zoe and get her to come too, but we decided not to involve her in any of this.'

'We don't have to tell her everything. We could say we found the hole and want to know what's down there.'

'You're right, I know you're right. And what's the harm in telling her anyway?'

'None.'

'Not even if the Watchers still exist? We might be putting her in danger.'

Michael gestured at the surrounding woodland.

'We're on our private property,' he said. 'Who's going to know what we're doing out here? Besides, Zoe won't tell anyone. It'll be fine.'

They covered the hole with a twisted, fallen bough and marked the site with a tent peg. Iris glanced at the hole and a sudden coldness settled over her skin.

'They really looked like deer bones?' she asked.

Michael's mouth tightened and he shrugged, his expression worried. They stared at each other for a long moment.

'We should head home,' Iris said.

She kept Gus at heel and with a last look to where the covered hole lay, she led the way back through Foxcombe Woods.

Chapter Twelve

Early next morning Iris watched crows circling, calling in the trees while others chased each other performing acrobatic swoops and dives. Finches and sparrows zoomed overhead and squabbled in the woods. Gus romped about, covered in dew that drew rivulets and sparkled in his tawny coat. He stalked scents and chased squirrels, real and fancied. Iris breathed deeply of the crisp air, feeling light and fluid all at once. The valley held a gold-tinged mist and looked, she imagined, as it had done for centuries. She almost expected to see Sam riding through or Gordon to be sitting, sketching the ruins. Michael and Zoe reached her, and they all continued, carrying spades and rucksacks, past the foundations of Foxcombe Manor. Iris glanced at her husband who talked to Zoe about her work, keeping their daughter's attention.

Half an hour later they pulled the twisted bough away and set to the earth with spades, moving the loam and any loose bricks to widen the hole. Finally, Zoe peered into the cavity.

'It's very dark down there,' she said. 'Are you sure about this?'

Iris wasn't but couldn't think of any other way.

'Your dad is, and I trust him.'

Michael was unpacking the rucksack and took out rope,

webbing line, torches and finally the orphan pouch, without the pouch.

'I did lots of research into climbing gear and the theory,' he said. 'I also watched abseiling and climbing videos online last night and I think we can manage. Plus, there's the pile of bricks to use as support, carefully, so it won't be abseiling as such. More like walking down a stepped wall with a harness on.'

Zoe looked as dubious as Iris felt. Picking up the harness Iris tugged the newly attached rings, one each back and front and on either side. She shrugged into the gear, feeling it strangely unfamiliar with its new purpose, and tried not to look at the cave-in hole. Michael ran the wide webbing line through each side ring, then round her bottom and attached the rope to the ring at the back. Gus sniffed at the rope and webbing line on the ground, looking unsure. Michael surveyed her, walking around, tugging the harness.

'It seems solid enough,' he said.

'That's your best reassurance?' Zoe asked, sounding concerned. She crouched and hugged Gus, who rested his whiskery chin on her shoulder. 'Seems solid enough? Honestly Dad, I'm really not certain about all this. Why don't you do it?'

'Because the harness best fits your mum. Any adjustments for it to fit me would take too long and then it would all have to be put back so she can use it as the orphan pouch again.'

'Besides I want to go down,' Iris said. 'It's not your dad's idea, it's mine. I want to know what's down there so I should be the one to go in.'

Down into the scary, dangerous, dark hole where all the bones are.

Zoe frowned, her fingers in Gus's collar, stopping the dog from investigating the hole. Iris took a breath, pushing unhelpful thoughts away, and tugged at the harness.

'Explain it to me again,' she said to Michael.

'It's safe, I promise. Look, the webbing line acts like an extra harness and a safety line but is also more secure as it goes around your bottom. That way if you slip it catches you from falling. The rope at the back allows me and Zoe to pull you up if anything goes terribly wrong. I've run both lines around a tree for extra safety and leverage. Have you got your gloves?'

Iris took her latex gripper gloves from her pocket and slipped them on; normally used for heavy duty farm work and draining the back-up generator, they smelt of diesel and oil. Michael bent over the rucksack taking out something round and metallic.

'Oh, and there's this,' he said.

'Are you joking?' Zoe asked.

Iris stared at the object in her husband's hands.

'Is that my colander?'

'No, it's your protective headgear. See, I've attached your old woolly hat to the interior and added straps, turning it into a handy helmet.'

He put it on Iris's head, tugging the woolly hat down and fastening the webbing under her chin.

'I look ridiculous,' she said.

'Well, you don't know that as you can't see.'

'Really?' She pointed to her head. 'You think I can't work it out?'

'Better safe than fashionable,' Michael said.

She turned to Zoe, who buried her face in Gus's fur, stifling giggles. Iris eyed her daughter.

'Given that reaction I think the cover of *Vogue* is safe. All right let's get on with it. Unless you've got some baking tray armour in there?'

'Just extra gloves for us to handle the rope.'

He adjusted the helmet, and she met his gaze, taking in his anxious expression.

'I'll be fine,' she murmured.

He nodded and managed a smile.

'Have you got a bag for the bones?' he asked quietly.

She nodded, knowing the cotton bag was folded and tucked safely into her back pocket. Suddenly she was no longer afraid. The woodland smells and the early morning light seemed sharper, dappling the hole. She fancied the lichen-covered bricks were inviting rather than slippery and foreboding. She shifted toward it and Michael touched her shoulder.

'Wait, I almost forgot.'

He took a slim torch from his pocket and turned it on. Even in the bright morning the white beam was impressive. He produced cable ties, gestured her to lean forward and deftly fastened the torch to the top of the colander. This time Zoe's laughter rang about the trees startling the birds and making Gus prance. Iris grinned and waited while they leashed the Picardy, tying him to the custom metal stake that screwed into the ground, which they used when camping or at county shows with the caravan. Father and daughter then donned gloves and got into position. At a nod from Michael, Iris sat on the edge of the hole with the brick pile to her right and below her. She shuffled along, turned slightly and her boot toes touched the top bricks. Slipping down she felt the rope and webbing tighten and looked over. Zoe, white faced, and Michael, jaw tense, were holding the lines taut while nearby Gus watched intently.

'Guys, you've got to give me some slack or all this is pointless. I've got my trusty colander – all will be well.'

They smiled tightly, identically, and loosened their holds. Iris drew a breath, looked at where to put her feet and hands and began the descent. Immediately Gus set to whining and then barking, the noise resounding amongst the trees. She called reassuringly to him and the Picardy quietened somewhat. Iris waited a moment and then continued down, talking to Gus as she did so. She could hear the odd whine but mercifully he refrained from barking again.

Descending, the air smelt dark and fresh and it got colder the lower Iris went, fogging her breath in the torchlight. The lichen-covered bricks were treacherous at first but dried out as she descended. The white beam illuminated the tunnel, finding cracks through the brick pile, making woodlice and spiders scuttle. But the bricks remained solid beneath her boots and gloved fingers, so the descent was easier than she had imagined. Near the bottom she looked up seeing blue sky meshed behind tree branches. She exhaled, thinking how very far away the surface seemed and then returned to the descent. Moments later she reached the tunnel floor. Her torchlight pierced darkness that stretched to her left revealing seemingly endless black. The brick pile on her right filled the tunnel, making it impassable.

'You okay?'

Michael's voice sounded distant and echoed slightly.

She looked up at their shapes against the daylit hole. She gave a thumbs up, shouted she was fine and unhitched the webbing line and rope. Iris then turned so the light swept back and forth across the brick-strewn ground, turning the bones starkly white. She crouched to one, hesitating to touch it and frowning at some sort of remnants of rubbery covering. Something glinted and she took her gloves off to retrieve a tarnished cufflink. She glanced at the brick pile.

Did someone lose this, and it bounced down all this way?

She studied the cufflink for a moment, feeling a raised emblem like a flower or tree beneath the dirt and discolouration of age. Pocketing it she then moved so the beam bounced off the tunnel wall on her right, turning it bright as day. Abruptly, Iris yelped and stumbled back. A skull, blank eyes staring, lay amidst the bricks and dirt. The darkness pressed in and the pearly bone seemed to glow in the torchlight. She stared at it, heart racing while trying to comprehend what she was seeing. Then, with faltering breaths she gazed at the bones littering the floor.

'Oh my God,' she breathed, 'someone died down here.'

It took her nearly twenty minutes to carefully place all the bones she could find in the cotton bag. Finally, with fingers sweating inside her gloves and silent wishes for forgiveness, she retrieved the skull, reverently adding it to the bag. She pulled the drawstring, looping and clipping the detached rope to it. She removed her gloves, took out her phone and typed a text message. She then climbed three feet up the brick pile until she got a signal and pressed send. A few moments later the bag began its ascent. Iris watched it go, worried it might hit the brick pile, but Michael's pull remained slow and steady. Zoe's dark shape against the daylit hole, arms outstretched, guided the rope in a straight line.

Everything will surely change now.

She was unsure why the thought saddened her. She didn't know the exact process but realised the authorities would have to be informed; wouldn't they? She glanced into the black stretch of tunnel and with her light illuminating it, it turned grey.

Whoever the poor soul in the bag is, it isn't Amy Dudley.

There had been a crack atop the skull in the bag but no holes on the left and, she reasoned, the number of bones meant a whole person must have died here. She looked up as Zoe caught the bag, pulling it to the surface and disappearing over the edge. In a few moments she knew the rope would return so she could reattach it to her harness and climb out. She retrieved her phone, staring at it before tapping out another text message, then climbed to the signal sweet spot and pressed send. Not wanting a reply, she hurried down almost slipping on the bricks. She paused, glancing up at the hole just as Michael's head appeared. He shouted something but she was already walking into the darkness and didn't hear his words.

Iris felt she had walked for hours. Looking at her phone it had only been twenty-five minutes but the tunnel and pressing darkness seemed to warp all sense. Twice she had negotiated scattered, fallen bricks but thankfully the ceiling had remained intact. Although the tunnel curved, given how long she had been walking, she estimated Foxcombe Manor couldn't be too far away. She recalled in Gordon's notebook that he had counted one hundred and fifty steps to where Amy Dudley was hidden but that had been from the now inaccessible trapdoor.

When I reach where the trapdoor caved in, I can count as I walk back.

The thought heartened her, and she walked quicker only to slow as earth began to scuff against her boots. Suddenly she stopped. Her light picked out a black mass strewn across the floor ahead. Swallowing, she looked up and exhaled at seeing brickwork still solid above her. She moved closer to the mass and while the ceiling remained unbroken her torchlight showed the wall had collapsed, creating a tide of soil and bricks. Nervous of the ceiling being weak Iris carefully studied the wall and noted that the mass had pushed through equally, the weight of the soil filling the wall space continuing to support the ceiling. Reassured, she hunkered down, trying to guess how far it went, if it were safe to negotiate or how long it would take to clear.

'Damn it,' she muttered.

She let her light play over the soil, punctuated by dirt-filled bricks, knowing she shouldn't try and cross it but reluctant to turn back. Some oddity amongst the mass caught her attention and she peered, then stood, trying to get a better look. It was about twelve feet away and seemed to be some sort of material. She studied the soil, bricks and root debris between her and the oddity, gauging if the heap would hold her.

'I don't need to walk on all of it,' she muttered.

Gingerly she placed her foot on the mass, testing it against her weight, and thankfully it held. She took two cautious steps onto the soil and brick heap, feeling it sink unpleasantly, and then she crouched, lying on her belly. Her outstretched hand reached the material and she pulled. It was stupidly heavy and resisted. Grunting, she rose and walked another three steps, hating the way the soil gave even more beneath her. But crouched over the material she was able to scoop the soil and move some bricks, freeing it while trying not to disturb the mass too much and cause herself to sink. Soon she cleared enough to lever the oddity out. In the torchlight the material became a canvas bag, rotting and stained, but still wrapped around a weighty box. Carrying it, barely breathing, she retraced her steps. Once off the mass she peeled the bag away and found the box whole.

She took off her gloves and with shaking fingers wiped soil from the lid and hinges. She ran a fingernail round the lid crease, easing any dirt there. Applying pressure, she felt the lid give and, needing more leverage, sat against the tunnel wall placing the box on her lap. With a quick breath she used both hands and exerted more force to the top. It shifted but remained stubbornly closed. She made an exasperated sound and then fumbled in her pockets with movements suddenly clumsy. Her fingers closed on her penknife. Slipping it out she opened the blade and inserted it into the lid crease. She twisted the knife, forcing the gap wider. Abruptly the box opened, and Amy Dudley stared up at her.

Chapter Thirteen

Later that day in the living room at Whitebarn, the walnut box and cotton bag sat innocuously on the coffee table belying their exceptional contents. Michael brought in a fresh cafetière while Iris kept glancing at the door.

'It's been nearly an hour. How much longer can she take?'

Michael took her mug, filling it from the cafetière. He poured his own cup and put Iris's next to her before settling on the sofa.

'It took us that long at the bank. I'm sure she'll be done soon.'

Iris picked up a novel only to put it down again. She rose, disturbing Gus from her feet, and paced.

'What if she phones the authorities from the study? We'd never know.'

'She promised not to. Not until she'd read everything. Don't you trust our daughter to keep her word?'

'I do. But…'

Suddenly the door opened, and Zoe came in with her lashes starred with tears. She walked to Iris, who opened her arms and hugged her daughter. Gus rose and went to them, tail wagging, to be included in the cuddle. Zoe bent to the dog, stroking his ears and running her fingers through his fur. She settled in an armchair, accepting a cup of coffee from Michael, and stared at the box and bag.

'I can't believe it. What happened to Amy Dudley is so sad and so wrong,' she said. 'We have to do something.'

Michael let out a breath. Gus nosed Zoe's hand and then leant against her legs. Iris perched on the arm of the chair, ruffling Gus's back.

'That's what we think too.'

Michael nodded and Iris squeezed Zoe's shoulder.

'We've given it a lot of thought,' Iris said. 'And we want to investigate Amy Dudley's death before we go to the authorities. To finish what Sam and Gordon started. It's what Josephine wanted us to do. We don't want there to be any doubt over Amy Dudley's murder to make sure she can rest properly in peace. What do you think?'

'I think it's the right thing to do. But not reporting human remains is illegal.'

Iris studied her daughter, noting Zoe's taut jaw and set expression that reminded her of Michael when he was being stubborn. But Zoe's gaze kept flicking to the table, and it contained only compassion. She squeezed her daughter's shoulder again, catching and holding her gaze.

'All right,' Iris said. 'What would the normal procedure be for finding bones like this?'

Zoe sipped her coffee while teasing Gus's shaggy fur through her fingers.

'Well, the police should've been called as soon as we found the remains and, in all honesty, we've should've left them there for the authorities to investigate. They take photos and send them to experts to verify the bones are human and their age.'

'I think that we can safely say they're human,' Michael said. 'As to their age we know or at least suspect that the skull in the box is from the sixteenth century. As to the other, I've no idea.'

'If the skull is truly that old then it'll be classed as "of antiquity",' Zoe said. 'In other words, of no interest to a criminal investigation.'

'And the other?'

Zoe looked unhappy, stroking Gus's head and keeping her gaze on the Picardy.

'To be honest, Mum, they both need to be properly verified even if we delay informing the authorities. We can't help Amy Dudley unless we definitively prove that's her in the box and the other bones could be anyone.'

They all stared at the box and bag. Iris's throat ached and she cleared it, rising and resuming her seat. Gus followed her, jumping on the sofa and putting his front paws on her lap. She settled the Picardy beside her and sipped coffee, trying to relieve the tightness in her throat. Zoe gestured at the table.

'Although after the quick look I had I don't think our mystery person is anyone who died recently – but bones aren't my area of expertise.'

'Your considered opinion is much more expert than ours,' Michael said. 'And it's a relief to hear you say that about the mystery bones.'

Iris agreed, feeling pleased that Zoe's opinion matched her private suspicion of who the bones were.

'If we do alert the authorities to the mystery person,' she said, 'do we have to tell them about Amy Dudley as well?'

'If they find out later that you didn't tell them you had two sets of remains you can't plead ignorance to the process and you could be prosecuted. At this stage it has to be both or none.'

Michael rose and built the fire. Iris toyed with her mug, trying to gauge her daughter's determination.

'What if we said none?' Iris asked. 'How would we go

about getting verification of Amy Dudley then?'

'In either case I'd need help; as I said, bones aren't my speciality.'

'You mean Will?'

Zoe nodded, her expression pensive.

'Ideally, yes. If we decide to do this under the radar, then I'll see if he's willing to help. If you do it officially, I can't say where the bones will end up.'

'The unofficial way, could it get you both in trouble?'

'I can't say it won't,' Zoe said. 'Arrant is an independent facility, but not above the law. However, I am allowed to take on private work. So, I could hide it under that umbrella for a little while. If anyone asks, I'll tell them the declaration is in the finder's hands and the remains have been passed to me and Will for verification.'

'How much trouble would you be in if it came to it?'

'Suspension certainly. In the extreme I could lose my job for not declaring and even be prosecuted. But it's all about timing. At the moment we've no reason to suspect the remains are part of any criminal investigation. They were found on private land and by turning them over to Arrant you're following the same procedure as the police would. In essence, as long as the remains are confirmed as being of antiquity and we declare them as such to the police and coroner after verification, we should get away with it. It's not perfect but legally we'll have covered our bases.'

'Wait, why are we telling the coroner?'

'When remains are verified as human the county coroner is normally informed. After they've been examined the bones are interred wherever the coroner deems appropriate. Basically, unless you accidentally dig up a family member you don't get a say in anything once the remains are declared.'

'All the more reason not to declare,' Iris said. 'We

don't want Amy Dudley taken away, verified and interred without our say or proper investigation. Do we?'

She studied her husband and daughter, feeling her determination as a bulwark against the emptiness, tethering her wholly and inextricably to saving Amy Dudley. She desperately wanted them to help her but didn't know how to ask. Michael rose from the fireplace and crouched in front of her, taking her hand.

'No, we don't.'

Zoe came and took their free hands so the three of them made a triangle supporting each other.

'Agreed.'

Gus, tail wagging, rose and tried to kiss everyone.

For the next half an hour they discussed how to proceed, what to tell Will and what not to in order to protect him. They spoke briefly of the Watchers and Ruth's death, but Michael and Zoe were convinced the first didn't exist and the second was a terrible coincidence. They were so adamant that Iris found herself swayed and reassured. Zoe took photographs of the skulls to show Will and see if he would be willing to examine the bones. Afterward Iris took the box and bag, locking them away in the safe.

Going into the kitchen she found Michael heating up a late lunch of vegetable soup while Zoe cut and buttered crusty bread. Iris opened a bottle of wine, pouring herself and Michael a glass, knowing Zoe wouldn't have any as she was driving. Her daughter arranged the bread on plates and distributed them on the table.

'Mum, whatever happened to the pocket watch in Aunt Josephine's letter?'

'It's in the safe with everything else.'

'Did you ever find out what the treasure was?'

Iris dipped her hand inside the neck of her long-sleeved

top and pulled out the locket fastened around her neck by a gold chain.

'This. It was inside the watch.'

'Wow, that's beautiful. Can I see it?'

Iris took it off and passed it to her daughter. Zoe held the locket, so it spun catching the light.

'It's gorgeous. Are you sure wearing it's safe? It looks really valuable.'

'I know, I only wear it in the house. I put it on just now from the safe.'

Zoe turned the locket over, examining the boar's head engraving. She tugged at the wings, but they didn't move.

'Doesn't open?'

'No, we tried.'

Zoe returned the locket and Iris resettled it around her neck, feeling the jewel warm on her skin. Michael poured soup and handed out filled bowls. Soon the sound of family lunch filled the kitchen and the talk turned to ordinary things. Yet, Iris knew, Amy Dudley was there. Her presence a fourth, silent member, waiting for them.

Chapter Fourteen

The bedside clock showed 1am when Iris gave up trying to sleep. She donned robe and slippers and accompanied by Gus went to the kitchen. Once she had made hot chocolate, she went to the living room with the dog following, bright eyed and happy to be with her. Iris then fetched her laptop from the study, pausing to watch the new camera monitors flick uneventfully through their cycles. Curling up on the sofa with the Picardy she opened the laptop and began to search for Gordon McCraken.

Nearly an hour later she found a website entitled, 'Victorian Murder & Mystery'. Iris read about murderous brothers John and William Lightfoot and the infamous William Palmer, before finding a section on Doctor Gordon McCraken. Gordon McCraken, the website stated, had once been a prominent, brilliant anatomist living and working in Edinburgh. In 1839–40, McCraken had been accused, imprisoned and acquitted of murdering his wife, Iona, and their stillborn child. According to the website, Gordon McCraken had been driven mad by the deaths.

He had left Edinburgh soon after his acquittal and, for unknown reasons, travelled to London. Here he had met and befriended a Doctor Tiberius Bennett and his sisters, Liberty and Verity Bennett. Having stayed with the Bennetts for a number of weeks McCraken had then persuaded Tiberius and Liberty Bennett to accompany him on a camping trip to Oxford.

It was there, the website stated, that the crazed Doctor had struck. A few days after the trio had been seen leaving Oxford, two of their hired horses were found wandering the outskirts of the city. This prompted a search which weeks later uncovered an abandoned campsite in nearby countryside containing personal property of the Bennetts. The police surmised that Gordon McCraken, in his lunacy, had kidnapped the siblings for ransom. None of them were ever heard from again despite a reward being offered by the surviving sister.

The website held a variety of theories as to the mysterious events surrounding the disappearances, but Iris knew them all to be false. With profound certainty she now believed the bones in the tunnel to be Doctor Gordon McCraken. She was equally convinced the Bennetts had also perished in the tunnel perhaps lost and starved or maybe crushed during a cave-in. From her dressing gown pocket, she removed the cufflink, now free of tarnish thanks to a mix of baking soda, aluminium foil and boiling water. She held it up, studying the thistle emblem in the light and the initials G intertwined with I on the reverse. Iris wondered if the cufflink had been commissioned to celebrate Gordon and Iona's marriage or an anniversary. With a sigh she placed it on the table and switched off the laptop, tiredness now dragging at her. Gus rose from the sofa and went to the French doors and nosed between the curtains, then cast a look at Iris.

'I see,' she said. 'Taking advantage of insomnia.'

Rising, she went to the dog, pulling the curtains back and opened a door, letting the Picardy into the garden. She tracked his pale form as he meandered about in the dark. Looking up she admired the wheel of stars, the air, fragile and sharp in her chest. Sudden barking rent the quiet.

Gus, in full voice, rushed to the garden gate. Iris called to no avail. Abrupt images of Ruth assailed her, halting her breath. The Picardy's noise continued, spiralling her anxiety, and suddenly Michael was behind her.

'He won't come in,' she said.

'The silent alarm's gone off.'

He held his phone, and she could see the text message from the security company.

'No one's in the house. Gus would know,' she said. 'It must be the storage container.'

She called her dog again, hearing desperation in her voice. Suddenly Gus fell silent and a moment later appeared out of the dark. Iris let him in then locked the French doors. She and Michael hurried to the study where the monitor showed the storage container door, grey in the dark, hanging open.

'What do we do?' Iris asked.

'Nothing. We stay in house, safe, until the police get here.'

Iris stared at the screens, letting out a breath when her animals appeared, unmolested. Gus weaved between her legs, nudging her hand. She fondled his ears, watching the stables and pigsties on the cameras; everything seemed shut and bolted. No person could be seen in any shot, either on the farm or at thc container.

'Maybe Gus scared them away?'

Michael, intent on the monitors, nodded, his jaw tense. They heard the police and the flash of sirens caught on the container monitors when they drove in.

'Well, if he didn't, they just did.'

Half an hour later, with a constable as escort and Gus at her side, Iris was allowed to check the farm. She was relieved to confirm only the storage container had been broken into. She then joined Michael at the container, its door now peppered with black fingerprint powder. Seeing the police officers Gus hid behind her legs and she hooked her fingers through his collar, speaking quietly to her dog. Tall spotlights lit the night and the container interior. Inside, a man in a white paper jumpsuit was packing up equipment and speaking to DI Fields. There was no sign of DS Dens.

'Everything all right?' Michael asked Iris.

'Yes, all okay,' she replied.

DI Fields reached them and got a nod from the constable who had escorted Iris.

'So, everywhere else is secure and undamaged. From what we're seeing here it seems the intruder got just inside the container before fleeing. We swept the area before allowing you to check the farm and found nothing untoward.'

'We think Gus may have scared them off,' Iris said. 'He started barking in the garden about the same time the silent alarm was triggered.'

The inspector glanced at the Picardy and then to the container door.

'That makes sense,' she said. 'It was lucky your dog was out so late.'

'Do you think it was the same people who broke into Ash House?'

'It would seem likely, I'm afraid. We'll post a car at the farm entrance, men inside the house and stationed near the container. You should stay at a hotel overnight, then at friends or relatives for a longer period. It's probable that the perpetrators will make a further attempt. Should that happen I'd like to be ready for them.'

The lights seemed too bright. Iris's grip tightened on Gus's collar and she clutched Michael's hand with her free one while her stomach hardened into knots. She shared a look with her husband which held total agreement.

'We're not leaving our animals or being driven out of Whitebarn,' she said.

Frustration flickered over the inspector's face then her expression became wooden.

'That's your choice. Although I am utterly against it in the circumstances. We cannot guarantee your safety if you stay here, nor can I authorise a surveillance operation with you in situ.'

Iris glanced at her husband, who licked his lips, swallowing convulsively. She briefly closed her eyes against the white lights.

'You think it's the same people who killed Ruth?'

The inspector's expression screamed 'obviously', but she said, 'Whoever broke into Ash House and this container didn't find what they were after. If you're determined to stay on your property, I strongly advise the container and contents be moved to a police facility. Hopefully then, the motivation to come here is removed. Although it is my duty to warn you, you may still be in danger.'

Iris caught Michael's gaze, thoughts flitting to the safe and its contents.

'We'd prefer you take the container than us leaving,' she said. 'We can give you an inventory easily enough. Will you take it now?'

The inspector eyed the grey behemoth, her mouth a thin line.

'Not now. It'll take time to arrange suitable transportation and storage. We should be able to move it later today probably in the afternoon.'

'Where will it go?'

'I'm not sure at this stage. Wherever we've got enough space. But don't worry, you'll get a receipt for everything. It'll all be returned to you once the case is completed.'

'Once the murderer's caught, you mean?'

'If the two are proven to be linked, then yes.'

'Do you think Ruth could've been murdered by someone other than whoever broke into Ash House?'

'Mrs Shaw, until we have evidence proving the break-ins and Miss Dunn's death are definitively connected, we cannot afford to make assumptions or sweeping statements. That is why we are investigating rather than surmising. Perhaps Miss Dunn was targeted by a psychopath and the break-ins perpetrated by mere opportunist thieves. For your sakes, let's hope so.' Her expression became frightening in its intensity. 'But if you insist on remaining here you should take extreme caution.' Irritation crept into the inspector's tone. 'Moving the contents of the container is better than nothing, I suppose.'

Beneath her fingers Gus shifted and Iris felt rather than heard his low growl. Michael squeezed her other hand, his gaze on the inspector.

'It'll have to be enough,' he said. 'We're not leaving.'

'That is your decision, naturally, no matter how foolhardy. Now then, we'll need tonight's surveillance footage.'

'We've already checked it,' Iris said. 'You can't make out who the two people are when they break in or when they run away. They're wearing dark masks and clothes.'

The inspector stared and then turned to the constable.

'Please accompany Mr and Mrs Shaw to the house and retrieve the footage.' Her gaze swept to them. 'The silent alarm will be reset once we've finished here. The lights and men will remain as I've said, until we remove the container. If you have any questions, please contact the station.'

Her attention returned to the container interior, clearly dismissing them.

Late that afternoon container and contents were hoisted and secured onto a transport lorry which then rumbled away from Whitebarn. At the front door DS Dens, his amiable face concerned, took the newly signed paperwork and a copy of the inventory from Iris.

'Mrs Shaw, are you certain you won't reconsider staying elsewhere just for a few days?'

Iris smiled at him.

'I understand your worry, Sergeant, and thank you for it. But this is our home, and I won't leave the animals. I'm sorry if it's causing the inspector some bother.'

'DI Fields is as worried about you being here as I am. It just comes across a little differently.'

'That's a very diplomatic way of putting it.'

The man flushed slightly and rubbed his chin.

'I know the inspector can come across as somewhat rigid and abrupt, and she believes her way is the best despite others thinking differently. But on this occasion, I think you should take her advice for your own safety.' He raised his hand, palm up in defeat. 'But I hear what you're saying, and you should know that a patrol car will continue passing the farm on a regular basis. That way response to any silent alarm will be that much quicker, as it was last night.'

'Thank you for letting me know. It's very reassuring.'

The sergeant looked as if he wanted to say more but didn't, for which Iris was grateful. Instead, the young man nodded goodbye and took his leave. Iris watched the now familiar unmarked car go, and noted another vehicle, pulling off the road and coming up the drive. The two met on the drive, with the strange car pulling over to let the police pass. DS Dens stopped his vehicle and a brief conversation through open windows ensued. The police car then continued on its way. The unknown vehicle drove to the farmhouse where it was parked next to the Land Rover. A stocky man alighted, and Iris recognised Will just as Zoe got out the passenger side and waved.

CHAPTER FIFTEEN

While Will set up his equipment in the cellar Iris made coffee telling Zoe about the break-in. Iris poured herself a cup, trying to remember how much she had drunk already but couldn't. Suddenly aware of the silence, she glanced at her daughter whose face was pallid and fingers trembling on her mug.

'Hey, it's all right,' Iris said. 'No one was hurt, and nothing was taken.'

'Only by luck. You and Dad could've been hurt, could've been…'

Tears streaked her face, and she clearly couldn't continue. Gus raised his head from where he lay in front of the Aga, his tail wagging and expression worried. Iris settled at the table and took Zoe's hands, forcing her daughter to meet her gaze.

'But we weren't.'

'What about next time?'

'We'll be careful.'

Zoe frowned and wiped her eyes with a proffered bit of kitchen roll.

'What does that mean?' She stared at Iris and her frown deepened. 'I don't understand, how are you so calm? How can Dad have gone to work like nothing happened?'

Iris studied her daughter, battling the need to reassure

with the need for discretion.

'Look, I wasn't sure whether to tell you or not, but we've taken precautions.'

'Like what?'

'Well, Thomas's boys are staying with us for a little while. They're set up in the old groom quarters over the stables.'

'Okay, and?'

'Let's just say they're putting their hobbies to good use.'

Zoe's eyes narrowed while her expression flickered through confused to thoughtful.

'Clay pigeon shooting. Shotguns and dogs?'

'Their dogs, certainly, and they're planning on roaming the fields and woods at odd times of the day keeping an eye out for anything or anyone that seems odd.'

She didn't mention the surprises Thomas's sons were currently placing about the farm. The flash alarms Luke had assured her were positioned so that only two-legged animals would trigger them. Luke had also installed extra surveillance in the form of motion and light sensors as well as hidden cameras hitched to the monitors in the study. He had also given Iris two cans of CS spray; one was now in the bedroom, the other in the Land Rover. She hadn't told the Wades everything but the break in on the farm had been enough to prompt Luke to offer his black-market engineering skills for good, if not entirely legal, use. She hadn't asked how he had got the equipment so quickly but the reasons for Luke's forced university hiatus were now clearer and Iris, sworn to secrecy, struggled not to tell Zoe.

'Suffice to say, we're safer now than we were before the break-in, okay?'

Zoe looked about to say something, but Will emerged from the cellar.

'I'm ready for the bones now,' he said.

Nearly forty-five minutes later Will finished laying Gordon McCraken on a trestle table. The newly erected halogen lights threw Gordon's bones into stark relief. Will peered and measured, studied and wrote with Zoe in tow. Iris, perched on the cellar steps with Gus, caught only the odd word while Gordon filled her gaze.

He looks vulnerable, too exposed. I wish we had left him under Foxcombe Woods.

She imagined taking him back to rest easily, peacefully under the earth and murmuring trees. She was suddenly aware Will was talking to her and re-focused her attention.

'Definitely of antiquity,' he said. 'I believe these remains are over a hundred and fifty years old.'

'I thought as much. Poor Gordon.'

Zoe looked alarmed and shook her head which thankfully, with his back to her, Will didn't notice.

'You know who he is?'

'No, not really,' Iris said, contriving a smile. 'It's just a name I've given him.'

'Well, you got the gender right,' Will continued. 'I would say he, Gordon, died of blunt force trauma. Do you see on the skull there's cracking? One injury, I think, is older than the other as it had time to partially heal. The one that killed him was significant. It fractured shards of bone and probably caused a bleed on the brain, if it didn't kill him outright.'

'Could falling rock have done that?'

'Certainly possible. There's other injuries to his bones that could be consistent with rockfall rather than a beating or accidental.' He crouched in front of her and gave Gus a tickle. 'Do you want to tell me what's going on here?'

Iris exchanged a look with Zoe, whose expression was closed.

‘I’ve only told Will we made the discovery on land Aunt Josephine owned which she willed to you,’ Zoe said. ‘And because probate is still going through it would be better if we verified before declaring.’

‘And I saw the photos and was intrigued,’ Will said. ‘Which is why I took this afternoon off and Zoe lied to her supervisor to get away.’

‘Which, as it turns out, wasn’t a lie. There *is* a family emergency.’

Will grunted, his attention fixed on Iris.

‘Now I’ve examined Gordon,’ he said, ‘I know there’s more going on than concerns over probate.’

Iris studied Will. His gaze was open and honest, trusting, and she hated involving him.

‘Can we say ignorance is bliss?’ she asked. ‘If this all goes wrong then you’re protected by not knowing.’

‘Exactly,’ Zoe said. ‘At the moment you can blame me entirely for not declaring and claim innocence over anything else which means any fallout will be on me.’

Will straightened, looking from Iris to Zoe.

‘True and I’m not happy about that.’

‘And we’re not prepared to put your career at risk,’ Zoe said.

Iris shifted on the step, trying very hard not to think about Ruth.

Or your safety. Please Will stay out of this as much as you can.

Will looked thoughtful, seeming to weigh Zoe’s determination and Iris’s silent entreaty.

‘All right,’ he said. ‘But I’m still not happy.’ He looked to the table and then to Zoe. ‘So, I’ve verified Gordon. What about the other one?’

Zoe swallowed and gestured to the steps. Iris lifted the box containing Amy Dudley, putting it on her lap. Will studied it, clearly curious.

'Let's put Gordon away,' he said. 'Then I'll take a look at what's in the box.'

Amy Dudley was amber and ochre in the light. She rested in the centre of the table, her Stygian eyes contemplative, patient. Iris found breath hard to come by and her fingers tightened in Gus's fur. She resisted the urge to rise and smooth the woman's bone. Will had been studying and measuring the skull for nearly twenty minutes and let out a breath.

'Antiquity again. More than four hundred years I'd say.' He looked at Iris. 'Does this one have a name?'

She hesitated; providing something false seemed blasphemous, as did giving none.

'Amy,' she said.

Will nodded and continued his inspection.

'Another blunt force trauma. Edges too defined to be rockfall I should say.' He glanced at Iris who schooled her expression blank. 'Right, ignorance is bliss.'

He sighed and, lifting the skull, replaced it in the box, closing the lid. Iris let Gus go and the dog wandered down the steps and under the table sniffing all the while. She noted Zoe, a pencil twirling from finger to finger, her gaze thoughtful and anxious all at once resting on Will.

'There's something else,' Zoe said to him. 'Something I need to ask you.'

'Go on,' Will said.

'You can say no.'

'Just ask.'

'We need to know who she is. Really know, I mean.'

Will's eyes narrowed. Iris's gaze darted from the box to her daughter.

'Zoe, what are you doing?'

'Mum, we have to know for sure, don't we?'

Iris swallowed, hating that Zoe was right, and gave a tight nod.

'Fine,' she said. 'But how?'

Zoe touched the box, her expression reverent.

'Will can extract DNA, can't you?'

'Possibly.' The word came out slowly and he frowned on it. 'But even if it's something I could sort out it's not enough. You need something to compare it to. A living relative.'

'I know,' Zoe said.

'Which means,' Will continued, 'you must have an idea who she is.'

'Zoe.' Iris's voice held a warning note.

'Mum, it's fine. Will, if you extract the DNA and we find a sample to compare it to, a living relative, you only have to say it's a familial match or not, right? You don't need to know who she is or who the living sample is – just confirm whether they're related?'

'Right. But I'll have to take Amy to a lab to do the extraction and sequencing.'

'So, you'll do it?'

Will looked at the box, his gaze seeming to pierce the wood and lead lining to take in the skull once more.

'I'll do it on one condition. When all this is over you tell me everything, deal?'

Zoe glanced at Iris, who nodded.

'Deal.'

Her daughter hugged Will. Iris placed both hands atop the box, battling a fierce desire to hold Amy Dudley close and never let her go.

Will was packing the last of his equipment in the car when Iris walked out with Zoe, who was carrying the box. She gave her daughter a one-sided hug.

'I'll start looking for relatives,' Iris said. 'See how far I can get.'

Zoe put space between them.

'It's not going to be easy. Amy Dudley didn't have children. So, as I said, it'll probably need a genealogist to find a living relative if there is one.'

'I know, but if I can get a couple of generations away the professional won't need to know who we're researching. They'll look forward, not back. And there was something in Sam's notes I think could help.'

Her daughter nodded, rubbing shingle with her toe and glancing at the car.

'Mum, there's something I need to tell you.'

Iris waited, holding onto Zoe's sleeve and trying to quell her rising anxiety.

'Has someone threatened you?'

'No, nothing like that. It's a good thing. At least I think so.' She drew a breath and let it out in a rush of words. 'I've met someone. Someone decent and I wondered if I could bring him to lunch on Sunday?'

'Oh. Well, that's lovely and of course you can bring him to lunch. But are you sure, given everything that's happening?'

'It'll be fine, and he already knows us. And no, I haven't told him anything and I won't so there's no need to worry. And Sunday is definitely okay to bring him?'

'Yes, of course. But how does he already know us? Who is it?'

Zoe didn't meet her gaze and settled into the car with the box on her lap and the door partially open.

'It's Theo, Theo Tallis. Rosalind's stepson.'

Her daughter glanced up, now holding Iris's gaze with entreaty in every line of her face.

'Right, well. That's good then,' Iris said through numb

lips. 'See you both, Sunday.'

The door shut. Will called goodbye as he drove away. The car dwindled down the drive to the road and disappeared. Iris stayed where she was, watching for long minutes after it had gone.

CHAPTER SIXTEEN

At just after 6.30 the following morning Lana Mitchell was halfway through her usual jogging route in Regent's Park. She entered St John's Lodge Gardens, ran past the gate lodge and around the flower gardens. Most joggers kept to the main walkways, but Lana loved the scents and colours of the all-year-round garden and so enjoyed the short, repetitious circuit. Checking her watch, she reduced to her cool-down pace, letting her heart and breathing slow. When she reached a hedged arch, she dropped to a walk, entering her favourite, most secluded part of the gardens. The stone laid path she reached stretched right and back to the park while dead-ending to her left with the 'Shepherdess' statue. Lana walked to the bronze figure and began her warm-down while relishing the elasticity of muscles and tendons. In the midst of a shoulder stretch she became aware of a blonde-haired man coming through the arch; grey suit odd amidst the greenery, with briefcase and phone call completing the incongruity. Irritated at being disturbed, Lana continued her stretches hoping it might dissuade the man away. He finished his call, slipping the phone into a pocket and stared about as if wondering how he had got there. He seemed to see Lana for the first time and approached, smiling.

'I wonder, could you help me?' he asked.

'The way back to the park is behind you,' she said.

She bent, stretching calf muscles, and noted the man's shoes stopping some three feet away. She straightened, not liking the proximity, to find an A4 glossy photo being held at eye level. Lana could clearly see the young woman, spreadeagled, gagged and chained to a bed. Her eyes were blackened, swollen shut. To the left of the bed somebody in dark clothes, mask and hood held a gun, pointing at the woman's head. Lana gasped, half falling, grabbing at the photograph. The man let her take it.

'Do as instructed and your sister will be released.'

Lana sank to the ground, her mouth opening and closing, eyes wide on the picture.

'What?'

'Oh dear, it's a bit of shock, I know. Still, if you keep your head it will soon be over.'

His shoes stepped forward and the briefcase was placed before her, then gloved fingers snapped in her face.

'Lana, focus on the case. Everything you need is inside. If you go to the authorities, alert anyone or deviate from the instructions your sister will pay the price. We *will* know. You are being watched.'

He walked away while Lana scrambled at the briefcase.

At 11am Lana bent and let the retinal scanner strobe her for the second time that day. The steel door swung open and she entered the safe deposit room, hearing the door shush closed. She paused as instructed and counted to twenty while desperately trying to stop trembling. Her legs were the worst, almost buckling her to the carpet. She swallowed, picturing her sister, and forced herself to stillness. Reaching twenty Lana moved through the room counting to the fifth Ficus and retrieved the briefcase she had hidden there before anyone else had arrived that morning. Her mind tripped over the instructions, panicked again at the thought of the motion and heat sensors while sweat dimpled her back. She moved on, checking the drawer stacks until she reached the first number on the list: 803.

Stopping and undoing the briefcase, Lana extracted what she now knew to be some kind of scanner and attached it to the drawer front. Pressing a button caused it to whir into action, emitting a steady light and faint heat. Lana glanced at the steel door, expecting it to swing open, spewing security guards, but nothing happened. Hope flared, painful and sharp in her chest, and she waited for the scanner to finish. She moved through the room scanning the three other drawers on the list and finishing at 1053. When all was done, she removed the flash drive from the scanner and stowed it in her pocket. She repacked and hid the briefcase and left the room, returning to her duties.

At 5.21pm Lana stared at her boss, willing him to go home.

'Don't work too hard,' he said.

She found a smile and shook her head.

'Just finishing up. I won't be long.'

He gestured goodbye and left. Lana waited, intent on the clock. At precisely 5.24, as instructed, she rose, made her way across the dim foyer and re-entered the deposit room. Inside, her hands slipped with sweat around the briefcase handle and she glanced at her watch, 5.27, three minutes before the cameras turned on. She hurried to the door, willing it to open more quickly, and stepped into the foyer as 5.29 became 5.30.

Just over half an hour later Lana unlocked an unfamiliar door to a flat in Marylebone. She paused in the final opening, listening to the silence. Clutching the briefcase, she entered closing the door behind her and stood scanning the white and silver living space. Two leather sofas occupied the laminate floor. They faced a coffee table and an expensive, real flame fireplace. Above the mantle a flat screen television was attached to the wall and tall floor speakers were strategically placed about the room. Three closed doors worried her. Moving inside, she placed the briefcase and her bag on the table and breathed the oddly unscented air.

'Where the fuck are you,' she whispered.

Skin crawling, she refused to sit down despite her unsteadiness. She checked behind a door, finding an achingly tidy kitchen. She went to a second door, pushing inside, and the scene punched her to the floor. Then crawling and sobbing, snot and spittle dripping to the floor, she groped for her sister's hand. Uncaring it was cold she cradled it and struggled up. Gasping, her mind a screaming blank at the syringe embedded in the soft elbow crease, she curled next to her dead sister.

It seemed to Lana hours passed. The night deepened, streetlights came on and finally she uncurled. Tendrils of snot clung to her lips and she felt numb inside and out. Not looking at her sister, Lana rose on disobedient legs, running a hand over her mouth and swallowed against the sandiness in her throat. She gained the living room and in the firelight the briefcase and her bag were exactly where she had left them. She fought the urge to scream and throw the case against the wall. Fumbling her bag, she emptied the contents on the floor and grabbed her phone. Sobbing she stared uncomprehendingly at a blank, unresponsive screen then stumbled to the front door only to fall against it and slide to her knees. She tried to think past the bastard phone, the briefcase and her sister's corpse. She struggled for the handle, but her hand refused to move. The firelight seemed to pulse, making the room sway.

'Help, please, help me.'

She shouted but it croaked out, her throat tight and unresponsive. Her body bowed, rubbery and suddenly unconnected, so she crumpled entirely to the floor. The door opened, shoving her back across the laminate floor. With heavy effort she turned her head, seeing the man's shoes from the park. The door closed and the legs put on a white paper coverall. The room grew bright and she realised spotlights had flicked on. She felt it when the fire went out, the heat disappearing. The man moved about taking things from the walls before going into the bedroom. Suddenly he was there, crouched, hooded head sideways, peering into her eyes.

'Oh good, still conscious,' he said, voice muffled through a face mask. 'I prefer to watch when they know what's coming. Like your sister did.'

He undressed her with latex gloves strange on her skin while removing her lavender suit and silk blouse, admiring her body as he did so. She wanted to scream, to run, but couldn't move. Terror made her bones watery. All the while tears fell, silent and without menace to him. He even wiped them away, once. She recognised the clothes when he re-dressed her. They were from her wardrobe. She tried to struggle, fuelled by fear and rage, and her little finger jerked. He smiled at that and she longed to spit and kick. The whole time he didn't stop talking.

'I've watched you,' he said. 'For a while now, out and about, but also while you were in here today. That's what I took off the walls – cameras to watch and transmitter blockers to stop your phone working, you see. I was only next door. It's one of the perks, watching like that. Didn't you wonder how the fire came on? It's remote controlled. Clever huh?'

'You wouldn't believe how easy it was to jam the heat and motion sensors at Goodwins. Our transmitter blockers are gone now of course. We can't leave any trace. Retinal scanners though, bloody things, nigh-on impossible to fool no matter what films portray. Cameras are a bitch as well. Cut the feed and it's obvious. Looping the images? Well, that's all bollocks unless you've got access, lots of time and the knowhow. But we're working to a bit of a deadline, that's why, if you're wondering, we needed you.'

She managed to swallow, and he noticed; a gloved hand caressed her throat.

'Funny, you never noticed your sister's face in there. No bruising. It was just make-up for the photo. She needed to be an accidental overdose or there might be questions. You were too shocked seeing her dead, I suppose, to wonder where the bruising had gone. No, she was like you are now, the whole time we took the pictures. She had an easy death, so there's that.'

Abruptly the stench of piss filled the space between them.

'Oh dear, you've wet yourself. Don't be embarrassed, it happens. Now, you're thinking about being paralysed, aren't you? It's the fireplace. It releases a nerve agent designed for specific muscle groups and its undetectable inside you and out.'

He met her gaze, the mask making him alien and distorted.

'Lovely flat you've got in Piccadilly, better than this. I'm popping back there, after, to replace your suit and blouse, swapping bags, stashing drug paraphernalia and whatnot. So it looks like you went home and picked up supplies. Nice colour on you, lavender. Oh, don't worry, if you'd tried to leave here earlier, I'd have got you anyway. So, don't feel bad that you got caught out by the gas. Right, upsy daisy.'

He lifted Lana as easily as if she were a rag doll and carried her into the bedroom, positioning her beside her sister. He squatted next to the bed, staring into her eyes.

'So, here's what's going to happen. I'm going kill you. Ah, there it is, fear response. I like that better than sex, really. Shame we can't have some carnal fun.' He paused, studying her body and then stroked her face. 'Still, I do enjoy my work. But don't worry, I won't being doing it with a blade or anything, more's the pity. Overdose like your sister. Shared experience for you, so there's that.'

Lana tried to squirm, to move, but her body felt numb as if it belonged to someone else. She was screaming on the inside while desperately straining to move.

'I imagine you're thinking about your family and friends finding out you have this nasty habit. Do you think it will make them grieve less?'

He held up a syringe full of liquid. Her eyes succeeded in widening, making tears fall faster. She didn't feel the needle but felt the drug sweep her; a fierce wind, scalding and savage all at once. It suddenly became sluggish. A coursing oblivion covering her like a cloak. The last thing Lana Mitchell managed was a smile, trying to spit at the man watching her die.

Chapter Seventeen

For Iris the week was slow and too quick. Handling everything with care, she and Michael spent two evenings re-reading Sam and Gordon's documents and studying the leather tome to ensure they hadn't missed anything important. The drawings of Leonardo Da Vinci held a special interest for Michael and Iris never tired of looking at them. She woke on Sunday morning sluggish in mind and body as if she hadn't slept at all. After breakfast and tending the animals she prepared lunch. Slicing shiitake and oyster mushrooms then adding pre-drained lentils, she tossed everything in a little olive oil. Transferring the mix to a saucepan where the red onion had already softened, she added basil and black pepper. Opening the fridge, she hesitated then muttering began moving things until,

'Michael! Where's the bloody garlic?'

Gus retreated under the table. Her husband wandered in from the living room with newspaper in hand.

'Not in the fridge I take it?'

'Clearly not.' She rummaged in a cupboard. 'Don't just stand there, help me. You used it last.'

Michael glanced into the saucepan and at the ceramic dish on the side layered with pasta sheets.

'Your famous vegetarian lasagne – Theo is honoured.'

'He won't be unless I find the bloody garlic!'

'You mean this garlic?'

She turned to find Michael holding the bulb and snatched it from him.

'Where did you find that – on some obscure shelf you left it on?'

'Behind the empty mushroom punnet. Where you left it, I think,' he said mildly.

She peeled and then pummelled the garlic in the presser adding it to the saucepan and placing the pan on the hot Aga plate. Michael settled at the kitchen table and Gus came out to sit beside him.

'Do you want to tell me why you're so irritable?' Michael asked.

'No.'

He turned a page with one hand while the other stroked Gus. She stirred the mix, folding the onion and mushrooms into the lentils while hearing the faint sizzle and inhaling the comforting scents.

'Anyone else,' she said.

'Sorry?'

'Zoe. She could've picked anyone else. Why him?'

'Maybe she likes him.'

'But why? He's smarmy, insincere and too bloody full of himself. Don't you think?'

'I don't know. I don't know him well enough to say.'

She turned to him feeling as if her muscles were grit and girders, all uncomfortable and taut.

'Don't be all reasonable and bland, it's annoying.'

Michael rose and gave her a hug she didn't return with Gus weaving between them.

'So, you're not irritated,' Michael said. 'Just annoyed with your husband for not pre-judging your daughter's new chap?'

She rested against him, breathing in his Michael scent,

and felt her shoulders loosening. Her fingers tousled Gus's ears and she sighed.

'I'm just worried, that's all.'

Her arms crept round her husband's waist and Gus was a comforting weight against her legs. Michael rested his chin on her head.

'I know, me too,' he said. 'But if Theo is a smarmy little toerag then Zoe has to find out for herself. You being all judgemental about him isn't going help and might push her away.'

She buried her head in his shoulder, muffling her voice.

'They're not here yet.'

He leant back, finding her gaze.

'Oh, I see, you're getting all your judgement and irritation out before the culprit arrives?'

'Maybe.'

'And you're buttering Zoe up with her favourite food to prove you're really all right with her choice of beau?'

'Beau? What are you, eighty?'

'Would you prefer lover?'

'Not especially.'

'Well, "boyfriend" reeks of permanence,' he said.

She stepped back, eyeing him.

'Aha!'

'What aha?'

'You don't like him either.'

'I didn't say that.'

'Reeks of permanence? That sounds as if you don't want Theo to be long term. Admit it, you don't like him.'

Michael returned to his seat, his expression prim.

'On with you, woman. You cannot trick me with your wily ways.'

Iris snorted and returned to the Aga. Gus followed and lay next to the Aga's warmth watching her. After a moment there was a rustle of paper and she glanced at Michael pretending to read.

'I will admit,' he said without looking up, 'that Theo wouldn't be my first choice. But there's not much we can do about it, is there?'

Iris pursed her lips, catching words before they fell, and returned to stirring.

Chapter Eighteen

Zoe and Theo arrived just before eleven in his black Mercedes. Iris opened the front door and Gus trotted out to greet Zoe. On seeing Theo, he pelted back inside, hiding behind Iris's legs. Theo presented Iris with a bouquet of flowers and a bottle of wine. Thanking him, Iris ushered everyone to the kitchen. Gus went under the table, keeping away from Theo. While putting the flowers in a vase she tried very hard to quash any thoughts on ulterior motives. Michael admired the wine and chatted to Theo about the journey from London while Zoe hovered.

'Mum, I'm just going to show Theo round the farm, okay?'

Iris nodded, face taut with a smile. They left through the back door and she resisted the urge to shoot the bolts behind them. Michael put the wine on the table and opening a drawer took out cutlery.

'Zoe seems nervous,' he said.

'I noticed. Probably the speedy drive up in his flashy Merc upset her.' She glanced at her husband. 'Sorry. I'll try harder.'

'Thank God, because I'm flagging already.'

Iris laughed and hugged her husband, suddenly feeling lighter.

Over lunch the conversation became easier. Zoe visibly relaxed and Iris managed to keep her concerns at bay. Theo made a few attempts to befriend Gus, but the Picardy remained wary, staying firmly at Iris's side. Halfway through the lasagne Michael went to the cellar for a second bottle of wine. Theo refilled Zoe's glass and topped up Iris's from the one on the table.

'I meant to say, I really enjoyed looking round the farm,' he said. 'It's an amazing place.'

'Thank you. It's hard work but worth it.'

'Of course. Well, it's clearly a labour of love. And Zoe says your reputation in Europe is second to none?'

'Something like that,' Iris smiled. 'The Sandy and Blacks are doing particularly well overseas at the moment.'

'Those are the pigs, right? And you've got sheep?'

'Boreravs. You might've seen them dotted about up in the fields.'

'We did. Zoe pointed them out.'

He tore a piece of garlic bread and popped a bit in his mouth. Michael returned and opened the wine before settling at the table.

'We also met Honky,' her daughter said.

Iris tried not to smile.

'Oh dear. How did that go?'

Theo raised his arm showing slobbery marks on his polo shirt.

'Nibbled,' he said. 'I should've had some carrot for him, I guess. His friends were much nicer.'

'Shiloh and Blue are definitely less demanding. Sorry about your shirt.'

'Not to worry. It was a pleasure to meet them all. Zoe says one of the horses is pregnant?'

'Yes, Shiloh. We put her to a friend's stallion last year.'

She finished her lasagne and wished he would stop

being nice about the farm.

'I have to admit,' Theo said, 'I know next to nothing about horses. But I did get to see some in action at the last Olympics. I accompanied Rosalind to watch them jumping and doing… dressage, is it called?'

'That's right. You were at the Olympics in Athens?'

'My father got the tickets for Rosalind. I found the whole thing exhilarating. Do you ride your horses at all?'

'I do, actually and I still ride Blue out regularly to keep her fit. Both excel at dressage in particular. As a breed Andalusians are renowned for it. The same friend with the stallion has been training us, but not with Shiloh since she fell pregnant. In fact, my friend should've been at the Olympic events you saw but broke her wrist. She's hoping to make it next year.'

Theo nodded, his expression interested and open. He nodded to where Gus lay next to Iris's chair.

'Zoe mentioned you have a special sheep-herding dog. He's a pedigree, isn't he?'

'Gus is a purebred Picardy sheepdog.'

'I thought pedigrees had fancy names.'

'He does, it's Voyager Le Plus Auguste. All Picardys born in 2004 have names beginning with V. We shortened the Auguste to Gus.'

'Ah I see. So, he's, Traveller Most Majestic.'

'You speak French?' Zoe asked.

'Oui,' replied Theo kissing her hand.

Iris swallowed, rising to make custard and take the apple crumble from the Aga. Zoe got bowls while Michael cleared the table.

'I'm really looking forward to this,' Theo said. 'Apple crumble's one of my favourites and yours certainly smells wonderful.'

'It's one of my favourites too,' said Zoe. 'And Mum

makes the best apple crumble of anyone I know.'

Iris smiled, her face aching at the compliment, and exchanged a look with Michael.

Surely, they'll run out of nice things to say soon? hers said.

Keep smiling. It can't last much longer, his replied.

The conversation turned to Michael's job and Iris studied Theo. The young man seemed utterly intent on what her husband was saying. Iris tried to believe it; the interest in Theo's expression, the way he nodded and picked up on key words to continue asking questions. He glanced at Zoe and smiled. Her daughter returned it and rested her hand on his arm. Iris looked away, mashing her crumble topping into the stewed apples.

What is it about him I don't trust? He's good looking, seems to really like Zoe and by all accounts he's treating her very well. So, what is it?

She returned her attention to Theo, watching his mobile features as he suddenly laughed. Yet to her it seemed forced, his smile not reaching his eyes and abruptly she knew.

No matter what he says or does, his eyes never change. He looks like he's constantly calculating, weighing everything up, and I don't like it.

Worry surged like a tide and she glanced at Zoe. Her daughter caught her gaze and surreptitiously gestured to the living room.

'Mum, have you got that book I asked about?'

'Ah yes, somewhere. I finished it a few days ago. Come and help me look.'

Iris rose with Gus at her heels and Zoe followed them into the living room. They went to the bookcase pretending to peruse the shelves.

'Have you found anything about Amy Dudley's family?' Zoe asked quietly.

Iris glanced across the room, checking the kitchen door was closed.

'Yes, actually. She had two half-brothers, one was mentioned in Sam's notes, and two half-sisters. We traced one, Frances Flowerdew, in a book about Tudor uprisings your father has.'

A clatter made her look to see the kindling basket overturned with wood all over the floor and Gus skittering away from it to collide with her legs. She staggered at his weight and then crouched, stroking and reassuring him. The Picardy's whiskery face was level with hers and his kisses wetted her cheeks. Iris then helped Zoe pick up the wood and replace it in the upturned basket with Gus nosing the odd stick.

'Frances was married to a William Flowerdew,' Iris continued, straightening, 'whose father instigated a chap called Ketts to rebellion. It's all very interesting actually.'

Zoe gave Gus a stroke and the Picardy rubbed his bearded chin on her sleeve with a goofball expression.

'Did Frances have any children?'

'We don't know. It got very vague,' Iris said. 'So, I took your advice and passed the search to a genealogist. I told the woman it's for our family tree and we think we're looking for cousins.' She picked up the kindling basket, moving it out of the way of Gus's questing nose. 'That way she won't ask too many questions and will hopefully come up with a living relative we can talk into helping us.'

'Clever.' Zoe took an audible breath. 'Okay, now tell me, what do you think about Theo?'

Iris paused and hated herself for doing so.

'He seems very nice,' she said quickly, 'and as long as he makes you happy that's all that matters.'

She looked at her daughter. Zoe's expression was wary;

her eyes narrowed.

'Really? Because he does make me happy. Very happy, in fact.'

Iris took a book from the shelf and held it out.

'Good. Here, you'd better take this, or it'll look like we left just to gossip.'

Her daughter took the novel and went back to the kitchen. Iris waited until the door closed then bent and hugged Gus while trying to not to feel guilty about disliking Theo.

An hour later, they all took a stroll around the farm. Gus ambled, sniffing, staying away from the stranger while Zoe talked to Michael. Iris found herself walking beside Theo.

'Thank you so much for having me,' he said. 'It's been great.'

'Our pleasure,' Iris said.

Theo's gaze roamed the drive and surrounding fields.

'I was very sorry to hear about Ruth Dunn,' he said quietly. 'I know it's affected Zoe badly and can only imagine how it's making you feel.'

Iris twisted inside but kept her face blank and eyes dry.

'I just hope they catch the bastard soon,' she managed.

'And that awful break-in. Nothing was taken, Zoe said. Thank goodness for decent security systems.'

Iris looked to where the container had stood. A deader, flattened patch of grass still showed where it had been.

'We were very lucky.'

He followed her gaze.

'I hear the police took your shipping container. Was that to keep everything safe?'

'Something like that, yes.'

'And now you can't even visit your belongings. I guess you don't even know where they are. Stuck in some police warehouse, I imagine. Personally, I'd be worried sick about damage.'

Iris considered the younger man. His expression was sympathetic and yet his eyes seemed to gauge her, watching for a reaction.

'I hope the police have the good sense to look after everything,' she said. 'Luckily, we do know where it is, some warehouse in Southwark. So, if it does go poorly, we know exactly who to blame.'

'Well, that's a silver lining then, isn't it?'

He twiddled a piece of straw between his fingers, gaze raking the paddock and fields. They continued walking, finding small talk in the horses until they reached Theo's car. The young couple got in, giving cheery goodbyes, and drove away. Watching them leave, Michael put his arm around Iris's waist.

'I've changed my mind,' he said.

'Oh yes?'

The Mercedes stopped at the end of the drive and turned right, pulling out smoothly and steadily. Michael's arm tightened around her.

'I don't like him,' he said.

She shifted to look at him and noted her husband's tense expression.

'Me neither,' she said.

Later that evening, Iris was trying to stay awake with the book about Tudor rebellions open on her lap and Gus warm against her thighs. On her other side, Michael suddenly swore and turned up the volume on the television. Iris looked at the screen seeing pictures of two women and went very still. The newsreader handed over to a live feed in London where a reporter looked grave.

'Following complaints about a smell, the bodies of

two sisters were found in this block of flats in Marylebone yesterday. The victims have been named as Lana and Stella Mitchell. Earlier Lana Mitchell's colleagues at Goodwins financial institution here in the City expressed their shock and sadness at her death. Her sister was employed by a major pharmaceutical company, Everson, who have yet to comment. Police are not looking for anyone else in connection with the deaths. The family have asked to be left in peace at this tragic time. Back to the studio.'

Michael muted the sound. Iris stared at her husband while the cracking and popping fire seemed overly loud.

Chapter Nineteen

Two days later, the Shaws were in London visiting The National Archives. As they walked past the man-made lake, the impressive entrance shone with glass and white stone reflecting sunlight. Iris tried to ignore the security guard, yet her heart became punishing in its beat. Then they were inside, showing their identification and being handed their reader's cards. Michael led the way, stowing their belongings in lockers then proceeding to the bank of computers overlooking the document reading room. Settling in office chairs Michael accessed the order forms while Iris took a piece of paper from her pocket.

'How sure are you they won't realise what the document is?' she asked.

He paused, eyes on the screen and fingers over the keyboard.

'We can only hope,' he said. 'I've never really noticed if those processing everything actually read the documents. Have you got the numbers?'

Iris passed the piece of paper to her husband.

'When were you here last?'

'A year or so ago for that paper I wrote about political interpretations of Henry VIII's wives. I went to a Swedish conference with it, remember?'

'I remember you went to Sweden.'

He smiled, scrolling through a form and tapping in information.

'I love how you take an interest in my career.'

'Why, Dr Shaw,' Iris said, 'how can you doubt my eternal interest in your conference papers? Do tell, how many piglets and lambs were sold last year?'

'Enough to keep the place running?'

'I love how you take an interest in our livelihood.'

They grinned at each other. Michael continued typing and then pressed return.

'That's it,' he said. 'Now we wait to be called. Come on.'

He rose and led the way into the reading room. The occupants seated at the green-topped, numbered tables and behind raised wooden partitions were hushed, absorbed in reading. Iris followed Michael and settled at an empty table. The air seemed heavy and she took off her jacket, which made little difference to the uncomfortable weight that seemed to press on her skin and in her bones. She glanced about, hating the waiting and wondered at Michael so seemingly relaxed. He gripped her fingers under the desk, and she knew then he was anxious too.

Twenty minutes or so passed in a fidgeting, sighing wait that pestered at Iris's nerves and made her jittery, convinced they were going to fail in their purpose. When their numbers were called it took an effort of will to rise smoothly and calmly collect the documents and boxes. They had ordered fifteen items for Michael and thirteen for her. Too many, they reasoned, might cause attention, yet they needed a goodly amount to cover their intended target, the coroner's report into Amy Dudley's death. Equally, to ensure their plan worked the requested documents were ranged between 1480 and 1663. They resettled at their table and began to sort through the items, taking care to read and peruse as if they all mattered. Eventually, Iris reached for the box marked 'Court of the King's Bench. November 1561 to November, 1562' and steadied her breath. Michael glanced at her and then about the room. She followed his gaze and, reassured no one paid them any heed, flicked through the box, taking documents out as if at random, searching, searching for the memorised Latin words from Gordon's notebook.

She scanned a page and found nothing she recognised. Putting it back, it refused to slip neatly amongst its brethren, poking out the box and creasing on its own weight. She slid her fingers inside the box and touched folded parchment at the bottom. Excitement and fear took hold in equal measure. She desperately hoped it was the report while believing it couldn't be. Still holding the first page she slithered the folded paper up its front and removed them both. Flattening the page, she studied the sepia whorls and loops, reading: *Super visum corporis domine Amee Dudley, nuper uxoris Roberti Dudley*. Trying not to smile and with shaking fingers she passed the parchment to Michael, who read it, his eyes widening, and schooled his face to blandness before nodding once. As planned, they continued for a further half an hour, reading things Iris couldn't understand and didn't care about. Her gaze kept finding the coroner's report on the table, tucked beneath two other documents and her thoughts were filled with Amy Dudley.

Just before 2pm they attached special mark up strips to five documents and took them to the record-copying counter. Iris held her breath while a woman smiled and nodded, scrutinising the paper strips and pages before punching numbers on a register. Michael paid the copy fee and they left to wait once again. Iris couldn't sit still and pretend she was all right, so they went to the archives cafe and ordered coffee she was too agitated to drink.

'It'll be fine,' Michael murmured, adding sugar to his drink.

'You can't know that. What if someone reads the document and figures out what it is?'

'What if they do? There'll be a first-class outcry and hoo-ha at finding it. The press will be all over it for a few days and then it will be safely stored. But we'll still get our copy. That's not what this is about.'

'No, this whole cloak and dagger routine is about keeping our interest secret. Away from anyone "watching". So, don't tell me that if someone realises what that parchment is, it won't bring attention on us, possibly from those we're trying to avoid.'

'Come on now, this is all just a precaution so we can get evidence of murder without alerting the authorities to our bony finds. Besides, we don't even know there's anyone "watching" out there.'

Michael sipped his coffee. Iris turned her cup round and round on its saucer, so the black liquid sloshed at the sides.

'Ruth knew, in the end,' she said. 'So did Lana Mitchell, I bet.'

'Now, you're being paranoid. Lana Mitchell's death was accidental.'

'You still don't think it was a bit strange her dying just after we'd visited Goodwins?'

'We've gone over this. The bank wasn't broken into. Lana Mitchell had no idea what was in our box or what we took. There would be no reason for her *accidental death* to be linked with us or our search.'

Iris tried to believe him. She sipped coffee while her thoughts tumbled over the news reports she had seen and read, trying to discern particulars from the scant details.

'I don't like the word accidental,' she said. 'It could mean anything.'

'Short of finding and disturbing her family or asking the police we'll never know what happened for sure.'

She looked away, unwilling to share her thoughts and worries any further.

Another half an hour passed before they could collect their copies and the originals. Returning to the document reading room they settled once again and pretended to read. Finally, at nearly 4pm, Iris began tidying up, replacing pages, and Michael followed suit. Under cover of filing she slipped the refolded original coroner's report into the box further back from where she had found it. Letting the parchment go felt wrong and she silently vowed to make its presence known as soon as Amy Dudley would allow.

Taking the copies, they left the reading room and gathered their things from the lockers, putting their documents away in Michael's rucksack. Iris concentrated on leaving, keeping a smile in place and following Michael. The foyer was busy, and she focused on the outside, just beyond the glass.

They're perfectly legitimate copies. We haven't stolen anything. Calm down.

She drew a breath and glanced away from the security guard, letting her gaze roam the crowd, and suddenly stopped. Michael was at her side in a moment.

'What's wrong?' he asked.

Iris peered into the throng.

'I thought there was someone I recognised, but he's gone now.'

'Who was it?'

'I could've sworn it was that chap who came to Aunt Josephine's house the day Ruth disappeared.'

Michael was looking too, scanning the crowd.

'The man called Sloane who deals in furniture?'

'That's right, but I can't see him now.' She gripped his arm. 'It's probably nothing. Just my imagination. Come on, let's go.'

He studied her face, and she managed a smile. Unhurriedly they left the archive building and all the while Iris's neck crawled as if beset by spiders.

Chapter Twenty

The following evening Iris surveyed her living room, checking the rearranged furniture against the sketch copied from Sam's notes.

'Move the bolster a little to the left.'

Gus, lying in front of the fire, watched with interest while Michael obliged by shifting the pillow across the floorboards. He stood back admiring his handiwork.

'That feels about right,' he said. 'How does it compare?'

Iris looked around.

'Perfectly. I'd say we have Amy Dudley's bedchamber and Sam's estimate of where her body fell to a tee. Now we just need Bob.'

'I'll get him.'

Michael went into the kitchen and returned carrying a bag. He took out a skull, turned it on its side and placed it at one end of the bolster.

'How's that?'

Gus rose, sniffed and nudged Bob. Iris went over and repositioned the skull standing over the improvised body.

'It looks like it does in the sketch. Although Bob has blue putty holding a tooth in which I don't think Amy Dudley would've.'

'Ah, that's where Bob got knocked off Roger's desk a couple of years ago. Apparently blue putty is the dental plan for life-sized replica skulls.'

She moved away, surveying the rest of the room again with Gus following.

'Why exactly does Roger have Bob? You said he's in the English department, not science or medicine.'

'Roger is an expert on horror and gothic literature as well as science fantasy which, incidentally, is wizards as opposed to space travel.'

'*Lord of the Rings* not *Star Trek*?'

'Exactly. Bob the skull has something to do with one of Roger's favourite authors and as such he must be returned unharmed.'

'Right, so how are we going to smack Bob without hurting him?'

'With my improvised candlestick. Won't be a moment.'

Michael went back into the kitchen and returned with a bottle of food colouring, an old pastry brush and one of her large Kilner jars. Tinfoil was attached to the bottom of the jar in a familiar shape.

'That looks like the candleholder base,' she said.

'It's meant to. When you told me you wanted to construct Sam's theory of how Amy Dudley was murdered I figured we would want something to simulate the candleholder rather than use a four-hundred-year-old antique for our experiment.' He showed her the bottom, tipping the jar. 'See, the foil is wrapped around a cardboard cut-out I made based on the candleholder and measurements Sam took which I verified against the real thing.' Gus sniffed the foil and wandered off to lie in front of the fire. 'Well, Gus is clearly impressed. But, apart from the intricacies of the silver base, it matches. Have you got a pencil handy?'

She found one.

'Can you mark on Bob where Sam indicated Amy Dudley's gouges were? The pencil will rub off easily enough.'

Iris did as she was bid.

'And the food colouring is for?'

'Not hurting Bob. Hold the jar please while I apply it.'

She took hold of the Kilner glass lid. Using the brush Michael applied the blue colourant from the bottle to the foil base. He then took the jar from her, holding it bottom up.

'I'll let it dry a bit and it'll still be tacky enough to work as blood,' he said. 'Get Bob and we'll start the reconstruction.'

Iris retrieved the skull while marvelling at the life-like quality in the moulded plastic.

'According to Sam's theory,' she said, 'Amy Dudley ran from her attacker, was caught and hit with the candleholder.' She swallowed. 'And then her neck snapped.' She moved to where they had stationed the sofa to replicate the bed. 'There were blood drops found on the hearth.' She glanced at the fireplace and positioned herself where the foot of the bed was represented by the sofa end. 'The attacker was blocking the door, so she would've had to run around him, going past the fire.'

Michael moved into position, still holding the jar up. Iris walked forward, skirting her husband and holding Bob at head height.

'Right. The attacker was quicker and grabbed Amy Dudley,' Michael said.

He caught her arm and she automatically twisted towards him. Suddenly Gus barked, rose and rushed between them. Iris reassured her dog and the Picardy leant against her legs while enjoying a tickle from Michael's free hand.

'All right,' her husband said. 'They struggle and the attacker grabs the candleholder from the table and…'

Michael brought down the jar and gently tapped Bob,

distributing blue pigment on the skull. They looked at the marks covering the pencil.

'It's not very scientific and I'm sure the professionals can verify it after we publish everything. But it proves it was possible,' Michael said.

Iris stared at the skull and shuddered, imagining Amy Dudley terrified and dealt such a terrific blow as to cause the gouges she had seen in her skull. Gus sat at her feet and she stroked his ears.

'It was more than possible,' she said. 'Between this reconstruction and him ruling out poison I have to agree with Sam about how Amy Dudley was murdered.'

'And, thanks to Gordon McCraken, we know that Lord Dudley wasn't involved.'

'So, the iodine method for fingerprinting is real?'

'Certainly is. The marks just don't remain visible for very long unless fixed with something called Benzoflavone.'

'Not something our Doctor McCraken would've known in 1840?'

'Unfortunately not. But nowadays you can buy such fuming kits off the internet. Again, once we publish everything the documents he found can be properly tested. I'm certain that professionals will confirm Gordon's discovery about the thumbprint on the message not being her husband's. Personally, I've no doubt Gordon was right about the prints and Lord Dudley's innocence.'

Iris gazed at Bob and then to the prone bolster.

'Right,' she sighed. 'So, both men understood how Amy Dudley was murdered but disagreed on who did it and neither knew why?'

'Except it was for something she had. Something dangerous to the crown.'

'I don't suppose the coroner's report helps with that at all?'

'It does not. But it does confirm the dents in Amy Dudley's skull and their depth. So, we're getting there.'

Iris placed Bob on the floor, at the end of the bolster. Using her phone, she took photos of the placement and then the rest of the room. Gus rose and wandered over to sniff Bob again. Michael picked up the skull before the Picardy could investigate too much. Gus, ears pricked, ambled toward the curtains and wandered into the dark behind, his back and tail still visible. Iris gestured Michael to turn Bob and photographed the blue deposits on him, bending forward to do so, making the locket swing under her top. She paused, heart quickening, and straightened with a hand going to the jewellery. Her thoughts flicked to Sam's notes and Gordon's theories, the coroner's report and Michael's historical research. The disparate threads seemed to knit together and she drew a sharp breath.

'Oh my God, Michael, what if…'

Behind the curtain Gus suddenly barked and began pawing at the French door. Frowning, Iris lifted the drape and Michael joined her. She stared into the dark garden, peering at the black fields and woods beyond that marked Whitebarn's boundary. Abrupt light burst among the trees.

'What the hell was that?' Michael asked.

Iris turned, dropping the curtain.

'It's one of Luke's flashes. Someone must have triggered it. Come on.'

Racing out the front door they met Thomas's younger son, Dan, running toward the pastures and far-away copse with his black and white spaniel at his heels.

'Where's Luke?' Iris called.

'Out there. Doing a round.'

Dan tossed Michael a torch and turned another on. Gus, long legged, tore ahead and then ran back to keep pace with Iris.

'He's not supposed to be *out* anywhere,' her voice was harsh with anger.

Fear tightened her guts, and she raced toward the pasture with Gus at heels. As she ran, Iris scanned the copse where the treetops were visible against the star-strewn sky. Michael's light swept up while Dan's swept ahead.

'Luke!'

The older Wade was standing where the shipping container had once been, staring at a white heap on the ground. His two Labradors sat patiently nearby, their yellow coats shining in the torch lights. Reaching Luke, Michael's light brought the white heap into sharp relief and the stench of blood and entrails was punchy. Whining, Gus circled the corpse.

'Oh no,' said Iris. 'Oh shit.'

Dan's dog was ordered back and settled next to Luke's. Iris caught hold of Gus, crouched and peered at the poor dead creature.

'It's not one of mine,' she said. 'It's not a Boreray. It's maybe an Oxford ewe.' She studied the gutted sheep. 'It's been slaughtered recently, I think.' She rose staring at Luke. 'What on earth are you doing out here?'

'I saw the man who dumped it,' Luke said, his voice monotoned. 'He ran through the pastures and into the copse, where I lost him. I was worried about the animals and came back. I got here just as he set off the flash.'

She clenched her fists to stop from shaking him.

'Bloody hell, Luke!'

Michael put a hand on the young man's shoulder.

'Thank God you're all right,' her husband said. 'Did you see who it was?'

'No, it's too dark and he was too fast. I didn't want to send the dogs after him in case they got hurt.'

'Well, at least you've got some sense,' said Iris. 'You

were supposed to just monitor the cameras and sensors so you would be *inside* if a flash went off. Not roaming around in the dark!'

Luke shrugged.

'No one's likely to come during the day so we thought night-time patrols would be a good idea.'

'What if it had been the killer? Gods Luke, didn't you think about that?' She suddenly noticed he was trembling and hadn't moved since they had arrived. Her anger drained away. 'Come on, let's get you inside. Michael can phone the police.'

'Those flashes aren't exactly legal,' Dan said.

'We don't mention that bit or even that you two were here. But they need to know about this poor sheep. Are there any more flashes in the copse?'

Dan shook his head, his expression in the torchlight worried and tight with fear. She found a smile, hoping it was reassuring, then took Luke's arm and led the way into the house.

When the police arrived, she kept them in the kitchen, feeling glad DI Fields and DS Dens didn't attend. No one questioned their version of events where, alerted by Gus, they had come out and found the butchered animal. Noises were again made about them leaving to stay somewhere else, but again they were strenuously declined. After the police left, Iris called Thomas, who drove over to Whitebarn to stay with his sons. Natasha, he told them, was visiting her sister in Ireland for a couple of weeks and didn't need to know about Luke's misguided heroics.

Iris and Michael tidied the living room, putting everything back in its usual place, helped by Gus, and finally made their way to bed just before eleven. In the bedroom the Picardy lay on his doggy duvet with a satisfied huff. Iris told him what a good lad he was and got into her pyjamas, feeling anxious and exhausted all at once. Michael lay on the bed, tiredness evident in his groan. Her fingers automatically sought the chain clasp on her neck to remove it and she stopped.

'Michael.'

Her husband opened his eyes and turned his head to her.

'Present, barely.'

'What if Sam was right about the why as well as the how?'

'That Amy Dudley was murdered for something she held, like what?'

She lifted the locket still secure around her neck.

'Like this.'

Michael sat up, frowning.

'Sam never mentions the locket and Gordon only in passing, so what makes you think it's all about that?'

'I don't know. But it suddenly struck me earlier, why *would* Amy Dudley hide this in the pocket watch? Why does anyone hide anything? To keep it secret and safe.'

Michael stared at the locket, his gaze narrowing.

'All right let's think about this,' he said. 'Sam believed Amy Dudley's clothes had been rifled by the killer searching for something hidden on her body. The locket's certainly small enough for that and the murderer didn't find it because it wasn't on her but inside the pocket watch the whole time.'

'And Sam never mentioned the pocket watch or the locket so he couldn't have found either one.'

'Plus, we know from Gordon that both were in her chambers when she was killed, one hidden in the other. Waiting, perhaps, to be handed to her husband, who Amy Dudley believed would be visiting for just that purpose.'

Iris settled on the bed and the locket filled her gaze while her mind crowded with Amy Dudley. She thought about the two men, separated by hundreds of years and their theories. Sam had been convinced that a faction of Lord Dudley's enemies had beget the Watchers and sent them to kill Amy Dudley for what she held and to ruin her husband, getting him hanged for her death. Gordon, however, had thought of Katherine Grey as being behind the murder and the heinous faction but equally with the intent of gaining what the poor woman held while condemning Robert Dudley to the gallows for the killing.

'If this locket *is* why she died, Sam clearly didn't know about it.'

She unhooked the clasp, taking the jewel off. Michael shook his head, clearly unconvinced.

'But why on earth would Amy Dudley be murdered for it?'

'I've absolutely no idea and I could be completely wrong. But at the very least we should try and get it open again.'

'You're right. Let's do some research. There must be ways jewellers get such stubborn items open. Perhaps some sort of oil or pick?'

She nodded, watching the locket twirl on its chain, making the gold and gems flash in the bedside light. She closed her fingers round it while Michael rose and opened the wardrobe door. He crouched and tapped the combination on the safe keypad.

The safe was a curious object, the large body embedded in Whitebarn's thick stone floor, with its, upturned, raised face taking up the entire bottom of the wardrobe. Her stepfather had commissioned the first one in the 1960s and kept the breed ledgers and his research, the lifeblood and success of the farm, locked inside. And although everything was digitally stored now, Iris still kept her stepfather's precious ledgers and invaluable early research inside. She felt by doing so she was protecting the farm, ensuring that the ledgers and research secured against any failure on her part to manage the breed programme. Keeping them at Whitebarn, rather than in a bank, felt as if her stepfather watched over the farm still and hadn't completely gone. More, that she hadn't abandoned or forgotten what she owed him and his life's work. Four years ago, at great expense and labour, she had updated the safe to a fire retardant and much stronger, modern version. Now, holding the jewel and feeling it warm in her palm as if a small bird sheltered there, she had never been more pleased at the investment.

'Iris?'

She looked at her husband, who held out his hand. She passed the locket over, startled by a flash of protective instinct, and resisted the urge to snatch at it. Michael, his expression understanding, held it carefully before locking it away with the other artefacts.

CHAPTER TWENTY-ONE

Earlier that same evening Zoe had barely closed her front door when someone knocked on it. She looked through the peephole and reopened the door with a smile.

'Will, I wasn't expecting you. Did something happen since lunch today?'

Her old friend came in, closed the door and followed her to the kitchen.

'Yes, actually. I wanted to let you know, I got a call just after I left the lab this evening. A friend thinks he'll be able to finalise the DNA extraction and sequencing in the next couple of weeks.'

'That's great. Did I know you'd farmed it out to someone else?'

She waved a mug at him and he nodded while taking off his coat and hanging it over a chair.

'Coffee please, decaf, if you've got it.'

Will moved about, picking up the pepper grinder and putting it down, shifting it to exactly match the salt cellar. She turned the kettle on and glanced at him.

'What's the matter? You look worried.'

He turned the pepper grinder round and round shedding black dots.

'I need to tell you something and I'm not sure you're going to like it.'

She frowned, trying to quell the anxiety pinching her guts.

'Is it about the skull?'

'No, that is, sort of.'

'Yeah, that doesn't help,' she said. 'Just tell me, please.'

He took a deep breath.

'I passed the extraction to someone else as it's not really my area of expertise. Given the way everything came about I thought it best to have the process done, let's say, outside of Arrant.'

She got the coffee from the cupboard, her mind flashing to his equipment and his readiness to take on the clandestine skull work.

'You've done this sort of thing before, haven't you?'

Will hesitated and with a sigh, said, 'If by "this" you mean had processes done off the books, then yes, on occasion.'

Zoe nodded, automatically spooning coffee and adding sugar to Will's mug. Her friend touched her shoulder and she glanced at him.

'It's never to do with criminal cases,' he said.

'It's none of my business.'

'It kind of is, now, so I want you to know. It has only ever been for specialised digs, treasure or heir hunters. When they need to verify certain things about sites or bones before they go public or put a claim in.'

The kettle clicked off and she automatically poured water into the coffees. Her thoughts were hard, and she struggled not to let them colour her voice.

'How long have you been doing it?'

'Since university. Most of my contacts are now trusted professionals who need a bit of extra money and don't ask too many questions.'

'An old buddy network for old bones, who knew?'

Despite her efforts it came out bitter. Will sighed again, shaking his head.

'I'd hoped you'd understand, especially now…'

'Oh, I understand, Will. You're my best friend and you've lied to me. For years.'

She took a sip of coffee, trying to ease her tight throat, and blinked, desperate to prevent tears falling. He put his mug on the side and took hers from unresisting fingers, putting it next to his. His arms encircled her, gently and then in a fierce hug.

'I'm so sorry. Can you believe I was trying to protect you?'

Tears ran hot on her cheeks and she wiped at them.

'Maybe.'

He shifted, looking at her.

'Zoe, I never wanted to involve you. It started as a favour to a mate's mate that turned into a way to make extra money. But we both know it's not exactly legal and I didn't want to put my best friend in that position.'

She hiccoughed a laugh.

'Doesn't say much about me, does it? I had no such worries about involving you in something not entirely legal.'

'Ah, but that's different. Yours is a one-off. Reaching out to a friend for help. Mine is an ongoing felony for strangers and money. You have to believe me when I say I was only trying to protect you.'

She stepped back and found a tissue. Will tugged her sleeve, catching her gaze.

'There's a bright side,' he said. 'I've been doing this sort of thing a while and never been caught. So, you don't have to worry about our bosses finding out and sacking us.'

She saw his anxiety warring with concern for her and

abruptly felt elastic. Tension she hadn't known was there drained away. She exhaled, enjoying the ease in her bones and muscles, and touched his arm.

'It's okay. I get it,' she said and managed a smile. 'And let's be honest, without your sideline where would I be?'

He let out a breath and hugged her again.

'Thank you for understanding,' he said.

'Thank you for helping me with my illegal activities.'

He barked a short laugh. They broke apart at the sound of knocking.

'That'll be Theo,' Zoe said, wiping her cheeks again. 'He's bringing dinner. Do you want to stay and join us?'

Will shook his head and reached for his coat.

'Thanks for the offer, but I should get going.'

He followed her to the front door. She opened it and Theo, smiling, held up takeaway food bags.

'Dinner is served,' he said.

Will moved past Zoe to leave. Theo's smile faltered and he stood aside, expression blank. Will gave Zoe's hand a squeeze.

'See you at lunch tomorrow?' he asked.

'Of course,' she replied.

Will smiled, nodded to Theo but got no response, so shrugged and left. Theo walked in, not stopping to kiss her, and went to the kitchen. He had pushed hers and Will's mugs to one side, spilling coffee in doing so, and was unloading the food when Zoe caught up to him. She poured the coffees away and put a hand on his back, feeling his shoulders tense beneath his coat.

'Hello,' she said.

He glanced at her and then became busy finding plates and cutlery.

'Hi,' he replied.

'Good day at work?'

'Busy as usual.'

'Thank you for bringing dinner. Why don't you let me dish up? There's wine in the fridge.'

He grunted and went into the hall to hang his coat. She peeled the lid from a takeaway carton and her stomach clenched at the pungency.

'What did you get?' she asked.

He returned, opening the fridge and taking out the wine, poured himself a glass.

'Vegetable curry, samosas, naan and some rice. Why?'

'It smells really potent.'

'The curry's a chilli thing. I thought you'd like it.'

'Oh, um, really spicy food doesn't agree with me. Sorry.'

'I've seen you eat curry before.'

'Yes, but normally a korma or the like.'

'Oh, for God's sake!'

He stormed out of the kitchen. She followed, feeling disjointed as if the ground rocked slightly back and forth making her perpetually unbalanced. Theo turned on the television and settled on the sofa while she stood to one side, confused.

'Why are you being like this?' she asked.

'Sorry. I got it wrong, obviously.'

'It's fine. You didn't get anything wrong. I can still eat the samosas and stuff. I'll just have something from the freezer with them.'

He sipped his wine, seemingly engrossed in the television. She perched next to him.

'Come on Theo, come and have something to eat with me, please?'

'I'm not hungry.'

She put a hand on his leg and felt it taut beneath his trousers. She rose and tried to think of something to say but his tight expression warned against it. She went to the kitchen, opening the freezer, and stood, staring unseeing into the cold depths. Closing the door, she turned to find Theo standing there. He opened his arms and she went to his embrace, relief flooding her. They stood like that for a minute or so.

'As first fights go,' she said eventually, 'that wasn't so bad.'

He kissed her forehead then moved away busying himself dishing curry onto a plate. She helped herself to samosas, rice and naan bread and, not wanting to upset him again, decided against adding anything from the freezer. They ate and the evening passed easily enough. Theo seemed fine but Zoe couldn't shake her anxiety and kept trying to make him laugh or connect, all the while wondering what she had done wrong.

Later that night Zoe woke to find Theo gone from bed. She sat up, worried he had left, and breathed easy on seeing his clothes. She looked at her phone seeing the time was just after midnight. Barefooted she padded downstairs and heard the murmur of his voice. Pausing in the doorway she saw his face illuminated by his phone screen. Not wanting to intrude she returned to bed. Minutes wound on before he came back, sliding under the duvet with cold feet making her gasp.

'I woke up and you were gone,' she said.

He spooned her with his breath warm against her neck.

'I took a phone call downstairs,' he said. 'I didn't want to wake you. It's a business thing. The guy never sleeps.'

She rolled over, seeking comfort in his closeness. His fingers trailed her spine, and he pushed her back, sliding on top of her. She looked into his eyes seeing only dark holes in the gloom.

'We're okay, aren't we?' she whispered.

He parted her legs with his knee.

'Of course we are,' he said, driving inside her.

She writhed and gasped, letting him pound away her disquiet.

CHAPTER TWENTY-TWO

The following afternoon, Iris, conscious of towing a loaded horsebox, slowly drove the Land Rover along Foxcombe Valley's overgrown track to park in the gravelled space. She let Gus out and unboxed Blue, who was already tacked up. Mounting and holding the reins with one hand, she took a notebook from her satchel. Ignoring Michael's compass, she studied her copying of Gordon's work. She then flicked through the pages to what she had noted of Sam's accounts. Gus gambolled over from investigating the grass and Blue lowered her head, so they touched noses. The Picardy then nudged Iris's boot in the stirrup, and she glanced at him.

'All right,' she said. 'I think we can find Gordon's campsite. Are you game?'

Gus, tail wagging, backed and gave a short bark. She laughed, put the notebook away and urged Blue along the track with Gus ranging ahead. The late September sun warmed woods peppered with red and gold leaves. Between branches the azure sky held crows and streamer clouds. The dappled grey's stride was smooth and near silent on the loam. Iris drew a deep breath of autumnal air and wondered if the desire to find Gordon's first campsite was really just an excuse to ride Blue out. She patted the mare's marbled neck murmuring to her horse and Blue's ears flicked back as she listened. Gus trotted beside the mare or quartered about and with abrupt rushes investigated the rustle and dash of squirrels and rabbits amongst the fallen leaves. Watching him and swaying in time to her mare's walk, Iris felt relieved at being alone. There was no one to judge her or anxiety over getting things wrong. She managed to banish all thoughts of Ruth's murder along with her disquiet over Lana Mitchell's death and tried to just enjoy the ride.

It took more than half an hour of easy riding to reach the ruins. Iris dismounted and led Blue, with Gus following, to the twines, which still denoted the library and the tent peg driven in where the trapdoor should have been. She turned, estimating distances, and checked her notebook before heading for the far corner of the manor, leading Blue. Here there was lush grass and Iris crouched imagining Gordon perhaps sitting there, sketching. Frowning, she retraced her steps to where a chimney had fallen in the library space, its bricks buried in the long grass. Some bricks had recently been moved, evidenced by the damp and soil covered faces newly exposed to daylight. She stared at them and then glanced about at the treelines.

Probably Michael kicked them when we were here or maybe Zoe.

Feeling oddly exposed, she re-mounted and, calling Gus, rode toward where the cave-in lay, suddenly needing reassurance that it was undisturbed. It took twenty minutes to reach the hole and Iris was relieved to find it covered by the fallen bough exactly as they had left it. Shaking her head at her anxiety she rode into the as yet unexplored woods.

Two hours later Iris drew rein, halting Blue, and stared about. A stream meandered to her left and she let the mare drink sparingly while Gus waded into the water, catching some in his mouth. She took a bottle from her satchel and swigged lukewarm water. Dusk was touching the lapis sky and gloaming filled the woods. The air had become sharper and she knew it would be dark before too much longer.

'Damn it,' she muttered.

Gus settled next to the mare, tongue lolling and clearly unperturbed about being lost.

'It's all right for you,' she said to him. 'You can catch your dinner and not worry about cooking it.'

She felt in her pocket for any stray pony nut missed from the handful she had given Blue earlier, but to no avail. Sighing, she took her mobile from her satchel and called Michael. His phone rang and rang and went to voicemail before she remembered he had a faculty meeting and then a leaving party, so it was most likely on silent. She ended the call without leaving a message and rang Thomas instead. The farm manager answered immediately.

'Wondered where you'd got to,' he said. 'I was about to come down to the valley with one of the lads.'

Abrupt images of Ruth, branded, strangled, and the slaughtered ewe swamped her thoughts. She blinked, anxiety spiking at the thought of Dan or Luke alone at Whitebarn.

'I'm fine, honestly,' she said. 'Just a little caught up in the ride and lost track of time.'

'Do you need me to come out?'

'No, that's okay. I'm not far from the horsebox now,' she lied, trying to think how to stall him. 'Actually, I rang to say I'm going to Ash House before heading home. I haven't checked it today so I might be a while yet.'

Thomas hesitated and she could hear the familiar sounds of pigs in the background.

'Text when you reach the horsebox,' he said.

'Will do,' she said with forced cheer and ended the call.

She rang Michael again and left a message asking him to ring the moment he got it. For good measure she texted him the same thing. Putting the phone away, she stared about the darkening woods feeling terribly alone.

'Where on earth am I?' she murmured.

Gus rose and nudged her foot, sitting back on his haunches and looking up at her. She couldn't help but smile at his expression.

'All right, sweet dog, I know you're hungry. If you can find our way back, I'll give you a steak dinner.'

Except for his tail, Gus didn't move. She sighed and stared at the trees, trying to decide which way to go. Her gaze returned to her waiting dog and an idea struck.

'Gus, where's Honky? Find Honky.'

The Picardy tilted his head then looked about and rose, trotting purposefully away before stopping to wait for her.

'Well, your direction is as good as any,' she said and urged Blue to follow him.

The woods had darkened so that Gus was a tawny shade when Iris next reined in, peering about. The sky between branches held the indigo and grey of twilight making a fallen bough seem black by comparison. She turned her phone to torch and raked the light over the mass of leaves and limbs, letting out a breath when she recognised the cave-in covering.

'Good lad,' she said to Gus. 'Whether by accident or not I don't care, we're nearly there!'

The Picardy's tail wagged as a pale feather in the gloaming. Blue tossed her head, eager to get home. Iris stroked the dappled neck, murmuring words of encouragement. She texted Thomas, lying that she had reached the horsebox, and put the phone away. Taking her bearings from the fallen branch she urged the mare toward the manor ruins.

Twenty minutes later she dismounted and hung onto the saddle with her legs threatening to give way. Gus was a warm shadow at her side. Holding the reins and her dog, Iris peered through the branches of a holly tree. The tree was an ancient one, nearly forty foot tall; it had grown at the edge of the woods and somewhat around an oak in typical ground-hugging fashion. By parting the branches Iris had ridden inside to a hollow space large enough to accommodate mare, woman and dog. Surrounded on all sides by thick branches and large, evergreen holly leaves all three were hidden from anyone at the manor ruins. Their concealment was assisted by spotlights, illuminating the pegged-out library and the men working there. Everything outside the brightness would be doubly hard to see for which Iris gave silent thanks even while terror congealed her insides.

What the hell is going on?

Five men were digging at Foxcombe Manor while another, his back to Iris, supervised. There was an excited cry and the men stopped work. The supervisor hurried forward, peering at the ground, and then crouched. He straightened holding something that shone white and yellow in the lights and, horrified, Iris recognised it as a leg bone.

They must be looking for the tunnel, for Amy Dudley. Horror skewered her. *Shit, the Watchers are real!*

The man placed the long bone in a clear plastic bag and gestured for the work to continue. He turned, walking toward where Iris and her animals were hidden, while taking out a mobile phone. The screen lit his face and Iris sucked in a breath at the unmistakable features of Stephen Sloane. He was too far away for her to hear the actual words but from the tone of his voice he was pleased. She waited, holding her breath, hand clammy and tight on the reins and the other warm in Gus's fur. Finally, Stephen Sloane ended the call and returned to the dig. She let out her breath, thoughts racing, incoherent and muddled. Gus whined and drew her attention, forcing her to focus. She took out her phone intending to call the police and hesitated, suddenly thinking about questions the authorities would ask when they reached the ruins. Zoe's career would be in jeopardy, so would Will's, and they might even face prosecution. The police would take Amy Dudley and Gordon.

I won't ruin Zoe or Will and the police can't have the bones.

She stared at the working men and Stephen Sloane, feeling sick as they desecrated Foxcombe Manor even as she wondered about the bone they had found.

The Bennetts. It must be them.

She felt a surge of satisfaction that the Watchers' search for Amy Dudley would prove futile. On the back of it her dense anger and sadness at their raping of Foxcombe and stealing the dead siblings coalesced into a hard core of determination. She slipped her phone into the satchel, knowing she wouldn't call the police. She studied the excavation, noting a couple of tents, ATVs and motorbikes and realised the Watchers had settled in for the night. Suddenly their intentions were clear to her; they were using this one night to get what they wanted and leave, preferably undetected. She recalled the moved bricks from earlier and understood the significance now.

They scouted it first to find out where to dig. But how did they know after all this time?

Under the reins Blue shifted, tossing her head, making the bit jangle. Iris's grip tightened, fear spiralling, and she stared at the men, willing them not to have heard. No one looked their way, Stephen Sloane didn't turn and she breathed again. Staying hidden where they were was clearly not an option. Michael was too far away to help and incommunicado. Thomas must be left at Whitebarn to protect his sons and the animals. Keeping to the woods she reasoned she could skirt the ruins and ride back to the horsebox unnoticed. The need to flee tightened her nerves as she whispered Gus to heel and mounted. Her hands shook as she quietly rode her mare from the protective holly bush.

They can't have found the Land Rover and horsebox or they wouldn't have started excavating. They probably don't even know the parking space is there.

She trusted Gus to stay close, knowing the Picardy had picked up on her fear and was unsettled by the strangers. Gus remained at Blue's side with ears swivelled toward the ruins but his attention on Iris. She gathered the reins and tried not to think about being chased. The risk to her mare racing through unknown, dark woods was horrendous. In a mad gallop or even controlled canter there was a real danger of Blue tripping on roots or snapping her legs in unseen rabbit holes. Iris knew Gus would never leave her side even if she were thrown. The idea of the Watchers hurting her mare or dog was a shaft of pain in her guts. She drew a long breath, banishing thoughts of splintering bones, Ruth's murder and Lana Mitchell. She nudged Blue to a walk and stole away as noiselessly as the loam allowed.

Iris rode deep enough into the woods to lose sight and sound of the men yet had to stay sufficiently close to keep her bearings. In the trees she circled the ruins, keeping Blue to a fast walk, and each measured hoof-beat seemed to thunder beneath her. The creaking saddle and jangling bit were too loud. She became convinced the sounds would reach the men and bit the inside of her cheek trying to keep her breaths steady and quiet while resisting the urge to push Blue to a trot. Gus padded silently alongside never more than centimetres from her stirrup.

The ride seemed to take an eternity. Then up ahead she recognised a fallen beech tree and knew nearby was the deer track leading to the car park. She stood up in her stirrups trying to see the faint pathway. Abruptly Gus growled, low and threatening. She halted Blue, fear making her heart a speeding drum. A shadow detached from a tree with a lit cigarette aglow in his mouth. Gus growled again, deeper more menacing.

'Best you keep that dog under control,' the man said.

Trembling with fear she tried to sound calm.

'This is private property. What are you doing here?'

Gus growled louder at the sound of her voice.

'If you don't shut the dog up, I'll shoot it.'

He lifted an arm leaving Iris in no doubt there was a gun. Gus stalked forward but halted at her shaky 'stay' while his growl never faltered.

'Please,' she whispered, 'don't hurt us.'

'Get down from there.'

Her feet seemed numb and wouldn't come free of the stirrups, making her sob. The man raised his gun toward the sound. Gus leapt and the weapon cracked. Blue reared, spun and bolted. Iris, screaming, barely kept her seat, losing her reins. Flung forward she clung to the mare's mane. From behind, the man yelled and the gun barked again. She cried out for Gus, desperate to turn back or slow down but Blue, thoroughly frightened, powered on. Branches whipped Iris with the air frigid and fierce. Fear for Blue gripped her and, talking as soothingly as she could, her fingers fumbled for the reins amidst the piston-like leg muscles. Gasping and finding the leather straps she pulled, begging her horse to stop, and managed to drag Blue to a blowing, steaming halt. She slipped from the saddle and sank to the ground, shaking too hard to stand. She wanted to scream for Gus and swallowed sobs. Rustling halted her tears and she gulped, struggling upright. Blue snorted and backed from the bushes. A shadow emerged, took form, and the Picardy launched into Iris's arms, felling her to the loamy floor.

Gasping and crying she held him close. Gus wriggled and tried to lick her cut and sore face.'Oh Gus,' she whispered. 'Oh Gus. You stupid dog, you scared the crap out of me. Oh Gus, thank God. Good boy.'

She cried more while hugging him fiercely and he suddenly whimpered. She scrambled to her feet and checked his fur with fingers that came away wet. Whispering comforting words her fingers found the wound in the gathering dark. She was relieved there was no hole or blood flowing; instead it only matted his coat. After a careful inspection, done mainly by feel, she determined a bullet had most likely grazed his side. She let go, trying to see if he limped or seemed in pain, but Gus merely trotted to Blue and touched noses with the nervous horse before licking at his side. Iris followed, talking reassuringly to the mare who rolled her eyes and skittered sideways. Catching the reins, Iris patted and stroked Blue while speaking softly. Senses alert for anyone approaching, she ran her hands down the mare's legs checking them for any injury or heat, relieved to find none. Still, it took long moments before she was able to mount the frightened horse. Toward the ruins the faint sound of a motorbike started up, then another and a deeper ATV and she knew the Watchers were looking for her.

CHAPTER TWENTY-THREE

Iris rode away from the noise of engines and the ruins trying to think through her terror. Above, amongst the branches, stars began to show, and the sky blackened toward night.

We can't go to the gate they could've sent someone to it. They might find the Land Rover now they know we're here. What do I do?

A horrifying thought gripped her, and she urged Blue into a dense thicket, fumbling her phone from the bag. She drew rein, breathing in the cool air, and tried to discern where the vehicles were from their sound. Gus crouched, a fawn shade amidst the dark trees, tense and alert. With trembling fingers, she pressed the contact, and the phone was answered immediately.

'Thomas? Listen, just listen.' She kept her voice low, hearing the fear in it. 'There might be bad people coming to Whitebarn, now, tonight. You have to be careful. If they come, call the police straight away.'

'Where are you?'

He sounded so worried she nearly cried again.

'I'm still in the valley. I know, I know, but I lied. I'm fine, but please, please don't leave your sons or Whitebarn. And don't tell the police I'm here. They mustn't come here. Even if I have to stay in the woods all night, hiding. Please don't leave the farm or tell the police about the valley.'

'Michael?'

'I can't reach him. He's still in Oxford. There was a thing after the meeting, a do.' A motorbike sounded closer, echoing amongst trees. 'Shit, Thomas I have to go.'

She rang off and urged Blue from the thicket, taking a line away from the ruins and the motorbike. Gus trotted at her stirrup, occasionally loping to keep up when she risked a trot through glades. She heard voices to her right and realised there were men on foot searching the woods.

For crying out loud how many are there?

Hearing the ATV rumbling somewhere behind and the higher motorbike engines further back, she reined Blue left.

We have to get out.

She glanced back where she thought the gate was and thought of turning, trying to slip by the men and vehicles, only to imagine dark figures at the gate opening fire. She shuddered and urged Blue to a faster walk then let the mare trot for a moment. Her thoughts lighted on Michael in Oxford and she wondered if she should ring him again.

Oxford is too far away.

She drew a breath, hope suddenly warm in her chest. She rode to a dense copse of firs, forcing their way into the black interior. Gus, a tawny shadow, dropped to the ground amidst the trunks, again licking his side, and she swallowed against fear for him. From the satchel she took out her phone and notebook. Risking the light from the screen she flicked through the pages until she found what she wanted. It was her copying of Gordon's journey from Oxford to the ruins. She re-read his account of the trail down the valley side and into the wood at the bottom of the track thence on to the Manor.

If we can get to the trail, we get out the valley and ride to Oxford.

She read Gordon's directions and sagged, overwhelmed

at the futility of trying to follow them. She took a breath thinking of her husband, Zoe and her animals. She stroked Blue's neck and the image of Gus lunging for the gunman skewed her fear into rage. She clenched her fists on the reins. Hunger gnawed at her, making her tired, and she knew it must be worse for Blue and Gus. She stared at the faint outline of the Picardy, now lying prone on his uninjured side.

Gus, my poor, brave boy. You saved me, saved Blue. I don't know how hurt you really are. We have to get out and get you to Pete.

She knew her only chance was to head to the ruins and follow Gordon's directions from there. She sent a text to Michael asking him again to call her as soon as he got the message and, telling him she loved him, resolutely put the phone away. The darkness after the screen light was dense, like a heavy, living thing pressing about her. She breathed deeply inhaling the fresh, oily fir scent then turned Blue from the trees. She kept an eye on Gus and was relieved when the dog rose to keep pace once again at her stirrup.

It took what seemed like hours to ride back, threading through the dark trees with terror like an extra rider gripping her. She heard and avoided motorbikes and an ATV but the dread of the hidden Watcher firing stalked her. Every shadow waited to pounce, to attack, and the only way Iris kept panic at bay was knowing Gus would alert her to a stranger's presence. The Picardy was vigilant, she knew, by his ears and body language just visible in the darkening evening. Twice he growled, swinging toward danger, stance tense and alert to the men searching for them. Gus's warnings enabled her to turn Blue to seek darker cover for the grey mare and avoid capture or worse.

They reached a treeline and the spotlights illuminating

the ruins seemed dazzling, flooding the area with brightness. Men still worked and the earth gaped from their shovels. A figure she knew to be Stephen Sloane paced the site, phone to his ear. She turned Blue back into the woods and kept trees between them and the ruins. The area that she suspected had been Gordon's campsite was mercifully untenanted. Iris put it behind the mare and rode in what she hoped was the right direction. Once a goodly distance from the ruins she risked taking out her notebook and studying it again by the phone's dim light. Alert to anyone coming, any sound, she orientated herself using the directions and knowledge of where the ruins were. Suddenly she gave a happy cry, fumbling fingers closing on Michael's compass in her satchel. She held it to her screen light, setting the course, and nudged Blue to a walk with Gus faithfully at her stirrup.

CHAPTER TWENTY-FOUR

By the time Iris rode from Gordon's campsite, night had truly taken over the valley. A full moon had risen giving an otherworldly sheen to the woods lighting Blue's coat, silvering Gus and worrying Iris. She could hear the ATV roar in the distance, back toward the ruins and the lighter cries of the motorbikes. None seemed to be heading their way, but she wondered how long that would last. Tight with fear, breaths shallow and fast, she concentrated on keeping Blue steady with the compass line and watching Gus for signs of his injury or if he sensed strangers.

Riding through the monochrome woods, the vehicle sounds faded, and she breathed a little easier. The black and white world warped all sense of time and it seemed hours later that the trees thinned with patches of grass stretching between them. Then, ahead and to the right, the valley wall loomed dark and silvered in the moonlight. It rose, immense and forbidding, seeming to reach the stars. She drew rein, swallowing on a dry throat, and panic fluttered likc bladed wings. Gus lay down with a groan and the dread swelled, threatening to overwhelm her.

'Gus,' she whispered.

In the moonlight the Picardy's tail fanned a little. She slid off Blue with legs buckling but she managed to stand, holding the saddle. Once steady, she walked stiffly to her dog and knelt to him. His breaths were shallow, and her fingers found the crusted wound in his side. He licked her hand, and she knew he was hurting. She stared around at the shadowy woods, listening for any movement, any sound of pursuit, and heard only the night.

'We can rest here, for a few minutes,' she said.

Gus put his head in her lap, and she stroked his ears with trembling fingers, whispering words of comfort while trying to keep the tears out of her voice. She peered ahead, wondering where the track started.

What if it's not there anymore or blocked? What if I can't find it?

She pushed the unhelpful thoughts away and, taking the bottle from her satchel, poured a small amount of water into her palm, which Gus lapped up. Holding the end of the reins, Blue snatching at the odd bit of grass, Iris sat with the Picardy, stroking him and ignoring her tears.

Time seemed stunted. The night was loud with silence when the whine started, coming slowly closer and growing louder. Iris, hearing it, knew at least one motorbike was headed their way. Gus seemed to understand and, with a sigh, rose. She hugged him, murmuring reassurance and crying into his fur. Gus turned his head, licking her hair and ear. She wiped her tears, rose and mounted, nudging the tiring mare to a walk with the Picardy padding alongside. From behind them the motorbike was a constant, persistent buzz getting ever closer and louder. It seemed to be weaving, left and right, scouring the woods. Iris's fingers clenched and unclenched on the reins while sweat trailed rivulets down her back. Her gaze cut to Gus, bleached white in the moonlight, loyally pacing at her stirrup. After what seemed eternity the trees unexpectedly ended, and Iris was staring up at the valley wall. Closer now, the motorbike was guttural, and fear froze her thoughts, her breath faltering.

Gus sat, his bearded face turned to her, trusting her. She stroked the mare and rode toward the foot of the valley wall. Suddenly, a lighter ribbon of earth snaked away, cut into the valley's face, and with a sob she headed Blue for the pathway.

Starting the ascent, the trail footing was uneven, peppered with stones, and she slid off Blue, knowing leading the horse would be safer with the drop so sheer on their left. The pathway was bright in the moonshine and just wide enough for the mare. Iris put Gus in front, fearful of him falling too far behind or worse and let the Picardy set the pace. His slow padding scared her, but Blue's plodding seemed just as tired as the mare stumbled in Iris's wake. They had been climbing for some time before the motorbike roared directly below, echoing from the valley wall and reverberating in the trees. Suddenly the noise stopped and Iris imagined the rider, staring up at the valley face. The motor gunned, and she stifled a cry, resisting the urge to halt and listen for its direction. With jarring, inhibited sounds the Watcher's motorbike began climbing the stone-laden path. Gus growled but kept moving, his pace quickening, and she hurried Blue after him.

All around the noise of the motorbike seemed to consume the night, rising and falling with agonising tones as it traversed the uneven terrain. Iris's breaths were sobbing now, the reins slick in her hands, and her voice sounded desperate urging Blue on. Ahead Gus vanished and she cried out, but moments later she mounted the lip of the valley edge and reeled back from the five-bar gate blocking the way. In the moonlight the galvanised steel shone and hung on the right from a drystone wall. Either side, the steep valley dropped away, making the gate the only way off the path. There was no hope of Blue getting over or round it. Gus stood before the gate and nosed at the padlock on its chain.

Behind them the motorbike was deafening, like thunder and gunshots. Groping in her pocket, Iris gripped the padlock keys, sweat making her eyes sting. The first one didn't work, and she sobbed, slick fingers almost dropping them, and fumbled the second into the lock. The steel parted and she shoved the gate open, walking Blue through. Abruptly, the bike bellowed and shot over the lip screaming toward them, headlamp blazing. Iris yelled, releasing a panicked Blue. Gus sprang forward, gripping the man's leg and yanking him off the bike, which screeched, spinning to crash against the wall. The Watcher staggered, yelling voice muffled by the helmet. He beat at Gus, who ferociously pulled at his leg. Suddenly, the Picardy let go. The man stumbled, arms windmilling and disappeared over the edge. The bike's raucous engine stuttered to silence. Gus crept through the gate to Iris and collapsed, panting on the ground. Numb with shock, she spied the mare's pale form against the dark treeline, head down. Sobbing and shaking she went to Blue, caught the reins and led the horse to Gus, kneeling next to her dog. A noise froze her and then, recognising it, fumbled her phone from the satchel.

'Michael. Oh Michael.'

She struggled for calm.

'Iris, where are you? What's the matter? Are you hurt?'

It took several seconds for her to speak and then relate a garbled account.

'I don't know what to do now. Gus is hurt, maybe badly.'

'We need to call the police, right now.'

'No, no we can't. Please, think about Zoe and Will. These people are monsters. Even if we called the police now the Watchers could find me first. I can get to Oxford on this track, I know I can. Blue's tired and frightened, but still okay. She can go a little further, but can you come and meet us with Pete?'

'I'll get him out of bed if I have to, and we'll use his Land Rover. What about Gus?'

'I'll try and put him on Blue and ride with him.'

Suddenly Gus raised his head, growling. She stopped talking, listening, breath held. Far below a whining motorbike sounded.

'Shit, Michael, they're coming. I have to lock the gate. It might hold them up a bit. We'll keep going, can you find us?'

'I've Gordon's directions and a map, I can find you with those. Call me if anything happens or you get scared. Be careful. I love you.'

Determination galvanised her aching body and telling Michael she loved him, Iris ended the call. She turned the location finder on and pocketed the phone. Leaving Blue near Gus she closed the gate and snapped the padlock shut. Somewhere below the motorbike rasped, weaving, searching the woods. She drew a calming breath knowing if she were anxious Blue would never stand still for what she was about to attempt.

In the bright moonlight she led the mare to a tree stump, looping the reins over a branch. She picked Gus up, heavy and warm in her arms and walked awkwardly to the mare. Climbing on the tree stump, her head was just above the mare's shoulder, giving her enough height to lift the Picardy. Speaking quietly and reassuringly, muscles protesting and aching, she managed to lift the dog as carefully as possible, conscious of his wound. She laid him across the mare's neck, just in front of the saddle. Blue snorted and shifted slightly, turning her head to sniff her friend, and Gus's tail waved. Murmuring reassurance, Iris mounted, holding the Picardy steady. Thankfully her dog remained relaxed and still while Blue seemed unperturbed about him being there. Iris turned the mare and, one hand buried in Gus's fur, rode slowly toward Oxford.

The swaying mare was comforting. The adrenaline had gone, leaving her hollow, everything hurting. Tiredness blanketed her mind and weighted her bones. She felt her eyelids dropping and forced them open, focusing on the moonlit trail, the silver form of Gus and Blue's ears. The stealthy exhaustion kept trying to claim her and she desperately fought against it. She rode in a trance, barely awake, and didn't know how much time had passed when she heard the guttural spluttering of an engine. Panicked, she turned for the treeline, her only thought to hide when she realised the sound came from ahead. Headlights pricked between the trees and suddenly a Land Rover towing a horse box came bumping into sight. With a sob she recognised it as Pete Maddox's and drew rein, waiting for help to get Gus safely down.

Late the following afternoon Iris woke when Michael sat on the bed. Panic gripped her and struggling to sit up she glanced at the doggy duvet. Gus lay half on it, half on the floor snoring with his cone of shame acting as an amplifier and paws twitching. On his side, in a wide, shaved oblong, his black stitches contrasted with a red and pink wound from which there was no tearing or bleeding. She exhaled a long breath and sat upright to hold Michael's hand.

'Did you and Thomas find anything?' she asked.

'Motorbike tracks, turned earth and our Land Rover with its tyres slashed. I think the padlock was picked as there are scratch marks around the keyhole. Otherwise, nothing.'

'They were there. They tried to kill me, us.'

'I believe you.'

'What do we do now?'

She accepted a cup of tea and drank, feeling the hot liquid wake her more.

'Well, we could publish everything we already have. The documents, coroner's report and the skull will be enough to cast doubt on Amy Dudley's suicide and accident theories.'

'But we can't prove it's her, not yet. We haven't got the DNA or a living family member.'

'And we may never get either.'

She looked at Gus, who farted, the wafting smell like sulphuric meat.

'What in heaven's name did you feed him?' she asked.

'For breakfast our hero had antibiotics, scrambled eggs and a bit of steak with his usual food. Pete said he needed protein and lots of love.'

'Well, he certainly earned both. He saved my life, twice. And Blue's.'

She felt her eyes hot with tears that spilt cooling to her cheeks, and she wiped them one handed. Michael took the mug and gave her a hug.

'Thank God for Gus,' he said. He broke away, holding her gaze. 'Maybe, given all that's happened, we should just publish everything. Get it over and done with?' He gripped her hand, his face etched with worry. 'You could've died, all of you.'

She thought about it, speaking to the police and going to the press. She imagined the headlines, the speculation and denials. Amy Dudley could be re-buried with no one knowing where; Gordon and Sam's accounts would be discounted, torn apart by academics, the press and the establishment. It felt like abandonment.

'What else can we do?' she whispered.

Michael sighed and she saw the same concerns in his expression.

'We go on and prove it's her. From what you told me the Watchers found the Bennetts' bones. It will take them a while to discover they're not Amy Dudley. So, we have a little time.'

She shook her head, trying not to think about gunshots and motorbikes.

'I can't believe the Watchers still exist and are still after Amy Dudley. Why? What on earth can be so important to keep killing people over?'

'I don't know. But I know they won't stop until they get whatever they're after. They've been at this for hundreds of years so it must be something powerful, worth all the secrecy and death.'

'The locket?'

'Perhaps, although I still fail to see how. Anyway, the hinge is definitely broken. Folded in on itself and clamping the locket closed. I'm trying to find a way to repair it without damaging or destroying the locket.'

She drew a breath and nodded, gaze going to Gus and then back to her husband.

'You know what I find really odd,' she said. 'The Watchers have never tried to hurt us before. I mean, yes, they've tried to break into the container, and they've left a dead sheep, but there's been no direct threat. Why is that?'

Michael frowned, his fingers stroking the back of her hand.

'They tried to kill you last night.'

'I think Gus killed the guy on the motorbike,' she shivered at the memory. 'Look, the violence and guns were a reaction to us discovering them, not a premeditated attempt at murder.'

'Do you think they murdered Ruth?'

She nodded. 'And Lana Mitchell, which I bet had something to do with Goodwins.'

Michael's silence made her realise he agreed, and it chilled her core. Her husband's mouth was a tight, downturned line and his gaze flicked from her to Gus.

'You don't want to publish everything right now, do you?' he asked.

Sadness and fear were like a fist in her guts but determination to save Amy Dudley filled the emptiness and pushed away feelings of inadequacy. Any thought of abandoning her provoked a sharp pain and swamped Iris with images of ruined skin and a pitiful body. She spoke slowly, trying to order her thoughts.

'I want to prove beyond doubt that the skull is Amy Dudley and I want to get the locket open. I want to let her rest peacefully and properly. But I don't know if we *should* carry on. It's so dangerous. I couldn't bear it if you or Zoe or anyone I love, including all the animals, got hurt.'

He hugged her again, rocking a little. Tiredness crept in, stealing her thoughts, and she rested against her husband letting him comfort her.

'We don't have to decide right now,' he said, shifting to meet her gaze. 'You're still exhausted. Go back to sleep and we'll talk some more tomorrow.'

She glanced at Gus, her thoughts syrupy with tiredness.

'The animals,' she managed.

'I'll look after Gus. Thomas and the boys are looking after the rest. Zoe will be here tomorrow evening. Go to sleep now, love.'

She smiled at him and gave into the weariness, snuggling under the duvet. Michael kissed her forehead and left with a whispered endearment. She turned on her side so she could see Gus still snoring and twitching on his doggy duvet. She watched, counting the Picardy's breaths, each strong and sure, until sleep took her.

CHAPTER TWENTY-FIVE

Iris woke, panting and rigid, nightmare images of Gus, Blue and Michael shot and dying imprinted behind her eyes. Tears were wet and unpleasant, running down the side of her face to gather in her ears. She wiped at them and sat up in the dark. The bedside clock showed 5.03am. She lay for a moment taking comfort from Michael's sleeping form while concentrating on breathing slowly and easing her aching muscles. Then, careful not to wake her husband, slipped from bed and knelt to Gus, stroking his head in the cone. The dog waved his tail.

'Good lad,' she whispered.

She rose, put her dressing gown on and silently opened the cabinet drawer. She removed an envelope and slipped it into her pocket. Aching all over and heavy with the nightmare, she went downstairs with Gus following. Iris debated trying to send him back to bed but knew the dog wouldn't go.

In the kitchen she made hot chocolate and helped Gus when he got stuck with the cone under the table, leading him into the living room. She curled up on the sofa with the dog and took the cone off.

'You can't lick the wound, though,' she told him.

He sighed and laid his head on her lap. She scratched around his neck smiling at his goofy, pleased expression.

Then, from her pocket she took out the envelope and removed Josephine's letter, re-reading it, crying and hugging her dog.

'Oh, Gus, I don't know what to do.'

The Picardy enthusiastically kissed her tears, making her feel a bit better. She wiped her face with a tissue and noted the light greying behind the curtains. Suddenly she needed to be outside in the autumn air and see her animals. She took clean clothes from the dryer and got dressed, keeping an eye on Gus to make sure he left the injury alone. She picked up the cone and he ducked his head, sidling away from her.

'All right. But the second you lick that wound it's going back on.'

She put it down and he padded over, nudging her with his nose. She stroked his ears, gave his ruff a final scratch and took him out via the French doors.

Honky was already awake and up when Iris reached his stable. The donkey gave a wheezing bray and ambled over. Gus nudged at the bottom door and Iris opened it, letting the Picardy inside. Honky gave another bray and snuffed his friend all over, blowing gently, ruffling the dog's fur. Gus licked Honky's knees, tail waving. Beams made up the side walls so the mares and donkey could keep each other company. Iris could see Blue lying down, dozing with legs gathered beneath her. On the far side Shiloh wandered in her box, mouthing at straw picked up from the floor. Blue opened her eyes and whinnied at Iris but didn't get up. Leaving Gus with Honky, Iris went inside Blue's stable and sat in the straw at the mare's head. She stroked the broad face and hugged her horse.

'Oh, you big, beautiful girl,' she said. 'Thank you for looking after us.'

Blue softly lipped her hair and blew lightly through her nostrils. Iris stayed like that for some minutes, enjoying being close to her horse until Shiloh, irritable in her last weeks of pregnancy, started kicking at her stable door. Blue heaved herself up and Iris rose too. She let herself out of the stable and did the same for Gus. The horse and donkey put their heads out, dapple grey and dark brown, nodding in the early morning, clearly enjoying the crisp air. She opened Shiloh's door and went inside with Gus following. The chestnut mare greeted her, nosing her pockets.

'Good morning gorgeous,' Iris said.

She ran a hand over Shiloh's neck, shoulder and belly noting how distended she was and how the mare's pelvis had relaxed ready for the birth.

'The little one can't be far off now,' she murmured.

Gus touched noses with the chestnut mare and sat protectively at her side, watching Iris. Shiloh dropped her nose to the dog and blew at his ears, tickling them. The dog shook his head, licking the mare in return and making Iris laugh.

'You guys are the best,' she said.

Gus waved his tail through the straw and Shiloh turned her head, investigating Iris's pockets once more.

'You hungry? An early breakfast won't do any harm.'

She fed the mares and donkey, Gus her constant shadow, and left a note for Thomas, telling him they had had breakfast then went back to the house. Curling up on the sofa with the Picardy again half on her lap she felt tired once more but hated the thought of sleep, dreading the nightmares. She put the television on low, hoping it might help her stay awake, and watched the sunrise through the French doors.

She woke from a dreamless sleep to sunshine flooding the living room and heard voices in the kitchen. She stretched and Gus twitched awake, yawned and got off the sofa, nosing the kitchen door open. She heard Zoe greet the dog and rose on stiff legs, easing muscles, pleased to find them less tender. On entering the kitchen, she stopped, heart suddenly leaden on seeing Theo talking to Michael while Zoe stroked Gus, looking at his wound.

'Mum!' Her daughter hugged her. 'Dad told me you got lost most of the night. Are you okay?'

She briefly met Michael's gaze. Her husband inclined his head, never breaking his conversation.

'I'm fine, honestly. Just tired,' she said. 'Blue and Gus took good care of me. They saved me from a night out in the woods, actually.'

Zoe released her and knelt to the Picardy, now hiding behind Iris's legs. The dog's gaze was on Theo as he absently licked Zoe's hand.

'What happened to him?' her daughter asked.

'He got caught on a branch. It was very dark out there.'

It was the same story they had told Pete Maddox. Zoe seemed to accept it easier than the vet had. Her daughter patted the Picardy, telling him what a brave boy he was. Iris greeted Theo and set the kettle to boil on the Aga while trying not to mind him being there.

'We weren't expecting you until this evening,' she said.

Zoe rose and got mugs from a cupboard.

'Well, we didn't have much planned today and when we found out what happened, I couldn't wait.' She glanced at Theo, still talking to Michael. 'Theo didn't want me driving so upset and he was worried about you too.'

Iris found a smile, but it felt tight and she hoped it looked sincere.

'That's kind of him.'

'It's all right if we both stay over, isn't it?'

She nodded, not trusting herself to speak, and made coffee for everyone. They settled at the kitchen table. Gus lay at Iris's side, head heavy on her foot. Michael's hand found hers under the table. Theo smiled at her with a concerned expression she found feigned.

'I'm glad to see you're all right and that Gus is too. How about the horse you were riding, is she okay?'

'Yes, thank you. Blue's fine.'

'That's not the pregnant one, is it?'

'Oh no. I wouldn't have ridden Shiloh out. Not when she's so close to foaling.'

'You must be excited about the baby. How long do you think it'll be?'

'Our vet thinks sometime this week or next.'

Suddenly she couldn't stand him any longer; the evaluating look made her feel ill. She rose and Gus did too.

'I'm sorry. I really need a shower then I need to get out to the animals.'

Michael rose and gave her a hug. Zoe looked worried.

'Don't you think you should rest today?' her daughter asked.

Iris leant against her husband for a moment and then moved away, kissing his cheek. She glanced at Zoe.

'I've had enough rest, love,' she said. 'Honestly, I can't stay in bed anymore. I need to work. We'll have a lovely lunch about one o'clock.' She looked at Theo. 'Please excuse me.'

She left with Gus, breathing easier when the door shut behind her and feeling sorry for having left Michael behind.

An hour later, Iris was weighing piglets in the barn when Zoe brought her a cup of tea. She smiled at her daughter and slotted the piglet into the orphan pouch to sip the drink.

'Thanks love, I needed this.'

Zoe returned the smile and gave the piglet a scratch on its head before settling on a wooden stool and flicking through the logbook. Iris studied her daughter, legs crossed, and chestnut hair held back with an Alice band.

'Have you done something different with your hair?'

Zoe flushed a little and touched the band.

'Yes, I'm growing it.'

She slipped the band off and shook out the once-sleek bob, now shaggier and longer. Iris felt a touch of disquiet she couldn't understand.

'It looks nice,' she lied. 'Do you remember when you were little how much you hated having your long hair brushed?'

Zoe laughed and replaced the band.

'I do. It's so fine it always got tangled and hurt to brush out.'

Iris put her mug down and flicked the log pages back to the day's date, entering the piglet's weight.

'Well, you wouldn't let me do it every day. You used to run and hide in here or somewhere on the farm to avoid me.'

'Until *The Family-Ness*.'

Zoe grimaced, making Iris chuckle.

'Fancy you remembering that!'

'How could I forget?' Her daughter shook her head. 'What was I, five? You sat me down in the living room, on a chair from the kitchen and played a game of pretend with a promise of ice cream later.'

'Which you got.'

Zoe snorted.

'You turned the TV on to show *The Family-Ness*.'

'You loved that cartoon.'

'Which you took advantage of while you pretended to play hairdressing. Wrapping me in a big towel and click-clacking the scissors all about my head. But it wasn't pretend, was it?'

'It was not. I freely admit I'd had enough of your tantrums when trying to brush your hair and the exhausting games of hide and seek trying to find you to brush said hair.'

Zoe laughed and ran her fingers through her locks, dislodging the band.

'And so you actually cut it all off while using cartoon Loch Ness monsters as a distraction. It was so short! Honestly, it bordered on child cruelty.'

Iris laughed and lifted the piglet out of the pouch, marking it with a special pen to say it had been weighed. She put it back in with its mother and picked up the next one.

'Made it so much easier to look after though, and once you had the ice cream you didn't care.'

'Hmmm, school wasn't much fun for a while though.'

'And now you're growing it again. This time you can go to a proper hairdresser to get it done. Unless of course you want me to do it?'

She popped the piglet into the pouch and, making scissor movements with her fingers, advanced on Zoe. Her daughter jumped up, backing to the door, and Gus barked.

'Oh no you don't, you wicked old woman. Keep your scissoring fingers to yourself!'

Iris grinned and retuned to weighing the piglet. Zoe settled back on the stool, stroking Gus.

'Mum, what really happened when you got lost?'

Iris schooled her expression to polite confusion.

'What do you mean?'

'This wound in Gus's side doesn't look like it was done by a branch.'

Iris silently cursed her daughter's work and training while trying to decide how to answer. Suddenly Theo came in, smiling and gaze raking over everything in his calculating manner. Gus padded to Iris, leaning on her legs and watching the newcomer.

'Hello, Theo,' she said. 'What can I do for you?'

'I was taking a wander round the farm and bumped into Thomas out by the horse paddock. He said to tell you Honky's got out again.'

Iris sighed and turned to Gus glancing at his wound.

'I'd better go with him,' she said, 'in case he licks at his stitches or overdoes it.' She handed Zoe the piglet, shrugged out of the pouch and placed it beside the pen on the workbench. 'You finish up here. There's two more to do.' She enjoyed the look of surprise on Theo's face, then turned to the Picardy. 'Gus, where's Honky? Find Honky.'

The dog tilted his head then trotted from the barn and Iris followed him.

They found Honky in the back garden eating grass and Gus dropped into herding pose. Michael, marking papers, watched from the patio. Iris went to see her husband.

'Why didn't you take him back to the paddock?'

'He wasn't hurting anyone, and I enjoyed his company.' Michael gestured to the shiny, damp table, recently cleaned. 'As you might guess, he came up for a slurp of tea.'

'Oh, for heaven's sake, bloody rascal.' But she couldn't help a smile. 'Did he get much?'

'About half a cup,' he said returning her smile with a grin.

She leant forward and kissed him.

'What was that for?' he asked.

'Looking after me and my donkey.'

'Ah, not guilt then, for leaving me alone with "the boyfriend".'

'Maybe that too.'

She called to Gus, who advanced on Honky. The donkey looked at the Picardy, gauging the distance between them, swished his tail and continued to eat.

'Where are they anyway?' Michael asked.

'In the barn weighing piglets last I saw.'

Her husband chuckled.

'Oh, I bet he loved that.'

She smiled and watched Gus rounding up a thoroughly uncooperative and mischievous Honky. The donkey, braying happily, kept constantly trying to break sideways checking on the dog while doing so and looking pleased with himself. Gus, playing the game, pretended not to notice until the last second before herding his friend the right way. She followed them from the garden and heard Michael chuckling as she went.

On returning to the paddock Honky bucked his way across the grass to greet the mares as if he hadn't seen them in weeks. Shaking her head and smiling at the donkey's antics, Iris called Gus to heel and headed for the barn and piglets. Passing the stables Gus slowed and halted, a low growl rumbling his throat. Iris swallowed, motorbikes and guns loud in her mind, and picked up a pitchfork. The Picardy crept forward, intent on Shiloh's stable.

'Thomas is that you?' she called.

The door swung open and Theo stepped out.

'Hello, only me.' He stopped at the sight of Gus and the raised pitchfork. 'Goodness, I'm sorry, did I startle you?'

Iris lowered the tool and called Gus to her. The Picardy obeyed while keeping his gaze on Theo.

'What were you doing in there?' she asked.

'Just waiting for you actually. Isn't this where the donkey lives?'

'Two doors down. But Honky's back in the paddock.'

'Oh right. I thought what with him escaping the field you'd bring him back here.'

She propped the pitchfork against the stable wall feeling his gaze on her and hating the fake interest.

'Why were you waiting for me?'

His smile seemed to falter momentarily and then returned.

'I wanted to ask you if it would be all right to take Zoe to the farmer's market tomorrow morning? I didn't know if you had any plans.'

'Only the usual Sunday lunch.'

'Right, so we'll be back before midday if that suits?'

'That sounds fine.'

Iris didn't move, enjoying the look of discomfort that flickered across his face. Theo glanced at Gus and sidled around the dog.

'I'll go and see if Zoe's okay with that,' he said.

She nodded and watched him go.

'You do that,' she murmured.

Iris looked at Gus who, she suddenly realised, was still growling.

At just after 4pm the following afternoon, Iris watched the Mercedes move down the drive, creating a dust cloud. Michael slipped his hand into hers and squeezed.

'How much longer do you think she'll put up with him?' her husband asked.

The sleek car pulled out onto the road and she felt a protective pang thinking of Zoe.

'I don't know, but I hope it's not too much longer.'

'You don't think she'd tell him about Amy Dudley, do you?'

'She said not. We had a chat about it this afternoon after lunch.'

They turned and walked into the house with Gus trotting ahead.

'Did you tell Zoe what really happened in the valley?'

'No, I managed to avoid it, but she wasn't happy about Gus's wound story.'

Michael led the way to the kitchen and poured two glasses of wine.

'We should decide what we're going to do about Amy Dudley.'

Accepting the glass from Michael, Iris settled at the table with Gus at her feet.

'I've been thinking about this all day.' She took a deep breath, pushing her anxiety and nightmares away, determination like a hard knot at the centre of the emptiness. 'To protect Zoe and Will I want to wait to publish until we get the DNA, which should be next week sometime. While we wait, I want to get the locket open.' She sipped wine not looking at her husband, afraid he was going to argue. 'Once we've got the DNA, we contact the genealogist even if she hasn't contacted us. If there's no living relative or she's still looking, we publish. But, in the meantime, if we feel there's any danger from the Watchers, we see them or anything, we call the police and publish.'

She waited, turning the glass around and around. Her husband's fingers were warm over hers, easing them from the glass, and he lifted her into a hug.

'I don't know if waiting is the safe thing to do,' he said. 'But I know it's the right thing to do. A week and half, and then we publish.'

She nodded into his chest and breathed in his Michael smell, never wanting to let him go.

CHAPTER TWENTY-SIX

Over the next two days, Iris's nerves were continually taut. She was caught between terror of the Watchers, fear for her family and determination to save Amy Dudley. She constantly questioned their decision not to publish immediately, finding herself endlessly torn; one moment sure they had enough to definitively prove murder and the next absolutely certain they didn't. Distracted, she took solace in the farm using her normal routine to smother the anxieties. Shiloh was particularly diverting, still irritable and increasingly restless; Iris knew the foaling was very near and kept a close eye on the mare. Gus became especially protective, spending any free time as close to Shiloh as he could either outside in the paddock or by her stable door.

On Wednesday morning Iris woke to Gus standing over her on the bed, whiskery face centimetres from hers. She struggled up and in the predawn light saw the clock showed 6.32am.

'Gus,' she whispered, 'get down.'

She shifted, trying to move the dog, but he only gave little whines and licked her cheeks. Switching on the bedside light she stared at the Picardy who waved his tail, chestnut eyes full of entreaty.

'All right, all right,' she whispered. 'I'm getting up.'

She managed to pull her legs free, knees to chest, and swing out of the bed. Gus jumped off and gave a huffing woof. Michael stirred, rolling over.

'Whassup?' he muttered.

'It's Gus. He's all riled up.' She pulled on a robe and put slippers on while eying the prancing Picardy. 'Not sure what's going on, but I'll see if he wants the garden.'

Michael blinked in the light, frowning at Gus's agitation. 'I'm coming with you.'

She made to protest but her anxieties stalled her and two minutes later they let the Picardy out the French doors into the garden. The early light brindled his coat and Gus loped around the house, barking at the gate.

'Check the monitors,' Iris said. 'I'll see if I can get him back in.'

She took off her slippers and grimacing at the wet grass hurried out. The Picardy was on his hind legs, forepaws on the gate, woofing. He stopped and looked over his shoulder when Iris approached. Tail waving, he got on four paws and nudged the gate latch. Suddenly Michael was there holding her slippers.

'The only unusual thing I can see is Shiloh pacing,' he said. 'She's got her tail in the air.'

'Oh my goodness, the foal might be coming.'

She pulled the slippers on while Michael opened the gate and they rushed to the stables with Gus loping alongside. Unbolting the top door, Iris swung it free and turned on the lights. Inside, the chestnut mare was now on her side breathing hard, sweat gleaming on her flanks and neck. She rolled to her knees and rose, pacing and lipping at straw.

'The foal is definitely on the way. But it's still early stages,' Iris said. 'Go get Thomas and the lads to watch her while I get changed, please?'

Michael was gone before she had finished the sentence. Gus rose on his hind legs, forepaws against the stable door, trying to see over the top and whining. In their stables Blue and Honky were both watching Shiloh through the beams. The donkey lifted his head, resting his chin on a spar, and gave a chuffing bray in response to the Picardy. Shiloh ignored them, turning to look at her belly and continuing to pace.

After a few minutes Iris heard Thomas and the lads approaching. She called out a hello, left the top door open and hurried toward the house only to realise Gus wasn't with her. Turning, she saw the dog still standing on his back legs at Shiloh's door. Shaking her head, she continued to the house and dressed quickly, trying to contain her excitement. She met Michael in the kitchen where, barefooted, he was putting the kettle on the Aga, soaked slippers discarded amidst the wellies at the back door.

'I'll get changed then make coffee and some breakfast for everyone,' he said. 'I've got time before work.'

She kissed him and pulled on her boots, putting her phone in a jacket pocket.

'I'll call Pete Maddox in a minute,' she said.

Her husband turned with a frown.

'There's nothing wrong, is there?'

'No, I don't think so. But its Shiloh's first foal and ours. I just want to be safe.'

He nodded, relief evident in his face. She kissed him again and went to her mare.

Two hours later and Shiloh had safely delivered a chestnut colt foal. Iris watched the little horse struggle to its feet looking startled when Shiloh nuzzled him, unused to touch. A few wobbling steps took him to Shiloh's side, the smell of milk drawing the foal. Blue, Honky and Gus were all in Blue's stall watching through the slats. The donkey and Picardy had refused to settle until they could see Shiloh properly. Blue, the tallest, was able to put her head over the slats and whickered encouragement. Pete and Iris had monitored the birth, which had thankfully gone well. Pete, having taken blood and checked Shiloh and her foal over, picked up his bag. They walked to his Land Rover, the vet advising Iris on how long to keep the foal inside. When she returned to the stable Shiloh and her foal were close enough to the slatted wall for the other three animals to sniff the newcomer, who flinched at the new noses and then settled to suckle, furry tail whisking. She resisted the urge to go inside, watching from the doorway where Thomas joined her.

'Good-looking lad,' he said.

She glanced at him, taciturn face schooled to blankness, but his eyes were merry and full of pride.

'He certainly is.'

'Decide on a name?'

Iris looked at the foal whose tiny chestnut flanks were quivering as he suckled, and she smiled.

'Red Jasper after the gemstone.'

'Suits him. Vet all right?'

'All good. I've got the paperwork to fill out and file later.' She smiled. 'Pete thinks Jasper's going to be a fine stallion.'

'Good stud.'

'We can hope and with his sire tipped to be an Olympian and Shiloh being such a wonderful mare I think we can safely say his chances are better than good when he's old enough.'

'Be the star of this place no matter what.'

They shared a smile, gazes returning to the foal. After a

few moments Iris sighed.

'I'd better get on with the rest of the day,' she said. 'Although I'm not sure Gus will want to leave.'

'Bide here a while longer,' Thomas said. 'Farm's taken care of.'

He squeezed her arm and, calling Peg, headed to the pigsties. Iris took out her phone and rang Michael then Zoe to share the news, all the while smiling and watching Jasper and Shiloh.

Early evening found Iris and Michael, along with Gus, watching the mare and foal. Shiloh hadn't been happy at first for Jasper to be introduced to Michael. Her ears had flattened, and head snaked forward ready to nip. Iris had reassured her with gentle words until the mare let Michael handle the foal as easily as Iris and Pete had. Jasper had certainly gained in confidence in the hours since his birth, investigating the stable, and Blue and Honky through the slats, touching noses with Gus and enjoying being petted. The sound of a car took the Shaws to the stable door and the sight of the now familiar Mercedes. The car stopped. Zoe and Theo got out and headed for the house. Not wanting to call out and cause Jasper any anxiety, Michael went to fetch them. Iris turned to the mare and foal, her heart suddenly heavy.

'Why is *he* here?' she whispered.

She had imagined, hoped, Zoe would come alone and now felt a family moment had been spoilt. Waiting, she heard their approach and Theo's laugh, and her shoulders became taut while she struggled against a fierce protective surge for Jasper. Then the light dimmed with three figures blocking the daylight framed by the open top door. Iris greeted her daughter and Theo without moving.

'This is Jasper,' she said.

'He's beautiful,' Zoe said.

'I've never seen a foal in real life before,' Theo said. 'He's smaller than I expected but look how perfect he is!'

Iris found a smile.

'You can be introduced, but one at a time. Shiloh's very protective so please do exactly as I say, or you might get hurt.'

Zoe came inside first and Shiloh whinnied, tossing her head, ears flat. Iris reassured the mare and gestured her daughter to hold out her hand to Jasper. The foal extended his nose, showing no signs of fear or anxiety. Stepping closer, Zoe was able to stroke Jasper's neck and his furry back, smiling all the while. She stayed that way for a few minutes stroking Jasper and talking to Shiloh, before leaving so Theo could repeat the process. It took Shiloh longer to allow Theo to pet Jasper and Iris found it hard not to order him out. In the end the mare relented when Gus crept out from behind Iris's legs to sniff Theo's trousers and then sat very close, watching him. Theo glanced at the Picardy and returned his attention to the foal, but Iris saw how he shifted away from the dog.

Walking back to the house Zoe fell into step beside Iris, who noted how tired her daughter seemed. Zoe's face was paler than usual and there were dark smudges beneath her eyes that Iris didn't like. She linked her arm through her daughter's as they walked.

'How are you, love?'

Zoe laughed.

'You are funny. I only saw you three days ago!'

'I know, I just worry is all. You look a bit tired.'

Her daughter glanced back at Theo walking with Michael.

'I'm fine, just busy at work.'

'Any news about our friend's DNA?'

Zoe shook her head, and they entered the kitchen. Theo settled next to Zoe at the table and covered her hand with his, cocking his head slightly. Iris pretended not to notice and busied herself at the Aga while Michael disappeared into the cellar.

'Mum?'

Iris briefly closed her eyes, wondering what was about to come. She turned.

'Yes?'

'Would it be all right if we stayed over and drove back early tomorrow?'

Her daughter's voice sounded strained and Iris wondered if they had argued. She paused, trying to think of a reason to say no, but found nothing plausible.

'I don't see why not.'

Theo smiled at her, his gaze intense, and patted Zoe's hand. Iris's jaw tightened and she returned to the Aga lest her expression give her away.

Hours later, the clock showed 4am and Iris knew sleep had fled. Silently cursing the Watchers and Theo she rose and, accompanied by Gus, made her way downstairs. In the study she unlocked her desk drawer and removed her notebook and laptop, determined to piece together anything that could explain why Amy Dudley had been murdered. In the kitchen she debated making a hot chocolate but settled for decaffeinated tea. She lit the fire in the living room and curled up on the sofa with Gus's head on her legs. Opening her laptop, she began a new document and, using her notebook, listed everything she felt was relevant. First of all was the locket, then she put Gordon's theory of Katherine Grey ordering the murder and orchestrating the Watchers. Sipping her tea, she turned to the Tudor family trees copied from Gordon's notes, tracing the line of Katherine Grey and wondering who the descendant was now, starting a search on the internet. As Gordon had done, she traced the ancestry through the Greys and Seymours to the Northumberlands but was surprised to find the line ended in 1865, something Gordon would never have known.

'The Watchers can't still be about Katherine Grey through the Northumberlands if they're all dead, can they?'

Gus waved his tail and sighed. She stroked his head for a moment, thinking. Then with brow furrowed Iris began to research Katherine Grey's other descendants, wondering if they could have a claim to the throne.

Over an hour later she stared, astounded, at the screen and then her notebook.

'Holy shit,' she murmured. 'They don't have a claim to the throne, they're on it!'

She re-checked her research and found the same thing; Katherine Grey's line went directly to Elizabeth Bowes-Lyon and thence to Queen Elizabeth II.

'Gordon was wrong. The Watchers have nothing to do with putting a descendant of Katherine Grey on the throne. If so, they've already succeeded and wouldn't be needed any more, surely?'

Gus yawned and she tickled his ears, wondering if she could bear to wait or just wake Michael now. The Picardy climbed off the sofa, wandering to the curtains, and nosed behind the drapes to the French doors. Putting down her notebook and laptop, Iris rose, stretching stiff legs and feeling hungry. She noted the time was nearly 6am and doubted she would be going back to bed. Opening the French doors, she pulled her robe tighter at the cold air and watched Gus's tawny shadow peruse shrubs and grass. Birds had started to sing even though it was still dark to her eyes and she gazed up at the cloud-shrouded sky. A slight sound made her look back and her breath hitched at the sight of Theo, dressed in a charcoal suit, groomed to perfection.

'Good morning,' he said. 'I wasn't expecting anyone to be up.'

He halted by the sofa and glanced at her laptop and notebook. She resisted the urge to rush inside and snatch them up.

'I couldn't sleep, too much work to do,' she said, wondering why she felt the need to justify herself in her own home to this man she disliked. 'Where's Zoe?'

'In the shower. She won't be long. I thought I'd make some coffee and saw the light on.'

'Coffee. Yes, of course. Please help yourself.' She gestured to the kitchen, hoping he would leave. 'I've got to finish up some farm figures but if you can't find anything let me know.'

Theo nodded and moved toward the kitchen. Iris hurried to her laptop and notebook. Picking them up, she swallowed and turned to find Theo standing in the doorway watching her. Startled, she fumbled the items and the notebook slipped from her grip to the floorboards. She bent, but Theo was quicker and scooped it up. They straightened and suddenly he was too close. His citrus aftershave was too strong and she felt strangely vulnerable in dressing gown and pyjamas. He held out the notebook and she took it, trying to smile, unable to speak. Gaze intense, his fingers grazed hers and she swallowed again, the base of her neck crawling. She stepped back and he smiled, shifting his weight as if to follow. Abruptly Gus loped in, catching their attention. On seeing Theo, the Picardy gave a short bark and, claws clattering on the floorboards, gained Iris's side. Theo's features had frozen when the dog entered and now, eyes narrowing on Gus, he backed away, turning and going to the kitchen.

Iris let out a breath she hadn't known she was holding. Putting her laptop under one arm and holding the notebook, she stroked the Picardy, murmuring what a good lad he was. Moving to the French doors she resisted the odd impulse to go outside and sit, locking the doors behind her. Instead, she closed them, wondering at her trembling fingers, and went to the study with Gus at her heels. She slid the notebook and laptop into her desk drawer and locked it, gazing at the monitors. They showed reassuring images of the stables, Jasper a smudge amidst the straw with Shiloh standing over him. She managed a smile and suddenly wanted nothing more than Michael's comforting presence. Attention still on the monitors, she straightened up some paperwork, absently closed the top drawer of the filing cabinet and left with her thoughts uncomfortably on Theo.

CHAPTER TWENTY-SEVEN

Later that same day, Stephen Sloane entered the Watchers' Park Street premises in London. He slipped his black mask on to cover the top half of his face, the eye holes enough to see by while leaving his lower face and mouth clear. He moved to the long dining room, breathing in the richly scented air and enjoying the opulence. His two fellow Watchers, known to him only as Briar and Thorn, were seated at the table where a large cafetière of espresso resided alongside biscotti and a plate of finger sandwiches. They were drinking the espresso, speaking in low tones, and greeted him, smiling beneath their masks. Stephen noted Briar's lips were cranberry-red today, marking the fine porcelain like blood. He settled and poured himself a coffee, stirring in sugar before speaking.

'The bones have been dated and, regrettably, they're not Amy Dudley.'

Stephen tried not to notice how the other man's jaw tightened. Briar laid a finger on Thorn's sleeve, her gaze on Stephen.

'Sloe, tell us about the bones,' she said.

'As you know there were no whole skulls recovered. From the quantity we believe there are three bodies. Two male and a female. They all date from the same period, that is the mid-1800s. Most likely the Bennetts, McCraken and/or Nightjar. It seems our lost Watcher may have finally come home.'

Thorn tilted his head, blond hair contrasting starkly with the black mask. He murmured something to Briar that Stephen couldn't hear.

'Indeed,' she said. 'Until Nightjar is conclusively identified it's another disappointment. We've spent years keeping watch on Josephine Guard. Now we're so close to fulfilment, yet Goodwins gave us nothing but an empty drawer. Foxcombe Valley nothing but a useless tomb.'

Stephen sipped his coffee, trying to ease his constricted throat, knowing how vicious Briar could get even to her own.

'Amy Dudley must be in there,' he said. 'Now we know the ruins are where Gordon McCraken and the Bennetts went, she must be. The valley could be searched again. Perhaps there's another way into the tunnel?'

'Perhaps,' Briar's tone was hard. 'But following the debacle with Iris Shaw, re-entering and excavating the entirety of the tunnel is too risky at this stage. We cannot risk exposure.'

'Look, what happened in the valley wasn't my fault.'

Thorn leant forward with fingertips white on the tabletop and eyes narrowed to slits behind the mask.

'Then whose was it, Sloe? Tell me, so I can rip their tongue out.'

Stephen's gaze locked on Thorn's.

'There's nothing to tell,' he said. 'It was an unfortunate occurrence. Nothing anyone could've done.'

Thorn snorted and sat back.

'I planned and executed the Goodwins raid,' he said, 'and the Mitchells' deaths perfectly. So many things could've gone awry, yet all went without a hitch.' A sneer thickened Thorn's tone. 'You had a remote, rural location in the middle of the night and still managed to botch it.'

Stephen's guts hardened and he fought the urge to punch the man.

'You want the rural location next time? Be my guest. I'll happily swap for the high-tech, easy kills you had!'

Thorn rose, knocking his chair over, fists clenched.

'Peace!' Briar called. 'Stop acting like bloody children.'

Stephen smirked, gesturing to the other to sit, making it an insult. Thorn gave him the finger, before righting his chair and resettling. Briar shook her head and took a sip of coffee before replacing her cup precisely on the saucer.

'Now, we must decide what to do next.'

Thorn shrugged, his expression bland, and lifted a biscotti, running it under his nose like a cigar connoisseur.

'I say we kill the Shaws and anyone else at that farm,' he said. 'Search the house until we find the locket.'

He ate the biscuit in two bites, his gaze on Stephen.

'God, you can be such a thug,' Stephen said. 'Do you know how difficult that would be to orchestrate and clean up? Not to mention the mess it would make with the authorities?'

Thorn wiped the side of his mouth with a finger delicately, like a cat washing.

'We'll make it look like an accident or a murder–suicide thing,' he said. 'We've done it before, look at the Mitchells, and we know the Shaws have got the locket.'

'Thanks to me,' Stephen said. 'Without my infiltration we still wouldn't know where it was.'

'Infiltration!' Thorn's laugh echoed about the large room. 'You conned your way in with that Dunn woman blathering about antique watches and jewellery. It was only blind luck that she blabbed about seeing the pocket watch and locket. If you'd gone up against the old woman, she would have seen right through you.'

'Oh okay, we're doing the pissing contest right now. Fine. I saw the aerial photograph of Foxcombe Valley in the old woman's living room. All you did was check the Land Registry. Briar made the connection between Samuel Banks's old house and Gordon McCraken and ordered us to follow the Shaws. Basically, you were nothing but an office clerk, Thorn.'

He sat back and Briar smiled at him. Thorn scowled and tapped his fingers on the table then swallowed coffee.

'We would've found the picture with or without you, Sloe, I'd have made the connection easily enough. Your contribution is merely that of a petty conman.'

Stephen's fingers ached and beneath the table he unclenched his fists while forcing himself to take deep, slow breaths.

'I discovered Josephine Guard had the locket. It's your out-of-control violence that cost us its hiding place. The tunnel was found because I noticed the photograph and the Shaws were stupid enough to peg out the ruins. So, you've done what exactly?'

'Everything that you were too much of a pussy to do.'

'Gee Thorn, I guess the way you tortured Ruth Dunn got us all the information we needed. Oh wait, no it didn't. She just died.'

Thorn grinned, his eyes alight in the depths of his mask.

'Oh, she died. Lovely and messy too. Once I realised she didn't know where the locket was, it seemed the right thing to do. The psycho act always throws the police off, you know that.'

'An act is it? Could've fooled me.'

'Why yes, *Sloe*, I imagine most people could.'

Briar tutted, breaking the tension and their locked gazes.

'Oh, for heaven's sake,' she said. 'Will you two stop

pissing all over the room and each other? You're both alpha dogs, very macho, very clever. Now, can we get back to the matter in hand?'

Stephen looked away from Thorn, taking a sandwich and eating it, thinking.

'I believe caution is still necessary,' he said. 'We don't know for certain that it's at the farm.'

Briar inclined her head, gaze amused despite the mask.

'Oh, I'd say it was a certainty as it's not at Ash House nor in the container.'

Stephen stared at her.

'How do we know it's not in the container?'

'It seems a police warehouse isn't as secure as the public are led to believe. Some rapscallion searched the thing, unobtrusively of course.'

Thorn smiled, showing perfect white teeth, and sipped his espresso.

'In that case,' the blonde man said, 'I reiterate. Fuck caution, kill the Shaws, search the farmhouse.'

Briar sighed and shook her head, her mouth turned down. Stephen pondered Thorn's idea, running through the variables, and could see the appeal but still the number of bodies in one place seemed incautious despite the possible, ultimate reward. He recalled the night of the dead ewe.

'They're not some prissy bank clerks or old age pensioners, Thorn. This lot have guns, dogs and some bloody booby traps. Flash bangs and the like. And there's the cop car that keeps going by.'

Thorn shrugged and looked at Briar, whose expression became thoughtful.

'Not to mention the silent alarm,' she said, 'and the cameras. Which we need access to the farmhouse to disable. We can't just pick the locks and walk in without setting the alarm off even if the place was empty. A difficulty in and of itself as the place is pretty much always occupied and with dogs too. And killing the Shaws would make it impossible for them to tell us anything useful.'

'Fuck that,' Thorn said. 'Let's just take one, say the husband, and torture him. Make the others watch, they'll soon tell us what we want to know.'

Briar considered him, exasperation apparent in her tight jaw and narrowed eyes. Stephen wondered, not for the first time, how much longer the woman would endure the thug.

'No, Thorn,' she said. 'It's too risky at this stage. There must be other options.'

Thorn grimaced, looking frustrated. Stephen drank his coffee and poured another, thinking about skulls and where they might be hidden.

'Do we think Amy Dudley is at the farmhouse as well?' he mused. 'That somehow they've found her?'

Briar looked at Thorn who raised both hands, palms up.

'Can't say for certain, but it's possible,' he said. 'They could've excavated the tunnel at a different point and found her. And with Zoe's job who knows what they might have done with Amy Dudley.'

Stephen frowned, his attention sharpening, feeling like he was missing something.

'Zoe Shaw does blood doesn't she, not bones?'

Thorn nodded.

'That's right, but she's got this friend, Will Pritchard. He's an expert in bones and I wouldn't put it past him to quietly examine Amy Dudley using Arrant's facilities if Zoe asked him to.'

Briar sighed and frowned.

'All right let's have a proper look into Will Pritchard and see if he's involved somehow. Other than that, we've got two possibilities. Either both skull and locket are at the farmhouse or the locket is, and the skull is with Arrant.

Arrant will be hard to breach but not impossible. Yet I am loath to take the risk unless we're certain Amy Dudley is there, and we've ruled Will Pritchard out of the equation. Equally, we don't know for certain that Amy Dudley has been found.'

Thorn smiled.

'Which means extracting the information from the Shaws.'

'Which means searching the farmhouse first,' Briar corrected.

'For fuck's sake, Briar, you said it yourself; it's not that simple. Despite everything we've done the place is never unoccupied. There's security and bloody dogs. Even watching them is a problem at such a rural, exposed location. It would be much easier to just remove the Shaws, disable the cameras, then search the place and torture them for any information.'

Stephen shook his head, irritated at the man's insistence at thuggery.

'Seriously Thorn, I understand that killing can be a useful means to an end but try using a bit of common sense. What if we can't find the locket or the skull and, like Ruth Dunn, the Shaws don't talk? Dead they're absolutely no use to us.'

'I agree with Sloe,' Briar said. 'At this point it's more of a risk torturing the Shaws than finding a way to search the house without them knowing.'

Thorn's eyes narrowed behind the mask.

'Like I said, take one of them then,' he said. 'Zoe, for instance. Leverage her to get the others to talk and hand everything over.'

'And have them go to the police?' Stephen asked. 'It's too chancy.'

Thorn cocked his head at Briar in a gesture Stephen

found annoying, as if the man were seeking advocation. But the woman ignored the motion, nodding at Stephen.

'Sloe's right,' she said. 'We must get them all away from the farmhouse so we can safely search it.'

Thorn made an exasperated sound. Stephen smiled as an idea formed.

'Something that will make them all come running, leave the house unattended and without the alarm set, for quite a while?'

Briar's expression became interested, her gaze riveted on his.

'You have something in mind?'

'I do believe I have.'

The Watchers spent the next hour making their plans. When everything was laid out in detail even Thorn seemed satisfied.

'It's a shame you'll have to search the farmhouse alone, Sloe. But if Briar and I are exposed it would be a disaster.' Thorn turned to Briar, his demeanour intense. 'Playing devil's advocate, if the search turns up nothing, can we then ditch the subtle approach and use more physical means on the Shaws?'

'We'll have to consider it, yes,' Briar said. 'We can't let the Shaws keep the locket or unravel Amy Dudley's death. But that doesn't mean you can go off half cocked. If necessary, we threaten them with torture and death, so they reveal the locket and skull whereabouts. Yet torturing and killing them would be entirely unproductive and could leave us back were we started with no locket and no skull. Manipulation and stealth are our best options. So, let's hope Sloe's search is fruitful.'

Stephen, finishing his third espresso, noted how Thorn kept returning to violence against the Shaws. He knew his was a more clinical approach to their work and Thorn's evident enjoyment of killing had long concerned him. He recognised it made the man dangerously impulsive and sighed, wondering if he might do something about Thorn. While he sipped the last of his coffee, he studied Briar. He knew her control was formidable as was her temper, icy to Thorn's heated rages. But he knew that Thorn bridled against her careful approach. In many moments of recklessness Thorn had raged at Briar for what he saw as ineffective plotting. Stephen liked to view himself as the moderate middle, calm yet capable. He watched Briar's slender fingers lift a cup to her lips and then pause.

'What about the dogs?' she asked.

'Oh, I've got an excellent poison for that,' Thorn said.

Stephen went very still.

'I'm not killing any dog,' he said. 'I'll use sedative. This is meant to be a covert in and out. If I start poisoning animals it'll raise suspicions.'

Briar smiled and sipped her coffee. Thorn raised an eyebrow.

'Merciless dispatcher of women and children, but won't harm dogs? That's new.'

Stephen stared at his cup, turning it round and round on the saucer. He imagined gutting Thorn, slowly, and looked up to find the man watching him.

CHAPTER TWENTY-EIGHT

Two nights later at close to 8pm, Stephen set fires in the woods above Whitebarn. He used oil drums he had placed there the night before to contain the blazes and added a few smoke bombs to the effect. As the flames gathered strength Stephen hurried back to where he had left the trail bike, uncaring if he set off any flash bombs this time, wanting the attention. He rode halfway along Whitebarn's drive with the headlights off then hid the bike in bushes near the house and walked further, pressing amongst hedgerows to watch through night vision binoculars. It took another ten minutes for the fires to be noticed by anyone at the farm. Fed by paraffin-soaked foam in the dark amidst the black trees, the flames seemingly raged through the woods toward the pastures where the sheep grazed.

Stephen counted the Shaws and all their lackeys as they raced to the woods and pastures in two Land Rovers, noting none had any dogs with them for fear of the flames. He knew it wouldn't be long before the fire brigade arrived and bet no one would return until all the animals were safely away and the fires extinguished. He retrieved the bike and rode slowly to the farmhouse. Switching off and parking in the shadows, he removed his helmet, sat and listened. Hearing only the faint commotion he had caused far across the fields, he settled his mask on and pulled his hood up. He then delved into his satchel and took out the house plans Thorn had given him. Walking round the house he found the kitchen lights on and through the window ascertained no dog was lurking about; it took only moments to pick the back door lock and slip inside. He hurried to the study, relieved to find the silent alarm off.

A huffing woof came from what the plans indicated to be the living room. Stephen took the cooked chicken breast injected with sedative from his bag. He weighed the meat in his gloved hand, wondering yet again at the dosage. Given what Thorn had told him about the size of the dog and breed he had guessed at the amount needed and erred on the side of caution. Stephen consulted the plan, and knocked on the living room door. The dog gave voice, claws scrabbling on laminate floor or floorboards as it careened toward the sound. Stephen swiftly retraced his steps to the kitchen and, pushing open that living room entrance, he threw the contaminated chicken inside. He shut the door as a large tawny shape spun and leapt toward him. The barking continued then trailed off to sniffing and he knew the dog had found the meat.

He checked his phone, setting an alarm for forty-five minutes. He took the dog taser from his pocket, putting it on the lowest charge and hoping he wouldn't have to use it. Consulting the plans, he searched the study first, deeming it most likely to hold a safe, but even the locked drawers yielded nothing of interest. In the hall he debated his next move and decided on the master bedroom, reasoning it a private space that the Shaws might use for anything secure. Gaining the landing, he caught a glimpse of the fiery woods then, hearing the thin wail of sirens, hurried upward.

Ten minutes later he found the safe hidden in the wardrobe and sat back on his heels, staring at the beast and wondering how far down it went. He shone a torch onto the keypad and, peering at it, it seemed to him some numbers were more worn than others. He punched the digits and hissed through his teeth when the safe remained locked. Stephen then tried various combinations, making a note of each set of numbers that failed. After fifteen minutes the safe stayed stubbornly closed and he pondered trying force, weighing the incriminating damage it would cause against his need to find out whether the locket or Amy Dudley were inside. Sounds halted his thoughts and he listened to the rise and fall of voices. Silently cursing he rose, gathering his belongings, and stole to the top of the stairs. From the kitchen he could hear a woman's voice punctuated by a younger male.

'I think we should go to the hospital,' she said.

'Honestly, Mrs Shaw, I'll be fine. It's only a superficial cut. You should get back to the flock.'

'They're out of danger now and your father and brother are managing them, don't worry. Here, hold this over the wound until the bleeding stops. Then we'll have a proper look at it and go from there.'

Reassured they would remain in the kitchen, Stephen crept down the stairs with his gaze fixed on the front door.

'How's it feeling?' she asked.

Stephen reached the door and eased the lock, one gloved hand on the handle while trying to discern an odd whining sound underneath the voices; he hoped it wasn't a vehicle.

'It's actually doing all right. I think the bleeding's stopped. I'm sure it'll be okay.'

Stephen quietly inched the door open, every nerve and fibre poised to flee should they leave the kitchen.

'Keep the pressure on, Dan,' the woman said. 'I'll get the first aid kit and see what's bothering Gus.'

Stephen pulled the door further open, almost wide enough for him to leave.

'Gus? What's the matter?'

The dog barked, loudly alert, and abruptly the whining made sense. Suddenly uncaring of noise, Stephen hauled the door open and ran for his motorbike. Seconds later more barking, louder, closer, followed. He mounted the bike and turned it on in one motion; spinning it round he saw a large tawny shape racing toward him. He gunned the motor, completing the circle, and sped down the driveway, helmet lost to the movement. In the side mirror the dog sprinted after him with a figure following. Stephen pulled the throttle, his only thought to escape. The dog dwindled in the mirror and darkness, so he risked a glance back to see it slow while the figure reached it. The bike wobbled, catching all his attention. He gained the road, wheels churning and squealing as he cornered too fast. He yelled, fighting to keep upright, but the bike slid under him, careening sideways and dragging him with it. He screamed, blinded by searing light, engulfed in noise and pain.

Iris, a firm grip on Gus, heard the crash and ran to the road only to halt at the mayhem. An articulated lorry was squealing and hissing to a standstill, a tyre skewered by a piece of metal. Remnants of twisted bike were strewn across the road and in the lorry's wake. There was no sign of the rider. The door opened and the lorry driver got out, his face stark in the streetlamps. He stumbled to her, eyes wide and sweat dimpling his face.

'He came out of nowhere,' the man said, numbly. 'I couldn't stop.'

'I know. It's not your fault,' Iris replied.

She wasn't sure he heard. The man swayed and abruptly sat at the side of the road, staring at the wreckage. With trembling fingers, she dialled the emergency services and spoke to the operator, summoning ambulance and police, letting them know what had happened. She ended the call and sat next to the driver with Gus at her side.

'The police and ambulance are on their way,' she said. 'I'll wait here with you.'

He nodded and seemed unable to speak. She rang Michael, who was with the fire brigade, and learnt that the fires had been deliberate and contained. She told him what had happened, and that Dan needed attention at the house. She knew Thomas and Luke would take care of the sheep and asked Michael to talk to and coordinate the Wades. Reassuring him she was all right, Iris rang off. Suddenly the driver threw up, leaning to one side and heaving until only bile was left. She gave him a tissue and saw he was crying. A few cars stopped behind the lorry unable to negotiate the wreckage. A couple of people got out of vehicles and came over to check no one was hurt. One gave the driver some water from a bottle. She still couldn't see the bike rider. Then sirens in the distance were a welcome sound.

Later that night she found Gus worrying at the sofa and found a chicken breast beneath it. Retrieving the meat, she stared at it then noted a slimy trail on the floorboards and suddenly understood; the chicken had slid under the sofa before the Picardy could eat it.

Nearly a week later in the blueing of the day, Iris was bedding down the horses when a familiar car arrived carrying DI Fields and DS Dens. She muttered to Blue about bloody police, pasted on a smile and went to greet them. Taking them to the kitchen she made cups of tea while Gus hid beneath the table. DS Dens seemed uneasy, his gaze narrowing on the inspector and fidgeting with his pen and radio. DI Fields looked serene, placing a leather folder on the table, but her fingers were hard on the notebook, flicking through the pages with undue force. Iris handed out mugs and settled, warming her fingers around her drink, and felt Gus lean on her legs.

'Is it about Ruth? Or the break-in?' she asked.

DI Fields' mouth thinned.

'Both, actually. It seems the man who broke in here last week is our killer.'

'What! Are you sure?'

'All the forensics indicate it, and we matched a fingerprint inside your container to the chap as well. So it seems he's behind everything.'

'And he's dead now?'

'Yes, unfortunately. I'm sorry to say the lorry decapitated him. It trapped his body beneath it and dragged the man apart. Obviously, he won't be talking.'

Iris was suddenly very glad she hadn't seen the rider.

'Do you know who he was?'

'It seems he had a few names but the one you'll know is Stephen Sloane.' Iris stared at the inspector and found her gaze returned by a hard one. 'You remember him, don't you, Mrs Shaw?'

She abruptly remembered the woods, being shot at, seeing the man's face illuminated by his phone. Gus hurt and Blue bolting. Fear and anger swept her in a hot wave, and she fought not to rise, not to scream or cry.

'Stephen Sloane,' she managed, sipping tea. 'Of course, the furniture chap. But I don't understand why he would kill Ruth and break into the container and here?'

DS Dens let out a breath and seemed about to speak but stopped at a small gesture from the inspector. DI Fields leant forward, her gaze still on Iris.

'We were rather hoping you could tell us,' she said.

The locket spun in her mind. Amy Dudley, sightless and all knowing, seemed to fill the kitchen, her name on

Iris's lips. Iris swallowed, dropping her eyes to her mug, and her fingers found Gus's warm back.

'I have no idea,' she said. 'Why would I?'

She glanced up to see the two officers exchange an exasperated look and her jaw clenched. DS Dens rubbed his forehead, eyes closed, and for a moment looked exhausted. Iris felt sorry for him, having to work long hours with the inspector and suddenly wondered if he had a wife and children to go home to. DI Fields drank tea, watching her, and the silence grew. Iris, recognising they were trying to get her to fill the quiet, sipped her own tea and ignored them. Seconds grew to minutes and still no one spoke. Finally, Iris grew tired of the game and smiled at the woman across from her.

'Would you like some more tea or should I contact my lawyer?'

'Mrs Shaw, we're just trying to help you.'

'Oh, in that case well done. You've caught Ruth's killer and the man whose been harassing us. I guess you know about the dead sheep and fires? Yes? All done by this Stephen Sloane, I imagine. So, just let me know when you'll be returning my great aunt's belongings and we'll be done here. Unless there's some reason you need to question me further, in which case I will be contacting my lawyer.'

DS Dens shifted in his seat, his expression uncomfortable. DI Fields frowned at him and sighed, returning her attention to Iris.

'We'll arrange for the container to be returned in a few days.' Her tone was resigned. 'There's some paperwork for you to sign.'

'That's fine,' Iris said, rising and collecting the mugs. 'Just show me where.'

The inspector opened the leather folder and indicated where Iris should sign. The forms duly completed, DS

Dens rose and stood near the kitchen door, fiddling with his radio, which crackled. DI Fields seemed in no hurry, arranging the paperwork neatly and closing the folder, sorting out her notebook and coat. Iris swallowed her impatience and stood holding the door open, watching the light fade in the hallway as the day darkened. Eventually the inspector deemed it acceptable to leave. DS Dens followed his superior from the kitchen, passing Iris still holding the door. He nodded to her with entreaty in his eyes, but she only shrugged. He smiled as if understanding and Iris liked him for it.

Once the officers had gone, Iris returned to the kitchen, settling at the table, and laid her arms there and buried her head in them. Gus was a warm, heavy presence at her side and she cried, cried for her stepfather and Josephine, for Ruth, for Amy Dudley and Gordon. She sobbed and felt light and dark inside, relieved Stephen Sloane was dead all the while knowing there were other Watchers waiting.

CHAPTER TWENTY-NINE

Three days later, Iris spent the morning checking the shipping container contents to make sure it was all in good order. Gus had tried to help but after a little while had been redirected to the farm to spend the morning with Thomas.

Just after midday she heard the door creak and Michael entered carrying a tray that held steaming mugs and sandwiches which turned out to be cheese. They moved a table and sat on Josephine's leather sofa eating in companionable silence. Michael glanced about, smiling slightly.

'It's a bit like having her back, isn't it?'

'I know what you mean. There's so many memories here.'

Michael looked around and sipped his coffee.

'How's it all going?'

'I've only got the pictures left. Everything else is accounted for and in decent condition.'

'That's good. Do you want some help? I've finished my lecture plans so I'm free.'

Iris eyed her husband, noting his serious expression. She put her mug on the table and turned to him.

'If I say yes, will you tell me what's going on?'

'With what?'

'With you. You've been odd since last night, preoccupied. Is it Amy Dudley or what happened with Stephen Sloane?'

Michael shook his head.

'Actually, no.' He sighed. 'Well, yes, I am worried about the Watchers. But this is something to do with work.'

'Why, what's happened?'

'There was faculty meeting yesterday, mostly about funding and the proposed reorganisation. Anyway, the upshot is, there's going to be forced redundancies in the next six months.'

'Oh, that's awful.'

'After the meeting morale was terrible. It's the not knowing that's the worst,' he said, taking her hand. 'So, I've been thinking. What if I leave now instead of after probate?'

'What! Are you sure?'

'Yes, very. I've thought of little else since the meeting, I was going to leave anyway, and this just accelerates things.'

'But you've worked so hard to get where you are and teaching there was something you always wanted.'

'I know, but it's not everything I want from a career. I'd love to spend my time writing historical biographies or about Amy Dudley come to that. And by leaving voluntarily now, it might save someone from being made redundant in six months.' He squeezed her hand. 'I've done the sums – we can manage on our savings until probate's done. What do you think, can you stand to have me around every day?'

'Well, the pigs do shit an awful lot, so an extra pair of hands is always welcome.'

Michael's laughter echoed around the container and, lifting her hand, he kissed her fingers. Iris grinned at his gallantry.

'So, you'll hand your notice in Monday?'

'Yes, I'll draft it tomorrow. I was thinking to ring Zoe later – I can tell her then.'

'Maybe ask how the DNA extraction is going.' Iris sipped some coffee, her thoughts on their daughter and her last visit. 'I'm worried about her.'

'Me too. She didn't seem like herself last week. I hate to say it, but I think it's Theo's doing.'

Iris remembered how vulnerable she had felt in the younger man's presence. Michael sighed and rubbed his jaw.

'Should we talk to her about it?' he asked.

Iris tried to imagine how any such conversation with Zoe would go and they all ended with shouting or crying. She patted Michael's hand, trying to impart some comfort when she felt none.

'We'll work something out,' she said. 'In the meantime, how's the locket coming along?'

'Ah well, there is some good news. The tools arrived this morning and I've got the instructions from the chap on the internet. I'm going to give it a go this evening.'

Iris's heart quickened and she swallowed, trying to temper her excitement.

'I really think it could be something.'

'I know you do, and I hope you're right, but we'll see.'

She nodded, knowing he didn't believe the locket was important. Yet every fibre in her being resonated that it was. Her belief that the jewel held a secret people were willing to kill for was as steely as her determination to save Amy Dudley. Michael finished his coffee and half turned to her.

'Have you heard from the genealogist?'

'Not yet.' She tried not to think what the silence meant. 'I was going to give her until Monday then call.'

Her husband nodded, his face drawn in the same unhappy lines that she imagined her own held.

'I know Stephen Sloane's gone,' she said, 'but we both know that he wasn't the only Watcher.'

Michael let out a breath, his expression suddenly relieved.

'I've been thinking the same. As much as I want to solve Amy Dudley's murder, to let her rest in peace, I think we need to set a deadline if the genealogist and the DNA don't come through.'

Iris swirled the dregs of her coffee in the mug, finding words impossible. Michael seemed not to notice her silence and continued.

'We're in a relatively strong position anyway. Better than when we started. The age of the documents and skull can be verified, which will help. We have the coroner's report, which is a truly phenomenal find.'

'But will it be enough to prove murder?'

'Not conclusively. But we've got the ruins, which support Sam's existence. The tunnel will help authenticate his and Gordon's accounts. The skull is the most important thing we have. I've been doing some research and forensics can do reconstructions to prove she was hit. Someone else can extract the DNA and do the genealogy bit. Not to mention the locket might hold some answers.'

Iris nodded and tried to ignore the hollow feeling in her chest, every instinct telling her to let it be and not show vulnerability. But the emptiness built and her fear of it shoved her words out in a rush.

'I feel like we're abandoning Amy Dudley if we publish without definitively proving murder and who she is.'

Michael looked sympathetic but she couldn't ignore how relieved he still seemed.

'I know it's hard,' he said, 'especially after everything we've been through, to think about stopping now. And who knows, we might get the DNA and the genealogist could find a living relative. But we have to face facts, it's more likely that it's not going to happen. So surely it would be better to publish now and be safe?'

'I know what you're saying makes sense, but I'm just…'

He covered her hands with his and took a deep breath.

'Iris, I know how much this means to you, but I've been terrified of losing you, of the Watchers, ever since you got lost in the valley.'

She stared at him.

'You've never said that. You told me it was all okay.'

'I didn't want to worry you or make you second-guess everything. I know how much Amy Dudley's peace means to you but I'm not sure I can take anymore. Not after you in the valley, fires and the break-ins. The not knowing, the stress of wondering what or who will be next is horrible. Please, can we end this?'

She saw the fear in his eyes and realised how much of a toll it had taken on him. She could feel the emptiness claiming her, the inadequacy and insecurities returning to cover her. Still, she projected the complete, confident Iris and somehow smiled.

'All right,' she said. 'We'll end it whether we get the locket open or not. I'll call the genealogist on Monday and regardless of progress or lack of it, we'll publish next week.' She continued to smile and mask her misery. 'When you call her later can you ask Zoe to get Amy Dudley back from the DNA chap and ask her if she wouldn't mind driving up one evening in the week with the skull? Will that be okay? Can you wait until Amy Dudley is here for us to go public?'

Michael agreed and she couldn't help but note how much happier he seemed. He finished the sandwiches as her appetite was gone. Then together they checked Josephine's pictures. While her husband chatted away about the future and publishing their findings, Iris felt nauseous and could only think of how they were failing Amy Dudley.

CHAPTER THIRTY

In London earlier that same afternoon, Zoe couldn't settle. She moved from living room to kitchen, picking things up and replacing them. She straightened the sofa cushions, thinking to sit and read, but the book held her for only minutes. The television lasted even less time. She wanted to call Theo, but he was away on business and the reception was so bad that he had to go to the hotel car park to call her. This meant their conversations were brief, sporadic and dictated wholly by Theo. Still, she rang anyway and, as they had for the last two days, her call went straight to voicemail. She didn't leave a message and, wondering at her restlessness, scrolled aimlessly through her phone.

She paused at Will's contact and bit her lip, glancing at the door. Then she shook her head, trying to ignore the quiver of unease the thought of calling him induced. She drew a breath to alleviate the tightness in her chest and recalled Theo's annoyance over her continued lunches with her old friend. No matter what she said, Theo was convinced Will didn't like him and had feelings for her. Theo hated her talking about him to Will, imagining that she painted him in all sorts of terrible colours and that Will was trying to undermine him. The ensuing arguments had been upsetting and confusing for Zoe as she didn't understand most of Theo's reasoning or how it was all her fault but realised it must be. Afterward it had taken a considerable effort on her part and a cessation of the lunches to mend Theo's broken trust in her. Since then, she only spoke to Will at work and still felt guilty for doing so.

Now though, she realised calling Will about Amy Dudley was something she couldn't tell Theo about anyway. She swallowed and with a trembling finger rang her old friend. Holding her breath, she listened while the tones rang and rang until going to voicemail. Surprised at how disappointed she felt, Zoe was suddenly overcome with a fierce desire to see Will. It swept her with an urgency that had her put her coat on, head out the door and onto a bus within minutes.

Travelling through London's autumn streets, she felt breathless and giddy. Staring out of the window, she relished the feeling of doing something. She pushed thoughts of Theo away while ignoring the unease contracting her guts and concentrated on getting to Will.

Nearing the right stop, she tried Will's phone again only for it to go to voicemail once more and her heart sank. She abruptly wondered at her actions, doubting her motives and feeling guilty at betraying Theo. Still, she reasoned that she needed to know about Amy Dudley and face to face was better than over the phone where someone might overhear or, worse, put things in writing. Suddenly she thought it would be for the best if Will wasn't in so she could say she tried and then go home.

Alighting from the bus, her phone rang, and the thought of Theo made her panic, wondering how she could explain where she was; but it was Will. She answered, hearing the relief and strain in her voice.

'Hi Will.'

She heard a gargle followed by silence and then footsteps. A muffled voice, female she thought, and a door being slammed.

'Will? Hello, Will?'

The gargle came again with a pitiful wheeze, then nothing. She stared at the phone, seeing it still connected, and, with a surge of terror, started to run. Breathing hard, she reached Will's block of flats and pressed every single intercom button shouting 'delivery' until someone buzzed her in. Ignoring the elevators as they would take too long, she used the stairs and raced to the second floor. Panting, she stepped into the hallway to find it hushed and normal. She hurried to Will's door and banged on it, calling his name, but received no answer. Suddenly she cursed, realising he could be anywhere. Staring at her phone she saw they were still connected. Holding it to her ear she banged on the door again and was rewarded with a faint echo on the phone receiving inside. Fearful and heartened she called his name again and tried the door handle which unexpectedly yielded. Shoving it open she rushed inside and found her friend in the kitchen.

Will was naked and curled on the floor. Blood pooled around his head while his face and body were a mass of bruising and cuts. A key shape was branded red and angry on his upper thigh. Dropping to her knees Zoe sobbed on finding a thready pulse in his neck and called an ambulance. She kept talking to him, pleading with him to stay with her while resisting the urge to turn him over and see what the head wound was, fearing she would make it worse. The paramedics seemed to take an eternity, but they arrived within minutes of her call. She told them what she knew and reluctantly stepped away, allowing them room to work.

Everything seemed dreamlike and bizarre, as if she was watching it from above. With bags of liquid attached to him, a pad on the side of his face and an oxygen mask on, they transferred Will to a gurney. Zoe heard enough to know he had been shot, had lost a lot of blood and had multiple fractures including his ribs and a broken arm and ankle, but was miraculously alive. The paramedics wheeled Will out of the flat and she stood in the kitchen doorway, staring at the scarlet mess that remained. There, covered in her friend's blood and beneath where he had lain, was Will's phone. Still in a queer daze, she picked it up and hurried after the paramedics.

Hours passed in a mustard-coloured waiting room. Zoe shared the wait and worry in numbed silence with Will's parents. Strangers, their anxieties palpable, came and went but she didn't properly see or hear them. Each time a surgeon or nurse appeared, her attention focused to needlepoint, but none called a name she recognised. She drank fawn-coloured coffee that tasted of sugar and little else. Will's parents seemed grey and stark under the fluorescent lights and she wondered if she looked the same. Finally, a surgeon said Will's name and approached his parents when they rose. Will's mother said something, beckoning her, and the surgeon nodded. Relieved and terrified, Zoe joined them.

'The surgery on Will's jaw and face went well,' the man said. 'He's currently in recovery before being transferred to ICU.'

Will's mother abruptly sat with her head in her hands and sobbed. His father swayed and Zoe caught the man's arm in a steadying grip.

'What happened?' Zoe asked.

'Well, the bullet shattered Will's left jawbone and exited from his neck,' the surgeon said. 'It missed the artery by an eighth of an inch. He's lucky to be alive.'

'Will he be all right?'

'We've repaired the jawbone as best we can, removed the fragments and wired the jaw shut so it can heal. We're hoping he'll make a good recovery, but it will be a long road.'

Will's mother took a gulping breath and rose to stand beside her husband.

'When can we see him?' she asked.

'A nurse will be along shortly to take you to him.' He looked at Zoe. 'Tonight, it will be immediate family only I'm afraid.'

'I understand,' Zoe said. 'And thank you, for everything.'

The surgeon nodded and left. Zoe clutched Will's parents' hands, taking comfort from their presence. Will's mother hugged her.

'If you hadn't found him,' she whispered. 'My Will would've…'

'It's all right. He's going to be fine, you'll see.'

Zoe stepped back and in her pocket her fingers curled around Will's phone. She remembered him telling her about his less-than-legal contact who had Amy Dudley. She waited until Will's parents left with a nurse and then went outside.

That evening in the kitchen at Whitebarn, Iris cooked dinner. She knew her husband planned to call Zoe after the meal and so ate slowly without enjoyment. So well versed at covering her true self, her misery went unnoticed by Michael, who ate with relish while talking about his resignation and writing plans. Only Gus seemed to understand her unhappiness. Under the table the Picardy lay his head on her lap refusing to move and she took comfort from his presence. Still, she could only delay the inevitable and finally the meal was over. Michael cleared the plates humming to himself and she couldn't stand it. Rising, she went to the living room and tried to settle. Her mobile phone buzz was a welcome distraction until she saw the caller was her daughter and she answered with a heavy heart.

'Hello, darling, how are you?'

'Not good. Mum, it's Will, he's been hurt.'

'What do you mean? How?'

'His place was broken into, he's been beaten really badly and, and shot. He's been rushed to hospital.' She started crying. 'Oh Mum, I found him. There was so much blood.'

'Oh my God! Where are you?'

'I'm at the hospital.'

'Do you want us to come?'

She heard Zoe control herself, the crying turned to hard breathing and then, 'No, I'll be fine. Will's out of surgery and he's going to make it. I just need you to check the safe and make sure everything is secure.'

'Why?'

'It was the Watchers. They tortured Will until he told them where she was. Mum, they've taken her. They've taken Amy Dudley.'

'How do you know that?'

'When I found Will he had brand marks as you told me Ruth had so I knew something was wrong. I've been going through his phone and I finally worked out who had Amy Dudley. I've just spoken to the guy. His lab's been broken into and she's gone.'

'Shit. Oh no, poor Will! Are you sure you don't want us to come?'

'I want to know everything else is safe from those bastards.' She heard the tightly controlled rage in her daughter's voice. 'I'm going to expose the Watchers to the press. Those arseholes are going down one way or another.'

Iris didn't know what to say and heard Zoe draw a deep breath.

'Mum, I've got to go. The police have arrived and want to talk to me. Just keep everything safe, please. It's all we've got left against those fucking Watchers.'

Zoe rang off before Iris could reply. She sat staring at the blank phone, her mind and body numb. She glanced up when Michael walked in carrying two glasses of red wine.

'Was that Zoe?'

She managed a nod.

'Did you ask her about getting Amy Dudley back?'

He handed her a glass of wine and she gulped a mouthful before telling him about Will and Amy Dudley.

'I really want to go to the hospital,' she continued. 'But I think we'd be better travelling to the city in the morning. That way before we visit Will we can put everything back in Goodwins.' She paused, thinking of Lana Mitchell. 'Or find another bank to use. This has got to stop. It's all too dangerous. I don't know what we were thinking. Now they've got Amy Dudley hopefully they'll leave us alone if we just hide everything away again.'

Michael slugged wine and she noted his paled face. Anger gripped her and she silently cursed the Watchers for all the harm they had caused. Putting down her glass, she rose and hugged her husband.

'I'm so sorry it's all so horrible,' she said. 'But it's nearly over.'

He felt rigid in her arms and she worried over his fear.

'The hell it is,' Michael said. Puzzled at his tone, she stepped back. His expression was hard and unforgiving. 'Zoe's right, those bastards need to be stopped. They've killed Ruth, tried to kill you and now they've hurt Will. We need to publish everything and expose them for the murdering arseholes they are.'

'But they might come here and without Amy Dudley how can we publish?'

'Screw that. We've got photos of the skull along with everything else.' He drew her back into a rough embrace.

'What do you say, shall we get the locket open and go to the press?'

'Are you sure?'

'Damn right. Let's see what the locket holds and talk to the genealogist in the morning. Then publish what we've got and expose the bloody Watchers once and for all.'

She hugged him, feeling elated and terrified at the same time.

Half an hour later she climbed the stairs to retrieve the locket, her thoughts heavily on Will and desperately hoping he was all right. Halting on the landing, she stared at her reflection in the window and suddenly Amy Dudley swamped her thoughts. In the glass the woman's dark image seemed to overlay her own.

'I'm so sorry they've taken you,' Iris whispered. 'But we're still going to do what we can to let you rest properly.'

She blinked and the reflection was her own again.

At the hospital Zoe gave a statement to the uniformed police officers and stuck to the absolute truth about how she had found Will. With difficulty she omitted any mention of Amy Dudley and the Watchers, reasoning she had no real evidence and no idea who the attackers were. She tried not to let her guilt and dread affect her, but it seemed to feed into every word until she became convinced the officers knew she was hiding something. The interview only took minutes, yet it seemed as long as the wait for Will's surgery.

In the end she only managed to hold on by focusing on Will and the DNA chap. Zoe knew any investigation into the skull and Watchers at this stage could lead to his and Will's careers imploding and possible prosecution. Besides, what did she really know? That Will had been attacked and left for dead. That she had found him by sheer good luck and by some miracle he had survived. When she finished, Zoe felt the policemen studied her too closely, for too long, before leaving. She knew they would be back to speak to Will as soon as he was deemed fit enough. In her exhausted state, she despaired.

CHAPTER THIRTY-ONE

At Whitebarn Iris placed the locket on the kitchen table. Michael laid out the tools and the sheet with the printed instructions. He positioned a reading lamp, so it illuminated the jewel and picked up the locket, which spun in the light while he studied it. Frowning, he palmed it, peering at the engraved back, and took a photo of it on his phone. Gus wandered in from the living room and leant against Iris, who was watching Michael.

'What's the matter?' she asked.

'I feel like I've seen this boar's head recently.'

'On the locket perhaps?'

He made a face at her.

'Very funny. No, somewhere else.' He handed her the jewel. 'Here. You get started on opening it up. There's something I want to check.'

She stared at him.

'You want me to open it?'

'You've got as much experience with stubborn, ancient jewellery as I have.'

'Great. Thanks.'

Michael grinned at her and left the kitchen. Iris shifted Gus, settled at the table and placed the locket on the waiting towel. The Picardy sighed and lay next to her chair.

'All right,' she told him, 'I can do this. It's not as if it's hundreds of years old or could hold the key to a centuries-old mystery or anything.'

Gus's tail waved and he put his head on her foot.

'Thanks,' she said. 'Your faith in me means a lot.'

She read the instructions then rubbed the balls of her thumbs over her fingertips, trying to stop them trembling. Picking up the locket, she turned it around and around while easing her fingernail into the freshly cleaned groove. She put some pressure on and grimaced at the solid resistance.

'Wishful thinking,' she murmured.

Taking a deep breath and using the delicate tools, Iris began work on the bent hinge. She soon realised how it was folded on itself and needed to be eased away from the spar so the locket could be opened. With one hand she inserted a tool that reminded her of a toothpick crossed with a flat-headed screwdriver, between the hinge and the spar. With her other hand she used a small pair of grippers on the hinge itself. She re-read the instructions and exerted careful pressure, feeling the hinge give a little beneath the grippers. She paused, drew a long breath and then continued. Time seemed suspended while she laboured until she heard the door open. Without losing pressure or grip she glanced at Michael returning. Along with his phone he was carrying a book she recognised and his laptop.

'Is that the book about Tudor rebellions?' she asked, returning her attention to the locket.

'Yes, it is. I think it's where I saw the boar's head.'

Iris frowned while easing more pressure onto the grippers and tool. She was rewarded by a slight movement as the two began to part. Michael settled at the other end of the table.

'How's it coming?'

'Slowly,' she murmured.

He grunted and began flicking through the book. Iris

tried not to be irritated by the noise. She focused all her attention on the minuscule movements needed to ease the hinge away while not damaging the locket. Gradually the joint peeled back beneath her ministrations. She took another calming breath, trying to shake the intense feelings, and glanced at Michael.

'What about the boar's head?' she asked.

'I'm not entirely sure. But in the back of my mind there's something about Mary.'

'Huh, good film but hardly relevant.'

She smiled at him and he grinned back.

'Oh, very good,' he said. 'But I meant Bloody Mary. Elizabeth's sister.'

Iris returned her attention to the locket.

'How many rebellions was she involved in?'

'A few. I'm still looking.'

Michael bent to the book once more. Iris slipped the toothpick blade tool further along the hinge and teased the golden edge upward with the grippers. Her hands ached and her eyes stung. She eased the tools away, putting them down and rubbing her cramped fingers. She considered how much more she had to go and with relief saw the hinge was three quarters released. She glanced at her husband, who was studying the photo he had taken and comparing it to the book.

'Have you found something?'

He nodded.

'Come and look,' he said.

She rose, dislodging Gus from her foot, and went to her husband. The book was open at a coat of arms. It depicted a red three-pointed shield surmounted by a yellow and red plume and surrounded by flurries of more red and yellow. A knight's helm hung from the top of the shield. A wide yellow band ran across the shield's centre which had in its middle a stylised black lion. But Iris's attention focused on the three ferocious white boar heads. Two positioned in the shield corners, one at the shield's pointed bottom. Iris bent, peering from the coat of arms to the photo on her husband's phone. All three boars' heads were identical to the one on the locket. She ran her finger over the picture, feeling breathless.

'Bloody hell! Whose coat of arms is that?'

Michael turned the page back.

'It belongs to the Wyatt family. And if I'm not mistaken, they had a pretty chequered history during Henry VIII and his daughter Mary's reigns.'

Iris stared at the picture and gripped Michael's shoulder.

'I knew it,' she said. 'I knew the locket wasn't just a random piece of jewellery. You look for any connection the Wyatts had to Amy Dudley or her husband and I'll get it open.'

She settled back to the locket and flexed her hands, trying to ease the last of the stiffness. She wiped the hinge with a cloth and reapplied the tools to the jewel. Curbing her impatience, she exerted the same minimal but consistent pressure and grimaced at the instant aching it caused. She heard a tapping and glanced at Michael to see he had opened the laptop and was typing; then the locket absorbed her attention. She didn't know how much time had passed when Michael suddenly spoke.

'So, Thomas Wyatt the Younger helped lead a rebellion against Queen Mary in 1554.'

'Six years before Amy Dudley was murdered?'

'Just so. There's a fair bit of dispute about the reasons behind Wyatt's rebellion. Some say it was in protest against Mary wanting to marry Prince Philip of Spain, others say it was about the Queen's intention to return England to the Catholic faith.' She heard Michael flick pages of the book.

'Frankly, I think it was more likely a mixture of the two.'

'Okay. But whatever the reasons, didn't the rebellion ultimately fail?'

'Indeed it did. Mary married Philip, much good that it did her, and ruled for a number of years. Hers was a terrible reign. She well earned the nickname Bloody Mary for all those she barbarically killed trying to drag England back to Rome.'

'What happened to Wyatt after the rebellion?'

'He surrendered and was thrown in the Tower of London. Before, during and after his trial he was savagely tortured. Mainly in an effort to get him to implicate the then Princess Elizabeth in the rebellion.'

'Goodness. Did he?'

'No, he did not. In fact, when he was about to be executed on Tower Hill, Wyatt made a speech taking full responsibility for the rebellion. Very clever actually because by doing so publicly he ensured that Elizabeth couldn't be implicated by rumour or someone else's false confessions.'

'That's amazing. Either he was indescribably loyal, or Elizabeth truly had no part in the scheme. Whichever it was Wyatt must have been a very brave soul to endure so much and not implicate Elizabeth to help himself.'

'Agreed.'

For a time there was silence but for the keys of the laptop. Iris focused on easing the hinge, feeling her foot going to sleep under Gus's head and trying to ignore it. Suddenly Michael gave a low whistle making the Picardy lift his head. Iris sagged a little with the relief and pins and needles rushed up her instep while she wriggled her toes.

'Did you find a connection to Amy Dudley?' she asked.

'No, but I've confirmed what I know about Thomas Wyatt, the rebellious younger Wyatt's father. He had history with Henry VIII and Anne Boleyn.'

Inching the grippers along she lifted another minuscule bit of the hinge and glanced at her husband.

'In what way?'

'Thomas Wyatt helped Cromwell with Henry VIII's controversial divorce from his first wife, Catherine of Aragon, which paved the way for the king to marry Anne Boleyn.'

Iris manipulated the tools to the last millimetres of the folded golden hinge. Michael continued, 'Wyatt was a royal ambassador and wrote a famous poem about Anne Boleyn likening her to a hind.'

'I've heard of that,' she said only half listening.

'Well, there was much more to the man's flirting than just that, if rumours are to be believed. There's a story about him making free with Anne's person at Hever Castle and another where the queen gave him a jewel which Henry VIII later discovered – he was not impressed.'

Iris continued to work on prising the final section of the hinge while Michael said, 'So, in 1536 Anne Boleyn was arrested, accused of plotting to kill the king, adultery and incest.'

'Incest?'

'Yes, she was accused of it with her brother, George.'

'Blimey. Was it true?'

'Highly unlikely as were all of the accusations. They were merely used to get rid of Anne Boleyn so Henry could move on and sire an heir. Anyway, four men and her brother were found guilty, hanged, drawn and quartered for carnal knowledge of the queen and she herself was executed. However, Thomas Wyatt was also arrested at the time, for dallying with Anne Boleyn, but he was released.'

The final joint suddenly unfolded all along the spar and the locket halves seemed to move slightly apart. She tried to quell her excitement but nevertheless her fingers trembled, and she swallowed. Taking a small pointed tool, not much bigger than a needle, she probed the groove between the locket halves, easing them apart.

'Michael, this is opening,' she said.

Her husband rose and stood behind her. The air in the kitchen seemed heavy and hard in her lungs. The two wings inched apart and then suddenly separated with something falling to the table. Iris stared at it, recognising a plaiting of intertwined reddish brown and black hair. Then her attention was entirely captured by the two wings of the locket and she turned them to the light. Each held a miniature portrait of fine detail; one depicting a man and the other a woman. Michael peered at one side.

'That's Anne Boleyn,' he said in an awed tone.

Iris murmured an agreement and then gazed at the man's picture. The heavy oils showed a strong face with a red beard and hair.

'So that must be Henry VIII,' she said, hearing the wonder in her voice. She studied it. 'A young Henry VIII, surely?'

She glanced at her husband, noting his look of stunned surprise, and frowned.

'What is it?'

Michael went to the laptop and turned it toward her. A portrait of a man sporting a red beard and hair filled the screen.

'Is that Henry VIII?' Iris asked.

'No, that's Thomas Wyatt.'

'You're joking?' She looked from the screen to the miniature. 'So, the picture in the locket could be either Henry VIII or Thomas Wyatt?'

'And the hair could be Anne Boleyn's twinned with Henry's or Thomas Wyatt's?'

'Bloody hell. Amy Dudley must've found this and

thought the rumours about Anne Boleyn and Thomas Wyatt were true. That Elizabeth was illegitimate. Is that what we're looking at here?'

Michael's face flushed and he rose, pacing the kitchen.

'It doesn't matter whether that's Henry or Thomas in the locket. What matters is that it's enough to cast doubt on Elizabeth's legitimacy. It would have been more than enough to cause a rebellion.'

'Shit, you're right. Then this is what the Watchers are after. This is why Amy Dudley was murdered.'

Michael abruptly sat and stared at the locket. Iris felt stunned, unable to breathe properly, and touched the gold rim while trying to pin down her fractured thoughts. The implications of the locket suddenly hit her, and she swayed, gripping the table edge.

'Oh my God, if Elizabeth I was ever doubted to be legitimate the monarchy could collapse or be severely damaged, no matter who was on the throne or how much time had passed.'

Michael nodded, his face pale in the stark lamplight.

'Either by rebellion or civil war in the past or today's press and anti-monarchists. They will take the royals apart.'

Iris sat and her fingers found Gus's fur while the memory of Foxcombe Valley and the shooting made her shudder.

'Oh shit, Michael. Not only have we got the locket, we've proof that Amy Dudley's murder has been covered up for centuries while a secret faction has been killing innocent people who have tried to find out the truth about it. Can you imagine the scandal it would cause if it was all made public?'

Her husband rose, poured two glasses of red wine and handed her one.

'It would be a disaster for the royal family because

at this stage we still don't know who orchestrated Amy Dudley's murder. The speculation on a member of the royal family, like Katherine Grey, being involved would be never ending.'

Iris sipped wine and glanced at the back door, seeking reassurance in the shot bolts.

'The Watchers haven't finished,' she said. 'The skull isn't enough. They're after the locket. What do we do?'

'Go to the press. First thing in the morning.'

She frowned, taking another sip of wine, and tried to imagine doing so. It would take phone calls, meetings, discussions... and then what?

'It would be never ending,' she said, echoing her husband.

'What do you mean?'

'Michael, don't you see, we would forever be the people who made the locket and all its connotations public. And I don't want us to be the ones who unleash a scandal that could severely harm or even destroy the monarchy. Can you imagine? We would never be left alone. The press would be all over us, not to mention the monarchists would hate us. Our lives as we know them would be over.' She ran a hand through her hair. 'I just want to let Amy Dudley rest in peace without the taint of suicide.' She gestured to the locket. 'Not all this.'

He sighed and settled into a chair.

'Yes, you're right. So, what about going to the police?'

Iris thought about it, talking to DI Fields. Explaining it all while handing the locket and Sam's and Gordon's documents over. And Gordon. They would take Gordon.

'And say what? We've got no actual proof the Watchers exist. Ruth's murderer is dead as far as they're concerned. Will could've been attacked by anyone.'

Michael looked grim.

'Not to mention implicating Zoe and Will in everything,' he said. 'And you're right, we've got nothing tangible to take to the police about the Watchers. So, we're back to the press.'

Iris turned the wine glass around and around, her gaze going from the miniatures to the braided hair and back again. She suddenly wished it had never opened, that it was all still secret and hidden somewhere the Watchers could never find it. Michael suddenly pulled the laptop toward him and started tapping.

'What is it?' she asked.

'Something's bothering me about the locket. I just want to check some dates. Ah, yes, here it is. Robert Dudley was imprisoned in the Tower by Mary until 1555 for his part in the Grey rebellion.'

'Right, so?'

'Well, given his noble status he was housed in relative comfort and allowed visits by Amy Dudley. It just so happens that during the same period Thomas Wyatt the Younger was imprisoned in the Tower for his rebellion.'

Iris's fingertips tingled on the locket edge with the painting depicting Anne Boleyn.

'Are you saying that Wyatt, knowing he was going to be executed, somehow got the pocket watch to Amy Dudley – is that possible?'

'It's not impossible. Perhaps there were secret messages between the prisoners who had rebelled against Mary? Or a bribed guard or two to safeguard the pocket watch to Dudley, thence to his wife? Only Wyatt never revealed the secret inside the watch. But however it was done, Amy Dudley came into possession of the pocket watch belonging to the Wyatts. She probably never thought to open it until the year she died.'

'That poor woman. Completely used, brutally murdered

and never left to rest properly.' Iris rubbed the golden edge, angry and sad all at once. 'And now what? We can't carry on like this, the Watchers won't rest. They need to be stopped.'

Michael shook his head, his expression morose. Iris dropped her hand to Gus, seeking comfort from the big dog's presence while Michael continued tapping on the computer. She found the noise strangely intrusive, scattering her thoughts, and she wished he would stop. She stared at the laptop back and her heart was suddenly furious in her chest.

'Wait, what if we publish everything we want to, anonymously? Online.'

Michael's eyes narrowed as he thought.

'That could work,' he said. 'We can put everything we know about Amy Dudley's murder, the coroner's report, Sam's notes and Gordon's discovery of the fingerprints online. Then send copies of everything to the press. We don't have to mention the locket or the Watchers.'

'Right. But that doesn't stop the Watchers.'

He stared at the locket halves and his expression hardened.

'What if we destroy it? Then everything's over, once and for all.'

Iris knew what suggesting that had cost him and tried to think her way through the connotations.

'But then we've got no proof as to why Amy Dudley was murdered. Does that matter?'

Her husband's expression turned thoughtful.

'I'm not sure. We haven't got the skull for forensic examination or the DNA as definitive proof of who she is and by that token we need everything we can get even if we don't publish it.'

'And would the Watchers believe us if we said we had destroyed it?' she asked, knowing the answer. 'They would want everything else as well. Sam and Gordon's notes, the coroner's report. We'd have to destroy it all and then they might still come after us because we know everything.'

'True. They don't seem to be the sort of people to leave loose ends behind.'

'Loose ends, that's a nice way of looking at us.'

Michael grimaced and studied the picture of the man in the locket. Iris drank some wine and the Watchers were large in her mind, swamping even Amy Dudley.

'They're going to come after it, no matter what we do,' she said. 'Why don't we publish about Amy Dudley's murder as we said, anonymously online and to the press without using the locket. Then involve the police. We could get DI Fields and DS Dens on our side. Show them the locket and explain about the Watchers.'

'Still no proof they exist.'

'Yes, but once we've told the inspector about the Watchers and how Stephen Sloane was part of it, she'll have to investigate.' An idea gripped her, making her breathless, and she swallowed. 'Michael, we can leave Whitebarn.'

'What are you talking about?'

'Look, the Watchers are bound to come here looking for the locket, right?'

'Especially after we publish anonymously online. They know we have it and might publish it or hide it again. They're running out of options.'

'So, we tell the inspector everything and let her have any surveillance she wants, with us out of the way.'

'We can't leave the animals.'

'No, we can't. But we can take them to Foxcombe Valley in makeshift stables and pens in the woods and stay there in the caravan while the police are at Whitebarn. The valley isn't exactly safe, I know that, but I'm willing to bet the Watchers will come here first. If DI Fields is here waiting for them, then it's over. She might even let police stay with us at Foxcombe as protection.'

'And if not?'

'We can make arrangements with Thomas, Pete and others to take the animals and we can go somewhere, even Scotland to stay with my mother for a while.'

She hated the idea but could think of no other way to beat the Watchers and keep everyone she loved safe. Michael looked dubious.

'But what about Zoe and Will? We can't risk them being prosecuted.'

'We don't need to tell the police about Gordon's body and we no longer have Amy Dudley, so that puts Zoe and Will in the clear.'

'What about the photos of the skull we're planning to publish?'

Iris's thoughts were clear and needle sharp.

'We took them before we realised what we had, then the skull was stolen from here. Who's going to say different and be believed? Not the Watchers, that's for sure.'

'Right, so the police catch whatever Watchers come here and then what? That might not be all of them, in fact it probably won't be.'

'True. But once we prove they exist the police will have to investigate the whole lot. Take down the entire faction. We'll be safe and so will the locket, at least safer than we are now.'

They stared at each other and Iris saw her relief mirrored on Michael's face. She felt a loosening in her guts and shoulders.

'All right, are we agreed then? We'll publish anonymously online and to the press, leaving out the locket and Watchers? Then go to DI Fields?'

Michael nodded, his expression determined.

'I'm not lecturing tomorrow, and I can easily move my student meetings, so I'll phone in sick. We can draft something and then find a suitable forum to post on.'

He took her hand, and she found a smile for him. Her heart and nerves were blurred bird's wings and the locket filled her gaze.

'Can you make a start on the draft now?' she asked. 'I'll take photos of the locket and then put it in the safe.'

Her husband rose and kissed her, before settling to the laptop. Iris arranged the locket halves on the towel and took photos. All the while, her thoughts ricocheted from Amy Dudley to the Watchers and spiralled amidst terror and anxiety. Taking the locket and with Gus following, she paused at the foot of stairs and turned instead to the study. Inside she watched the cameras wheel reassuringly through their cycles, showing nothing untoward. She checked the silent alarm was on and the front door was locked before taking the locket to the safe.

CHAPTER THIRTY-TWO

Zoe couldn't remember getting home from the hospital nor going to bed but woke the next morning fully dressed on top of the covers. The sun was streaming through her window and in a panic she called the hospital, to be told Will was resting as comfortably as could be expected and, yes, she could visit.

An hour later she entered the ICU ward and swallowed at the sight of her best friend. He had a tube in his nose and was attached to various machines. The left side of his face seemed to be all metal wires and padding with his left eye bruised and swollen shut. The white of the cast on his left arm, foot and ankle contrasted with the blue bed covers. Her vision blurred with tears and she couldn't speak past her constricted throat. Guilt left her empty and distraught then filled with shame. She longed to hold him and stroked his uninjured right hand. His good eyelid flickered slowly open and his gaze focused on her.

'Hi Will,' she whispered.

He squeezed her fingers, and she felt her tears fall warm then cold on their clasped hands.

'I'm so sorry.'

A nurse appeared and Zoe said hello without moving or taking her eyes from Will's.

'He's on morphine for the pain and knows he can't talk,' the nurse said. 'But he's managed to write some things down for his parents and the police.'

'The police have already been?'

The nurse's mouth drew down in a thin line and her expression was disapproving.

'First thing this morning.' She produced a small whiteboard and a pen while looking at Will. 'Do you feel up to it?'

Will let go of Zoe and held out his hand for the board. With deft movements, the nurse gave him the board and set the pen in his hand, so the nib rested on the white surface. She caught Zoe's gaze.

'You'll need to steady the board for him and I'm afraid you can't have long.'

She checked the machines and left with a nod. Zoe held the board and Will moved the pen laboriously across the white surface. She read the shaky words.

'"Cop no rembr." You told the police you can't remember what happened?'

Will wrote a 'Y' and his gaze on hers was steady if a little glazed in his pale face. She read fear and determination beneath the exhaustion and medication.

'But you can?'

He pointed to the 'Y' with the pen.

'Oh shit, Will, why did you lie?'

He wrote a 'U' and his gaze never left hers. She abruptly sat, resting her forehead on his arm and cried. She felt his wrist move and she looked through blurred eyes to see him writing.

'"Tel me,"' she read and looked at him. 'About the skull?'

He pointed to the 'Y' again, his movements slow and his breathing harsher. She glanced about wondering how much time she had and where the nurse was. Then in hurried, whispered words she told Will everything about Amy Dudley and the Watchers.

CHAPTER THIRTY-THREE

At just after 7am that same morning, Iris stowed a shotgun and a box of shells beneath the bed. Michael, emerging from the shower with a towel wrapped around his waist, stared at her.

'Where did you get that?'

'It's Thomas's. I borrowed it.'

'What did he say?'

'He doesn't know. I used my spare key and took it from the lock-box in his Land Rover. I told Thomas you're poorly and took it after he left with the lads for the top pasture.'

'Right. Is that wise?'

Iris sat on the edge of the bed feeling tiredness weigh her mind and body like old iron muffled in wool.

'I don't know,' she said. 'But it makes me feel better.'

He settled next to her and put an arm round her shoulders. She rested her head against his naked chest.

'It's nearly over,' he said. 'Everything's ready to publish and the press packs are done. We just need to find the right forums to post on this morning.'

She closed her eyes, letting her weariness take over for a moment.

'Thomas was so nice about doing the feeds without me,' she murmured. 'I felt terrible lying to him.'

She looked up at Michael and he leant back so he could see her face.

'As soon as we've spoken to the police, we can tell him everything,' her husband said. 'He'll want to know why we're moving the animals to Foxcombe Valley anyway.'

She nodded, her throat tight, and tears inexplicably stung her eyes. Abruptly Gus rose from his bed, staring at the open doorway. A growl, low and menacing, rumbled in his throat. From downstairs came the quiet sound of the front door closing and footsteps on the tiled hall. Iris froze, held against her husband and felt his muscles taut around her. She stared up at him, seeing her own terror in his expression. Gus took a stalking step toward the threshold, his body tense, and his growl deepened. Iris rose, crossing the room, and silently closed the bedroom door. While Michael pulled on some clothes, she took the shotgun out and loaded it. Together they manoeuvred a chest of drawers in front of the door and settled on the end of the bed.

'We should call the police,' Michael whispered.

Iris nodded, her gaze on the door while her husband took out his phone. Iris listened, straining to hear anyone coming up the stairs, but heard only silence and Gus's low continuous growl. She put her hand on Michael's, halting his motions.

'Wait,' she murmured. 'Listen.'

They listened to the increasingly loud silence punctuated by Gus's growls. Iris rose, carrying the gun, and went to the door. Still she heard nothing. Putting her head to the jamb join she closed her eyes, trying to feel anyone moving, breathing beyond the wood. From below came the faint sound of footsteps and the front door closing again. Frowning, she glanced at Michael.

'That sounded like someone leaving,' she said. 'Could Thomas have come in for something?'

'The front door was locked, but he does have a key for emergencies.'

Together they moved the chest of drawers from the doorway and cautiously opened it a crack. Hearing and seeing nothing untoward they opened it entirely. The hallway was hushed, and sunlight spilt through the landing window. No sound came from below. Gus shouldered passed Iris, trotted out and down the stairs. She retrieved the gun and with Michael beside her followed the Picardy, still hearing nothing unusual. Downstairs, they moved cautiously through the kitchen and living room, finding nothing worrying, nothing disturbed.

'It must've been Thomas come back,' Iris said. 'Maybe he needed something from the study?'

'Odd he didn't say hello, though.'

'Probably thought you were sleeping, and I was upstairs with you.'

She went to the study, opening the door to find it looking normal. She glanced at the monitors seeking reassurance, only for them to blankly look back.

'Did you turn the cameras off?'

Michael came in.

'No.' He looked at the panel. 'Shit, the alarm is off too.'

They stared at each other. Suddenly Gus's barks rent the air and he scrabbled at the front door. Iris, thoughts full of blood and guns, raced upstairs rather than risk opening the door. She stared out the landing window. A horse truck was pulled up to the stables and a figure wearing a black mask stood by the lowered ramp. Even as Iris watched, Shiloh was led out to the ramp by a second masked person while a third figure followed, leading Jasper after the mare toward the lorry.

'What the fuck, they're stealing the horses!'

She ran downstairs and, flinging open the door, raced to

the stables with Gus loping ahead, barking. Behind her she heard Michael following, calling the police. The tableau at the stables froze, staring at the charging, enraged dog and woman. Gus rammed into the thief leading Shiloh, fastening on a leg. The man screamed and dropped the rope. Spooked, Shiloh reared, dancing sideways off the ramp and Jasper, snorting, tried to follow. Blue and Honky started neighing and kicking at the stables. The figure holding the foal dragged at Jasper's head, swearing. Iris raised the shotgun.

'Get the fuck away from my horses or I'll shoot,' she yelled.

Suddenly the lorry's engine started and Iris realised the third thief had disappeared. The one holding Jasper tried to drag the foal into the lorry. Jasper neighed and leant back on his haunches, desperately trying to get to his mother. Shiloh's reply was deafening. She reared, striking out at the thief holding her foal. The man ducked, barely avoiding the lethal hoof, but hung on to Jasper. Iris raised the shotgun, firing into the air. Jasper whinnied, high pitched and terrified, eyes rolling white. Shiloh screamed and lashed out again, catching the thief in the back. He hurtled forward, crashing off the side of the ramp, face crunching into the metal and tearing the mask off. On the ramp Shiloh snuffled her foal while Jasper trembled and gave little whinnies of fright. The lorry's gears crunched and the engine revved. Michael hauled the door open and scrambled inside the cab. The engine died. Iris heard a scuffle and then her husband emerged dragging the slight, masked figure with him. He put the person into a half nelson, driving the thief to their knees. Gus was still worrying the first robber, whose screams had turned to sobs.

'Gus, leave,' Iris called.

The Picardy let go and backed, growling, his teeth

showing. The thief scrabbled away further into the lorry while Gus stood guard between the robber and the horses. Iris saw little blood though the torn jeans and knew the dog had barely grazed the skin. In the distance sirens sounded. The figure on the ground gave a moan and lifted his head, then collapsed into unconsciousness. The face was a bloody mess thanks to the ramp and gravel, but Iris had recognised it, nonetheless.

'What the hell?'

She exchanged a bewildered look with Michael, who suddenly bent and pulled his captive's mask away. They stared at the thieves, then each other.

'I don't understand,' Iris said.

The police car turned into the drive, storming along and spewing dust behind it. Iris hastily lowered the shotgun and slipped into Blue's box. She unloaded the spent shell and stowed the firearm in the shadows. She was checking Shiloh and Jasper as the police officers reached the lorry.

Nearly two hours later, the police left Whitebarn having taken statements following interminable waits and questions in the farmhouse. The thieves had long been taken to the station. In the yard the lorry was being put onto a police tow truck. Thomas and the lads led the horses and Honky to the paddock. The sky had darkened with grey clouds and, shivering, Iris closed the front door. She went to the kitchen and kissed the top of Michael's head where he was settled at the table.

'I tried calling Zoe,' Iris said, 'but she didn't answer.'

'Try again,' he said.

Iris took her phone out of her pocket just as it started to ring. Glancing at the screen, she answered.

'Oh darling, I'm so glad you rang.'

'I've just left the hospital,' Zoe said.

'Right, the hospital.' She exchanged a look with Michael. 'How's Will?'

'He's conscious and doing okay,' Zoe replied. 'He hasn't told the police anything.'

She drew an audible breath. 'Here's the thing, Mum. The chap who had Amy Dudley rang me. He managed to extract the DNA before the skull was taken. It's now sequenced and ready to match to a living relative.'

Everything else fled Iris's thoughts and she gripped Michael's shoulder.

'Shit, that's amazing.'

'Yes. He's willing to either hand the results over or match it to a relative, for a fee. Will was supposed to pay him but…'

'How much does he want?' Iris interrupted.

'Four thousand pounds.'

'Done,' Iris stated.

They agreed the details and Iris steeled herself to speak.

'Zoe, there's something…'

A beeping sounded and Zoe said.

'Mum, sorry, I've to go. Work are calling, probably about Will. Love you. Talk later.'

She rang off and Iris stared at the screen.

'I didn't get a chance to tell her.'

'Don't worry, we can call her again. Now tell me, what did she say and how much is it costing us?'

She told Michael about the DNA and his expression became jubilant.

'If we can find a living relative and prove it's Amy Dudley, it will add so much weight to our narrative.' His expression faltered. 'But I don't want to wait to publish.'

Iris silently agreed, imagining Watchers breaking in, stealthy and dark. Finding her and Michael helpless and asleep before cutting and slicing. Branding.

'Same here. I want to publish as soon as possible so we can get the police involved. Get everything over and done with. So, Zoe said she can get pay for the DNA tonight. I'm thinking if the genealogist hasn't found a living relative, we just publish anyway and add the DNA evidence later.'

Michael agreed and put the kettle on while Iris rang the genealogist.

CHAPTER THIRTY-FOUR

Zoe ended the call with Arrant laboratories. Her supervisor had been horrified at Will's attack and insisted she take the rest of the day off. Zoe caught the bus home thinking to eat, shower and change then head back to the hospital before her meeting with the DNA chap that night. Walking along the road, her thoughts full of Watchers and Will, she noted a police car outside her house. She slowed, Amy Dudley's skull swamping her mind, making her guts tighten. She halted, wanting nothing more than to turn and go back the way she had come. She shook her head, reasoning that it must be about the attack and they would only come back. Besides, what if they had seen her already? She strode on and hoped she didn't look as guilty as she felt. As she approached the car a man and a woman she didn't recognise got out. The woman was in uniform while the man wasn't.

'Zoe Shaw?'

'Yes?'

'I'm Detective Inspector Gareth Ross with Major Crimes and this is Sergeant Green. Can we talk to you inside, please?'

She asked to see identification, which they produced. She stared at the badges, worrying about Watchers and knowing she would have no idea if they were fake or not.

But feeling she had little choice she led the way into her house. On reaching the living room her phone rang and she answered.

'Sorry, Mum, I can't talk right now. The police are here. I'll call you after.'

She ended the call without giving Iris a chance to speak and offered the officers seats. They settled on the sofa and she took the chair, making an effort not to fiddle with her jumper.

'Is it about the attack?' she asked in what she hoped was a calm voice.

'I wouldn't really call it an attack,' Ross said. 'More of a robbery gone wrong.'

She bristled, heat flooding her at his tone.

'Will could've died so I think attack is entirely appropriate under the circumstances,' she snapped. 'And I don't appreciate you trying to lessen what happened to my friend.'

The officers exchanged a puzzled look and Ross leant forward.

'I'm sorry, Miss Shaw, but who's Will? Does he work at Whitebarn?'

'What's Whitebarn got to do with anything? I'm talking about the attack yesterday on my friend Will, at his flat here in London.'

The two looked at each other once again and a dark feeling gripped Zoe.

'What is it? What's happened at Whitebarn? My parents are all right, aren't they? Of course, they are, I've just spoken to Mum. Sorry, I'm babbling. Just tell me, please?'

Ross cleared his throat.

'An attempt was made this morning to steal two horses, a mare and a foal, from your parents' farm.'

'Oh my God! What happened?'

'We have reason to believe the thieves knew the usual farm routine and expected the horses to be unguarded. Fortunately, your parents were unexpectedly at home. They discovered the thieves in the act of taking the horses and were able to alert the authorities while preventing the perpetrators from leaving.'

'Thank God for that. What bastards would try and steal Shiloh and Jasper?'

'How do you know it was those particular horses, Miss Shaw?'

'You said a foal. The only foal is Jasper, and it stands to reason that to take Jasper they must take Shiloh as well. The foal wouldn't be able to leave without his dam, he's not weaned yet. Besides, Shiloh would have raised merry hell if they had tried to take him without her.'

Ross nodded and his sergeant wrote something in her notebook. Zoe, watching, suddenly felt a chill creep across the back her neck.

'Why are you here?' she asked.

'We're getting to that,' Ross said. 'Do you know a man called Theodore Tallis?'

'Theo's my boyfriend.'

'When did you last see Mr Tallis?'

'I don't understand, what's that got to do with anything?'

'Can you answer the question please, Miss Shaw?'

'Fine. I saw Theo four days ago just before he went on a business trip to Wales.'

'And you've spoken to him in that time, yes?'

'Yes, he's rung several times. Although now I think about it, not for the last two days. But the reception is terrible where he is. Look, what's going on?'

'I have to tell you, we arrested Mr Tallis this morning.'

'Arrested? What on earth for?'

'He was caught trying to steal your parents' horses.'

'Don't be ridiculous! Theo would never do such a thing.'

The officers gazed at her sympathetically. Zoe looked wildly about, seeking escape from these people, from what they were saying. Her thoughts battered as if caught in a tornado. She desperately wanted Theo to appear and tell them what a mistake it all was. The officers kept talking, asking questions. She seemed to see herself from outside and hear her answers as if spoken by someone else. Her thoughts became numbed and she responded automatically to what was put to her. Suddenly she was at the front door and the officers were leaving. Sergeant Green paused at the threshold.

'Is there anyone we can contact for you?'

Zoe struggled to focus on her.

'No,' she managed. 'I'm going to call my mum.'

The officer nodded and left.

Two hours later Zoe settled at the kitchen table at Whitebarn. Michael made cups of tea and Iris held her daughter's hand while trying to find words that could comfort.

'I don't understand,' Zoe said for the second time. 'Theo's a thief.'

Iris sighed; the revelations were still raw in her own mind and she couldn't imagine how Zoe was feeling.

'Theo's not just a thief,' she said gently. 'He's a black-market trader. Specialising in protected wildlife and high-end animals.'

'And Rosalind is in on it as well?'

'I'm afraid so. She was here too. Driving the lorry they were going to use to take Shiloh and Jasper. It was such a shock.'

Michael grunted agreement while the kettle boiled.

'I nearly broke the woman's arm before I realised who

it was,' he said.

'How do you know all this?' Zoe asked. 'Could it be a mistake?'

'I'm sorry, Zoe, but no. Rosalind turned on Theo the second they got caught, spilling everything to the police and us on the driveway. Apparently, they've been doing it for years under aliases but because we knew them, they had to use their real names. The police had been tracking their aliases for months when they suddenly disappeared.'

'But why Shiloh and Jasper?'

'Shiloh because they had to take her to take Jasper. He was the one they really wanted for a Saudi buyer, it seems, wanting an Andalusian stud with a pedigree.'

'And Jasper's sire is tipped to be an Olympian,' Zoe said, her mouth tightening.

'Exactly. All that interest in Whitebarn, the horses and staying here was Theo laying plans and understanding our routine. According to Rosalind, they found out about Shiloh being pregnant at Josephine's funeral and it went from there.'

'Bastards,' her daughter muttered, eyes tear bright. 'How did he do it this morning?'

'Theo assumed I would be up in the top pasture as usual with Thomas and the lads for half an hour with Michael having left for work.'

'Thank God you guys were home.'

'I have to say he scared the bejesus out of us. We thought he was a Watcher. Anyway, Theo got in the house using a duplicate key he had made. Probably stolen while he was staying here.'

Zoe looked appalled and Iris squeezed her hand.

'Clearly the man has no conscience,' she continued. 'Anyway, once inside, Theo then turned off the cameras and silent alarm. He even took the papers, birth certificates and everything for both horses from the study, presumably to destroy them. The police found forged documents in the lorry including fake passports for both horses. It was very well planned.'

'And me. He used me, didn't he?'

'Oh darling, I'm so sorry.'

'He lied about everything. Everything.'

Zoe's face was streaked with tears and Iris couldn't bear it. She swallowed her fury at Theo and hugged her daughter. Gus's whiskery face appeared at Zoe's side and he nudged her with his big Picardy nose. She hiccoughed and stroked his scruffy head. He put his front paws on the chair edge and licked her face. Iris let go and her daughter hugged the dog.

'Oh Gus, I've been such an idiot,' Zoe whispered.

Iris rubbed her back and Michael put the mugs of steaming tea on the table. Gus got down and Zoe rose and washed her face of tears and Picardy kisses. Iris settled next to Michael and held his hand, conveying her worry with a squeeze. He nodded and went to their daughter, giving her a cuddle and whispering words of comfort that Iris couldn't hear. She drew a long breath, determined not to let Zoe see how upset she was. She joined their hug and then they all settled at the table with their tea.

'So, we've got an appointment to see the genealogist this afternoon,' Iris said. 'Do you fancy coming along?'

'Sure, why not,' Zoe's tone sounded flat.

'She wouldn't explain her findings over the phone,' Iris continued brightly. 'Apparently it's too complicated. We're hopeful, but your dad's not convinced.'

Michael grimaced.

'I just think if she's found a living relative, she would've said. How complicated does it have to be?'

Iris tried very hard not to feel anxious about the visit.

Instead, she talked about what they had found inside the locket and showed Zoe what they intended to post online and to the press. She explained their plan about the Watchers and the police. Zoe seemed to be listening but there was a blankness to her expression and her gaze wandered around the kitchen. Tears began tracking down Zoe's cheeks again and she suddenly buried her head in her arms on the table, sobbing.

'Oh sweetheart,' Iris said. 'I know. It's horrible.'

She pulled her chair to sit next to her daughter and stroked her hair. Zoe raised her head and took the tissue Michael held out.

'Why, Mum? Why did he do this to me?'

'Because he's a heartless monster and a complete arsehole. Hopefully he'll get his todger cut off as punishment.'

Zoe hiccoughed a laugh and blew her nose.

'Todger and ball sack,' she said.

'Both. With no pain relief,' Michael said. 'By a man called Trevor who'll use a blunt spoon.'

They were all chuckling now.

'Or at the very least go to prison for a long time,' Zoe said. 'Bastard deserves that.'

'I think we can all agree there,' Iris said.

Zoe took her and Michael's hands.

'I'm so sorry I brought that scumbag into our lives as much as I did,' she said.

'It wasn't your fault,' Michael replied. 'He would've found a way in somehow, used me or your mum to get the information he needed, I believe that utterly. Arseholes like Theo will always find a way to manipulate their way to what they want.'

'Thank God I never told him about Amy Dudley,' Zoe said.

Iris squeezed her daughter's hand once more and Michael nodded, looking relieved. Zoe continued, 'Okay. I'm going to feel crap for a long time about what he did to me, but thankfully it's over. Shiloh and Jasper are safe, which is the main thing. The bastard will get what he deserves at least in terms of prison and that's as good a revenge as any.' She drew a deep breath and managed a smile. 'All right, tell me again about the locket and publishing. I didn't really take it in before.'

Iris's thoughts seemed to have coalesced with telling her daughter the first time.

'Before I tell you again, I think we should get Thomas in here and tell him too.'

'I thought we were going to wait until after we'd published,' Michael said.

'I know, but I'd rather tell him now, get the animals moved and then publish. That way they're all out of any danger that much sooner.'

Zoe frowned.

'What do you mean move the animals, where to?'

'Foxcombe Valley. Look, I'll tell you everything once we've got Thomas in here.'

So saying, Iris rose and with Gus at her heels fetched the farm manager's purloined shotgun and went to find her oldest friend.

CHAPTER THIRTY-FIVE

Late that afternoon, the Shaws entered Theresa Thirsk's yellow-bricked terraced house in Oxford. The genealogist was a stout and smiley woman in her mid-forties who chatted easily while leading the way through a narrow hallway festooned with photographs of her family and cats. She ushered the Shaws into what must have once been a dining room but was now a comfy office. A desk, impressive computer array, two floor-to-ceiling bookcases, photocopier and filing cabinet dominated one half. The other half held a large table which was covered by a patterned silk cloth. Chairs were grouped about the table.

Theresa gestured for the Shaws to be seated, offering tea or coffee. Iris, fretting about Watchers and the animals being moved, asked for water. Michael and Zoe opted for tea. It seemed to take a long time for the drinks to come but eventually Theresa returned carrying a tray with teapot, cups, milk and sugar and glass of water. She was followed by a tubby tabby cat who disappeared beneath the table. Iris was suddenly glad they had left Gus with Thomas preparing the makeshift pens and the animals to be moved. Theresa fussed, pouring and furnishing everyone with drinks while Iris's impatience tightened to breaking. Finally, the genealogist took a seat next to the table and smiled at them.

'All right, so I began with this name you gave me. From there it was a bit difficult as the family seemed to vanish. But after quite a lot of digging I followed them to Wales where they flourished. However, by the eighteenth century there only remained a daughter of the line, who married into a well-to-do family.'

In a practiced movement she turned two inches of cloth, revealing the top of a big sheet of paper filled with names, dates and lines. Iris bit back a sigh, realising with a sinking feeling that the woman wasn't going to be hurried to the present day. The Shaws rose and Michael peered at the paper tracing the lines with a finger.

'A Hester Mason who had three boys,' he murmured.

Theresa picked up her tea and took a sip.

'Indeed. The family continued in Wales for some time.'

Iris longed to yank the cloth away but settled in her chair, gripping the glass of water. She noted Michael's jaw was set and Zoe looked irritated. Theresa seemed unaware of their impatience and merely ploughed on.

'It increased over two generations with mainly boys. Not such a good thing when the First World War broke out as most of the sons were too young to have married but were old enough to fight. Sadly, nearly all of them did perish in the war,' she said. 'But one eldest child married in 1902 and lived long enough for the line to continue. See here.

The genealogist folded more cloth back revealing a few descendants. Iris bit her top lip and fought the urge to hasten the woman, fearing it would take longer if she were brusque. Michael sipped his tea, his gaze nailed to the paper. Zoe's knuckles were white where she gripped the table edge as if wanting to pull the cloth to one side and reveal the whole tree beneath. Theresa ran her fingertip along the names and turned the cloth once again.

Theresa pointed. Iris put her glass down and followed her finger.

'Lawrence,' she read aloud. 'Died in 1915. His wife, Ethel, never remarried and she died in 1918.'

Michael murmured something about the First World War. Theresa turned the cloth a little. Zoe followed the line.

'But they had two children,' she said. 'Twins, born in 1904, a daughter called Emily and a son, also named Lawrence.'

Theresa nodded and replaced the cup on its saucer, turning it just so.

'Yes, it seems Lawrence was a family name. Now, I do have more information, but I haven't added any of it to the tree yet. You rang before I could finish it.' Theresa sounded put out. 'But you were so insistent on the phone and I do have the results, so here we are.' Her smile looked forced and Iris wanted to yell at her to hurry up. The genealogist picked up her teacup, contemplating the contents, and continued, 'You will, of course, get the finished tree. But as you wanted to know today, you'll have to bear with me as I tell you my final results rather than my preferred way of unveiling them for you.'

'That's great. Thanks,' Iris managed. 'We appreciate you doing this at such short notice. Please continue, it's fascinating.'

Theresa preened a little, her expression mollified. She put the teacup down once more, removed glasses from her pocket and put them on. She produced a sealed envelope and handed it to Michael.

'Inside you'll find my invoice,' she said. 'As discussed on the phone I will expect payment today as you'll have all the information. I've a card machine if cash is an issue.'

She smiled at them and opened a notebook, turning pages and making small sounds to herself. The Shaws exchanged glances and Michael shook his head, looking as exasperated as Iris felt. The genealogist turned a few more pages.

'Aha, here we are.' She nodded and looked at them. 'The boy twin, Lawrence, did marry. But he didn't have any children. The girl, Emily, also married. I've got here that her husband died in 1930 and Emily herself a year later at the age of, yes, twenty-seven.'

Iris frowned trying to work out what all the dates meant.

'So, her twin brother, Lawrence, if he were alive would be over a hundred by now.'

Theresa's lips pursed and she nodded.

That's right. Lawrence actually died a few years ago. His wife, who was some ten years younger than he was, passed away two years ago.'

Michael looked unhappy and Zoe wooden with her expression shuttered closed. Iris settled deeper into her chair, despair covering her like a thick blanket.

'That's it then,' she said.

'Actually,' Theresa said slowly, 'Emily died in childbirth but the child, a son, survived.'

A bright thread twisted through Iris. Michael looked sharply at the genealogist.

'What happened to him, Emily's son?'

Suddenly the tabby cat jumped onto the table. Theresa tutted and immediately lifted him.

'Apologies, Franklin is meant to stay outside when I've got clients. Aren't you, you naughty boy? But he does love to sit on the paper and sneaks in when I'm not looking. Come along, Franklin.'

She carried the cat out. Michael rested his hand on Iris's arm, and she found a smile for him. Zoe's finger's beat along the table edge and her expression was tight with frustration. Theresa re-settled in her chair and bent forward, fussing with the cloth covering the table and tree. Iris gripped her hands together to stop from shaking the woman.

'Please,' she said. 'Tell us about Emily's son.'

'Of course. His name is Colin Hall, and he lives in Cardiff with his wife, Gail.'

'He's alive?'

'Oh, very much so. Now, they have four children and seven grandchildren,'

Iris let out an explosive breath and found she couldn't stop smiling. *Twelve living relatives*. She looked at Michael and saw her relief mirrored in his expression. Zoe chortled and hugged her father. Theresa continued ignorant of the Shaw's jubilation.

'I couldn't find any link to your family at all.'

The genealogist looked at Iris who frowned.

'I don't understand,' she said.

'That's why you employed me, wasn't it, to find your cousins from this family line?'

Michael and Zoe became still while Iris managed a nod.

'Ah, yes,' she said. 'That's right. Oh, what a shame we're not related. Still, it's wonderful to know. Thank you. And we can take the information about Colin Hall now, can we?'

'Certainly, it's all public information, births, deaths and marriages. And your tree, don't forget.'

'My tree?'

Theresa's expression flitted with annoyance which she smoothed away and smiled.

'Naturally, I had to investigate your family tree as well.' She produced a rolled page tied with a green ribbon.

'I completed it first, please do make sure it's all in order.'

She held out the parchment. Iris took it, unrolling and glancing at the contents. She went still and re-read names and dates.

'This can't be right,' Iris said, looking from the page to the genealogist.

A frown pinched Theresa's eyebrows together.

'I assure you it is,' she said, bristling.

Iris turned the parchment to her and pointed.

'No, look, here. You've listed Walter and Josephine Guard as being my father's aunt and uncle, but they're my mother's relatives.'

Theresa consulted her notebook, turning the pages rapidly until she stopped and read a section. She looked at Iris and smiled.

'Absolutely not. Mr and Mrs Guard were your father, Adam's relatives. Would you like me to explain my findings?'

Iris rubbed her forehead and then glanced at Michael who nodded.

'Please do,' she said.

'Adam and married your mother, Trudi in 1954. A year later they had you, their only child. And I'm so sorry but as you know he passed away a few days after you were born.'

She paused, looking sad. Iris swallowed and felt Michael's hand on hers but couldn't look away from the genealogist. Theresa continued.

'Your mother re-married a month after Adam's death and you both took the new chap's name.'

'Patrick Glass.'

'Yes, that's right. Adam's mother and father passed away in the sixties and seventies respectively. Adam's father was an only child. His mother, your grandmother, had a brother, Walter, who did marry but he passed some years ago childless and his wife, Josephine, passed a few weeks ago. Your mother is an only child, and you have no other living relatives, I'm sorry to say.'

She turned the notebook so they could see her research.

Iris couldn't focus and her hands were too numb to take the book.

'But they never said. They must have known, but they never said.'

Iris felt bereft and angry, leaden and lightheaded, unable to comprehend what was happening.

'We should go,' she said abruptly. 'I want to go.'

Michael's grip tightened on her hand then let go. She heard him speaking to the genealogist, taking the information about Colin Hall and paying the woman, but it all seemed distant noise. Someone, Zoe, she realised, touched her shoulder.

'Mum, we're going.'

Iris managed to stand and found a smile for Theresa.

'Thank you,' she said. 'For everything.'

Theresa nodded and moved quicker than Iris would have thought possible. The genealogist hurried out and led them out to the narrow hall, nearly tripping over Franklin on the way. At the front door Iris followed her husband and daughter outside and thanked the woman again. Theresa didn't smile and pecked a nod as she closed the door.

Outside Iris' barely felt the chill autumnal air, her mind tripped over her own family revelations and she was suddenly breathless. An unexpected memory of her stepfather, laughing and running alongside her pony took Iris by surprise. But suddenly Patrick faltered and staggered, covered in blood and his face shattered. Iris gripped the cold brickwork and closed her eyes against the world abruptly tilting like a fairground ride then drew a deep breath and followed her family to the car.

Chapter Thirty-Six

In the parked car Iris rang her mother and asked about Adam, Walt and Josephine. Trudi's cool manner flattened her anger and she listened in disbelief to her mother's reasoning. Ending the call, she tried to digest what had been said and shifted so she could look at Michael next to her and Zoe on the back seat.

'That woman is unbelievable,' she said. 'Mother made Walt and Josephine promise never to speak to me about Adam, or she wouldn't let them see me.'

'But why?' Michael asked.

'Because, supposedly, it was just too painful for her to talk about Adam, and she didn't want me asking questions or being told things by others. But now… now it's fine to talk about him apparently. Mother then reminded me what an awful thirty-six hour labour she suffered with me. Then she told me that Adam had died in a plane crash travelling home because and I quote, "you were being born".'

Silence filled the car. Michael shook his head.

'Well, I don't quite know what to say.'

'Oh, there's more.' Iris heard the bitterness in her voice. 'After my step-father died she thought telling me about Adam would just drag all the unpleasant memories up for her and she couldn't cope with it.'

'Is that why she went to Scotland so soon after your

step-father died, she couldn't cope?'

'That and because, so she says, Whitebarn was just too bleak and dismal for her to stay.'

Zoe sat forward her expression confused and dark.

'Why didn't Walt and Josephine say anything after Grandma left?'

'According to her, Walt and Josephine agreed not to say anything because of the state I was in.' Iris recalled her devastation at Patrick's death and the ongoing trauma it caused her, recognising that discovering Walt and Josephine's deception would have broken her trust in them completely, leaving her entirely alone. 'I guess they just felt it was better for me, to carry on with Mother's lies.' Her thoughts flailed around her mother and their difficult relationship. 'When everything is over, I need to go to Leith and get her to talk to me properly for once.'

She shifted back in her seat, fighting off tears. Michael and Zoe seemed to understand, neither pressing her further or attempting to fill the silence.

The drive back to Whitebarn blurred for Iris. She stared, unseeing, out of the window with her thoughts chaotic, fastening on slivers of her childhood, rushing to grief for those gone and for her own ignorance. Her memories and emotions were like speeding mercury that slipped and slid through her. A part of the conversation with her mother was on continual loop and she couldn't understand why. She forced her focus on the snippet of conversation, trying to discern its importance.

"I'm sure they felt as if Adam dying and Patrick's suicide were somehow my fault."

She shook her head, feeling angry. She knew in her very bones and soul that Josephine and Walt would never blame her mother for such things. No one would. But oh, she now realised how Adam's death had driven her mother away from her emotionally and physically. More, how Patrick's suicide must have compounded her mother's fear and desperation which had literally made the woman run from her past and only child. Iris felt sick and saddened that something so falsely felt could have caused so much damage. Her breath hitched and she swallowed. Something broke open inside and lightness was released to wash over her in a tingling wave, making her gasp.

'It was no one's fault,' she whispered.

Michael glanced at her, but she ignored him, too caught up in the revelation that stormed her thoughts and smashed into the emptiness like a tsunami.

'It wasn't my fault,' she said in wonder.

'What wasn't?' Michael asked, his eyes on the road.

She looked at him with new eyes and a wellspring of conviction. Suddenly she knew he would understand and would never judge her.

'My stepfather's suicide. It's wasn't my fault.'

Her husband frowned and glanced at her again.

'Of course it wasn't.'

'But I've blamed myself, don't you see, for all these years. It's what drives me to make Whitebarn a success, but it also makes me feel unbalanced and empty. As if nothing I do is good enough. It's made me hide from you, from everyone, in case I let you down or if you leave me.'

She was crying now. Michael turned into a lay-by and stopped the car. Iris heard the rear door open and then hers let in cold air. Zoe was kneeling beside her and hugging her. Michael, seatbelt off, was doing the same and she was enfolded by her family. Iris cried for all the times she had been distant with them; driven by her insecurities and feelings of inadequacy to hold them at bay. Abruptly she felt weightless with bones and muscles turned feathery. She touched her daughter's face and then Michael's, feeling awed by their love and concern. Michael wiped her eyes and she laughed, letting him, with no thought of how it might seem vulnerable to do so.

'I think,' she said, 'I need a cup of tea and something to eat.'

'Me too,' Zoe said.

Michael kissed her cheek, smiling and said, 'Definitely. And we need to talk about all this properly.'

'After Amy Dudley,' Iris said.

He took her chin, looking into her eyes with a serious expression that brokered no disagreement.

'Promise? No more hiding?'

She returned his gaze with steadfastness and her new conviction fragile but firmly in place.

'Promise,' she said.

An hour later in the kitchen at Whitebarn, Iris stared at the laptop screen. On the table lay four packages ready to be sent to national newspapers. She touched one and glanced at her husband and daughter standing side by side.

'We're sure about this?' she asked again.

Zoe nodded. Michael rested a hand on her shoulder.

'We are. We have Colin Hall, now. Zoe can pay for Amy Dudley's DNA results later tonight. Then talk to Will's friend and see if he'll match it to Colin as quickly as possible, if the man's willing to help.'

'I can't see why he wouldn't,' Zoe said. 'We can keep Colin's identity out of it so he'll never be in any danger. Then we can just add the result to the findings we publish now. It'll be fine.'

'I know, I know,' Iris said. 'And it's sensible rather than waiting, but still…'

Someone knocked on the back door and they stared at each other. On the floor at her side Gus lifted his head but made no sound.

'It's me,' came Thomas's voice.

Michael let him in. In the late afternoon light, dirt showed black on his face and hands. He looked tired but smiled at them.

'Animals are moved. Lads are with them in the valley. Just need you lot.'

His gaze flicked between them and his expression was concerned.

'Right,' said Iris, 'that's it then. Give us half an hour, Thomas, and we'll be there.'

The farm manager nodded.

'I'll wait outside with my shotgun and Peg.'

He left and, in his wake the Shaws were silent, staring after him. Iris swallowed, the realisation of Thomas's words and actions tightening her chest. She turned to the screen and with a quick, decisive movement uploaded their findings to the first forum, ensuring everything loaded properly and was public. Michael watched for a moment then kissed the top of her head and left the room. Iris repeated the upload to three more sites while Zoe moved about gathering supplies and putting them into waiting rucksacks and bags. Michael returned, carrying his oversized holdall, which Iris knew now contained the contents of the safe. She gave each site a final check, noting comments already flashing up and the views climbing rapidly. She shut the laptop down, slipping it into a rucksack and gathered the press packages. Gus rose and followed her to where Michael and Zoe were waiting. Thomas, seeing them coming, opened the door and ushered them out. Iris locked the door, and they made their way to the drive where the farm manager's Land Rover was parked next to theirs, now hooked up to the caravan newly brought out from the barn. Iris stopped and looked back. Whitebarn seemed a stranger to her, silent and empty as it was. The comfort of home, she reminded herself, is never contained in bricks and mortar but in those that inhabit them. She tried very hard to believe that but still hated leaving her home at the mercy of the Watchers. Michael ushered Gus into the Land Rover, and Iris got into the driving seat. The engines seemed very loud and Iris checked the mirrors, feeling suddenly exposed. Then, with a sense of relief, she followed Thomas to Foxcombe Valley.

Over the next two hours Iris and Thomas settled the animals in their makeshift pens and gave them their evening feeds while the lads set up their tents near the caravan. Zoe had left, driven back to London to pay for the DNA results and to visit Will. Her daughter chafed at the fact that she had to work in the morning as normal, but Iris had promised to let her know what happened with DI Fields.

Later that evening, dusk was blueing the sky when she and Michael returned to Whitebarn to meet the police. Approaching the farmhouse Iris recognised an unmarked police car as DI Fields parked outside. She frowned, looking about.

'I thought there would be more of them,' she said.

Michael parked the Land Rover next to the car.

'I expect she wants to hear what we've got to say first. Setting up a surveillance operation can't be easy or cheap. They must need a very good reason.'

'Well, let's hope we can convince her then.'

She and Michael got out of the Land Rover and went to the inspector's car, but it was empty.

'That's odd,' Iris said. 'Where do you think they are?'

Michael was looking at the farmhouse.

'Perhaps they've gone round the back to see if we're in?'

He didn't sound convinced. Iris felt uneasy and the evening gloom seemed suddenly full of shadows.

'You don't think the Watchers are here, do you?'

'I don't know, but I don't like this. Let's get back in the Land Rover and call the inspector.'

They did so, locking the doors, and Iris took the can of CS spray out of the glove compartment, putting it in her bag, then rang DI Fields. It was answered after the first tone and, following a brief conversation, Iris rang off.

'They're inside,' she said. 'Apparently we've had a break-in.'

They got out and hurried around the side of the house, finding the lights in the kitchen on and the back door unlocked. Inside they found their home in disarray with chairs overturned and food cupboards open and the cellar door off its hinges. They discovered DI Fields and DS Dens in the living room, which looked like a tornado had gone through it. The sofa and chairs were in pieces with the cushions, backs and underneath slashed open. All the cupboards and drawers had been emptied out and strewn across the floor. Even the curtains had been sliced to ribbons and hung in ragged strips. Iris felt sick and gripped Michael's hand, staring at the destruction. Standing amongst the debris, DI Fields looked angry while DS Dens's expression held only disgust. He moved toward them, his hands out, palms up, as if in reassurance, but something ugly flickered in his gaze.

'Michael,' Iris said, suddenly alarmed, and fumbled her bag, taking out the spray.

But DS Dens was quicker, and his hand closed around her wrist like a vice.

'Where the fuck is it?' he growled.

Comprehension hammered her, winding Iris and stealing her voice. Terror spiked as she stared at the contorted face and rage-filled eyes. Michael yelled, swung round and punched Dens in the head. The man reeled, dropping Iris's numbed wrist, and the can skittered to the floor. Recovering, the Watcher drew a wicked, serrated knife and dropped to a fighting crouch, advancing on Michael.

'You stupid fucker,' Dens remonstrated.

Iris yelped and ran for the kitchen to find Fields blocking the way, pointing a taser at her chest.

'That's enough,' Fields said. 'Put the knife away. Michael, do anything stupid again and I'll unload 50,000 volts into your wife.'

'Fuck that,' Dens said. 'I say we cut them and brand them until they tell us where the locket is.'

'Don't be an idiot,' the inspector sounded exasperated. 'If we do that, they could die without telling us. Or lie. Let's do this civilly. To start with.'

Dens grunted what Iris took for agreement but the Watcher held the knife ready on her husband. Fields, keeping the taser and attention on Iris, bent and gathered the CS spray. Straightening, she said, 'Both of you, put your phones on the floor and then get in the kitchen.'

Iris, muscles watery and unsteady, did as bid followed by Michael. In the kitchen Dens secured them tightly to chairs with duct tape and cable ties, muttering obscenities as he did so. Fields righted another chair and settled in front of them, taser pointed at Michael. A little in front of Iris, Dens rested the knife point against her ribs, digging it in. Her gaze blurred with tears and she felt urine warm between her thighs. Fields noticed and wrinkled her nose.

'I'll make this simple,' the woman said. 'Tell us where the locket is, and you get to live.'

'I don't believe you,' Iris managed.

'What, because you know who we are, we have to kill you? Oh, grow up, Iris. The only reason we've had to kill people is because we haven't found the locket, yet. Once we've completed our mission we'll do with the locket as we must, disappear and no one will ever find us. You will both be the victims of robbery gone wrong, much like your mate, Will.'

'You nearly killed Will,' Iris said.

Fields shot Dens a dark look.

'That was a mistake,' she said. 'Which is why he is on his very best behaviour and doesn't have a gun.'

Dens gave the finger, which Fields ignored.

'Tell us where it is,' she said. 'We take it and leave. It's that easy.'

'It's not here,' Michael said.

Dens hissed between his teeth.

'Fucking liar!' he spat.

He moved quick and sure. Iris heard a crack and Michael's chair tipped, slamming to the floor. She screamed and struggled to get free.

'Leave him alone,' she yelled.

'For fuck's sake,' Fields said. 'What is wrong with you?'

She rose and pulled Michael up, chair and all. Iris stared in horror. Her husband was slumped forward, head to chest and breathing harshly. Blood trickled from his nose and mouth. Dens stood to one side, a manic grin lighting his wholesome face and making him ugly. Fields tilted Michael's head and studied the damage.

'Jesus, I think you've broken his nose and how's he supposed to tell us anything unconscious?'

'Doesn't matter,' Dens said. 'I'll slice him up while the bitch watches. She'll soon tell us anything we want to know.'

'Or she'll tell us anything to get us to stop, you idiot. While we're chasing down her lies or wasting time with torture, someone could turn up. Then what?' She shook her head and returned to her chair. 'No, the best way to get Iris to talk is by letting them live afterwards.'

Dens eyes narrowed and he fingered the point of his knife.

'You're wrong,' he said. 'The quickest way to get the bitch to talk is to fuck up her husband. And then, if that's not enough, we'll do her daughter too. She'll talk to save them.'

'And you think she'll believe you'll let her live afterwards? Or that she'll want to, with them dead? For God's sake stop being a twat and use your brain for once in your life.'

Iris swallowed and tried to think of something, anything to get them out of this. She took a breath, striving desperately for some calm. Her heart was so rapid she feared she would pass out and Dens would murder her and Michael in the blackness. She was suddenly aware of a queer silence and that the Watchers were staring at each other. Dens's eyes were glittering slits while Fields' gaze was hard and intent.

'Do as I say,' the woman said.

'Fuck you, Briar,' Dens hissed. 'These arseholes have already published too much.'

He stepped in front of Michael and put the knife point over his heart. Iris whimpered.

'Please, don't,' she whispered.

'Move away from him,' Fields said, 'or I'll shoot.'

Iris stared at the taser pointed at Dens's back. The man glanced at his fellow Watcher, snorted and turned to face her.

'You're weak,' he said in a voice tight with rage. 'You think I can't move quick enough to avoid that.'

Fields, still pointing the taser, slipped the CS spray from her pocket and waved it at him.

'You're not quick enough to avoid this.'

Dens's breathing seemed too loud in the quiet room.

'You,' he sneered. 'All your plotting and planning has only made dead Watchers. We're doing this my way.'

'I don't think so,' Fields replied in an icy tone. 'You're nothing but a thug, Thorn. Unworthy to be a Watcher. Whether I put you down now or later doesn't bother me. Fucking Neanderthal.'

Abrupt red suffused Dens's face and neck and he leapt forward, straight into the fine CS spray. He yelled in pain, slashing at Fields with the knife. She cried out, firing the taser. The barbs stabbed into Dens and he fell rigid to the stone floor. Sudden flames burst as the CS spray ignited from the taser. Iris screamed and screamed. Fields crumpled across Dens's legs, blood spreading from her. The bitter smell of burning flesh and smoke engulfed the kitchen. Iris struggled against her bonds, yelling for Michael to wake up. Suddenly, the back door flung open. Thomas, shotgun raised, thundered in. Cursing, he placed the weapon on the floor and, tearing off his jacket, used it to smother the flames.

'Thomas, thank God,' Iris sobbed.

The farm manager stumbled to her through the acrid air.

'Ambulance coming,' he said. 'Get you outside.'

'Michael first, he's hurt,' Iris coughed. 'Please Thomas.'

Thomas knelt to her husband, slashed the duct tape with his penknife and cut the cable ties. He hoisted the unconscious man on his shoulder and carried him out. In a moment he returned and cut Iris free. Coughing, they staggered outside where Iris collapsed on the grass next to Michael. Thomas went back into the house while she scrabbled to her husband. In the light from the kitchen, she checked his wounds. The side of his face was already bruising, and his nose was a bloody mess, but his breathing was strong. She whispered his name, trying to stem her tears, and held his hand. Thomas returned, his expression grim.

'Both already dead,' he said.

'Good,' Iris said.

Thomas checked Michael over and murmured a reassurance to Iris before sitting next to her. She took his hand in her free one.

'Thank you,' she said. 'You saved us.'

He kissed her forehead.

'We're family,' he said. 'I was never going to let you be here alone.'

'You didn't say.'

'Didn't want an argument.' He shook his head. 'Shouldn't have checked the farm first. Never thought.'

Iris glanced at the smoke-filled kitchen, dread and fear still ripe.

'None of us did,' she said.

She rested her head on Thomas' shoulder, gratitude flooding her, letting her oldest friend's strength and unwavering love support her shattered nerves. Sudden sirens were shockingly loud. The glimmer of red and blue lights reminded Iris of Aunt Josephine. She sobbed and clutched Michael's hand harder. With a reassuring pat, Thomas rose and went to direct the paramedics. Iris whispered words of love and comfort to her unconscious husband and prayed to whoever would listen to help him.

What seemed like hours later the paramedics told her Michael would be fine and loaded them into the ambulances. They gave her pain relief and as the medication took hold, the jolting drive seemed to happen to someone else, while her muscles turned rubbery.

‘Zoe,’ she whispered.

Thomas squeezed her fingers.

‘Fine. On her way. Gus is with my boys. Safe with all the others.’

The drug iced her wits and worries, making everything distant while leaving a metallic taste in her mouth. She struggled to speak then between one blink and the next; darkness prevailed.

CHAPTER THIRTY-SEVEN

In London four days later, DI Gareth Ross surveyed the opulent dining room at the Watchers' Park Street premises. Papers and ledgers were stacked all along the table where six officers were going through them while another two brought more in. He approached one officer and peered at the document in the woman's hands, noting the date of 1934.

'Any real names yet?' he asked.

The officer shook her head.

'All I've got are details of searches. They used codenames for the artefacts they sought and their members.' The woman looked sickened. 'The Watchers weren't so sparse about the lengths they went to, to achieve their ends.'

The other officers gave murmurs of agreement, their disgust apparent even in the low tones. Ross poured a cup of coffee and tried not to let his own revulsion show.

'We've only three codenames for the last fifteen years,' he said. 'According to the records, anyone else they hired were mercenaries. So, if the Shaws are to be believed the two who died at Whitebarn last week were Thorn and Briar. Logically that means Sloe was Stephen Sloane and the whole black nest has been eradicated, which is something.'

No one spoke, heads bent to their work, but Ross noted the tightened atmosphere and rigid jaws of his fellow officers. That two of their own had been Watchers was a confidential matter known only to those on the taskforce. But it was a knowledge that left a bitter aftertaste for them all, especially in light of the dreadful deeds and killings contained in the records, along with the utter contempt the two had shown for procedure and the law. Their whole careers had been lies used to facilitate their grisly activities and every officer present took their betrayal and murderous actions personally. The fact that the bloody faction had finally been destroyed was scant comfort after all the death and destruction the Watchers had caused. Ross sipped coffee and pondered the society, wondering how it had ever come to be and what their agenda had been that could have stretched over so many years. The doors at the far end of the room opened and his sergeant came in carrying a large wooden box.

'Guv,' she said, 'you need to see this.'

Ross gestured her out and followed her to a room that had once been a study. The oak panels honeyed the room, making it a sanctuary that belied its masters' depravities. Yet the art and sculpture it held was tainted in Ross's opinion and he ignored it. His sergeant placed the box on the desk and opened the lid. Ross stared at the contents, his heart suddenly a trip hammer, and reached for his phone. He dialled a number which was instantly answered.

'Sir, we've found her,' he said.

CHAPTER THIRTY-EIGHT

Oxford, May 2008

Early morning mist made Foxcombe Valley a magical place. It covered the ruins of Foxcombe Manor like a fine cloak and dew sparkled the grass beneath it. Iris settled on the new bench and gazed across what had once been Sam's home, glad of her warm coat.

'Safe now,' she murmured.

For yesterday the final certification from the council had been awarded and Foxcombe Valley was now officially a private nature reserve. A tawny shape loped out of the mist and Gus ran to her, breaking her reverie. The Picardy nudged her hand for a stroke and, reassured she was fine, dashed away again to chase squirrels and ghosts. Four figures approached and she rose, kissing her husband and hugging Thomas while Zoe helped Will, still using a cane, to sit on the bench. Zoe fussed with his coat and Will withstood her ministrations patiently, then smiled, batting her hands away. She grinned, kissed his cheek and, settling next to him, took his free hand in hers.

'The flowers have come up well,' she said.

Iris looked about and nodded, pleased at her efforts with the wildflowers. Kingcups, English bluebells, forget-me-nots and dog roses were already blooming and others such as cornflowers and foxgloves would soon join them. Iris had made sure that this small part of Foxcombe Valley would always have something flowering whatever the season. Amidst the grass and wildflowers, the open grave was a chestnut and black accompaniment, with the headstone a grey and silver marker. The removed earth had been carefully positioned so as not to crush the wildflower meadow. As Iris gazed about she noted four crows perched in a nearby oak almost stripped of leaves. The birds seemed unusually still and quiet and she had the queer impression they were watching the meadow. She turned and studied where Michael and Thomas had earlier placed the oak coffin on a temporary plinth nearby ready to be interred. Iris had waited with the dead while her husband and Thomas had gone to help Zoe with Will. Now Iris glanced at the coffin and then to her husband. Michael nodded and gestured to Thomas and together they moved to the plinth. Iris watched her husband moving easily and steadily with no sign of trauma. She silently thanked any deity listening for their good fortune and for Thomas. Because Michael had fully recovered and Will was on the mend, so much so that the young couple were leaving for a long weekend in Paris the next day. She smiled as her daughter rose to stand next to her, one hand on Will's shoulder. Looking at them all, her family, a brightness spread through Iris, warming her soul.

'Thank you all for being here to witness this very special occasion,' she said. 'You all know how extremely privileged we are that permission has been granted for us to bury this poor soul here.'

She vividly recalled the visit made to surviving members of the Kilbride family when she had been to see her mother in Leith three months ago. The current Lord Kilbride had been shocked and saddened by Iris's unpublished revelations concerning Gordon McCraken's legacy and death. Using DNA, they had matched the bones to the man, proving beyond doubt who Gordon was. Lord Kilbride, having read Gordon's own accounts showing his deep love of the valley, had readily agreed to the burial taking place at Foxcombe Manor and had been instrumental in securing the necessary permissions. In the next few weeks, the Kilbride family planned to visit Gordon's grave and hold an official memorial, but for now Iris continued.

'We know this is the right place, the only place he wanted to be.' She moved to the coffin and touched it reverently. 'Rest easy, Gordon McCraken, now and always.'

Half an hour later Iris took off her gloves and settled on the bench with Will, watching as her daughter replaced her in helping Michael and Thomas finish filling in the grave. The sound of dirt whisking in the air was somehow comforting and the spring sun was warm on her back. Gus reappeared and cavorted about before dashing away again. Will handed her a Thermos mug full of coffee which she sipped gratefully.

'How are you finding living at Ash House with Zoe?' she asked. 'It's been, what, two months now?'

Will nodded, his smile a stretched, tight thing on his scarred face.

'Well, thank you.'

His words were slow and a little slurred, but his speech was improving all the time. Still Iris noted the frustration in his expression at not being able to convey himself as he would like. She touched his hand.

'It must seem odd after your flat.'

'Odd. Big. But good.'

Will's fingers touched his pocket in an unconscious gesture while his gaze slipped to her daughter and stayed there. Iris smiled.

'I hear the new premises are nearly ready,' she said.

He flashed her his tight smile and nodded.

'Working again soon,' he said.

'In your own company. I'm so proud of you both.'

'Zoe's company,' Will said frowning, clearly confused. 'Not mine.'

'Married people share everything,' she said.

He turned to her, eyes wide and face flushed.

'How?'

She pointed to his pocket and he laughed, a relieved sound which caused Zoe to look over and Iris waved to her daughter. Will touched her arm.

'Wanted to show,' he said. 'And ask you and Michael.'

Iris nodded, put down the mug and turned slightly, shielding Will with her body. Will took out the box and showed her the engagement ring before slipping it away again.

'Beautiful,' she said. 'And I know Michael will agree that we are over the moon for you both. When are you going to do it?'

Will pinked, looking pleased and suddenly shy.

'In Paris.'

She clasped his arm, trying to contain her excitement so as not to alert Zoe, but leant forward and kissed his scarred cheek. He looked startled and then smiled.

'Wedding at Whitebarn though,' he said.

It was Iris's turn to look surprised.

'Are you sure?'

He nodded and tilted his head toward Zoe.

'Home,' he said. 'It's her special place.'

Tears fell hot and then cold on her cheeks and she hugged him. Something nudged her leg and she looked at Gus's grinning face, his big Picardy nose nudging her again. At her feet was a large, dead rat. Stifling a sigh, she told her dog what an excellent boy he was and gave him a fuss. Gus made a happy sound and loped away. Smiling and shaking her head, Iris reached for her gloves.

Later that day the bustle and noise of Oxford was a distant, indistinct thing in the cool interior of St Mary's church. The Shaws, Thomas and Will along with Colin Hall stood by the newly opened vault while a priest solemnly commended the earthly remains of Lady Amy Dudley to their final rest. Iris listened feeling light and dark. The turmoil of the last months was vivid in her mind and ignited raw emotions. She knew her experiences with the Watchers were horrors that would never fully leave her, engraved forever on her bones and in her soul. Yet she knew just as well that the struggle, the terror, had been worth it. The emptiness still lurked, some days stronger than others, but with the help of her family and a therapist it was becoming more controllable and better understood. And now she knew she could make peace with it and be whole at last.

She watched the box containing Amy Dudley enter the hole which to her seemed a quiet place, serene and dark. Somewhere Amy Dudley could finally rest easy and be at peace. The priest finished and they all bowed their heads in prayer. Then Zoe helped Will to a pew while Thomas and Michael spoke to the priest and Colin. Two men covered the hole with the newly commissioned and engraved stone while Iris moved to the only other person who had been allowed in the church during the service. The man sat two pews back with a newspaper under his arm. Without greeting, she settled next to DI Gareth Ross.

'Glad you could come,' she said.

'We both know that's not true,' he replied mildly. 'But thanks for saying it.'

She inclined her head.

'You came, you saw, you know she's truly in there. We've met all the conditions and I hope never to see you or your bosses again. There, is that better?'

He grunted and held out the paper.

'You seen this, this morning?'

She glanced at the fold seeing a headline announcing the discovery of a priceless locket from the sixteenth century to be on show at the British Museum.

'I did. I see some convenient expert verified the portrait in the locket as Henry VIII.'

'Naturally. And of course, the jewel was a commissioned gift by Thomas Wyatt for the king on the eve of his marriage to Anne Boleyn.'

Iris snorted and looked away, watching Amy Dudley being sealed in.

'Well, at least our troubles avoided a scandal for the royal family,' she said, hearing the edge in her voice.

She glanced at Ross, seeing the sympathy in his expression.

'You and your family went through a lot to make this happen. You should be proud of yourselves. You quite probably saved the monarchy from not just a dreadful scandal, but perhaps from collapse.'

Iris thought of all the documents, artefacts and leather tome locked away once again in the safe at Whitebarn. She looked to where Zoe sat next to Will, cane in hand. She shook her head, knowing they would never be the same. She glanced at her husband, who smiled at her and she again gave silent thanks for those deities who surely looked after them. Sudden, nightmarish images of burning flesh, shots in the night and blood made her jaw clench. With an effort of will she banished them and took a breath to dispel the abrupt and brutal fear that swamped her. Using techniques her therapist had taught her she got herself controlled. Next to her, Ross seemed to understand and waited until she had collected herself and then continued.

'The National Archives are issuing a press release concerning the coroner's report in the next few weeks.'

'I know. We've been in contact with them,' she said.

If Ross was surprised, he didn't show it and tapped the paper.

'Was the exchange worth it; locket for skull?'

She suddenly smiled, relishing the moments to come.

'Well, we've had the results from the forensic expert for a while now.' She felt Ross tense but merely watched the gravestone being tapped into place. 'They confirm Amy Dudley was murdered. Bludgeoned to death and, after detailed examination of the coroner's report, candlestick and Sam's notes, the experts concur her neck was most likely snapped after the bludgeoning. Then there's the verification we've had that the message to Amy Dudley was indeed a forgery and not from her husband.' She now glanced at Ross, who looked stunned. Iris continued, 'Along with that, as you know, the DNA matched to Colin's and proved who she is. So, yes, locket for skull was absolutely worth it. Being able to put Amy Dudley to rest properly and peacefully is beyond any price.'

'But you never published those forensic findings proving murder. You never mentioned these experts to us, why?'

She turned to him, trying to convey her determination.

'We never wanted to cause a scandal for the royal family, DI Ross. We just wanted to prove Amy Dudley was murdered and for her to rest in peace with no taint of suicide. We knew if your bosses discovered our conclusive findings they would try and take her away again and gag us from telling anyone what we knew, even anonymously.' She looked pointedly at the paper now held limply in his grip.

'For fear of what else might come to light.' She nodded to the gravestone now fixed in place. 'This way Amy Dudley is safe for eternity. Beyond you or your bosses.'

Church bells tolled the hour. From outside the church the clamour of the city seemed to grow louder. The sound of vehicles stopping and voices was suddenly noisy. Ross looked from the doors to Iris, a dreadful suspicion forming on his face.

'Who's out there?' he asked.

'The press. Here for interviews and photographs, not to mention the odd television crew. We've even been given authorisation to film in here. So no one will ever be able to disturb Amy Dudley again without us or the world knowing it.'

'Oh my God.' He looked shocked then quickly sobered. 'But you can't say anything to them about the locket or the Watchers, it's in the agreement.'

'Oh, we know that,' Iris said. 'But there's nothing in the agreement to say we can't publish our definitive forensic proof that Amy Dudley was murdered nor the DNA match and genealogy proving who she is. We made very sure of that. There's nothing in anything we published to implicate the royal family as no one knows exactly who orchestrated it all, so there'll be no devastating scandal with the new forensic evidence or with us claiming authorship.'

Ross looked as if he might speak but then only shook his head. Iris smiled, enjoying his discomfort.

'My husband might even write a fictional account of things,' she said. 'All speculative, obviously.' She rose still smiling at him. 'We'll be starting soon and letting the press know exactly where Amy Dudley is. So, if you leave by St Mary's Passage you might avoid being seen. And we wouldn't want any awkward questions asked about why a detective inspector from Major Crimes is here, would we?'

Iris watched Ross hurry to the small side door and gave him a little wave as he left. She retraced her steps and let her fingers rest on a cool gravestone near Amy Dudley's. She traced the name and date engraved on the old stone and whispered, 'Sam, you were right. Amy Dudley was murdered. We found out the how and the why, but we will never know the who. I'm sorry for that. But know that the Watchers will never hurt anyone ever again.'

Iris patted the gravestone of Sir Samuel Banks, then lingered at Amy Dudley's and read the newly engraved inscription.

'Here lies Lady Amy Dudley. Sadly taken from this world too early at the hands of others. May she rest now forever at peace with her soul soaring free.'

Iris bowed her head, making a silent promise to Amy Dudley that her fate would never be hidden or false again. Then, holding Michael's hand, she led her family out to address the waiting press.

EPILOGUE

London, December 1560

From a chamber in the Houses of Parliament, Sir Samuel Banks watched the snow fall and vanish into the busy brown Thames. The part of his attention that remained in the room noted the ceremony was coming to an end and he re-joined it wholly. Removing the seal of sheriff's office from around his neck, Sam gave it to the clerk and received the official release from his duties therein. With a ragged sigh he left the chamber as the new man was being sworn to duty. Out in the cold corridor he fingered his new ruff, itching under it with a curse that caused two bewigged and perfumed men to frown in passing.

'Beshitten place,' he muttered.

Sam moved on, seeking the treasurer's offices to pay his release fee. He thought longingly of the nearby Golden Lion, where Hugh and Henry waited with ale and pie. Trying to move quickly through the corridors he was hampered by slow walking courtiers, nobles and parliamentarians. Some looked sideways at him while others did so more openly, all with distrust. Sam resisted the urge to shove them out of the way and fingered his dagger hilt.

Someone caught his elbow and Sam swung, fist ready to punch, only stopping a hair's breadth from landing the blow. The young page looked terrified, letting go and stepping back, causing those walking by to curse him.

'Sir Samuel Banks?'

Sam lowered his fist.

'Aye, and you should be wary of catching folk off guard.'

'My apologies but I've been sent to fetch you.'

'You're too late, lad. Ceremony is done. All that's left is to pay my fee and I'm away for my supper.'

'It's not for the ceremony.'

The page motioned him to the window. Sam followed the lad to the quieter spot with his guts tightening and his gaze cutting everywhere. The younger man noted his wariness and looked about with narrowed eyes, then bent to Sam's ear.

'You're to come with me and attend the Queen.'

Sam rocked back.

'Here?'

The young man nodded.

'Jesu,' Sam muttered. 'What now?'

But realising there was no choice, he gestured the page to lead on.

The chamber he was taken to was hung with overlapping tapestries to keep the heat in. A window showed snow still falling thickly outside while inside lit torches held in sconces and candles made the chamber bright and welcoming. Underfoot, thick rushes gave off dried thyme, rosemary and lavender scents, helped by the roaring fire. Three chairs were grouped about the hearth and a table. One seat was occupied. Sam went and knelt in front of Queen Elizabeth, bowing his head with the fire hot on his back.

'It is my desire that you be seated, Sir Samuel Banks,' she said.

Sam rose, took the chair indicated and studied the Queen of England. Her white skin seemed to glow in the firelight. Flames winked on the seed pearls in her burnished hair and ruff while the jewels in her bodice and gown twinkled like coloured stars amidst golden and emerald cloth. On her lap a small dog stirred under slender, beringed fingers. The blonde animal gazed at Sam before dismissing him and closing its eyes again. The Queen's feet, clad in embroidered white leather, rested on a stool that nestled amongst the rushes. Next to her the table held a book, sheaves of documents, a small hand bell and a goblet. He looked to find Elizabeth watching him with an intensity he disliked and schooled his features to impassivity. She smiled slightly and inclined her head.

'Ah my old hound, still as prudent as ever. How fare things at Foxcombe Manor?'

'Very well, thank you, Your Majesty.'

They continued to speak of ordinary, family things. All the while Sam surreptitiously watched the Queen, uneasy that Elizabeth was unattended and at Parliament in such a manner, feeling it boded ill for their meeting. He glanced at the other chair, wondering who it was for. The subject moved to the state of the roads and his journey to London.

'You brought scant retinue?' the Queen asked.

'My eldest son, Henry, and my lawyer, Hugh Longfellow is all, Your Majesty. I am a modest man of modest means and feel no need for myriad men at arms.'

'No doubt you feel your modest means are better suited to advancing those less fortunate than yourself. Such as finding children and rat catchers new and promising, if somewhat unorthodox, careers.'

Sam held himself very still and pretended a nonchalance he didn't feel. That Elizabeth knew of Eleanor Rose Archer and her father was a surprise, but he would be damned if he showed it. The Queen's eyebrows lifted and then she surprised him by smiling.

'Fear not,' she murmured. 'I think the investment an interesting one and well thought out.' Her tone darkened. 'My people should not be ill-used as scapegoats for others with less intelligence than credit is given them.'

Sam frowned, not fully understanding. Elizabeth stroked her dog and stared into the fire, her expression startling in its sudden weariness. In that moment she seemed very young and Sam remembered with a start that the Queen had only had her twenty-seventh birthing day in September. Then, Elizabeth shifted, the expression vanished and instead he felt the weight of her gaze once more.

'Did you discover who arranged Lady Dudley's final meeting?'

The question was abrupt, and he knew she sought to take him off guard, but he kept his expression calm and merely shook his head.

'I regret not, Your Majesty. If there were a missive concerning the meet, then it's likely destroyed.'

Her gaze was sharp, and she studied him for a long moment before seeming to reach a decision. Elizabeth picked up and rang the bell. Immediately, the chamber door opened to admit a short man with a grey pointed beard who used a heavy walking stick. William Cecil, Secretary of State, entered slowly. Sam's boyhood friend wore a dark doublet and hose with little embellishment. He warded against the cold with an open-fronted, fur-lined robe and removed his tall hat, revealing scant grey hair when he bowed to the Queen. Elizabeth motioned the man to rise and gestured to the empty chair. Cecil settled himself there and didn't look at Sam, who noted his old friend looked as if exhaustion was his only business. Glancing at Elizabeth he saw her gaze had hardened while her fingers tapped the table, drawing their attention.

'Gentlemen, we will have this discussion only once. Sir Samuel, I know who penned the missive arranging Amy Dudley's final meet. Moreover, I have the letter she sent to Lord Dudley that prompted the reply reportedly from her husband. This, as you know, set about events which ended in her ladyship's untimely death.'

Sam stared at the Queen unable to find words. His mind reeled, leaping from connotation to connotation. Cecil looked unhappy and Elizabeth angry but still he couldn't understand how this had happened.

'Majesty,' he managed, 'who sent the reply?'

'Cecil will tell you,' she said, her tone malicious and pleasant all at once.

Cecil looked away, his throat bulged on a convulsive swallow and when he spoke it was as if he found the words hard to utter.

'In the weeks before her death the letter Lady Dudley sent to her husband was discovered. It seems her ladyship felt she had learnt a secret that could threaten the Queen and panicked. She asked her husband to relieve her of the secret.'

Sam's thoughts darkened on Lord Dudley and his hand tightened on the goblet. The Queen tutted, a small sound, but Cecil flinched at it. Sam's gaze narrowed on his old friend and thoughts of Lord Dudley slid from him. He sensed a game he knew nothing of being played and it had naught to do with his lordship.

'You say Amy Dudley's letter was discovered,' he said. 'But mayhap you mean intercepted.'

Elizabeth looked approvingly at Sam while Cecil watched the flames.

'Aye, you could frame it as such,' the man admitted.

Sam resisted the urge to shake him and carefully eased

his fingers from their clamp on the goblet. Elizabeth stroked the dog on her lap, but her gaze was pinned to Cecil.

'Stop this mummery, Cecil, and be honest in your dealings here,' she said. 'So far your foolish duplicity has brought me naught but blood and dishonour in this affair. So, I am forced to take measures that right your wrongs. Tell him.'

Cecil pecked a nod, all colour now drained from his face.

'As Your Majesty commands,' he murmured.

The Secretary of State straightened and pulled at his doublet, settling it better, and then stared at Sam as if by doing so the Queen disappeared.

'Lady Amy Dudley discovered a locket of a two-winged design,' Cecil said. 'Along with the usual portraits, it contains a small plait of hair fashioned from two heads. One painting is of Queen Anne Boleyn.'

'And the other?' Sam asked.

'Is of my father,' Elizabeth interjected. 'The king. The locket once belonged to my mother. It was a gift from Sir Thomas Wyatt to celebrate her marriage and his role in it. After my mother's death it somehow found its way to Wyatt's son, who entrusted Lady Dudley with it when he languished under pain of death in the Tower.'

Sam stared between the two figures, one regal, the other a shrunken thing, that held the fate of his country in their hands.

'Did Amy Dudley know who gifted the locket to Anne Boleyn?'

Cecil shifted uncomfortably, his gaze again on the fire.

'The boar's head, the symbol of the Wyatt house, is etched upon the locket back,' he murmured.

Sam closed his eyes, yet despite the darkness beneath his lids he saw all too clearly.

'The portrait of King Henry,' he said tiredly, 'could be easily mistaken for Thomas Wyatt. So, Lady Dudley sent to her husband, terrified of what she had found. But her letter never reached him.'

He opened his eyes to see Cecil's misery and the queen's anger as confirmation of his thoughts. He stared at Cecil understanding an abrupt stab in his guts.

'You damnable whoreson,' he muttered.

Cecil bowed his head. Sam's jaw clenched, breath hissing through his teeth, and he half drew his dagger. He rose, intent on Cecil, who shrank back, but Elizabeth cut through his murderous rage.

'I think not,' she said, raised hand stalling his stalking, and continued, 'No matter if I believe striking Cecil is deserved, I would be forced to condemn you for killing an unarmed man in my presence. Is he worth leaving Foxcombe Manor, and those within, without you?'

Breath heaving in his chest and sweat cold on his brow, he was suddenly held fast by thoughts of Gwynn at home and Henry waiting at the Golden Lion. With a curse he forced his dagger into its sheath, tearing his gaze from the man that was once his friend, and resumed his seat. He gulped wine, swilling it in his mouth, trying to drown the bitterness on his tongue and throat.

'Tell me,' he managed.

At his harsh tone Elizabeth's gaze narrowed but she gestured to Cecil, who seemed even smaller now. The man coughed and looked away from them both, unwilling or unable to meet their anger.

'As my Queen commands.' He sounded resigned. 'The locket has been known to us for many years. But we had no clue as to its whereabouts. Moreover, the threat it poses is newly made since its origin as a gift from Thomas Wyatt to King Henry and Queen Anne was once well known. Alas, as with so many things from that turbulent time, the origin and knowledge of the locket's very existence faded. Two years ago, at the ascension of Her Majesty, I created the Watchers to search for the locket. I knew the jewel could become a threat, but I believed it was something easily discovered and dealt with.'

'Until Lady Dudley, unknowing custodian of the locket for many years, finally opened it and panicked over the portraits and the hair,' Sam said.

'Just so.' Cecil sighed. 'I aroused the Watchers and sought to remedy the matter without alarming Her Majesty.'

'Remedy the matter?' Elizabeth's voice was acerbic. 'You created a vengeful, secret society without my knowledge. A society that is now so entrenched that to eliminate it is nigh on impossible without causing a scandal amongst the nobility whose youth populate the Watchers as if it were a high honour.'

Cecil shook his head and seemed about to speak but Elizabeth's unforgiving look stalled him. The Queen continued, 'Rebuking and renouncing those sons and even daughters would cause outcry amongst the most powerful. As you have advised, such an outcry could lead to a rebellion in its own right! I could almost forgive that you have wittingly unleashed a wicked society on my reign. But not that it has already lost the dangerous political asset it was created to find, while murdering at will it seems!'

Cecil shrank from Elizabeth's rage. Sam ruthlessly bludgeoned his own down, drowning out his wrath at Cecil for all the harm he had done and the needless deaths he had orchestrated. Cecil's breathing was loud, punctuated by the crack and spit of the fire, and the man visibly controlled himself, saying, 'I can only repeat once more my deepest apologies for my actions, Your Majesty.'

'Little use to Amy Dudley,' Sam said scathingly, taking

no pains to hide his contempt for the man. 'Or the other innocents who died at your Watchers' hands. And what of the Justice of the Peace, Reynard? Was he so brutally slain at your order?'

Cecil's gaze tightened and his expression became wooden.

'We discovered that Reynard was penning a missive betraying his fellow Watchers to Lord Dudley. Something that could never be allowed.'

Sam recalled the tiny piece of blood-splattered parchment in the dead man's fingers.

'So, you sent the Verney brothers to butcher him in his own home and steal the message.'

'It was necessary. As was all else,' Cecil said stiffly, unable to meet Sam's eye. 'To protect the Crown.'

'Necessary? Letting your beshitten Watchers murder an innocent woman and make it look an accident or worse? Then to consign that poor woman's soul to labour under the terrible sentence of suicide, perhaps for eternity? I hope you and your godforsaken Watchers sicken and die on your necessities!'

Weariness and sorrow engulfed Sam, making him heavy and his wits leaden. He fought the emotions off, staring at the man he had once called friend. His thoughts sharpened on this arranged audience.

'Your Majesty,' he said carefully. 'I must wonder why you've taken me into your confidence and beg to ask the question.'

Elizabeth sipped her drink and seemed to consider her answer. She gestured to the Secretary of State.

'Trust in Cecil must be rebuilt,' she said. 'His counsel is too valuable to me to discard or punish publicly over this. It is true his Watchers have proven themselves little more than feral beasts. But the locket remains a serious threat.

A threat these Watchers have proven undeniably that they will devote themselves to as their sole duty of finding and destroying; to protect the Crown at all costs. Such loyalty is not set aside lightly.'

Suddenly Sam felt trapped by the knowledge he had been given and blurted, 'You would have to hang me before I would join them, Your Majesty.'

Elizabeth smiled as if he had confirmed her own conclusions.

'I would never command that you wed yourself to such a dark society, my old hound. I recognise that your morality would soon turn you from me and the Crown should I venture such a notion. No, it is because of your true nature I ask a different service of you.'

Sam swallowed, feeling abruptly nauseous.

'Ask, Majesty?'

Suddenly Elizabeth looked weary and she nodded.

'I ask it of you, my old hound. My most steadfast friend. These Watchers are not to be trusted. Yet I found myself disagreeably yoked to them due to Cecil's zeal and the threat of the locket. I need someone I can trust to guard against the Watchers. To stand apart from them and mete out discipline in its most brutal form when they go too far; as I and only I command.'

Sam stared at her and then at Cecil, who looked shocked.

'Your Majesty,' the secretary said, 'I must protest. It would be unwise to put your confidence and your secrets into one man and bestow such power upon him.'

The look Elizabeth gave Cecil was withering.

'Do not seek to lecture me when you have brought us here with your murderous, uncontrolled faction,' she said. 'Be thankful you're not in the Tower.' She turned her gaze to Sam. 'What say you, Sir Samuel Banks?'

Images of Amy Dudley running for her life, smashed

and snapped to death, crowded Sam. A dagger splitting doublet and skin, splattering blood while puncturing heart and lungs and then the victim, Daniel Fleet, tossed into the river like rubbish. Lord Dudley's men threatening his family and injuring Hugh. Only they weren't Lord Dudley's. They were Watchers. Men working for Cecil.

'I would ask a question, if I may,' Sam managed to keep his tone even despite his inner turmoil. Elizabeth motioned him to continue. 'Why set me to investigate Lord Dudley's involvement in his wife's death if you knew he was innocent of it?'

Elizabeth drew an audibly sharp breath and her gaze turned stony. A part of Sam panicked that he had gone too far, but the words could not be unsaid. He met her gaze mildly enough, masking any fear until her expression softened and he let out a breath. If Elizabeth noted it, she made no comment, saying, 'After Cecil told me of the Watchers and how they had murdered Lady Dudley, he revealed the letter that her ladyship sent to her husband may not have been her first to him concerning the locket. Your investigation was paramount in uncovering Lord Dudley's intentions.'

Sam thought through the implication of her words.

'You needed to know if Lord Dudley's man Blount sought the locket at Cumnor Place or merely attempted to sway the jury to protect his master. Blount's actions and my conclusions proved his intention was merely to sway the jury to accident or suicide.'

Cecil remained sullenly silent while Elizabeth indicated her agreement.

'Equally, I wanted the Watchers stopped,' she said. 'Something Cecil could not enforce without revealing who was behind Amy Dudley's death to Lord Dudley or his men.'

And, thought Sam, risk unmasking the Verney brothers

as Watchers working for the Crown within Lord Dudley's household. The political ramifications of such a revelation were myriad and unpleasant. Elizabeth nodded as if understanding his thoughts.

'Would Lord Dudley, had he known of it, offer me the locket seeking no more than my thanks?' she mused, as if to herself. When neither Sam nor Cecil answered, she stared into the fire and continued, 'No matter now.' She sighed and looked very young again. 'I will never have a man hold sway over me and his wife's death has ensured Lord Dudley can never attain higher than he is.'

Her sorrowful tone matched her expression and the silence stretched, with Sam loath to break it. Finally, Elizabeth looked at him.

'What say you, old hound, will you take this oath and guard against the Watchers for me?'

Sam drew a deep breath of fire-warmed air, thinking of Gwynn and his family, of his queen and country, all of which he loved beyond words. He knew then where his duty and heart lay, no matter the cost.

'Your Majesty, I am honoured, but I cannot take such an oath.'

The Queen's gaze narrowed, and she tilted her head, clearly seeking an explanation. Sam continued.

'My wife and family have endured and suffered through my absences over my many years of loyal, and might I say, exemplary service. This investigation into Lady Dudley's death placed them all, my children included, in mortal danger.'

Sam stared at Cecil, who swallowed and shifted in his chair. 'Even my home, their home, came under threat of destruction from the Watchers.' He looked to the Queen, hoping desperately for understanding. 'Afterward, I swore an oath that my work for Cecil was done, that never again would my family be forced into such a vulnerable position and on no one's orders would I leave them.' It took all his skill and wit to keep his tone from cracking. 'It is an oath I cannot, will not, break.'

He managed to keep his expression calm and watched Elizabeth, wondering if his refusal would mean the Tower. His queen seemed porcelain, so fine and remote did she look in the firelight. Yet, the gaze she returned was sympathetic, if belied by her foot-tapping on the stool. She pursed her lips and nodded, letting Sam breathe a little easier. Her expression became thoughtful and another silence stretched, winding into minutes. Finally, she said, 'It is an admirable promise you've made and one, I believe, that should be kept.'

Relief made Sam light headed. Cecil frowned and seemed about to speak but thought better of it at a look from Elizabeth.

'Cecil,' she said, 'that will be all.'

With a start, the secretary stiffly rose and bowed to the Queen. Then, with a final worried look at Sam, left the chamber. Elizabeth idly stroked her dog's ears while her gaze remained on Sam.

'So, what say you if I were to propose an arrangement that was advantageous to us both, old hound?'

Wondering at what trap she planned, Sam said, 'Arrangement, Your Majesty?'

'Indeed. Should you take the oath to guard against the Watchers, I would place your entire family and any retinue you deem worthy, such as your lawyer, Hugh Longfellow, under my personal, royal protection. Any who raised a hand against them would be as if they raised a hand against me.'

Sam felt his jaw slacken.

'More,' the Queen said, 'I will confidentially confer upon you the ability to secure any you deem worthy to train and aid you in your duty against the Watchers. In this way any discipline that requires absence from hearth and home can be meted out by those you trust, allowing you to remain at Foxcombe Manor.'

Sam stared, thoughts spinning on the implications in Elizabeth's offer. Suddenly he thought of Hugh's unwavering devotion in their hunt for the murderer and to the Crown. Unbidden, the image of his second-born son, Tobias, and the lad's studious, caring nature seemed to merge with his youngest son Ned's eager mind. He imagined the three of them working with his first-born, Henry's fiery ways and fighting prowess. Suddenly he recognised Hugh and his sons carried the best parts of himself and knew they would be able to help him, meaning Gwynn need never be alone again. Yet imagining Foxcombe Manor ablaze and his family in peril tempered his reasoning. Elizabeth waited, bright eyed and curious, and he knew he must answer.

'I thank Your Majesty for such considerations,' he said carefully. 'Yet while your personal protection is a princely gift, I see naught in such an arrangement that would save my family should vengeful Watchers attack Foxcombe in the dead of night.'

The Queen looked taken aback and Sam silently cursed his lack of diplomacy. But once again, Elizabeth surprised him by smiling.

'For shame,' she said in an amused tone. 'It sounds as if you doubt my ability to be everywhere at once.'

Sam inclined his head, not trusting himself to speak. The Queen's expression became thoughtful once more and she sipped her drink.

'None will know of your oath nor any duty regarding the Watchers done by you, or others in your service, at my command,' she said. 'Not even Cecil or any that come after him. Secrecy will be paramount, 'twixt you and I alone, bar those who choose to take the oath and serve.'

Elizabeth paused, watching, letting the silence, save the fire-crack, grow. For Sam, time seem thickened, while he battled to regain his wits and digest all that had been said. Abruptly his fractured thoughts narrowed on the secrets in the Leonardo Da Vinci tome, the library to be built and its hidden tunnel meant for escape in emergencies. The tunnel, he now thought, would prove invaluable for anyone coming and going undetected from Foxcombe Manor and, as such, would need to be added to the tome. He shook his head, forcing his focus on the wider implications and trying to engineer some clarity. Elizabeth coughed, a delicate sound that drew his attention. She said, 'And as a grateful monarch for the services which you have already given to the Crown, I will set aside an annual sum for you and your family for the entirety of my reign, however long that may last.' She named an amount that sent Sam's mind reeling even more. Elizabeth continued, 'So, my old hound, will these arrangements allow you to keep your promise to your wife and family while taking an oath to protect your Queen and country by guarding against the Watchers?'

Sam sipped wine, trying to think through his shock. With an effort of will he focused on Elizabeth's offer and imagined telling Gwynn. His wife, he knew, would despise the service itself, but not its purpose. Equally he knew the money Elizabeth proposed would provide his sons with something they could otherwise never obtain; independence from service to others and the ability to choose their own path, rather than one based upon rank and financial need. If his sons chose to take the oath and be trained by him, then so be it, but the money would allow them a freedom of choice many never knew. While being an obvious piece of blackmail on Elizabeth's part, he knew it would be something Gwynn would welcome as eagerly as he.

Abruptly Amy Dudley spun in his mind, beckoning and beseeching. He suddenly recognised her actions had been to protect the Queen and England, unthinking of her husband using the locket for gain. That Amy Dudley had been ultimately manipulated by Cecil, her death needless and her soul now tainted beyond his salvation crashed over Sam, washing away any remaining doubt. He straightened his shoulders; Amy Dudley must not have died in vain. She could not be left to languish under the taint of suicide for naught. His wits cleared and resolve hardened, Sam rose and knelt before Queen Elizabeth.

'I agree to your proposal, Your Majesty,' he said. 'And gladly take this oath. To guard against the Watchers for you and for England, during my lifetime at the very least.'

Here ends the final instalment of The Watchers Trilogy.

For more information on the Watcher's trilogy
please visit my website - www.miaemilie.com

ACKNOWLEDGEMENTS

I would like thank my friends, Gilly Banfield, Ian Whitmill and Jo Roberts for giving me their unfailing encouragement, time and invaluable help in completing this novel. My thanks also go to my friend and fellow indie author, Christine Hammacott of The Art of Communication, whose talents has produced yet another brilliant cover for my novel and whose ongoing support, imagination and advice is immeasurable. My editor, Andrew Chapman, has, as ever, my heartfelt thanks for his keen insights, in-depth knowledge, advice and unflagging patience with me. I would also like to thank my proof-reader, Helen Kavanagh, for her appreciation of the story arc while managing to keep my narrative under control. Particular and grateful thanks goes to Shirley Hitchman and Sue Jeavons of the UK Picardy Sheepdog Club for all their wonderful insights and advice which kept Gus true to his Picardy nature. I would also like to thank David Priest for his crucial advice concerning the relevant processes and procedures of the National Archives. As always my very special and eternal thanks to my Mum, Dad, husband, family and friends, without them none of this would be possible.